WWW.SIRENPUBLISHING.COM
EROTICA ROMANCE

SEX RATING: SCORCHING

SIREN SEX RATING

SENSUAL: Sensual romance with love scenes comparative to most romance novels published today

STEAMY: Heavy sexual tension; graphic details; may contain coarse language

SIZZLING: Erotic, graphic sex; explicit sexual language; may offend delicate readers

SCORCHING: Erotica; contains many sexual encounters; may contain unconventional sex; will offend delicate readers

SEXTREME: Excessiveness; many instances of unconventional sex; may be hardcore; not for the faint-hearted

REVIEWS for Gracie C. McKeever's
Beneath the Surface
[The Matchmaker, Book 1]

"Ms. McKeever has created a tight family group around psychic telepath Angela, whose words of wisdom and guidance help all around her. There's a strong sense of realism and locale in this book that really drew me in, and the attraction between EJ and Tabitha just grabs you. Even their banter is sexy, so you know that when they finally go to bed it's not just sex, it's something else, something amazing. The supporting cast is just as great, from bitchy Jade to lovable Frankie, the fast-talking sisters and the rest of Eric's family. With plenty of romantic twists and entanglements, this will keep you reading to the very last page. You're sure to love it—and there's more to come in this fantastic series. Keep a look out for the next book! **5 Magic Wands**." — **Autiotalo, *Enchanted Ramblings***

"*Beneath the Surface* is Book 1 in The Matchmaker series. The story is a phenomenal start to the matchmaking talents of Angela Calminetti, EJ's sister. Angela wants all her siblings and family happy and in love. She uses her telepathic abilities to make sure that this happens.

EJ and Tabitha, they have to struggle to make it to happiness, the two are stubborn and try to best each other. But they are miserable without one another. EJ knows Tabitha is the one because she reminds him of his first love Sinclair. Sinclair committed suicide when EJ was much younger and he has never really trusted his heart to another woman. Tabitha is different, for the first time in years EJ wants to tell her the truth about his telepathic abilities. Tabitha has had a rough life and is not very trusting of anyone but Eric James seems like he is worthy of her trust. Gracie C. McKeever shows that the bond between EJ and Tabitha will be long-lived and everlasting. And that the two are each others pretty match. *Beneath the Surface* is an outstanding book that is captivating. I definitely recommend this for readers. **4.5 Stars**" —**Chantay, *Euro Reviews***

"*Beneath the Surface* is the first book in The Matchmaker series and a wonderful beginning. Tabitha is a great heroine with plenty of backbone to stand up to whom and whatever. This makes reading about her a pure joy. EJ is not your typical author and it doesn't take much to transform him into incredibly sexy and totally hot. This couple has a fiery relationship both in and out of the bedroom and readers won't be able to get through the pages fast enough. The love scenes are full of desire and fraught with sensuality. Gracie McKeever has penned a book that will have readers desperately seeking the next volumes in the series. **4.5 Blue Ribbons**" —**Angel,** *Romance Junkies*

"Ms. McKeever captures intense love scenes loaded with earthshaking passion and desire. Eric and Tabitha burn up the pages of this book every time they give into the uncontrollable longing inside of them. At times, I felt like a voyeur watching the steamy embraces. Their passion is only the backdrop for an intense connection that bonds these two souls into one. The feelings and link they share [are] very special and unique. It is what we are all searching for out of life.

I will read *Beneath the Surface: The Matchmaker* many more times through the years to remember the beautiful love story of Eric and Tabitha. I look forward to the next installment of the series. **4 Hot Tattoos**" —**Ophelia,** *Erotic-Escapades*

"Ms. McKeever has succeeded in taking an often-used story line and breathed new life into it. Both Tabitha and Eric are full of such life and anguish that you laugh and suffer right along with them. This author has the talent to draw you into her story and you can really feel the sexual chemistry between the hero and the heroine. The author also sets things up so there will be more books in the series, something I will look forward to. I highly recommend this book. **4 Flowers/Excellent**" —**Char,** *May Reviews*

"EJ and Tabitha are a wonderful couple, and throughout the book, I enjoyed the interaction between them, especially how their past makes them closer. Stubborn isn't strong enough to describe these two, but their resistance to taking a chance at love never gets to the irritating stage. Their chemistry is excellent and the desire they feel never fades as the super hot sex gets better with each encounter. Definitely have a significant other available when this book is done. The interaction with the sisters was good and brought a break from the intensity of EJ and Tabitha's developing relationship...The paranormal link is very well-done, and was not only a selling part of the book but completely plausible. *Beneath the Surface* is an entertaining book and I look forward to reading the rest of the Vega siblings' stories when they come out. **4 Stars/Orgasmic**" —**Anya Khan,** *Just Erotic Romance Reviews*

"What do you get when you take a man and a woman with very different personalities, add an impossible to resist sexual attraction, and some meddling family members? You get Gracie C. McKeever's *Beneath the Surface*, one heck of an enjoyable read. Not only does it turn up the heat, it will make you laugh and cry and look forward to the next tale in Ms. McKeever's The Matchmaker series.

EJ is the type of man that it would be easy to underestimate. Only as you get to know him, do you see beneath his laid back exterior. When EJ decides to woo a lady, he does it relentlessly and with style. Tabitha's cold, business-like exterior protects a heart and soul that have been sorely battered. When she confronts her past, it will bring tears to your eyes. With interesting secondary characters to move the plot along and add some spice of their own, *Beneath the Surface* flies by at a quick pace.

Witty banter and complex characters make *Beneath the Surface* a delightful, engrossing read. Gracie C. McKeever has certainly caught my interest and I will be eagerly awaiting her next tale. Don't miss out on this wonderful new series." —**Vicki Turner,** *Romance Reviews Today*

Books by Author

THE MATCHMAKER
Beneath the Surface
Terms of Surrender
Manifest Destiny

SISTERS OF EMSHARRA
Guardian Seductress
Predator's Salvation

Single Titles
Spells Cast in Shadow

Coming Soon
In Plain Sight
Beween Darkness and Daylight
Eternal Designs

Published by Siren Publishing

ABOUT THE AUTHOR

Gracie McKeever is an author from the Bronx, and aside from several side trips along the way, has lived and worked her entire life in the New York City area. She has been writing since the ripe old age of seven when two younger brothers were among her earliest, captive audience for various short story readings and performances.

An eclectic and voracious reader whose audience has grown outside of the supportive family members, she's had the great fortune of being able to incorporate two of her favorite passions and talents—reading and writing—as a book reviewer for several online e-zines, both as a regular staff member and freelancer.

Her short stories, novellas and poetry have seen exposure in various lit and art magazines and other venues—online and in print. Of particular note, heard over the airwaves on KFJC's morning show, Dancing In The Fast Lane With Ann Arbor (Unbedtime Stories) out of Los Altos Hills, CA (*New Life Incognita* was the story of the month for March 2000). She's also proud to be a member of the ("Worlds' Oldest Active Homeless Paper") Street News family and has seen numerous articles, poems and novel excerpts published within its pages as well as having had a poetry reading on Pseudo On-line Network (Street News Review).

In 2001, Gracie caught the erotica bug, sinking her teeth into her first erotic e-book for a review, and hasn't looked back since, an instant affinity for the genre spawning her first erotica title, *Beneath The Surface*, published in 2006 by Siren Publishing, Inc.

Visit Gracie's website at www.graciecmckeever.com.

BENEATH THE SURFACE

The Matchmaker
Book 1

Gracie C. McKeever

EROTICA ROMANCE

Siren Publishing, Inc.
www.SirenPublishing.com

Beneath the Surface
The Matchmaker, Book 1

Gracie C. McKeever
Copyright © 2006

Prologue

Wantagh, Long Island

"EJ needs to settle down," Angela Calminetti opined. "I worry about him."

"All you worry and think about is that all our unmarried siblings need to settle down, Angie."

"Well, you all *do*."

Evelyn chuckled at her oldest sister's oft-repeated conviction and reached into her handbag for her Camels before she remembered she was sitting in Angela The-Surgeon-General's kitchen and that her sister didn't allow smoking in her house, even when her five kids weren't in the vicinity. Instead, she extracted and opened an emergency piece of Godiva chocolate, glaring at Angela as she popped the creamy candy into her mouth and unconsciously moaned when it melted on her tongue.

"I'd rather have you fat than in the hospital wasting away from cancer some day."

"Oh, you're so melodramatic." Between her oldest sister and her youngest brother, she was going to have a fatal nicotine fit long before cancer got a hold of her.

"Here, have a big dose of caffeine instead." Angela giggled, dark brown eyes sparkling as she ignored her youngest sister's pique and poured first herself, then Evelyn a cup of espresso. Pushing her sister's cup across the oak table she asked, "Now, where was I?"

Evelyn huffed and shoved a stubborn black curl behind her ear. "Like you don't remember."

"Don't be such a grump."

"You want to fix up all our unmarried sibs so we can all be as happy as you and Freddie."

"Hey, don't knock it until you've tried it."

"I did, remember?"

"I know, but at least you're not as bitter about your divorce as Donna is about hers."

"Tell me about it. That girl could give Lorena Bobbitt a run for her money." Evelyn lifted her cup and took a sip of her espresso, thankful for at least one chemical rush today, especially if she was going to get into a session of psychoanalyzing her other sibs with Angela.

Granted, each and every one of their siblings—and Evelyn included herself and Angela in the mix—had enough angst and complexes to keep several psycho-therapists busy for years to come, though Evelyn didn't think her brothers and sisters were anymore dysfunctional than any other brothers and sisters from a relatively large family.

Sure, Donna-the-cynic came off as a man-hating maniac capable of dismemberment when she got on one of her all-men-are-dogs rants. Evelyn knew, however, the bold threats and harsh sentiments were all an act to cover up how hurt her sister had been when her husband of just nine months did the unthinkable and left Donna for the "other woman" who turned out to be her husband's pregnant ex.

Once burned, twice shy, goody-two-shoes Emilia hadn't dipped her toes back into the dating waters since discovering, shortly after giving birth to their son, that her husband of fifteen years had been unfaithful for most of their marriage. Anthony was eight now, and Evelyn didn't think her sister had had an orgasm—self-induced or otherwise—since his arrival into the world, poor woman.

Nick, the perennial bad boy could be an arrogant womanizer on his worst days, and an irresistible cad on his best, but Evelyn remembered how difficult it had been for him coming up dyslexic in a home full of academic over-achievers, even down to his baby brother. She remembered how hard their father had been on Nick, harder than on any of the other Vega kids. She remembered too how Nick had rebelled and acted like their father's approval didn't matter to him; remembered how he had gone out of his way to be independent and tough, as if he didn't want or need any of his siblings' or his father's love.

Of all Joe and Viviana's kids, Nick was the most private, at least as much as Angela would let him get away with, which wasn't much.

Flirtatious free-spirited EJ was so busy trying to make everyone happy he had half-convinced himself and his family that he had long ago gotten over losing his soul mate in high school. But Evelyn knew he wasn't fooling anyone, least of all her and Angela.

Then there was oldest sister Angela, the general and organizer, buddinsky sibling supreme with a heart as big as her determination and passion to see each of her brothers and sisters happily committed and wasn't afraid to use every skill in her idealistic arsenal, short of an old-fashioned shotgun wedding, to match all her siblings up.

Shrugging now as she put her cup back on its accompanying saucer on the table Evelyn said, "To tell you the truth, I wouldn't mind putting my hand in the fire again."

"See! That's the kind of positive thinking I'm talking about. The kind you and EJ have. You're not afraid to get back on the horse after it's thrown you."

"Thanks for the metaphor." Evelyn frowned at the gleam of hope lighting her sister's eyes again, hating her current dry spell more than Angela would ever know. She wasn't, however, willing to engage in casual sex just to appease her libido and end it, at least not anymore. She had her vibrator for that, and for now, it would have to do. "I don't know if you can put me and baby brother in the same category though. He's too much of a confirmed bachelor to think about settling down." Though EJ rode a lot of fillies, he never gave them a chance to throw him before he jumped off in search of another mount.

"Oh, pish-tosh." Angela waved a dismissive hand in the air.

Evelyn laughed and thought how much her sister reminded her of Martha Stewart. A less white bread, swarthier, Italian Martha Stewart of course. From the hand-sewn calico aprons and curtains in the kitchen, to the homemade baked goods that always filled the porcelain cookie jar on the counter to the immaculate spic-and-span floors and surfaces throughout the house, Angela Calminetti could have given the infamous domestic diva a run for her money any day.

Evelyn always felt like she was visiting their mother when she stopped by her sister's home and didn't know how either woman kept things so clean and orderly most of the time with so many kids in the house—Angela with five of her own and their mom with six.

"EJ just doesn't know any better. The right woman would change his tune in no time flat, I'm sure of it," Angela said now.

"And I take it you have just the woman in mind?"

"As a matter of fact I do. Your personal shopper."

"Tabitha?" Evelyn gawked. "You can't be serious."

"She's perfect for him, Evie."

"They're oil and water."

"My point exactly. Opposites attract."

Evelyn frowned. She didn't think her sister realized the opposites in this case wouldn't attract and blend as much as rip each other apart.

Tabitha was the sweetest kid, but a little on the uptight side, or what their other brother Nick would colorfully describe as having "a stick up her ass," while EJ wouldn't hesitate trying to get the stick out, either by shocking her with his down-to-earth sense of humor or putting her panties in a tangle with his lust for life and good dirty fun.

Would that be such a bad thing for the kid? Evelyn wondered as she considered the ramifications of putting EJ and Tabitha together. Oil and water. Night and day. Hot and cold. Uptight and easygoing. Each could be without the other, but separated were a far emptier existence than the sum of their parts together.

"You're thinking about it, aren't you?" Angela prodded.

Evelyn shrugged, but didn't say anything. It wasn't like she hadn't pictured EJ and Tabitha together before; she had thought they'd make a great couple, her thinking in synch with Angela's.

This would have to be handled very carefully. Unlike Nick who ate up his sisters' efforts and attention as much as he ate through the women they pushed his way, EJ took particular umbrage at any familial interference in his love life.

"Of course you're thinking about it," Angela said as if she'd heard her sister's thoughts.

"It's just that Tabitha is so…so serious. I don't think she knows how to have a good time."

"Don't you see, that's where EJ would come in. He could rub off on her and she could rub off on him. Besides, we're not all meant to be free-spirited party girls like you."

"Party women," Evelyn corrected.

"Oh, that's right. You did just celebrate a fortieth birthday."

"Bitch."

Angela giggled. "So, we're in agreement then. You'll help me make this work?"

Chapter 1

Manhattan, New York—One Year Later

EJ Vega rued the day he'd let his sister talk him into this wardrobe makeover.

He'd be the first to admit he was fashion-challenged and hadn't kept up with the latest styles and trends since he'd left the corporate life along with replacing all his subscriptions to *GQ* and *Maxim* with subscriptions to several writers' magazines. He'd been getting along fine for a couple of years now without power suits and ties, which was one of the reasons why he loved freelance writing so much. He could get up, sit at the computer with five o'clock shadow, in his underwear or pajamas if he wanted—not that he did that often—and still get a full day's work done with no one the wiser or complaining about his unorthodox appearance.

EJ had left a successful six-figure job in advertising and most of its trappings—including Armani and Boss—behind because he had more important messages and stories to offer than what could be conveyed in the confines of mahogany lined boardrooms and ass-kissing pitch meetings. He did not want to go back to that cutthroat existence, wasting away spiritually, wasting his talent on the unworthy, too happy now doing what he'd always wanted to do: write.

He frowned at his computer monitor now as if it were at fault for his quandary, wondering when he'd reach the end of this image profile, wishing there were some way around it, but obviously there wasn't. If there were a way, Evelyn would have found it, his sister was always willing to use her connections or turn the screws if she had to. This fashion consultant, Tabitha Lyons, must have been immune and resolute where this area of her business was concerned. The woman required a profile from *all* her applicants, and that included the brother of one of her "favorite and most loyal clients," did not move forward without having an image profile.

Thorough did not begin to describe Ms. Lyons—the only thing she hadn't asked for so far was his blood type—and EJ wondered if this particular idiosyncrasy transcended other areas of his sister's personal shopper's life.

There was no picture on her website, *LyonsStyleInc.com*, and he had spent more time imagining what the mysterious ball-busting consultant looked like instead of filling out the profile. EJ pictured a sexually frustrated, white-haired, thick legged, matronly woman with nothing else better to do with her time than charge exorbitant fees and shop for strangers.

Not that he couldn't afford Ms. Lyons' $150-an-hour charge. He could afford her fees when he'd been in his nine-to-five job—which more often than not had been a seven-to-seven—money was not really the issue, as much as the time filling out this survey was taking away from his writing but he couldn't get his sister to see this.

'Think of it as an investment in your future as a best-selling author.'

Good old Evelyn, always with an answer for everything.

EJ did not want to think about the upcoming national book tour that was going to take even more time away from his writing.

He was already well into work on his second book, a how-to on reading body language, and looked forward to fulfilling the commitment he had made to Renegade Publishing. He had signed a contract for a two-book deal and accepted the seven-figure advance on the basis of *Reaching Out.*

More than anything, he wanted to start work on his third book and first true novel.

The phone rang and eager for the break, EJ leaped from his swivel chair. Any other time, a ringing phone was an unwelcome interruption that he usually ignored and let his voicemail answer. This time he checked the Caller ID and grinned at the familiar name on the readout.

Jade Aliberti. Ad executive supreme, a blast from his not-so-distant past.

EJ's penis twitched and convinced him to answer the call over all his intellect's objections.

"How's the hottest new author gig going?"

He smiled against the mouthpiece as he ensconced himself in a corner of his green leather sofa before sliding a hand inside his jeans and cupping a quickly rising hard-on. Jade's deep sultry voice did it to him every time. Or perhaps he'd been without longer than he thought. "Where are you?"

"In the neighborhood and I figured I'd give my favorite freelancer a ringy-ding."

He got harder, having a particular weakness for alliteration, and she just made the simple job title sound so naughty and sensual.

He pictured her in the driver seat of her silver Lexus convertible, long golden-blond tresses blowing in the wind behind her, a reminder of a past from which he was so far removed and wished never to return. Except for her, his on-again, off-again partner.

He couldn't call her a girlfriend, they were too casual for that, though their relationship was steadier than he'd shared with most women he'd slept with over the years. Jade was the perfect fuck-buddy. No strings, just out to get her swerve on, and in the bargain, he got on his. "You're looking for an invitation?"

"Do I need one?"

"Mi casa, su casa."

"Not in a long while."

He didn't want to think of all the late nights he'd put into his writing while the world went by him, didn't want to think that he was missing anything. Even if it was being between Jade's sexy shapely thighs and inhaling her heady woman's scent, a willing prisoner with her long legs wrapped around his waist. "I'll buzz you up as soon as you get here."

"I'm on my way."

EJ leaped from the sofa, replaced the cordless in its base—he'd learned the last time his agent hadn't been able to reach him when he'd let the battery run down and couldn't find the handset—and went back to his computer. He winced at the unfinished profile. Hell, he'd have to finish this another time. Ms. Aliberti was a known quantity with whom he wanted to deal. The faceless Ms. Lyons was so far a ball-busting tigress he had yet to tame.

The buzzer sounded, and EJ rushed to the eat-in kitchen of his large loft apartment—one of the only major trappings he had kept from his former life and rang the downstairs bell to let Jade in, glad that today was one of his non-pj wearing days.

Whistling, he practically skipped to the door, opening it up with a flourish and freezing when he saw Evelyn on the other side.

"Well don't look so pleased to see me, and close your mouth before you let in the flies." She handed him her handbag and micro-trench before pushing past him to get into the loft.

"What are you doing here?"

"Tabitha says she hasn't seen an image profile from you yet. I just wanted to stop by and see what was holding things up."

Hell, these two women were going to be the death of him!

EJ hung his sister's bag and coat on the oak coat tree adjacent his front door, and peeked into the hallway to see if Jade was on her way up. "You could have called first."

"I knew you would ignore it like you always do."

He grunted, unwilling to admit or deny.

"Expecting company?" Evelyn arched a brow, a knowing grin on her face as she took a seat in the spot he'd just vacated.

Sometimes he wondered if she had the gift too. Their oldest sister Angela had it, nothing as strong as his however, but one of the main reasons, despite the twelve-year age gap, he and Angie were so close. Of course, this didn't count the closeness he shared with dear sweet buddinsky Evelyn, especially right now.

"Not that it's any business of yours, but I was."

"You'll just have to get rid of her."

"How do you know it's a her and not my editor or agent."

"I don't think that's for your editor or agent." Evelyn waved at the substantial bulge in his jeans. "Or for me for that matter."

"Not likely," EJ muttered as he took a seat at his computer and swiveled around to face her. "For your information, I was working on the profile before you came up."

"Mmm-hmm." Evelyn stood and made her way across the floor, high-heeled pumps sounding on the parquet. She leaned over his shoulder, perused the screen then gently cuffed him. "You're not even half-way done."

"I was getting there."

"You're not taking this nearly as seriously as you should. This is important. It's your future."

"I know the game, Evie. I played it for years."

"You don't act like it."

"I don't see why she needs so much information. She's only going to be shopping for my clothes, not marrying me."

Evelyn covered his mouth and glanced over both shoulders with a flourish. "Please don't utter such sacrilege. If the woman could hear you, she'd have your head."

EJ chuckled against her hand before she removed it. "She can't be that bad, can she?"

"She can and she is, and not even those big pretty dimples of yours are going to save you from her wrath if you cross her."

"Are you trying to scare me?"

"I'm trying to prepare you. Tabitha is all business, and she takes her duties very seriously. She is not *just* a shopper. She is a fashion and style consultant, and when you meet with her, you'll see exactly what I mean."

After everything he'd heard about Ms. Lyons, he was not so sure he wanted to meet the little retail Nazi. He was definitely sure he didn't want to take the next step and have her snooping around in his closet. He could see the woman now, fainting dead away at the hopelessly its outdated, unconventional contents.

He'd given his designer pieces to his older brother Nick—who happened to share EJ's previous profession, and had his same measurements and taste in clothes—and the rest to Goodwill when he'd left his job on Madison Avenue, getting a fresh start on his way to "starving artist." Any new clothes he'd purchased over the last few years had been strictly casual, some utter vintage and thrift shop mainstays.

EJ had learned early on from his mother never to do things half-assed, and had celebrated his thirtieth birthday almost four years ago free of corporate agendas and restraints.

He had kept the essentials—his loft in the village, a generous 401K and other sizable earnings and investments that had tided him over while he wrote and gained publishing contacts freelancing his articles—and a functional new Jeep for which he had traded in his BMW.

Now Ms. Lyons would be coming here to tell him, EJ was sure, that his wardrobe was a mess and needed to be completely overhauled. Hell, no thanks to that.

The buzzer sounded and Evelyn folded her arms across her breasts again, gave him a challenging glare that dared him to shirk his duty. "I'm not going anywhere, so get rid of her."

"Dammit, Evie..." EJ pouted, feeling like a spoiled kid that had been denied a treat in the candy aisle of the supermarket. He stalked to the kitchen to give Jade the unwelcome news—that an emergency had come up and he'd have to take a rain check on them hooking up.

Damn, he could just scratch her off of his booty call list.

EJ came back to the living room and Evelyn pointed him to the swivel chair before he could flop on the sofa.

"You've got work to do and I'm here to make sure you do it."

"If I didn't know better, I'd think you were working on commission for Ms. Lyons."

"Tabitha Lyons doesn't need me to drum up business for her, believe me. Consider yourself lucky that she's taking you on."

EJ sat down and turned to face the monitor. He re-read the question he'd been stuck in the middle of and commenced to answer it before glancing over a shoulder to see what Evelyn was doing and found her settled back happily flipping through his latest *Writers' Digest* magazine.

"You can't be serious about hovering over my shoulder while I do this."

"I most assuredly am. You've already proven you can't be trusted." She lowered the magazine to peer at him. "I'm here to make sure you finish the profile and send it along so we can move to the next step."

The in-person interview. Like he could forget about it. "Is it really necessary?"

Evelyn gave him a sympathetic look, but he wasn't fooled for a minute. Underneath the soft hazel eyes was a sharp businesswoman waiting to pounce on any weakness. She hadn't succeeded more than a decade on Wall Street for nothing.

"Personal shopping is a process, and Tabitha needs not only to know about your lifestyle, but to see how you live, what you wear. She has to meet you so that you two can establish rapport.

You wouldn't want to hand over your credit card to just any old body, now would you? A certain level of trust is absolutely necessary."

He saw her point, but was loath to admit it.

Why did this entire process feel like a total invasion of his privacy? The woman hadn't even set foot in his house yet.

EJ spent the next forty-five minutes going through the survey, filling it in as completely as possible—favorite color, favorite materials, favorite foods, zodiac sign, hobbies…he felt like he was filling out an online dating survey—before hitting Send.

Maybe it wasn't too late to call Jade back.

Evelyn was behind him in a flash, leaning over his shoulder as if she'd heard his thoughts.

"See, now was that so difficult?"

"Painfully."

"Wise-ass." She cuffed him again, then threw her arms around him in a bear hug. "You won't be sorry, I promise you."

EJ watched her head for the front door, followed her and was at the threshold as she slid back into her coat and shouldered her bag. "You're leaving so soon?"

"My work here is done for now."

"What a relief."

"Next comes the face-to-face."

"I can't wait."

"Expect Tabitha to give you a call soon."

"I'll be right here with bells on."

Evelyn smiled, reached up to muss his hair before heading down the stairs.

EJ closed and locked the door in case his sister got any second thoughts about how he needed to spend the rest of his Thursday afternoon, then ran for his cordless, hoping it wasn't too late to make amends to the luscious Jade. It had been too long since he'd gotten some. He deserved the release now more than ever after the harrowing experience he'd just had filling out that questionnaire with his older sister looking over his shoulder and making him feel as if he were still a creative with a print deadline hanging over his head.

He had a sneaking suspicion Evelyn had gotten a real kick out of him squirming, probably liked getting back at him for all the times his mother had made her and his other siblings sit through one of his one-man shows as he'd acted out his stories as a kid.

He smiled at the memory of his teenage sisters and older brother putting off playing and dates to be a captive audience to a seven-year-old imagination.

"Give me one good reason why I shouldn't just hang up on you?" Jade answered her cell.

"I can give you several. If you'll come over, I could give you full-fledge pitch," EJ said and listened to her sultry chuckle drift over the phone line. "Am I forgiven?"

"We'll see once I get to your place."

* * * *

EJ grumbled and reached for the clock at his bedside before he remembered he hadn't set the alarm in years and no longer needed to get up for the corporate grind.

He reached for the cordless instead.

"Who's calling at this hour?"

Jade's question made him check the LCD on the clock, his frown deepening.

Seven o'clock! He'd kill Evelyn if she were calling him with some more bullshit about that profile. He'd sent it already, give him a break!

EJ snatched the receiver out of its base. "Hello," he rasped.

A barely audible gasp greeted him before a long pause.

"Who is this?"

"I'm sorry if I woke you. This is Tabitha Lyons of *Lyons Style, Inc.* Have I reached Eric James Vega?"

God, no one addressed him by his full name like that except bill collectors or his mother when she was at the end of her rope with him and that hadn't happened since he'd been a teenager. Otherwise, his family and most of his friends called him EJ. And EJ Vega was the pseudonym he used for his writing.

"No, but you've reached EJ Vega."

"Mr. Vega, as you know, I require a face-to-face meeting with all of my potential clients before I take them on."

"So Evelyn told me. Does anyone ever call you Tabby?"

"Not if they want to live to tell the tale."

He laughed, liked her quickness, and didn't need to hear her gritting her teeth to know she was angry. He could feel the irritation in her silence, but came up against a solid wall when he probed for more of her thoughts and feelings. Not a surprise since he'd never met her and wasn't in physical contact, but it never stopped him from reaching out and trying to read someone, especially after what had happened with Sinclair. A needless tragedy he had yet to get over. "I'll make a deal with you. I won't call you Tabby if you don't call me Eric."

"I'm sorry, Mr. Vega, I don't operate that way."

"So we're back to Mr. Vega."

"We never actually got away from it."

He smiled, unperturbed. "Okay, it's killing me, but I'll compromise. How about I call you Tabitha, and you call me Eric." He could almost picture her ramrod straight posture as she sat trying to decide how much to give in or if she should give into him at all.

A ball-buster, like he thought, and obviously a workaholic. Seven-freaking-o'clock-in-the-morning!

Expect Tabitha to give you a call soon.

Well hell, it wasn't like Evelyn hadn't warned him.

"Eric and Tabitha will be fine," she stated, her tone so cool and formal, EJ pictured pursed lips and a highborn retrousse nose.

"Now that we have that out of the way, when would you like to meet, Tabitha?" He couldn't help digging, knew that his familiarity, even with her previous permission, stuck in her craw. Good. If he had to suffer at such an ungodly hour, then why shouldn't she?

"How's Wednesday next week sound? My office at..." she paused for a moment, and EJ closed his eyes, imagined her consulting an electronic calendar. She probably had a BlackBerry or some other handheld or laptop chained to her hip when she wasn't at her computer—God, how he did not miss that aspect of his nine-to-five—because Ms. Lyons always had to be on point, and definitely wouldn't double book herself. That would be a business faux pas.

"Since you're not much of a morning person, Eric, how about afternoon, say two?"

He grinned at her emphasizing his name and her allusion to his before-noon fetish, liked that she could give as good as she got. "Sounds good to me."

She gave him the address and directions, made sure he repeated them before she prepared to sign off. "Good, I'll see you then, Mr. Ve—Eric."

"Old habits hard to break?" He chuckled. "I'll see you Wednesday." He hung up the cordless before she could respond and turned to Jade who was leaning up on her elbow, chin poised on her palm, intently staring at him. He tumbled her onto her back, eliciting a soft whimper and shudder when he slid a finger into her vagina, cupped her mound and found her wet. Good. He needed to relax and this was one of the best ways created he knew of to do that.

"Who was that calling this time of morning?" Jade asked, smiling as he straddled her.

EJ was already hard, just her hands on his waist had him ready again. Or it could have been the phone call for all he knew, Tabitha Lyons' low seductive voice ringing in his ear, the memory of her irritation still shivering down his spine.

He wasn't sure which had him so aroused, just knew he had to feel a woman's warmth surrounding him, feel her soft flesh surrendering to his hardness in ecstasy.

And Jade was here. Jade was so here.

He reached inside the top drawer of his bedside table and extracted a brightly colored foil packet from the party batch of condoms Jade had brought over. She liked colors. EJ didn't care as long as it did its job. He quickly ripped open a bright red one—Jade's favorite—donned it in record time, then slowly slid his penis inside her, rolling his hips as soon as he was balls-deep in her wet cunt.

"Well?" She lifted a perfectly waxed brow, but gasped at his powerful thrusts that almost made her forget what she wanted to ask him. She unconsciously arched her hips to take him deeper. "Who was that?" She clenched her pussy muscles around his cock as if to emphasize her question, made him groan.

"That was my personal shopper." He leaned in to bury her lips beneath his, dipped his tongue into her mouth in a scorching French kiss. He'd seen the follow-up questions written all over her features and didn't want to discuss Tabitha Lyons with her.

She belonged to him. A gentle mysterious secret he wanted to hold close to his chest for a while, revel in the knowledge of their subtle tenuous connection and imagine what it would be like when he met her and tried to remove that very big stick from her ass.

Chapter 2

Tabitha re-read Eric's dossier—she still wasn't used to calling him that, especially since she had yet to meet the man—for the fifth time since she'd received it, sat back in her executive swivel chair and grumbled.

EJ Vega. The perfect name for a former ad man. Slick, like his butter-melting voice.

Slick men didn't usually intimidate her, she didn't allow them to. But she could only imagine what she was getting herself into with Eric, especially if he looked as slick as he sounded, especially if he resembled his older sister in any way. Tabitha expected a totally arrogant and spoiled Lothario. How could he be anything but, the youngest of six children, four of whom were sisters who'd probably doted on him in typical big-Italian-family fashion?

She was beginning to dread the upcoming face-to-face as she had no other business meeting.

Thirty-three, Single, Freelance Writer, Sagittarius, forty-four inch chest, thirty-one inch waist, six-three, one-ninety-five, blue eyes, black hair, bronze complexion, big dimples... Great, a class clown and a procrastinator to boot.

Sheesh, the man sounded like a male model, and she didn't need to see his smart-ass mention of the dimples to think this. She only had to picture a taller, bigger, masculine version of Evelyn.

Okay, reality check. The man was, or would soon be, one of her many paying clients, and she would treat him with all the respect and dignity befitting all her clients. No special treatment. No favoritism. No nepotism.

Tell that to Evelyn.

Already Tabitha had made several concessions, pushing Eric's application through channels and to the top of a slowly growing waiting list. She never did that, and if it weren't for how she felt about Evelyn—a modicum of affection and cautious friendship, more than she felt for most people—she never would have broken protocol now.

After a full morning of shopping for one of her well-established clients, and rushing back to the office to have a few minutes to reintroduce herself to Eric on paper, she was now eager to meet Evelyn's brother, if for no other reason than to appease her curiosity.

And find out if the crack about big dimples was true.

She wondered what else on him was big, then immediately castigated herself for the errant thought.

This wasn't like her, never had been. She had no time for frivolous attachments, or even more frivolous wet dreams and fantasies. She most definitely didn't have time for a too-sexy-for-his-body Italian Stallion Dr. Phil wannabe.

Okay, that was a little harsh, especially since she'd read and enjoyed his articles and advice columns in various magazines. She particularly found his articles in *Prevention Magazine* about suicide and suicide prevention along with body language informative and riveting. She hadn't expected someone with his background to sound so insightful and sensitive.

She'd instantly liked his voice, surprised that his writing interested her since she wasn't usually on the receiving end of advice, self-help or how-to. She was more a doer than a follower; all the help she'd ever gotten throughout her life coming from herself before Dr. Phil and his brethren had come onto the scene.

So fine, he could write, turned an evocative phrase and inspired. Tabitha could almost see how he'd landed a big time New York contract. She just didn't want to have to deal with the ego that was probably attached to the writing talent that had wrought a seven-figure book deal.

She tapped her solid gold Mont Blanc pen on the glass table as she glanced at the wall clock across her office. Tabitha wanted to get out all her nervousness our of her system now before he arrived, put her best foot forward, her only foot, the triple C's—calm, cool, collected. No weaknesses. All business.

Difficult promises to keep when she remembered his voice on the phone.

Once she had gotten past her shock at the smoky, sleep-touched voice, she'd settled down to typical business mode. Her initial reaction—a liquid warm feeling low in her belly—had lingered throughout her conversation with him, intermittently rising and falling with the sound of his deep baritone, reacting in kind to the gentle earthy rhythm of his masculine timbre.

Tabitha stood and paced across the office aware that if Eric had arrived her secretary Cynthia would have let her know. She peeked out of her office door anyway and found an empty reception area. Well, except for Cynthia intently typing at her computer.

She surrounded herself with individuals as hardworking and organized as herself. Half the time they either didn't take lunch unless they were forced, or took a break on the fly, often eating at their desks the way she did.

She couldn't remember Cynthia taking lunch today. Except for a couple of breaks and trips to the copier and fax, she was at her desk most of the afternoon.

She wondered if Eric had stopped by during one of those brief afternoon breaks, found the office empty and decided not to wait. She wouldn't put it past him to be contrary, especially in the name of proving her wrong and dropping by a little early, and berated herself for pre-judging the man before she'd even met him.

She wasn't usually so critical, at least not sight unseen, but something about Eric Vega put her on the defensive. Maybe it was that nonchalant tone she had heard on the phone, maybe it was something else. The voice of a player, a free spirit, someone with no restraint, prone to excess.

Tabitha frowned. She'd had enough experience with all of the above from her mother and several foster parents as a child and then in her teens, and could well do without each now.

"He hasn't shown up yet, Tabitha," Cynthia said without looking up from her monitor.

Was she that transparent? "I just needed to stretch my limbs. Besides, it was getting a little stifling in the office. You know how I like to be on the go."

"I know."

Tabitha saw a grin that reminded her she may have capable and serious people working for her, but that didn't stop them from being fun-loving busybodies. *Can't win them all.*

The lettered glass door opened and someone stepped in.

The interruption was enough to make Cynthia look up from her computer and Tabitha duck back into her office quietly closing the door.

She wouldn't dare be seen waiting on pins and needles for him.

Tabitha stood with her ear against the door feeling like a teenager spying on the boys in the locker room while she listened to Cynthia give her greeting spiel followed by Eric's response.

She closed her eyes for a second as his voice washed over her, allowing herself the rare extravagance since she wouldn't dare indulge the simple auditory treat while in his presence.

The intercom on her desk sounded. She started and ran to answer it, silently thanking Cynthia for her discretion. "Yes, Cynthia?"

"I have your two o'clock here, Tabitha. Mr. Vega?"

"Send him in." Tabitha sat behind her desk and hit Escape on her keyboard.

Eric strolled in just as his dossier reappeared on her screen, and Tabitha swallowed at the sight of him, suddenly wishing she had stuck with her usual formality when they'd been on the phone and kept their relationship on a strictly last name basis. She didn't want him to get the wrong idea, especially since her own treacherous hormones already had the wrong idea and had her pussy muscles clenching in response to his tall height and broad shoulders filling the doorway as he paused on the threshold.

Instant attraction. Not only was it not good, it was unprecedented.

Tabitha stood up behind her desk and proffered a hand across the glass top as he approached, thinking Evelyn had somehow bamboozled her and that her brother's profile did not do him a bit of justice. There was nothing about the man that needed to be "made over."

He was inhumanly gorgeous, the black hair he had mentioned in his profile was sleek and wavy, worn in a longish but masculine and neat style combed back off his forehead and glistening beneath the fluorescent lights of her office.

Tabitha slowly moved her gaze down, taking in the aquiline nose, angular jaw, and cleft chin—the cleft he had neglected to mention in his profile as he had mentioned his dimples—immediately drawn back up to his indigo eyes, ridiculously long-lashed, so dark and intense they almost looked black.

She almost smiled when he grinned and she noticed the big dimples to which he had previously alluded, mentally taking his measurements and surprised he had been so accurate with his description. Most men—most people—boasted, overcompensated for some shortcoming or were too humble with their self-assessment. Rarely had she met anyone who'd been so accurate. Accurate and modest. *God, the man can't be this perfect!*

Tabitha slid her gaze down further to take in his outfit and amended her last thought. Today was not Friday, but he was definitely dressed down.

Okay, he *wasn't* perfect. Thank God for small favors.

His sense of fashion seemed to come straight from a discount store. Actually, a discount store would have been a step up. She could easily see the man perusing the aisles of a neighborhood thrift shop. Not that there was anything wrong with that. She frequented some of the better thrift shops herself when she was on the hunt for that perfect item for a client and not that his clothes were ill fitting, quite the contrary.

He had the kind of body on which clothes hung well, any clothes, pulled off the casual ragged, torn-up look with sensual style rather than coming off as a slob.

Tabitha glanced at her clock as he caught her smaller hand in his big one and gently squeezed. The resultant energy tingled all the way up her arm until she thought he had one of those practical joke buzzers in his palm, but there was nothing touching her palm except his smooth, warm skin.

He noticed the direction of her glance and grinned, showcasing those dimples to their fullest effect. "Come on now, you have to admit I'm on time."

Tabitha arched a brow. "Just," she said coolly.

"Let me guess, you're the type who turns up to all her appointments at least a half-an-hour early, am I right?"

"Why don't you have a seat and we can get started," she said, ignoring his quip. That he was so on target about her was totally beside the point.

He released her hand slowly, his body heat and intensity overwhelming and invading her comfort zone so much, it made her think twice about walking across the room to close the door before she finally did just that.

When she got back behind her desk and sat down, Eric was still standing and running a hand over the glass top admiringly, glanced up at her with a knowing look.

"I knew you'd be a glass and chrome type."

Tabitha glanced at him with a start, entranced by his long fingertips stroking her desk, imagined him caressing her skin instead of the smooth cold glass, her body wantonly arched beneath his manipulations. "Excuse me?"

"I got a definite vibe from your voice on the phone the other day." He glanced around her uncluttered office and nodded. "Cool, Spartan, functional."

His matter of fact appraisal made her feel as if her character had just been attacked, that maybe she should defend herself, but he spoke up again before she had a chance.

"Don't get me wrong. I like the look. It suits you."

"Not quite an apology."

He arched a lush brow. "Do I owe you one?"

"No, I suppose you don't. You were just making an observation after all." She leaned her elbows on the desk, folded her hands and leaned her chin on her clenched fingers as she looked at him. Two could play the intuitive game. "What type are you?"

"Eclectic, whatever feels good at the moment."

"Mmm-hmm." Just like she thought. A free spirit. He probably would have been right at home at Woodstock.

"Is this part of the interview process?"

"Everything you say to me here is basically part of the interview process. I get to know what you like, your general style, it helps me when I finally have to go and pick things out for you. That is, if you're not with me at the time I make the purchases."

"You mean I have that option?"

"If you have the time, of course you do. Most of my clients don't use the option. Time constraints are one of the main reasons people hire me in the first place. Your time is valuable, so why not let me do what I do best while you're using your time to do what you do best?"

"I like that philosophy."

Most men did. Most of her clients of the male, no-time-or-desire-for-frivolous-nonsense persuasion where shopping was concerned, did. Must have been something in the Y chromosome, some anti-shopping gene.

Tabitha looked at her monitor and hit the Enter key twice to make room for additional information. "Now, you mentioned eclectic..." Tabitha paused to glimpse his outfit. Not quite as out there as some of the Woodstock fashions she had seen, but definitely unconventional for the business world in which she moved. The white T-shirt tucked into a pair of blue wash-and-wear Levi's hinted at firm well-muscled abs that tapered down to a slim waist, would have been more suitable attire for a *Grease* revival. Same went for the black distressed leather blazer that clung to his broad shoulders and had Tabitha's fingers itching to divest him and see if his physique was as hard as it looked.

He had the anarchistic artist look down to a science, and she wasn't sure yet whether or not was a façade, or a well-honed image he'd perfected just for their meeting today, because Eric seemed like the type to go out of his way to shock.

Eric finally took the seat across from Tabitha's desk, resting his right ankle on his left knee and giving her a good view of a comfortable, well-worn black desert boot.

"So, let's get back to your sty—"

"I don't like suits and ties. I did the whole corporate dress for success deal years ago, and I'm not interested in reimmersing myself. What you see here is as dressy as I usually get."

True, the customer was always right, but Tabitha took offense at his tone, as if he was too good for a suit and she wasn't; as if he were attacking her tastes without even knowing what she might have planned for him.

"There are a lot of things we can do with slacks and a suit jacket that don't involve a tie."

"There are a lot of things I could do with a tie that don't involve clothes at all."

If she'd had liquid in her mouth, she might have spewed it across the desk in his face. As it was she had to tamp down a strong urge to laugh, and instead frowned to show her displeasure.

Her look didn't go a long way to putting him in his place, however.

He simply grinned at her, a smug boy who had just put his second grade teacher on the spot with his risqué comment in front of the class.

"Other than the suit and tie aversion—"

"I'm fairly easy."

She just bet. "That helps a bit." Although she didn't consider the subject closed by any stretch of the imagination.

He'd insulted her and Tabitha did not take well to insults. Rather than dwell on it though, she typed in "easy and casual" on his profile, then peered at him. "Would it be safe to say blue or black are your favorite colors?"

"Today they are. Tomorrow it might be something that's at my fingertips when I reach into my closet."

Tabitha shifted in her chair, crossed her legs to stem the sudden flow of wetness in her panties. She'd never found wise-asses a turn-on, but there was something intrinsically sexy and inviting about his grin, something raw and challenging in the depths of those indigo eyes.

She highlighted and underlined "easy and casual," already envisioning him in a charcoal single breasted suit and vest to highlight those beautiful dark eyes, and a black T-shirt underneath. There, no tie! "Any colors or materials you don't like?"

He shrugged, but rather than give off uncertainty, the motion emitted his indifference.

Tabitha stopped herself from flinging her mouse over the pad, and stared at him across the desk as he merely arched a thick brow. "This is not the best way to build rapport, Eric. I need cooperation from you to make this work. This relationship has to be a two-way street, give and ta—"

"Okay, okay." He chuckled, put up his hands as if in surrender. "You're absolutely right. I have to apologize for dragging you into this."

That was more than she expected, but less than she deserved, and Tabitha waited for the other shoe to drop. She was sure he had something up his sleeve, especially when she realized what he had said. "Dragging me into what?"

"Vega vendettas and power struggles."

"I'm not following."

"I have to be honest, my sister damn near twisted my arm to sell me on the idea of a makeover and personal shopper."

"You don't have to feel obliga—"

"*But*, now that I'm here I'm getting used to the idea of having a fashion consultant."

"Let's get something straight, I can't work miracles."

"I don't expect you to."

"And I won't do anything to your wardrobe you don't want me to do."

"I leave myself and my wardrobe at your total discretion, Tabitha."

She stopped herself from sputtering at his silky warm murmur, the sound of her name on his lips, still waiting for that big size twelve desert boot to drop.

At the thought, he did lower his right foot to the polished parquet floor, rolled his chair closer before leaning his elbows on her desk.

Tabitha purposely held her ground, though she was tempted to roll her chair back an inch or two, his clean musky scent riding the wind to her nostrils and making her light-headed.

It should have been illegal for a man to smell as good as he looked.

"Well, ah, that's good to hear."

"And I promise to cooperate and be a good boy for the rest of our meeting."

She didn't think he could or would keep that particular promise, not even if he tried, not a "good" bone in that big well-built body.

"Scout's honor." He raised his hand and grinned at her silence.

"Were you?"

"Was I what?"

"A Boy Scout."

"Even better. I was an Eagle."

She wasn't that up on what the qualifications for an Eagle Scout were, but she was sure they were pretty extensive and doubted that Eric's footloose and fancy-free mien had held him in good stead with the fraternity.

"I could show you my merit badges," he said at her doubtful look.

"I bet you could." *What did they give merit badges out for*? She was certain he'd excelled in totally different areas of achievement and socialization than had the rest of his troop. And despite his aversion to suits and ties, she could imagine him in the little green shorts uniform, politely helping an old lady across the street and shamelessly flirting with her all the way.

Tabitha bet he had nice legs too, to go with the rest of that hard body she'd been secretly ogling since he'd arrived.

"What about you?"

"Me?" She raised a brow.

"I can see you in a little Brownie's uniform selling cookies door to door."

The double entendre didn't escape her—she knew he'd meant it not to— his smile slow and seductive as he sat back in his seat waiting for her response.

"I was entirely too busy with more important activities to indulge in that particular whimsy." Too busy surviving, she thought.

Tabitha had never had to sell cookies door to door, but she'd had to barter, borrow and steal for a meal more times than she liked to count.

She especially remembered a period when her mother had neglected to come home for several days after Tabitha's father had left them. Everyday for a week she had come home to an empty house, and an even emptier refrigerator before going out to the neighbors to play "Whimpy from Popeye" with promises that her mother would gladly pay them Tuesday for a meal today.

No, hawking hundreds of boxes of overpriced cookies for top-selling honors and a cheesy overrated prize had not been high on her list of eight-year-old priorities.

"So, back to least favorite colors and materials?"

"I'm not too fond of orange and pink, unless they're on a woman. As for materials, I like anything that's washable."

She wanted to ask him if that jacket he was wearing was washable since it looked like it had been through the ringer. Distressed leather had been a trend back in the 90's, which looked to be about when he had bought the jacket. Of course, leather and blazers were pretty timeless...

"Before you ask, yes, it is."

"I'm sorry? Yes, what is?"

"The jacket's washable."

Her jaw dropped but she quickly coughed into a fist to cover her shock. "What are you, a mind reader?" she asked and watched as he fidgeted in his seat, for the first time since he'd come into her office looking uneasy, as if she had hit a nerve.

"I read facial expressions and body language, remember?"

Tabitha recalled a couple of articles and his observations about what certain expressions meant, wondered if she had used the one that had given her away in the seconds between his washable comment to his confirming that his jacket was.

She took out her BlackBerry and pulled up her schedule. "How about we set up an appointment for me to visit your closet?" The quicker she got this man out of her office the better. He was entirely too unsettling, especially that way he had of seeming as if he were crawling around in her head, siphoning her thoughts.

Not to mention her totally out of character physical reaction to him—like she'd been sleepwalking through a non-existent sex life and her hormones had only jolted to wakefulness when he walked in the door twenty minutes ago.

"You're done with me?" he asked.

Not nearly. "For now."

Chapter 3

She'd shot his concentration to hell and thrown him into instant writer's block. EJ knew it was infantile to take such a defeatist stand. Normally he didn't put any credence into or own writer's block. He personally thought the syndrome an all-purpose excuse for unproductiveness, laziness or procrastination—the first and second of which he almost never laid claim, the third…well, he was still working on that—laying the blame squarely where it belonged: with himself. Except it was so much more attractive and easier to lay the responsibility for his block on one uptight fashion and style consultant than to face the fact that he hadn't been able to put an intelligible string of words together on his computer screen since he'd left her office two days ago.

The thought of her haunted him—almond eyes, oval face, high cheeks, slightly upturned nose and full cupid's bow lips—all went a long way to putting the rock-hard in his cock. Shit.

He didn't think he had ever seen a woman who made tweed look sexy. Ms. Lyons did it effortlessly, teasing him with her classy lines, strutting around that beige and cream office in her brown pantsuit and lightweight chocolate turtleneck beneath, making him wonder exactly what was under all that elegant durable material.

Okay, so she was attractive, exceptionally so, her exotic features, especially those limpid, whiskey eyes hinting at a drop of Asian blood, as intoxicating as the color of her eyes. The sculpted cheekbones reminded him of a proud Native American heritage, accenting her strong ethnically mixed face. Everything about her was earthy and solid, and made him think of foreign tropical islands, warm summer breezes and hot sand against copper tone skin.

Jesus, either he needed a vacation, or he needed to get laid, probably and preferably both. If Tabitha were amenable, he could kill two birds with one stone.

EJ smiled, sliding into the fantasy of propositioning the prim and proper Ms. Lyons before he abruptly pushed back from his computer, almost tipping over the swivel chair he rose to his feet with such force.

He staggered back from the chair, raking a hand through his hair, closing his eyes, and taking a deep breath to try and exorcise her pixie's face from his mind. No go, still there, worse than ever. Or better, depending on his frame of mind, and his frame of mind obviously wanted to be on her. Damn it.

Maybe working up a sweat would take his mind off of her, steer it back to his work-in-progress. It couldn't make things any worse. As it stood, he'd written exactly three words—two of them several times over—filling the blank screen like an infatuated school girl trying out the last name of a crush with her first name to see if they were a good match.

Tabitha Lyons, Tabitha Lyons, Tabitha Lyons. Tabitha Vega. Tabitha Lyons-Vega.

EJ hit the deck and gave himself fifty, a quick set of push-ups that would have made a rampaging drill sergeant smile, but barely put a dent in taking the edge off of his tension.

Hell, he was going to have to go full out, totally obliterate the woman from his mind with an adrenaline rush. There was no other way. It wasn't like he didn't need it, the sedentary life was starting to catch up with him more than he wanted to admit. Things had been bad enough when he was in advertising, the biggest source of an aerobic workout coming from hop-scotching across the country for yet another campaign pitch or meeting. Half the time his credit card got more of a workout than he did, and he had enough frequent flyer miles on it to go to Mars and back.

EJ wondered what she was doing right now, mentally kicking himself for letting his mind drift back to the little lioness. Hell, he hadn't been in her company more than a half-an-hour and the memory of her burned through his gut like spicy Italian cuisine.

He had shaken her hand and been lost ever since, an electric shock jolting through his body, brutal like a lightning bolt. He'd felt the small hairs rising on his arms, never had as visceral a reaction to anyone, male or female, and didn't think it was just because she was a hot looking woman. There was more to her than that, more to his attraction.

EJ saw past the stuck-up attitude, past the perfect clothes, every long chestnut hair in place, unnecessary make-up skillfully applied and an erect carriage making her seem at least five inches taller than what he knew she was, everything so on point he thought her farts would probably smell like potpourri.

He realized almost immediately that it was all effected to cover her underlying sadness. She'd been hurt, badly, and was trying to hide beneath a veneer of cool professionalism.

She couldn't hide from him though. Not for long.

EJ finished a round of sit-ups—ten quick sets of ten—bounced to his feet heading for his stationary bike at the far end of the living room when someone knocked on his door.

He grabbed the towel from the handlebar of his bike and draped it around his neck as he headed for the door, determined to get rid of whoever it was and get back to his work-in-progress.

* * * *

Tabitha listened to the sound of bare feet padding to the door, ears finely tuned to whatever might be going on behind it, and preparing herself for just about anything.

Anything except the sight of Eric shirtless and in a pair of navy sweat pants that did little to detract from his overall sleek look.

She inhaled and his scent wafted to her. God, even his sweat smelled good!

He stood holding the door, his eyes slowly widening at the sight of her on the threshold. "Oh, shit! We had an appointment."

"Yes." She nodded. "Yes, we did." She waited, staring at him, did not even want to begin to wonder what or who was the source of his perspiration and breathless state. "You forgot."

"No, I didn't forget. Not totally. I mean I remembered this morning when I got up that we had an appointment. I just lost track of time in the interim and—"

"Please spare me." She put up a hand, motioned to pass him and enter the apartment.

He opened the door wider and stepped aside.

She stopped several feet inside, admiring the unexpected order and cleanliness.

His taste in clothes may have been suspect, but his decorating style was flawless. Or maybe he'd hired a professional like her to secure the smooth eclectic look of his loft.

She had a particular weakness for polished wood floors, loved the purity of uncovered parquet, but appreciated Eric's only concession, a Persian area rug in the region right in front of the door where she was standing, pumps sinking into the luxurious turquoise material.

Tabitha noticed his workstation right away—the black flat screen monitor on the desk, the black lacquer entertainment center on the opposite wall housing a small CD player, a twenty-seven inch flat-screen TV—and liked his state-of-the-art taste in electronics. The rest of the shelf space around the house was filled with hordes of framed family pictures that she liked as well, thought the personal touches gave nice insight to the man; more insight even than his over-protective older sister Evelyn gave with tales of growing up a tomboy in a house with three older fashion-plate sisters, two bratty younger brothers and one bathroom.

She smiled at the thought now as she admired Eric's living room and thought his furnishings indicated that there was hope; he wasn't totally clueless about what was going on in the outside world where style was concerned. But then he was a man, drawn to anything with gears, electricity and an engine. Now fashion…

Tabitha started when she felt his hands on her shoulders, glanced at him over one and saw that devastating take-no-prisoners smile. Her vaginal muscles tightened in response to his closeness and heat.

"Let me take your coat," he told her as she let him slide the trench off of her.

Watching him saunter to the coat rack to hang it up Tabitha noted he had the most delicious male butt, round and tight in every place it should be, making her imagine what each steely cheek would feel like cupped in her hands as he pumped into her.

Tabitha shook her head as if she could shake off her sudden desire. She didn't need this sort of trouble in her life, didn't want it. She was still stinging from the last time she'd let her hormones get the better of her and mixed business with pleasure and thought she could play the no-strings-attached game with the big boys.

She regretted the way she'd treated Michael while in her new and not necessarily improved, selfish mindset, hadn't enjoyed playing against her nature for the short time she was with him. She'd decided if she couldn't win the game of love and romance her way, then she'd rather not play it at all, unprepared to compromise her principles of commitment just for the sake of scoring a hard dick and available male body.

How she'd handled Michael after this epiphany had been the biggest mistake she'd made in her twenty-eight-year-old life, and she didn't intend to make it again.

Tabitha clutched her leather satchel close to her middle as she drifted towards the entertainment center, drawn by all the similar faces smiling out at her from the shelves, bodies poised in varying degrees of relaxation and formality.

She saw Evelyn's familiar face peeking at her from one group shot that also showed Eric surrounded by several kids as well as his own brother and sisters.

She smiled at their expressions—Eric's playfully harried, and Evelyn's supremely sisterly and aunt-like.

Everyone looked happy. More than happy. They looked serene, at peace with themselves and each other and comfortable in the knowledge that they would always have each other.

"Evie must have mentioned the lot of us to you."

Tabitha started again, then nodded as she turned to see him behind her, patting his face and chest dry with a towel before he flung it to land on the bike handle several feet away.

He had the most disconcerting habit of sneaking up on her and it was starting to catch up with her more than she wanted to admit.

At least he could have exercised the common decency it would have taken him to put on a shirt and cover up those hard, glistening, bronzed pecs and abs, for Christ's sake.

What ever happened to the sedentary lifestyle writers purportedly led? From the look of Eric, evidently, it was an urban myth.

Tabitha didn't feel she had the right to mention his state of undress, especially in his own house, despite her momentary discomfort, despite the fact that they had an appointment and he hadn't seemed to remember until she'd shown up at his door a couple of minutes ago.

"Are you like Freud and have several of the same pantsuit in your closet at home?"

She glanced at him, saw the grin as he eyed her outfit—a sensible gray tweed pantsuit and a black turtleneck beneath—and knew she wasn't going to like the next words out of his mouth unless she stopped him from saying them first. "We're not here to analyze my fashion choices, Eric. We're here to analyze yours."

His eyebrows shot up, a mischievous gleam lighting his eyes as he bowed at the waist and made a sweeping gesture with his hands. "Analyze away, ma'am. My closet awaits."

She followed him, passing the green leather sectional and entertainment center towards a large bedroom to their left, paused on the threshold immediately engulfed by the scent of him—a combination of sandalwood, citrus aftershave, shower gel and shampoo all blending into the potent masculine cocktail that was Eric.

She glanced around and took in the full effect of the color scheme, could feel him in every bold stroke of paint, versatile traditional wood furniture, the walls and fixtures a comfy combination of blues and browns. "I like it," she stated.

"Glad to hear it." He sidled past her and opened up the door to what she thought was another room, but was actually a walk-in closet. "It's all yours."

She wandered closer, not knowing what to expect where Eric was concerned, still surprised by the scarcity she found.

Wow, Adonis had an Achilles' heel!

Tabitha had never met anyone with so little fashion sense. The man had a Hawaiian shirt hanging in his closet, always a fashion faux pas in Tabitha's book, unless you were in Hawaii.

Rows of jeans, a few pairs of khakis, a couple of pairs of dress slacks, not one suit in sight, everything in monochromatic shades of brown, blue, and black, except for the Hawaiian shirt, of course. And he had the nerve to make fun of her outfit? Maybe *he* was like Freud and kept his wardrobe simple so that he could concentrate on more important things, like his writing. Who was she to argue with the logic when the man had walked with a seven-figure advance? He must have been doing something right.

Tabitha tapped her chin with her index finger, contemplating. She hated to gut his wardrobe; this was devastating for most people. Maybe she could update the pieces, take in a shirt, remove cuffs from the pants, work with the functional pieces already occupying a hanger and add on from there. This would take some time. "Are you color blind?" she blurted.

"As a matter of fact…"

"Oh! I didn't mean to…"

"I'm not."

Tabitha stared at him, felt heat rising to her cheeks and knew they were suffused with color. "That was not funny."

He chuckled. "It's not my fault you didn't give me a chance to finish and jumped to conclusions. Which you seem to do quite a bit, right?"

"I do not!"

He gave her a knowing smile but said nothing and Tabitha silently fumed.

The arrogance of the man. How dare he presume to know her!

Jump to conclusions? The only thing she wanted to jump was his lovely bones, but damned if she would let him know it any time soo…

Tabitha turned to him as he moved closer, her gaze straying down to the bulge in his pants, the looseness of the sweats doing precious little to hide the solid evidence of his arousal. Her nipples tightened at the sight, painfully erect and hard against the ribbed lamb's wool material of her turtleneck, fingers itching to cup him and make him gasp at her audacity, show him that he didn't know her as well as he thought he did.

God, what was it about the man that made her want to do shocking things?

Whatever it was, she was sure she could do without it, could do without him and those generous luscious lips that were slowly making their way towards her as he leaned forward.

Her eyes drifted to his, noticed the glimmer in the dark indigo depths.

She closed her eyes against the light, looking directly into his eyes was like looking into the sun, discombobulating and dangerous. She tilted her head to one side, felt him do the same, felt his mouth against hers, a brief touch, just a hint of a kiss, butterfly wings brushing her lips as his hand came up to collar the back of her neck and press her closer.

A buzzer sounded somewhere in the distance and Tabitha tried to pull away.

He held her in place though, stroked the base of her neck with his tongue, licked his way up her throat until he reached her earlobe, firmly took the small kernel of flesh between his teeth, then kissed it as if to soothe his bite. Or make a promise. "I'll be right back."

* * * *

Oh, shit! Oh, freaking hell, he was in trouble.

He'd kissed women before, hell, a lot of women. But he'd never had his world turned so thoroughly upside down by the simple contact of lips to lips. Shit, not even lips to penis had ever made him feel as vulnerable and excited as Tabitha's full mouth on his, had ever made him anticipate that live-wire tingle through his body when he caught her neck.

He could still see the colors, a vivid display of light bursting bright in front of his eyes in an exhibition to put a Macy's Fourth of July celebration to shame, colors intermittently pinwheeling and sparkling like a variegated ring of fire before he was able to see normally again.

He remembered his reaction to her handshake, but not even that memory had been able to stop his touching her. Like a cat he was nervous, yet too curious not to tempt fate again. He wanted to feel that excruciating energy that was too enticing to resist.

EJ finger combed his hair, forking both hands from forehead to nape several times before hitting the downstairs buzzer in the kitchen and sauntering to the front door in the living room. He was not surprised when he opened it to find Evelyn trudging up the last several steps.

"Hey baby brother."

He frowned but accepted the kiss she planted on a cheek, and distractedly returned it as she pushed by him to stand in the foyer.

"Is Tabitha here?"

"She's in the bedroom," he said, then quickly added, "surveying my closet."

Evelyn raised her brows, skimming her sharp hazel eyes over his half-dressed state, thankfully letting the rest go unsaid. He didn't think he could take his sister's ribbing, however good-natured it might be, yet too shaken by the touch of Tabitha's lips.

Just a kiss.

"What are you doing here anyway?"

"Anyone ever tell you you're a lousy host?"

"Especially when my guests pop up unannounced."

She pouted, looking suitably chagrined for about two seconds before she pasted a bright smile on her face and hooked both of her arms through one of his. "So, tell me how it's going."

"Is that what you came here for?"

"I had a few free moments after a late lunch meeting, was in the neighborhood and decided to drop by and see if you guys needed an impartial point of view."

"Impartial? From you? Not likely."

She playfully punched his arm just as Tabitha came in from the bedroom.

"Hi, Evelyn. How are you?"

"I thought you might need me to run a little interference for you with my brother. He can be a bit of a rapscallion at times."

"More like interfere," EJ mumbled.

"Don't be such a grouch."

"I can handle him okay."

Damn, she said that so quickly EJ almost snapped his neck to stare at her and see the serious look on her face.

Did she know how perfectly fuckable she looked right then? So prissy and sure of herself, he wanted nothing more than to throw her down on the rug, and plunge his cock into her wet depths until he brought tears to those whiskey colored eyes.

He wanted to mess up her hair, run his fingers through those glistening chestnut waves and see if they were as soft as they looked. He wanted to grab her by those long tresses, tilt back her head so that she would see who was going to be kissing her senseless, fucking her blind.

Shit, he was getting hard again. Well, he hadn't actually been soft since Tabitha's arrival, and doubted that he'd ever be soft again with her in the immediate vicinity. EJ shifted his weight from one leg to the other trying to surreptitiously adjust himself.

He was sure his sister knew what he was doing, but noticed Tabitha glancing around the living room as if she hadn't gotten the full treatment when she'd first arrived. She seemed so absorbed in her examination that a troop of naked Chippendale dancers could have marched into the room and she probably wouldn't have batted an eye.

Why the idea of her batting an eye and noticing a bunch of half-clothed men sparked his jealousy was beyond him. EJ barely knew the woman, and couldn't understand this sudden and unfamiliar spate of possessiveness, but there it was.

"I'll meet you back in the bedroom. I'm going to finish my examination of your wardrobe." Tabitha excused herself and left the room.

Evelyn stared after her, then looked at EJ. "So, you two seem to be getting along okay."

"Why wouldn't we?"

"No reason." Evelyn shrugged. "Guess I'll leave you guys to it then and be on my way."

EJ was of two minds as he walked her to the door: eager to pick up where he'd left off with Tabitha, and half-afraid of her overwhelming effect on his libido and psyche.

This was ridiculous! A minute ago he was having caveman fantasies about conquering her full-lipped mouth and plundering her pussy, now he was afraid of being left alone with her?

No way! She was only what? Five-five, maybe five-six tops and at a hundred-and-thirty pounds? A deadly combination of toned muscles and voluptuous curves sure, but smaller than his six-three, almost two hundred pounds by far. He could handle her.

I can handle him okay.

EJ swallowed as Evelyn leaned in at the door to peck him on the cheek.

"You be nice to her."

"You don't trust me?"

"I trust you fine. It's your libido that's suspect."

"You leave me and my libido alone."

Evelyn giggled, fidgeting with the strap of her bag for a moment.

EJ peered at her—stomach dipping at the look on her face—and impulsively broke a cardinal rule for him: lowered his shields to scan her thoughts. Just a brief mental touch, lightly brushing the surface of her mind to see what had her uncharacteristically on edge.

He'd suspected all along Evelyn had had an ulterior motive behind this whole makeover business, and he was sure Angela, the family's self-professed matchmaker, was in on the plot too.

Glimpses of them at Angie's kitchen table, Tabitha's name coming up in conjunction with his, vague images of a sisterly pact.

Evelyn shifted her weight, her restlessness confirming what he'd just seen, what he'd just felt. Nothing close to guilt—his sister had little self-blame in her, unapologetic for the life she led or the things she did with her family in mind—but he definitely felt her uneasiness.

He wanted to read her but good, almost regretted that he hadn't probed her when she'd first come to him with her personal shopper suggestion but for the fact that it had brought Tabitha Lyons into his world and into his bedroom.

What was done was done. He couldn't change it even if he wanted to.

But neither would he let Evelyn completely off the hook for her prying.

"You've pulled some elaborate schemes through the years to hook me up, Evie, but this is over the top even for you."

Evelyn blinked. "What scheme?"

"Tabitha. Me. You and Angela behind the scenes."

He saw the slight shake of her hand as she clutched her bag, knew he'd hit his mark before his sister rebounded with her usual unmitigated flair.

"Don't be paranoid. You needed a personal shopper—"

"So *you* said."

"And I introduced you to one."

"Hmph." He crossed his arms over his chest.

Evelyn stared at him, her uncertainty clear in the unusual brightness of her hazel eyes. "You're not going to do anything rash, are you?"

"I'm not sure yet."

"EJ…"

"I'll be nice to her. It's not her fault I've got two buddinsky sisters."

Evelyn sighed with relief. "I'm glad you're being so reasonable about this." She leaned in to give him another peck on the cheek as if to secure his assurance before she stepped into the hallway. "Love you."

"Don't think I won't get you two back for this." EJ grinned and closed the door after her.

Chapter 4

Tabitha stood in front of his closet extracting and examining each piece of clothing, appraising its worth and assessing its salvagability before putting it back to go on to the next piece.

Maybe this wouldn't be so bad after all. She'd found some gems during her search. Deep in the bowels of the closet, including several vintage Oxford shirts in solid shades of light blue and white, and two double-breasted blazers—one olive, one navy—designer pieces at that, and apparel she expected to find in the closet of a former Madison Avenue ad man.

Where had all his stuff gone? Surely he'd had more dressy outfits than what was here?

Tabitha put back the last piece, withdrew from the closet and closed the door, feeling momentarily disoriented standing in his large masculine bedroom.

She wandered over to the king size four poster bed, ran a hand over a mahogany knob, surprised to find such a quaint piece of furniture in the house of a comparative playboy, until she remembered his comment in her office about what he could do with a tie.

She paused at the foot of the bed. Visions of herself naked and on her back in its center, spread eagle, arms and legs tied to each post danced in her head only to be replaced with fantasies of Eric in the same position.

She had a hard time deciding which image turned her on the most, her thong getting soaked at just the thought of having his big hard body helpless and at her mercy or the other image of her at his mercy. *God, a girl could go crazy trying to chose a method of orgasmic torture!*

Eric chose that moment to amble back into the room, smiling at her as if he knew exactly what she was thinking.

Tabitha squirmed and craned her neck to glance into those sharp indigo eyes rather than avert her gaze. She'd almost forgotten how much taller than her he was. How much bigger, stronger and harder.

She liked the way his broad shoulders filled the doorway, tapering down to washboard

abs she couldn't help but admire despite her strong wish for him to put on a shirt and spare her hormones the resultant trauma.

Tabitha let her gaze roam further down his body, gaze locked on his hands resting at his sides, focused on the long fingers, wondered how they would feel inside her, caressing her labia, pinching her clit, igniting nerve endings that had long gone unignited.

God, this was crazy! She'd never had this intensely carnal reaction to any man, and she'd been exposed to quite a few as good-looking, virile and big as Eric.

Blind dates arranged by well-meaning acquaintances that had almost ended in date rapes. A couple of aborted wham-bam-thank-you-ma'am sessions of which she'd come to her senses in the middle of and just in time to avoid a bigger mistake than accepting the ill-advised date in the first place had been. Little foreplay, no foreplay, the closest she'd come to even remotely enjoying herself was the one time she'd given into her baser nature and taken her pleasure without regard for what she was giving back.

Poor Michael.

But nothing, no *one*, had affected her the way Eric was affecting her now.

What was it about him? Or maybe her long-neglected libido was catching up with her. More like punishing her for her concentrated disregard.

How long had it been? Eighteen months? Two years? She'd lost count after Michael, throwing herself into growing her business to the exclusion of everything and everyone else.

"So, where were we?"

Tabitha jerked up her head and stared when he clapped his hands and rubbed them together as if he were ready to dig into a juicy meal...and the look in his eyes told her that she was on the menu.

She glanced at his hands again. They looked capable of doing all sorts of naughty things to her body if she let him, and she was sure he wouldn't have a problem obliging her if she showed the tiniest bit of interest. She knew the type. Too sexy for his own good, and he knew it.

How many women did he have on the side, at his beck and call? How many had become notches on his bedpost? Did she really want to become one of those notches?

Problem was, she wanted to do naughty things to him as much as she wanted to let him do naughty things to her. These longings alone should have been enough to make her run from the room screaming into the evening for refuge at the very least if not a nunnery.

Instead, Tabitha held her ground and cleared her throat as he traversed the floor. "We were surveying your wardrobe."

"No." He shook his head, moved forward, and bent close to her ear. "If I remember correctly, we were somewhere around here..." He dipped his head low, planted a gentle kiss on her neck, his light whiskers tickling her skin, speeding her pulse.

Tabitha closed her eyes, gritting her teeth against the heat rising in her body, her skin so sensitized to his closeness, she thought she'd spontaneously combust if he touched her again.

"And here," Eric whispered and took her hands in his as he sidled behind her.

"We shouldn't...I can't." That didn't come out nearly as firm as she meant it to. Was it any wonder he dipped his head again to suck and nibble the skin of her neck? Her squeaky uncertain voice practically gave him carte blanche where her body was concerned.

He pressed close and she felt the heat of his erection against her buttocks and gasped when he slid a hand around to the front of her pants and eased down the zipper.

This was totally out of order, totally. She should stop him. *Someone* needed to stop this.

He cradled his chin against her collarbone, his breath warm and enticing against her throat as he slid his hands inside her thong and thrust a finger into her.

Tabitha gasped and arched her body, moving closer to his hand, gently pumping her hips, pulling his finger deeper as he palmed her sex. He slid in another finger and she bucked as he held her against him with his free arm.

"Easy baby. Easy," he murmured as he removed his hand and turned her around to face him. He raised his fingers to his mouth, licked each of them in turn and smiled. "I bet you'll feel as good to sink into as you taste."

It'll be a cold day in hell before you find out! Tabitha wanted to scream it at him, but couldn't get the words out of her mouth. She just silently stared at him as he bracketed each side of her face with his hands, and bent his head to take her mouth with his. He slid his tongue past her lips, polishing her teeth before thrusting further, searching for her tongue and finding it shamelessly willing and receptive as she kissed him back, tasting herself on his lips.

She felt like a marionette with arms dangling uselessly at her sides before she moved them up between them and rested her palms flat against his hard moist pecs. She felt his heart pounding in synch with hers, the evidence of his ardor as much a turn-on as his mouth.

With her finger she slowly circled each nipple in turn, thrilling to him shuddering beneath her hands, her own heart trembling with triumph, warm blood pumping through her veins straight to her head, sizzling her brain cells.

It was a short-lived victory as the buzzer sounded from the kitchen, again.

Eric cursed under his breath and Tabitha caught something about "Grand Central Station." as he stalked out of the room and headed for the kitchen.

Not a moment too soon, she thought, shakily zipping up her pants and running her hands through her hair as she headed for the cherry-framed mirror hanging behind the bedroom door.

Anyone looking at her face would know she'd just been thoroughly kissed—her lips were puffy, her face flushed—kissed and almost stripped bare right here in this bedroom.

How far would she have let him go? How far would she have let herself go?

Each question was moot because she knew the answers: as far as he wanted.

Her secret was out. She wanted him, and he knew she wanted him, knew she hungered. His fingers had been dripping wet with her juices when he'd removed them from her cunt. There was no hiding or denying her lust.

Tabitha quickly rummaged through her bag for her lipstick, unsteadily reapplied the bronze tint as she glanced in the mirror, finally able to get the coat on straight, and determined to leave regardless of whom was at the door this time.

She headed for the living room on rubbery legs, silently thanking the stranger downstairs for saving her from herself.

* * * *

Tabitha squared her shoulders and took a deep breath before stepping across the threshold into the living. She froze several steps away from Eric standing in the foyer with the new arrival.

Blond, blue-eyed and graceful, she was as beautiful as a runway model and just as tall. Her endless legs elegantly showcased to their best advantage in a black peach-skin mini skirt, a voluptuous figure sure to hold her in good stead with Victoria's Secret's hottest paragons. It held her in good stead with Eric, obviously.

Tabitha looked at them standing close and thought how perfect they looked together. She almost laughed out loud at the cliché, but didn't want to be rude, so instead cleared her throat to catch Eric and Ms. Secret's attention.

"EJ, why didn't you tell me you had company?"

Eric turned to her then, smile as boyish and innocent as if he hadn't just had his fingers in her snatch five minutes ago.

"It's not a problem. I was just leaving."

"You were?" Eric arched a brow.

Tabitha nodded as she approached the coat rack to retrieve her trench. She draped it over her folded arms rather than put it on, sure her temperature wouldn't be dropping any time soon, not even once she got outside into the early fall air. "I got what I needed for now. I'll call you to get more details before I start shopping for any items." She swallowed, looked at the way Ms. Secret stood next to Eric, her posture plainly indicating ancient history, current intimacy. Possessiveness.

Jesus, why doesn't she just raise up a leg and piss on him!

Tabitha didn't know why she was so upset. So what, Ms. Secret was obviously one of the aforementioned notches, and from the looks of it, held a special place in Eric Vega's bedpost notches' Hall of Fame. She'd been proven right about him, just hadn't expected to be smacked upside the head with the evidence of his Casanova ways so soon.

She turned to Ms. Secret, politely smiled and proffered a hand.

"Oh, you're right. Pardon my bad manners," Eric said. "Tabitha Lyons, this is Jade Aliberti, a friendly rival from my Mad Ave days. Jade, Tabitha's the personal shopper I was telling you about."

Telling her about? He'd spoken with Ms. Secret about her?

Jade put her hand into Tabitha's, nipping in the bud Tabitha's paranoid moment as she gave it a bone-crunching squeeze.

A warning, or just plain, old-boy-network assertiveness?

Tabitha squeezed back. "Nice to meet you," she said and watched Jade bare her teeth in a Hollywood-perfect facsimile of a smile.

"Same here," Jade said.

Tabitha turned and headed for the door, stopped with her hand on the knob when Eric called her name and sauntered behind her.

"You'll call when you're ready to do this?"

She frowned, silent for so long Eric chuckled at her obvious confusion.

"The shopping. You know, credit card and all that jazz."

"Oh, of course. I couldn't start anything without you."

"I'm glad you said that, because I think I'd like to accompany you, on that first spree at least, see if our tastes mesh."

"I'm sure they don't."

"Well we'll just have to find that out now, won't we?"

Tabitha turned the knob, opened the door and stepped out into the corridor. "I'll call you, and we'll set something up."

* * * *

"So, that was your personal shopper, huh?"

"One in the same."

"She seems like a nice person."

EJ grinned, thought about how nice Tabitha's pussy felt in his hands, how tight and wet she'd been. "Nice" was not the best word to describe Ms. Lyons. Naughty. Succulent. Ready. He'd take his pick. "She is," he agreed rather than go into any more detail.

"Well, as long as she gets the job done."

EJ expected her to do nothing less, knew a workaholic when he met one and couldn't wait to change her all-work-and-no-play ways. "I'll know soon enough."

"Speaking of getting the job done, I know a publicist who would be perfect for you."

"Jade, we already talked about this."

"I know, and I still think you're making a big mistake by handling the publicity yourself."

EJ frowned. "I'm not that long out of the business. I know how to work the system."

"But why should you waste your energies doing that when you can leave the legwork to a professional? No offense."

"None taken." Hadn't he just had this discussion a couple of weeks ago with Evelyn before she'd convinced him to hire a personal shopper and get a makeover? Were all the women in his life in cahoots with each other? "All I'm saying is, why should I waste perfectly good money paying someone to do something I can do myself?"

"Trust me, it wouldn't be a waste. She's good at what she does…and while she's doing what she does best, you can concentrate on what you do best and write."

Hadn't Tabitha said almost the exact same thing to him only days ago? And wasn't more-time-to-write one of the main reasons he'd hired Tabitha? At least originally. Now he wasn't so sure how wise hiring her had been, not when he hadn't written more than a page in his manuscript since he'd met her.

"Besides, you'd be doing me a favor," Jade said.

"A favor?"

"Well, she's new to the business…"

"Ah, I knew it."

"She's good, EJ, really good."

"So you said."

"She just needs a break."

Damn. The magic words. He was a sucker for helping out someone who "needed a break"— and Jade knew this—had had enough breaks along the way to reaching his own goals to realize how important luck and opportunity was to someone just starting out.

"You'd be helping a newbie reach her dreams." Jade batted her big baby-blues at him, prodding as if she'd read his thoughts.

He thought about probing her, discounted it immediately when he remembered how unsuccessful he had been in the past.

Once in a while he came across an individual who was either naturally resistant to his attempts at a mental scan or, like Jade, so strong-willed and defensive, he couldn't get past her shields to read her even when he tried.

He had a feeling Tabitha fell into the latter category, looked forward to testing that theory, and didn't feel a lick of guilt at his uncharacteristic nosiness.

Had he been half as nosy with his girlfriend Sinclair back in high school, he might have been able to save her.

EJ determinedly shook off his depressing train of thoughts, peered at Jade and asked, "What's in it for you?"

"Besides the knowledge that I've done my part to launch the career of a promising bright young star? Not a thing."

"You are so full of it, Ms. Aliberti."

"No, but I'd like to be." The words came out on a low enticing murmur as she winked at him, moved closer and wrapped her arms around his waist.

EJ eased out of her grasp, took a couple of steps back.

He needed some distance, some breathing room. He was still recovering from the spell that Tabitha had woven over him with her sultry, whiskey colored eyes and sexy pouting lips. He was nowhere near ready for a round with Jade.

At least his mind wasn't ready. His body was another story, cock hardening as if in dissension, making its displeasure with him known as it throbbed in his sweats.

Jade stepped closer, tilted her head to one side, staring at him. "Is something wrong?"

EJ shook his head, pivoted and headed for his workstation. He took a seat in the swivel chair and turned to face Jade. "Let's discuss this publicist."

Jade instantly brightened, came over and planted her shapely derriere on the corner of his desk. "So you'll hire her?"

"After we hammer out some details first. Like what's her fee schedule, the scope of her duties, you know, the whole business spiel."

"I'll set up a meeting for you two. How's that sound?"

Sounds like I've had more meetings set up for me in the last week than I had my entire career on Madison Avenue.

Wasn't nearly close to the truth, but the exaggeration helped keep his mind off of his aborted encounter with Tabitha, and how much he wanted her.

He needed the diversion that his writing just wasn't providing at the moment. Maybe hiring and working with Jade's protégée and marketing *Reaching Out* would satisfy that need.

"Do you have a resume for this very talented and gifted publicist?"

"As a matter of fact I do." Jade dipped two fingers into her bag, emerged with one neatly typed, eight-and-a-half by eleven piece of paper and handed it to him.

"Sure of yourself, huh?"

"Sure of what a warm and philanthropic guy you are."

EJ rolled his eyes. "Yeah right." He quickly perused the curriculum vitae, instantly recording vital statistics and work history highlights, before flipping over the paper and quickly jotting down several questions to ask Ms. Jodie Klein.

"Should I tell her to give you a call?"

EJ glanced up from the paper just in time to see Jade cross one curvaceous thigh over the other, her black mini seductively riding up to barely decent proportions. She leaned forward, palms resting on his desk as she gave him a bird's-eye view of her fantastic cleavage. His cock stirred, but not painfully so, nothing he couldn't tame with a little effort.

But why exert the effort?

This was Jade! On-again-off-again, get-his-groove-and-freak-on, call-him-in-the-middle-of-the-night-I'm-coming-over-to-rock-your-world-better-than-any-woman's-ever-rocked-it-before Jade.

Any other time he'd have shamelessly flirted with her, if not outright gotten down to the nitty-gritty. Any other time, he'd have glided a palm up her legs by now to see if she had on stockings and garters or plain old panty hose. Any other time he'd have slid a hand under her skirt and between her thighs to check if she were wearing any panties.

Except this wasn't any other time and hadn't been since that pixie-faced woman had walked into his life.

Damn, what was he thinking?

He'd never been indecisive about what to do with a woman who was throwing herself at him before. Rarely turned down accessible pussy, just went with the flow and saw where it took him.

"So, I can tell her it's all right to call you?" Jade repeated, arching a brow as she waited.

He glanced at her, noticed her irritation and something else glinting in those blue eyes.

Probably confusion since he'd never said no to her before.

Like he was about to do now.

EJ stood, went to the door, and held it open. "Yep, tell her to give me a call."

Jade blinked, hopped down from his desk and sauntered over as EJ extended her leather jacket. She took it, sweetly smiled. "So, uh, you'll call me after? Let me know how it goes?"

"You bet."

Chapter 5

Jade could still smell that Tabitha woman on EJ, the bitch's cloying scent adhering to his skin like some sort of parasite, smothering his familiar piquant musk.

She could only imagine what they'd been up to before she'd arrived, but from his reaction to *her*—he'd stepped away from her! Stepped a-*way* as if she were a dirty street person—there was no telling how far they had gotten.

Jade thought it must have been pretty far, far enough to make EJ turn down *her* advances.

He'd never turned her down before. If she came over to his apartment, or he hers, or even if they met at the apartment of an acquaintance for some sort of get-together, they never left each other without getting off. If it was nothing but a quickie during their lunch breaks, or a blow job and a little cunnilingus in a restaurant bathroom before they each ran back to their offices, somewhere along the line she and EJ came together for some toe-curling love-making.

Admittedly, their trysts had been few and far between of late, and that was something she had been working on correcting. Before that cat-eyed bitch walked into the picture.

Could she have poured on the sweet and innocent act any thicker? Batting those big hazel eyes at EJ as if he was Superman and she was Lois Lane.

Give me a break!

Jade sat in the front seat of her Lexus now, put her Chanel handbag on the passenger seat beside her, removed her compact and opened it to glimpse her face in the mirror. No broccoli in her teeth, every golden-blond hair in place, make-up immaculate and smooth.

What reason could EJ have had to deny her unless he was falling under little Ms. Personal Shopper's negligible charms after only a few days of knowing her? How much more entrenched in his life would she be weeks from now? A month?

Jade didn't intend to find out, had been around too long, worked too hard and gotten rid of far worthier romantic adversaries than to allow some new Jill to just step into the picture and take EJ away from her. She'd scratch out Ms. Uptight Personal Shopper's eyes first.

Jade turned the ignition, started her car and pulled out into the relatively light early evening traffic. She wasn't sure where she was going, she just knew she needed the comfort of a bracing shot of good liquor and even better company.

As she made a right at the next light, she realized just where she needed to go and steered her Lexus uptown, aiming for the east side and her favorite bar and restaurant. Her heart palpitated with nostalgia and first-date anticipation, as if she were on her way to a rendezvous with EJ at what had turned into their preferred haunt.

Jade had to admit now the "friendly rival" comment EJ had used to introduce her to Ms. Uptight Personal Shopper had been pretty accurate, even if it did rankle her.

Even when they'd been rivals—EJ's agency competing with and beating out her agency for the right to do the advertising for several big-name accounts—EJ had always been a charmer, friendly outside of the confines of their respective offices without rubbing Jade's nose in her agency's flops.

In this way, he actually hadn't changed much since high school—always the charmer, always the crowd pleaser, an estrogen magnet wherever he went.

But Jade hadn't known exactly how charming and gracious EJ had remained until—a year after they'd first "met" at some official business function at The Waldorf—her agency finally beat out his for an account.

Jade had been out celebrating, her agency's director in the midst of toasting her and her team for winning the coveted multi-million-dollar account, when EJ sauntered to the bar from across the restaurant where he'd been having dinner, and congratulated her accomplishment.

Far from drowning in his sorrows, he seemed genuinely happy for her success, a fact that didn't fail to surprise as well as turn her on.

Jade watched as he hobnobbed with her associates, accepting their good-natured ribbing and promising redemption.

She refused to believe he could be as nice as he appeared, that his girlfriend's suicide hadn't irrevocably damaged his spirit, and just knew that he was harboring some deep dark animosity, if not for Sinclair for checking out on him so early, then for the cruel world that had taken her away from him.

But then she realized she was judging EJ by most of the boys she'd associated with in high school, most of the executives in her agency now, all men, and even a few women like herself with giant-sized egos who would cut a rival's throat as soon as look at her to hook an account.

As the evening progressed and her gang left the bar to take two prime tables in Smith and Wollensky's dining area, EJ smilingly lingered at her elbow, showing no signs of disinterest or wanting to leave, nor any signs that he recognized her or had heard anything untoward about her and Sinclair in high school. Of course, it helped that Jade and EJ had gone to different high schools, their only connection being Sinclair Donatelli with whom Jade shared one class: creative writing.

Also, despite his allure and charming personality, EJ had been a serious student with no time for frivolous rumor mongers and backstabbing cliques; too wrapped up in his family and very few close friends, especially Sinclair, to entertain the negative social aspects of high school.

After Sinclair's suicide, he'd retreated even further into his school work and family, until by the time graduation had rolled around, he had totally disappeared from the social scene and Jade's radar, rendering all her, to that point, well-planned machinations with Sinclair, her supreme sacrifice, null and void.

To think she had let Sinclair kiss her; had let that awful girl touch her! Which wouldn't have been so bad had she acquired her principal target.

Rather than bringing Jade and EJ together, Sinclair's death had made it impossible for them to ever meet in high school without EJ becoming suspect. Jade had never forgotten him though, had been lost from the first moment she'd seen him at her school's campus visiting Sinclair and made her wonder what the Goth girl had that she didn't; what the Goth girl had that could hold the attentions someone like EJ.

Jade had had her doubts that she'd completely escaped the high school gossip structure before her introduction to the adult ad man EJ, but at his total lack of recognition, she didn't consider the doubts anymore, was relieved and looked forward to them making a fresh start.

Surely enough years have gone by for him to have gotten over the girl by now.

Jade turned to face him full now, one elbow on the shiny mahogany bar top as she held onto her brandy. "Shouldn't you be getting back to your...date?"

"Is that a not-so-veiled attempt to get rid of me, or find out if I was dining alone?"

She chuckled. "Definitely not the former. I already know you're not dining alone."

"And how do you know that?" He grinned.

Her stomach somersaulted, collided with her heart and sped it to Mach-10. He had the most gorgeous dimples! They had been one of the first things she'd noticed about him and, from afar, fallen in love with in high school. "Because no one who looks like you dines alone."

He frowned, but didn't stop leaning on the bar, his relaxed posture contradicting the serious penetrating look on his face.

God she was a sucker for blue eyes, despite having a pair of her own. Hers didn't come anywhere near close to the hypnotic beauty and intensity of his; she knew it was a cliché, but she could actually drown in them, and didn't think twice about diving into their dark depths.

She could almost understand why that pathetic Goth girl had rather died than disappoint or hurt EJ with her and Jade's antics.

Almost, Jade thought, because only a weak loser would go out like that and not fight for her man. Just went to show, Jade had done the right thing befriending Sinclair, getting her confidence enough to influence the girl's already questionable judgment. Sinclair hadn't been good enough for EJ, hadn't deserved him and certainly wouldn't have known what to do to keep a shining star like him happy.

But Jade knew what to do and was more than willing to do it.

"I could say the same thing about you," EJ said now. "But then you aren't alone, are you?"

Jade shook her head rather than spoke, occupied her mouth wetting her whistle instead, trying to ease the sudden dryness of her mouth. No other man, past or present, had ever made her nervous before. Men trembled in her presence, not the other way around.

"Hey Jade! We're waiting for you back here."

Both she and EJ turned to the caller, the art director from Jade's agency who had created the dynamite mock-up that had knocked off the client's socks. He stood at the threshold of the dining room, waving at them.

"You're being summoned," EJ said.

"You guys start without me," Jade called back.

The art director nodded and headed back into the dining area.

"You'll be missed."

"I'm sure."

EJ laughed, the deep honeyed timbre reverberating down her spine and pooling like liquid heat between her legs. "I like you, Aliberti. You're a straight shooter."

"Are you?"

He moved nearer, slid his free arm around her waist and leaned close to her ear, slowly tracing the outer shell with his tongue, and creaming her panties when he whispered, "Let's go find out."

That night was the beginning. Not of hand-in-hand moonlit walks and whispered sweet nothings, but the foundation of a friendship that was based on more than just sex. The sex was good. The sex was great, just not the end-all and be-all. Jade wouldn't have stuck around all these years if she had believed the relationship was all about sex and not shared interests and likes or similar senses of humor.

Not that she'd been sitting at home twiddling her thumbs nights.

She and EJ were not exclusive, though he was one of the most stable and constant forces in her thirty-four-year-old existence. No matter what was going on in her life, or where she was, she always found herself drifting back to him and him drifting to her.

Jade hated the terminology, had never thought of herself as much of a "drifter." She was a determined individual with purpose and goals, and when she put her sights on something, she wound up walking away with the prize.

Somewhere along the line she had gotten sidetracked, dropping her guard and forgetting to protect her borders against outside interferences. Interferences like Ms. Uptight Personal Shopper.

She was going to have to step up her program and face the challenge; she hadn't faced one in a while outside of her job, and decided she needed the practice. After all, nothing worth having was easy to get.

And Jade Aliberti always got what she wanted. Always.

* * * *

Evelyn couldn't wait to get back to her office to call Angela, had almost dialed her on her cell from the car, but decided against it as conversations between her and her sisters tended toward the gesticulating emotional side, especially when they were discussing family matters.

She touched base with her secretary, Daphne, as soon as she got back to the office, picked up her messages and made a few phone calls to her clients before telling Daphne she didn't want any interruptions for at least the next half-hour, and shutting herself in her office. She was glad she pulled in the type of commissions and had the rank that warranted such freedom, but knew she earned every unchecked moment.

Angela interrupted the answering machine and picked up just as Evelyn prepared to leave a message. Evelyn understood why the delay when she heard the ruckus in the background. It sounded like her two nieces were giving their mom a way to go.

"The purchase price of my two youngest has just gone down to fifty cents a piece," Angela said and Evelyn chuckled. She imagined Danni and Tina tying their mother to a homemade stake in the backyard of their suburban ranch house before they unraveled Angela to let her answer the phone.

"Oh, don't you laugh, *auntie*. They're just like you were when we were coming up."

"Come on now, I wasn't that bad. Besides, you used to love my tagging along when we were kids."

"True, true."

Evelyn wasn't surprised by her sister's ready agreement.

Angela had never made any bones about wanting kids of her own since she was a kid herself, the maternal instinct burning bright in her from kindergarten on. She'd practiced her mothering skills on her dolls and her younger siblings every chance she got.

Evelyn remembered many a day of Angela visiting a girlfriend's house for a play date with Evelyn and EJ in tow in their little red wagon. She'd gotten a lot of pre-teen raised eyebrows and a few cancelled play dates, but it never deterred her from bringing along any of her brothers and sisters who wanted to come along for a ride. Angie's motto: take me, take my brothers and sisters. "So what were they doing to get you all flustered before I called?" Evelyn asked now.

"The usual. Valentina's teasing Danielle about a crush this boy at school has on her, and Danielle's fiercely denying it. You know the damage to her tomboy image would be irrevocable if the rumors are true, or much worse got around."

Evelyn laughed, always entertained one way or another when she called her sister, flashes of the same sort of disagreements occurring at the Vega house, especially when Evelyn started to sprout little buds and all three of her older, earlier endowed sisters had made it a day of celebration when they took her out to get her first training bra. The teasing from then on had been endless and merciless, especially since Evelyn at fourteen had been a later bloomer than any of her sisters in addition to having been a diehard tomboy who hadn't wanted anything to do with breasts. At least she hadn't before she discovered, as her three older sister before her had discovered, the persuasive power a pair of mammary glands held over the opposite sex.

"So, any news on the romance front? Can I assume I will be sending an invitation to Tabitha for EJ's surprise party in a couple of months?"

"Hold your horses, sister dear. I think it's a little too early to start sending out *any* sort of invitations regarding those two."

"Shucks, and I had such high hopes."

"Don't give up hope just yet. The situation is promising."

"Spill it. How are things coming along?"

Evelyn smiled. She could see her sister ensconced in her family room recliner/rocking chair and getting ready for a juicy tidbit. "I dropped by EJ's today to check in."

"And was Tabitha there?"

"Indeed she was."

"Give, Evie, give."

She gave Angela as many details as she could about her abbreviated visit, Angela held rapt attention until Evelyn had finished, if her sister's silence on the other end was any indication.

"I know EJ's a pretty fast mover, but do you think they, you know, did anything?" Angela asked in a demure un-Angela-like tone.

"If the look on Tabitha's face was anything to go by, they came pretty damn close."

"How did she look?"

"Blushing and trying to hide it. I've never seen her blush. She's too in control to let anyone know they've gotten to her to that point."

"Leave it to EJ." Angela laughed. "What about him? How'd he look?"

"You know EJ. He's like Nick. He acts like he doesn't care when it's plain that he does."

"*Acts like* being the operative words."

This was true enough.

Evelyn remembered EJ's finger-combed hair, the color creeping up his neck at the mention of Tabitha in his bedroom. She knew EJ hadn't been as unaffected by Tabitha as he'd tried to pretend, knew that whatever had gone on in that bedroom to put the flush in her brother's and her friend's faces had nothing to do with fashion consulting and everything to do with lust.

She wondered what Tabitha's reaction to arriving in the middle of EJ's workout had been. *Had* she come in the middle of it, or had she been a part of it?

"He looked...diddled," Evelyn said, and listened as her sister chuckled and clapped her hands with what could only be described as childish glee.

"So you think they're getting along okay?"

"Like I said, it's early yet, but they seem to...vibe." She couldn't come up with another word to describe what she'd felt flowing between the pair, the current that had filled the air for just the brief moment that Tabitha had come out of the bedroom to say hi to Evelyn. For that instant, the room had sizzled with Tabitha's and EJ's curbed energy, palpable, like a fourth entity in the room.

"He was angry, wasn't he?"

How did the two of them do that? Just pluck thoughts and emotions out of thin air, and with such accuracy? She'd felt the connection at EJ's and she felt it now over the phone with Angela, a sensation of fingers caressing her mind.

Evelyn wondered vaguely if her sister's uncanny link and insight had anything to do with the New Age spirituality that Angie had been practicing for the last two decades. Crystals, aura and chakra readings...even Danni was into it, following in her mother's footsteps wearing different color crystals for different effects and meditating in full lotus position.

EJ wasn't nearly as spiritual, a former choir boy, now the typical lapsed Catholic—baptized in the faith, bred under his devout mother's and the Pope's edicts, but questioning most of the beliefs with which he'd been raised, and barely stepping into a church since he'd reached his late teens.

He and Angela seemed to have nothing in common where religion was concerned except the one time Evelyn remembered walking in on them during the performance of some ritual that involved lots of burning green and white candles, chanting and half lotus positions.

To this day the episode still mystified Evelyn, despite her sister's hurried and vague explanations about a ceremony for promoting positive energy and healing.

Evelyn had just assumed what she'd seen was another manifestation of her sister's rebellion against the doctrines she and her siblings had had rammed down their throats as kids. She hadn't thought the ritual an example of Angela's new burgeoning faith, or that she'd been trying to help EJ over his grief after Sinclair.

She knew now that the connection she'd witnessed between oldest and youngest sibling had been something sublime, proof positive of the special gifts that Angela and EJ had always had, and the beginning of the family's acceptance and understanding of those gifts.

* * * *

Evelyn had a flash now of EJ's last words before he'd closed the door in her face, the warning in his tone before he went back, Evelyn knew, to get busy with Tabitha.

Regardless of his affection for his sisters, or the circumstances that had brought Tabitha to him, she knew he wasn't going to let her and Angela off the hook as easily as it had taken him to throw Evelyn out of his apartment.

She didn't worry too much about it though. Sure, he'd been angry, but he wasn't nearly as angry this time as he had been the last time Angela had tried to fix him up with one of her husband Freddie's co-workers.

This particular intended for EJ had been sweet like Tabitha but, unlike Tabitha, was a typical blind date with a "wonderful personality," in no uncertain terms, what most men would call a dog.

Evelyn didn't know if EJ's level of anger then said more about whether or not he was shallow, as much as his level of anger this time said about Angela's instincts about her brother's preferences in women improving.

"He was angry," Evelyn finally said, "but it's nothing he won't get over."

"If he inherited anything from the Vega blood, it's resilience and forgiveness."

"I'm not so sure about the forgiveness part. At least not until he gets us back."

"Another strong component of the Vega blood: revenge," Angela wisely said and laughed. "So should I be expecting a visit from baby brother sometime soon?"

"I think you should."

Chapter 6

Tabitha made it to work later than her usual seven, but still bright and early at eight Monday morning, unlocked the heavy glass doors to her outer offices, made a beeline for her private office and closed the door.

She had a half-hour to read her e-mail, go over potential client image profiles and sort through requests from her older clients, before Cynthia and a couple of other early birds arrived.

When she sat down behind her desk and booted up her computer, the last thing on her mind was what work she wanted to clear up before the day officially started.

The first thing on her mind was a man, one Eric Vega—tall, broad-shouldered, sexy and a brazen flirt, among other things—thoughts of him plaguing her since she left his loft last week three days ago.

Normally, Tabitha didn't put much credence into Zodiac signs, but in his case she made an exception, recognized several distinctive traits of the Sagittarius he professed to be, especially in his flirtatiousness and outrageous candor, at least where sex was concerned. She had yet to test him on how honest he was in other areas of his life, still hung up on that tie comment he'd made in her office, revealing and candid enough in itself.

She'd never before thought of herself as a nympho or a sexual freak, but that vision she'd had in his bedroom wouldn't let go, had her squeezing her legs together and desperately fidgeting in her seat searching for relief. The image of Eric's wrists bound to his bedposts so intense and real she felt as if she'd done the knots herself and was now eager to try bondage when it had never been a conscience consideration before.

She usually had more control over her urges. What was wrong with her?

Tabitha pondered the latest symptom of her carnality for only a minute before she closed her eyes to recall that imaginary scene in his bedroom, and the actual one—his hand in her pants, fingers inside her, breath warm and seductive in her ear—that now had her nipples hardening against her silk top.

She immediately felt wetness seeping from her vagina.

This was not good, too early in the morning and the wrong place for these shenanigans!

Cynthia would have said there was never a wrong place or time for making whoopie, but then her secretary was a newlywed with the fresh glow of a one-month-old marriage hovering over her body like a halo publicizing her sated woman status for all the world to see.

How could he do this to her when he was nowhere in the vicinity? The arrogant sexy pig!

Okay, no use whining over spilled juices. She'd just have to take care of this while she had time. Granted she didn't often indulge in self-titillation, and certainly not at the office. Indeed, most who knew her probably thought she was still an untried virgin and didn't know where all her parts were much less how to get at them and stimulate them to fruition. But she had enough experience with her body to get herself off. She just preferred a partner, more accurately one who knew what he was doing, and cared enough about her pleasure to do it. Having had only three actual lovers since she'd turned eighteen, she had rarely come across men who fell into both categories at once.

Perhaps some shenanigans now *would* be good since she was meeting him a little later in the day to start shopping. She didn't want to be loaded and pent up with so much sexual frustration the mere sight of him sent her into an emotional and physical tailspin, creaming her panties even more than they were now. If this kept up, she was going to have to start wearing Depends! Either that, or carry extra underwear in her handbag.

Tabitha spread her legs slightly, pussy throbbing with anticipation as she slid her hand into the waistband of her skirt, gliding down into her panties until she'd reached her slit. The crotch of her underwear was moist and the flood had only begun. She teased her labia and vulva with her fingers for several silent moments, intensely focused as she was with any goal she had her eye on attaining, determined to reach it. She gently rolled and pinched her clit between forefinger and thumb before she drove her middle finger into her hot sheath and clamped down on it as if it were a hard pulsing cock.

Tabitha thrust and made circles with the digit, riding her hand and stimulating the bundle of nerves near the entrance of her vagina, writhing in her seat when she reached her G-spot. She thumbed her swollen clit and plunged her finger in a steady rhythm until she felt herself creeping towards climax.

Poised on the precipice, trembling and hot before the gathering force of her orgasm pushed her over the edge, Tabitha released a long deep moan, incredulous, the animal sound shocking her with its unfamiliarity. It concerned her for only an instant before she completely gave into her hunger and tumbled headlong into rapture—waves and waves of cold heat suffusing her belly—that left her perspiring and whimpering in her chair.

Tabitha came back to herself several seconds later, and instantly glanced at the clock across the room, wondering if she'd locked her door.

No sooner than the thought formed in her brain did someone knock.

She started, sat up straight in her chair, opened her handbag on the desk, rummaged through it for a moist towelette—she never left home without them—and quickly cleaned herself up as best she could.

"Tabitha, you in there?"

"Be with you in a minute, Cynthia!"

Tabitha threw the towelette in the trash, quickly glanced at herself in her compact mirror and didn't recognize the glazed bedroom eyes and smudged lipstick of the wild woman looking back at her. She'd been biting her bottom lip so hard she'd bitten the light burgundy hue clear off.

God, what had the man done to her?

Over a weekend she'd turned into a profligate wanton prone to uncontrollable urges, and engaging in early morning sex acts in her office when she should have been conducting business!

And the entire time she'd convulsed in the throes of passion, she thought of him, seen his face with her mind's eye, his gaze intent upon hers, smiling as he watched her bring herself to completion. Looking like the proud teacher of a prized and favorite student who'd just worked out a difficult math problem on the blackboard.

Tabitha gritted her teeth, more frustrated now than she'd been when she'd arrived with that man's image firmly imprinted on her brain cells, taunting her, the release she'd just experienced all but forgotten.

"What were you doing, catching a nap?" Cynthia teased once Tabitha opened the door.

"Of course not!" Tabitha blurted much too quickly and loudly she realized when she saw the arch of Cynthia's eyebrows. "I was in the middle of responding to a client and I didn't want to stop the flow before I answered the door."

Cynthia grinned. "Oh, I thought maybe you had given into a basic human necessity for once like sleep, Bionic Woman."

Tabitha felt herself blush, the heat of blood rushing to her face so concentrated she thought she might be having a hot flash. If Cynthia hadn't come so close to the truth, the situation might have been funny. "You leave me and my basic necessities alone," she mumbled.

Cynthia offered a stack of messages. "These came in Friday while you were out and after you called in the last time."

Tabitha took them. "Thanks." She sifted through them quickly, saw one from Eric that had come in at eight-thirty that morning and showed it to Cynthia.

"Oh, yeah, that one came in as I was walking in the door. You must have been involved in your e-mail and didn't hear the phone."

"I guess so."

The man must have had radar, his call coming in somewhere between her thrusting her finger into herself, and climaxing. Sheesh!

What was he doing up at such an early hour?

Tabitha would have liked to believe he was as hot and bothered by the thought of her as she was by the thought of him, unable to sleep or function as usual. Not that he had a snowball's chance in hell of relieving himself with her. He could damn well suffer in silence like her.

"He was just calling to confirm your appointment for later this morning," Cynthia said then stepped back, peering at Tabitha from top to bottom as if seeing her for the first time.

Tabitha put a hand to her hair, face tingling still, wondered if evidence of her earlier activities was on her person, something she'd missed. "What?"

"I like that outfit!"

"Oh, please, this?" Tabitha raised her arms away from her body and glanced down at royal-blue silk blouse, burgundy flower-print skirt, royal-blue pantyhose, and matching burgundy suede pumps. "It's not like I haven't worn this before, Cynthia. You've seen me in it."

"Maybe, but there's something different about the way it's looking on you today. The skirt is more flouncy and flirty. The blouse falls on your body more sensually."

"Will you stop."

"I'm serious, it's like you have a...glow."

"Don't be ridiculous!"

Cynthia chuckled, undeterred by her employer's glare. "Probably has something to do with that hunky new client." She pointed her chin at the message in Tabitha's hand.

Tabitha frowned. She had a special aversion to the term "hunk" or any variation thereof.

Her mother had had a penchant for using the all-encompassing description quite frequently to describe men she found attractive, which consisted roughly of most of the male population. To say Denise Sayer Lyons wasn't very discriminating was an understatement.

This alone would have been enough for Tabitha to question her parentage, despite her tender eight years. At one point she had even considered the possibility that she had been adopted, so much more exotic looking and darker than both her parents, that she couldn't imagine being the natural child of so pale a pair of Caucasians.

She remembered her mother during one of the woman's more plastered and mean days—with the usual glassy faraway look in her eyes—nipping the adoption theory in the bud when Tabitha overheard an argument between her and the man Tabitha had grown up knowing as her dad. She found out then that her biological father had been a "hunky" rock musician that Denise, the wild and undisciplined devotee, had met and screwed backstage after a concert.

Her mother hadn't even known the man's name!

Oh, what the sisters at St. Anthony's Catholic Orphanage would have to say about that, Tabitha thought now, wincing at the memory of a ruler smacking her knuckles or bottom for what the nuns deemed soul-forfeiting transgressions. At the time the category included anything from profanity to smoking, both of which Tabitha had done with great regularity, if only to give the black-clad celibates conniptions and something to think about when they were bruising their knees doing penance and reciting their Hail Marys.

Come to think of it, her earlier act of self-love ran pretty high on their burning-in-hell meter of sin too. Poor her.

"Hunky?" Tabitha arched a brown now at Cynthia. "You don't be careful, I'll tell that new husband of yours."

"I love Dillon with all my heart, but I'm not blind. The guy is hunky." Cynthia stared at her as if waiting for a response, and when she didn't get one, she asked, "Don't you think so?"

"He's a client like any other. Nothing more, nothing less."

"Oh, he's a client all right, but he's not like any of the other stuffy old clients already in your stable. No offense. He's a fresh piece of prime meat."

Tabitha just grinned, shuffling her messages as she went back to her desk. She sat down and glanced up at Cynthia poised at the door. "Get back to work, you."

"Want me to hold your calls?"

She took a minute too long to think about it before Cynthia was closing the door with an "I'll hold all calls" in her wake.

Tabitha put her messages down next to her phone, staring out over the empty expanse of her large glass desk. Barren. Unlike Cynthia's cubicle with the swarm of framed family photos on every available surface and others pinned to the two tack boards. Nephews and nieces, mom and dad, brothers and sisters, new husband…

It reminded Tabitha of Eric's entertainment center, the simultaneously full empty feeling she had gotten perusing the shelves of pictures, and coming to the realization that she had nothing like that sort of support system in her life. No siblings or cousins to argue or fight with growing up. No aunts and uncles by whom to be spoiled. No sister to have lunch with at a sidewalk café the way Evelyn had been having lunch with her older sister Angela when Tabitha had bumped into her client one day on the upper east side.

She realized that if she dropped dead today or tomorrow, there was no one to mourn her, no one to really miss her, the bastard child of a manic-depressive groupie mother and nameless, faceless rock musician father. Sure, Cynthia and the rest of *Lyons' Style, Inc.* employees might miss her for the time it took them to start a collection and notify all her clients of the sad news, but other than a job and a paycheck, what was she to them, really?

Vogue might miss her, but once the initial shock of her mistress's unmoving body wore off, a long period of time past before anyone checked on the rotting-corpse smell in apartment 2A, and hunger set in, Tabitha reasoned she might become convenient kitten chow for her practical and self-possessed little beast.

She swallowed, not used to all the deep reflection, definitely not prone to the maudlin self-pity that was beginning to pervade her chest. At least not before she had met that maddening man with the big, close knit family of which any former abandoned-orphan-sexually-abused-and-neglected-foster-child would be envious.

Envy. Another emotion for which she would have gotten a sound whack across the knuckles had she allowed the nuns to know she harbored it. So she'd hidden her jealousy of the cute little girl four years younger than her and who had been placed with a nice couple from the suburbs. Or the plainly Caucasian gap-toothed boy her age who had been adopted by a nice couple from upstate New York.

Either she'd been too young, too old, too female, or too ethnic, but never just right for a family to want her, or a stable couple willing to take her in. And the ones that did take her...well, they had left a lot to be desired on the altruistic, good-parenting-skills meter.

Hell, she was doing a lot of soul searching this morning. Amazing what a round of early morning masturbation could dig up and do for the spirit. She guessed she had Eric and the memory of his sexy smirk and wink to thank for providing the shovel.

Tabitha answered several e-mails and returned her calls from Friday before she finally, quickly dialed the number Eric had given Cynthia.

She couldn't get out of it. His call warranted a response, she just determined she would make it short and to the point. There was no need to get personal or go into details. Because the longer she stayed on the phone with the man, the more chance she ran of having to close herself up in this office for the rest of the afternoon to masturbate the day away rather than confront in the flesh the inspiration behind her urges.

Coward.

She winced as if from a physical blow, the term was not something she usually thought of in conjunction with herself.

Eric answered his cell on the second ring, sounded winded, voice shaky and fading as if he were on the run.

"Hello Eric, it's Tabitha returning your call."

"Hey, Tabitha!"

He sounded genuinely happy to hear from her, voice silky smooth despite the bad connection. It made her heart beat that much harder at the idea that she had been denigrating the man since she'd walked in the door this morning at the same time she'd been using the memory of their time together as a prelude to pleasuring herself.

"I'd just wanted to confirm that we're still meeting later this morning," Eric said.

"Yep, at eleven—"

"In front of Macy's."

"You've got it."

There was a long pause into which Tabitha could have rammed her entire wardrobe, which was pretty substantial by some standards, and she held her breath before Eric spoke again.

"Is there something wrong, Tab?"

"Nothing except you calling me out of my name."

He chuckled on the other end, and Tabitha saw the big dimples as if he were standing right in front of her, felt as if he had been with her in spirit all weekend anyway.

And soon he'll be with you in body.

God, what was she going to do with him?

If she were telegraphing her emotions so obviously over the phone that he could, through static and a bad connection, pick up on her mood, she was in trouble. It was a good thing she knew about it now so she could act and steel herself accordingly.

This meeting was not a date, they weren't in a relationship other than client and personal shopper, strictly business. That was it!

Suitably self-chastised, Tabitha took a deep breath and said coolly, "I'll see you at eleven." Then she disconnected the line before he could argue or otherwise comment.

Chapter 7

EJ stared at his cell, shaking his head as realization dawned that she had actually hung up on him. Anyone else on the other end and he would have deemed the act rude, but for some reason coming from Tabitha, it just seemed like business as usual, her way. Blunt and to the point and not her problem if someone didn't like it. Charming.

He grinned, looking forward to his meeting with her now more than ever.

A challenge.

He'd been looking forward a lot lately, more productive—finishing two articles and two chapters in his work-in-progress—and busier the last couple of hours than he'd been the last couple of days, like the U.S. Army, doing more at five a.m. than most people did the entire day.

Jodie Klein had shown up bright and early at eight this morning, as per their discussion Friday. She had another resume with her and a giant portfolio with samples of her limited, though impressive, work.

He liked her ideas and energy, knew a real go-getter when he saw one, went with his gut and hired her on the spot, and thought himself lucky to have her on his team.

EJ then gave Kyle Torrence—freelance graphic designer who had worked on several ad campaigns on which EJ had been Creative Director and now EJ's web designer—a call to hook him up with Jodie and see what they could come up with for his website campaign.

That comment Tabitha had made about his not being a morning person must have chafed more than he realized. He'd been getting up long before noon the last couple of days, and getting in several hours and chapters of writing when normally he would have just been getting up.

The early hours hadn't yet caught up with him though he was still keeping his usual late schedule, up until the wee hours researching and outlining when he wasn't actually writing.

Once he had touched Tabitha, even if it had only been a tease—had gotten the initial rough meeting out of the way, and had decided he was going to have her—EJ had been able to write, firm decision releasing his creativity.

EJ pulled into his sister's driveway in Wantagh forty-five minutes after hanging up with Tabitha. He turned off the ignition and got out of his Jeep as his sister came out and stood on the front steps as if expecting him.

He hadn't felt her touch as he'd driven through her tree-lined neighborhood, didn't think she had scanned him on the way, and finally decided she must have been forewarned by Evelyn.

"EJ, I've been expecting you."

"No kidding." He walked across the freshly mowed front lawn and instead of going into her outstretched arms, he put her in a gentle headlock and mussed her hair.

Angela giggled. "This is no way to treat a grandmother."

EJ immediately released her and caught her by the shoulders. "Who and when?"

"Oh, no one's pregnant. Perhaps I should have said a potential grandmother. You know I'm at that age. You owe me a little more respect than manhandling me like one of your nephews."

"And you owe me a little privacy."

Angela opened the front door and led the way into the house as EJ followed. "Whatever on earth are you talking about?"

"Evelyn, Tabi—"

"Don't tell me you're not happy with her."

EJ sighed, forked a hand through his hair, took a seat at the table in his sister's sun-drenched tangerine colored kitchen and Angela immediately offered him a cup of her famous espresso.

"Thanks," he mumbled and took a sip. "Whether I'm happy with her or not isn't the point."

"What is, EJ?"

"Look, I didn't come over here to argue about this."

"Didn't you?"

"Angela." He closed his eyes and gritted his teeth as Angela took the seat across from him and reached for his hand. EJ opened his eyes and glared. "You've got to stop doing this."

"What? Helping you find your soul mate?"

"You know I don't believe in that New Age…stuff, Angie."

"You used to."

"No, I used to humor you," he lied. "Besides, I could find my own soul mate *if* I wanted to."

"You can find a woman. We all know you've got more than enough experience in that area, but the question is, can you find the right one?"

"And the answer is 'none of your business.'"

She squeezed his hand and returned his stare. "I hate seeing you like this."

He raised his brows. "Like what?"

"So unhappy, in denial."

EJ jerked his hand out of hers, lurched to his feet and paced in front of the table. After several seconds, he paused and scowled at her. "I'm not a grief-stricken teenager anymore. I got over it a long time ago."

"Did you?"

He curtly nodded and sat back down across from Angie. "Sinclair is ancient history." *And even if she wasn't, you can't cure what ails me with burning candle rituals anymore.*

"That's what your mouth says, but your heart tells a different story."

EJ smiled at her response to his unspoken thoughts and last statement. "Will you stop acting like you know every little thing that goes on inside me and I don't."

"It's not that you don't know what's going on. It's that you're ignoring it, ignoring your nature, acting against it."

"How do you know what my nature is?"

Angela gave him one of those sage looks that used to annoy the hell out of him when he was a teenager. He didn't know what pissed him off more, the fact that she was usually right, or that she didn't have a qualm about sharing her perceptions with him any chance she got.

He guessed he should have been grateful that she cared so much, but sometimes she could be more interfering and smothering than their mother where his love life was concerned.

"I know you, EJ. None of us has seen you settle down with one woman for more than a month. It's not healthy."

"Yeah, but it's fun."

"You see what I mean? You try to come off as this carefree gigolo playing the field when what you want most out of life is to settle down and be with one woman."

"Please don't project your ideals onto me."

"I'm not. They're your ideals. You just won't admit it."

He might as well be trying to dust cobwebs off the moon for all the effect his objections were having on his sister. He'd known ahead of time that coming over was going to be a waste of time, but he couldn't not come, he couldn't let her interference go unaddressed.

EJ took one last gulp of his espresso, wiped his mouth with the napkin beside the cup and saucer and stood to leave.

Angela caught his hand, peered up at him and whispered, "You couldn't have saved her, EJ. Sinclair was too troubled, too far gone for you to help."

He swallowed hard, felt his Adam's apple bobbing and hoped his sister didn't notice it. "I know that," he murmured.

"She wouldn't want this for you."

He was almost afraid to ask, but did anyway. "Wouldn't want what?"

"You to be afraid to feel as deeply for someone else as you felt for her."

"Who says I'm afraid?"

She just stared at him, said nothing.

"Look, I've got to go. I have an—"

"Appointment with Tabitha."

"Before you get that glow in your eye, it's not a date. It's business. We're going shopping."

"Sounds like real serious business."

"It's her business. As you well know."

Angela rose and slid an arm around his waist as she walked him to the front door. She stood on her toes to kiss his cheek, palmed his lightly whiskered jaw and smiled. "Think about what I've said, okay?"

How could he not? Which was exactly what she'd been counting on, he knew.

* * * *

EJ cut it close, walking over to Macy's on 7th Avenue from the parking garage on 31st Street between 8th and 9th Avenues, arriving with only five minutes to spare—late in Tabitha's book.

He caught sight of her before she saw him, noticed her tapping right pump, arms folded across her rounded breasts in a closed-off, stay-away stance that didn't scare or fool him one bit.

He smiled as he neared and she still hadn't seen him, sidled to her left and tapped her right shoulder from behind.

When Tabitha turned and didn't see anyone on her right, she pivoted to her left and in that unguarded instant when she recognized him, he saw the smile in her eyes and knew he had her.

"On time is not late, contrary to some opinions."

She turned without saying a word and headed through the revolving doors of Macy's.

EJ followed her into the store immediately entering the Men's Wear section, confronted with ties, shirts, suits and more ties.

He shivered, uncomfortable not just because it had been so long since he'd been in this particular department store to do any serious shopping, but for the mere fact that he was in his sister Emilia's territory.

He loved his sister—loved all of his siblings, he truly did—but Tabitha had had enough exposure to the Vega females in Evelyn and Angela. He didn't want to overwhelm the poor girl with his family before either of them was ready. Not to mention he did not want to get embarrassed in front of someone he wanted so bad he couldn't think straight and he would definitely be vulnerable if they bumped into Emilia. Bossy Evelyn was a bad enough influence. He didn't want to add Emilia the Saint to the mix of him and Tabitha and give his sister a chance to interfere in his embryonic relationship with a fresh woman.

Tabitha didn't seem to notice his uneasiness, busy browsing the tie racks before she came back to where he had paused in the center of the floor, frowning at him before her eyes lit up as if with sudden understanding. "I know how you feel about suits, but I thought we'd start with your least favorite items first and get them out of the way."

"But I don't want—"

She put a finger to his lips and he immediately shut up as a waft of her soft vanilla musk tickled his nostrils. "We'll get all-purpose shirts and ties that can go with anything, so it won't matter what sort of suit, or dress slacks and jackets you buy."

"What if I don't want any ties?"

"Just trust me. There'll come a time when you'll need one. Like if you're asked to speak at some writer's convention or conference. You'll want to look your best, and make a good impression now won't you?"

"Who says I'm going to be asked?"

"I've read your writing. You'll be asked, trust me."

EJ was so flattered the irony of the situation was almost lost on him—the personal shopper pitching to the former ad man.

He silently followed her to a table of shirts and watched Tabitha automatically pick up his size in several different colors. She turned to him, put each shirt against his chest, explaining as she did that the trick to finding a flattering shade was to hold the shirt under your chin to see how it reflected on your face.

EJ assumed that aqua, dark-blue striped, red and purple were good shades for him from the choices she made.

She settled on six shirts in varying colors and patterns that he never would have bought for himself, but decided he'd go along and trust her.

After she made the selections and handed them over to EJ, she made a beeline for the ties in the same hue as the shirts she'd picked. She selected six designer silk numbers. "We're going to punch up sedate suits with boldly colored shirts and brightly patterned ties," she said, then surprised him when she picked up one plain cotton long sleeve and one short sleeve black T-shirt on their way to the dressing room. She explained that she "had plans for the T-shirts."

Finally, she brought him to the suits and helped him pick out several to try on, assuring him that they weren't going to purchase them all, just wanted to look at a variety.

He tried on the suits and shirts in the order that Tabitha told him to, and as he got to the last suit and modeled it in front of her, he realized how much her opinion mattered to him, how much he wanted to look good for her. How much he wanted to please her.

"Now this works just like I thought it would!"

"Like you thought, huh?" EJ raised his arms from his body and did a 360 in front of the mirror as Tabitha came up behind him and smoothed the lapels of the charcoal jacket.

He turned to glance at himself in the full-length mirror, admiring the fit of the suit, the color coordination. The T-shirt beneath the vest was dressy but not stifling.

"I pictured you in something like this when I was at your loft the other day, knew it would look good on you."

"You did, did you?"

"Well, it does doesn't it? And don't even bother to lie."

He looked at himself in the mirror again, then turned to her with a grin. "It looks great."

"And you're not even wearing a tie."

"Means we can save them for something else more useful," he whispered and chuckled when she blushed.

"C'mon. We're about done here." She pushed him towards the fitting room and pulled the curtain closed without another word.

* * * *

They spent another couple of hours in Macy's, more looking than actual purchasing and EJ came away with not only two suits, some ties and shirts, but a small idea of what a personal shopper's job consisted of, along with a new respect for Tabitha and her profession. More respect with each passing minute that his feet throbbed in a pair of Nike cross-trainers.

He'd had no idea that taking off and trying on clothes was such hard work.

"Can we break for something to eat?" EJ suggested, gave her a hopeful look. "I haven't had anything since breakfast; it's almost four and I'm starved. I'm sure you are too?"

Tabitha looked at her watch as if to confirm the time. "Wow, I had no idea it was so late!"

"So? Can we?"

"Can we what?"

God save him from a woman with a purpose. "Break for something to eat. My treat. Somewhere in the Village maybe. A sidewalk café."

"There are plenty of places around here to e—"

"I'd like to beat rush hour traffic and be closer to home. Besides, if I know you, I'm sure there are some places in the area to do some shopping."

"You're full of surprises, Eric"

"I may not do a lot of shopping, but I know there are some funky little clothing boutiques in the Village where we can do some browsing if not actually purchasing." He saw the glitter in her eyes before he finished his sentence, wondered what he was getting himself into.

"You're exactly right. And I know a couple of spots that have some dynamite designer shoes that would go great with that charcoal suit."

"Great."

* * * *

"Tell me about yourself."

Tabitha chuckled, covering her discomfort sipping her café latte and wiping her mouth.

"What's funny?"

She smiled, shook her head as she glanced past him for several long moments before finally getting her fill of narrow cobblestone streets, comedy clubs and growing pedestrian traffic in the Washington Square Area where EJ had settled.

"I'm serious, Tabitha. I want to know about you."

"There's nothing to know. You're my client and I'm your personal shopper."

"C'mon now. You know there's more to us than that."

She nodded as if agreeing, then she opened her mouth to dispute. "That was a mistake. It shouldn't have happened, and I intend to make sure it doesn't happen again."

His cock twitched at the challenge in her voice, blood pumping through his veins like lava as he picked up the gauntlet. "Why?"

"Why?"

"You heard me. Why? Why shouldn't it have happened?"

She leaned across the table and said through her teeth, "You know perfectly well why."

"Because you're my personal shopper? What rule book are you working from?"

"The rule book of business: never screw the client."

He knew the book well, used to live by it in advertising, just didn't think that it applied to their relationship. It wasn't like major multi-million-dollar deals were riding on whether or not they slept together. They weren't rivals, or business associates. Just client and personal shopper.

What possible repercussions could come from them sleeping together?

EJ thought about it for a moment, couldn't come up with anything and decided to attack her from a different angle. "You know it's not fair, you're knowing everything about me and my knowing nothing about you."

"Not everything."

"What do you want to know that you don't know already?"

Tabitha shrugged then licked her lips, and EJ had to restrain himself from leaping across the table to take her mouth with his. He settled for staring at the glossy effect her tongue had given to her full lips, imagined what his penis would look like sliding in and out of that giving and firm orifice.

He stopped his train of thoughts dead in their tracks when he glanced into her almond-shaped whiskey colored eyes, thought she looked incredibly young and vulnerable right then pushing a leaf of her spinach salad back and forth across her plate.

EJ felt her sadness, saw the mass hovering around and clouding her aura, but he could not read her and he'd been trying all afternoon against his better judgment. Because something told him this woman wasn't what she seemed and preferred that no one, especially him, got past her cool untouchable façade.

Somewhere along the line, he knew he was going to have to tell her about himself, his own personal credo about respecting privacy demanding it but not now. He was too much of a coward and procrastinator, enjoying the pure simplicity of her ignorance. No fear. No disbelief or judgments. No accusations. No Salem-witch-hunt-questions.

And he'd gotten enough of the latter in his life as a child to welcome the absence of all the above, had learned to hide what he could do, even from his family, Angela the one person who knew and then only because she was like him.

EJ remembered the first time his oldest sister had realized he was gifted, the way she'd gawked when he'd correctly predicted everyone's cards when he'd done his magic act at his oldest nephews' fifth birthday party

The rest of the family had thought nothing of it, only that he was a well-trained magician who had studied his craft well enough to pull the wool over everyone's eyes, even the adults. But Angela'd known there was more to EJ's act than just slight of hand or well-executed tricks.

She'd taken him aside to ask him how he'd done it, how he'd guessed with such accuracy though she already knew. When he confirmed her suspicions, there was no shock or askance look, only acceptance and...pleasure. As if she was glad she wasn't alone in the world, wasn't alone in the family with her gifts.

Just coming into her own with New Age religion, Angela took him under her wing, helping EJ to identify the scope of his own power, learn its limits; helping him hone his talent.

Before Angela's training, monster migraines plagued him. He had learned to live with the pain, the disjointed voices in his head, hadn't known their source until his sister explained he was hearing other peoples' thoughts. Once she identified the cause, and given him several survival tips that involved meditation and erecting psychic walls to maintain his sanity, EJ was able to curb the attacks, and block out the voices unless he was purposely scanning and wanted to hear an individual's thoughts.

Before Angela, he hid his mind-reading abilities beneath a veneer of good instincts, people skills and excellent intuition., but with Angela he was free to explore, free to strengthen his innate talents, no longer needed to lie.

It took his sister to make EJ see even had he been stronger, practicing his skills all along and with a purpose, he couldn't have saved Sinclair Donatelli.

"Sinclair was mentally ill, a drug user. Two strikes you couldn't have overcome, EJ," Angela told him after the funeral. "You couldn't have known what she was planning. She didn't want you to know."

A long time past before he could admit his sister was right, and even then, he couldn't absolve himself of all blame.

Sinclair had been his best friend, his lover, and even without the gifts EJ thought he should have known that she was in pain, too much pain to face another day.

* * * *

EJ peered at Tabitha across the table, wondered what lay behind those calm but expressive eyes, wondered what thoughts were in her mind.

He didn't think her sadness was anywhere near as complete and far-reaching as had been Sinclair's, but he didn't know.

He knew he was rationalizing, of course, giving himself a reason to invade her privacy guilt-free.

EJ reached across the table and caught her free hand in his, knew that he was stepping over her imaginary, do-not-cross line, but couldn't help it. Something in her called to him—her sadness, her mysterious past, her mental walls—made him want to know more. "I'm serious, Tabitha. What is it you want to know about me?" He knew he was taking a chance—that she might ask him something he wasn't prepared to answer—but decided it was a chance worth taking, if it meant she'd open up. A little, just a piece was all he was asking for.

"I think I know more than enough about you, Eric," Tabitha said. "More than enough to do the best job that I can for you."

"What if I'm not talking about job related?"

"I'm sorry, but that's all I have to offer."

Liar, he thought, and would prove it if it were the last thing he did.

Chapter 8

Tabitha was proud of herself.

She had managed to not jump his bones all afternoon, and considering the level of lust that had been building up inside her from the time he'd tapped her shoulder until now, that was saying something. Just sitting here outside the fitting room, imagining his tall broad frame without any clothes on was driving her crazy.

Tabitha shifted in her big comfy velvet seat, crossing one thigh over the other just as the curtains rustled and Eric stepped out of the fitting room sporting a mint green dress shirt, purple silk tie and purple dress slacks.

He looked great. Okay, reality check. The man looked great in anything. He'd looked great in all seven suits he'd tried on at Macy's though he'd only bought two. And he'd looked great in the several outfits he'd tried on here at *Mikail's* boutique. Especially the dark gray polo shirt and gray pleated and cuffed chinos that flatteringly fell on his slim hips, hugged his hard butt just so, and displayed what looked to be an impressive package to its fullest advantage.

God, she wanted to touch him! She wanted to slide her hands under his clothes and fondle those firm muscles, feel them twitch beneath her fingers, feel his warm pliant skin beneath her palms and know that she affected him the way he affected her.

"You like?" Eric raised his arms from his sides, repeating the motions he had executed at least twenty times today, grinning as he did a 360 and stopped to face her.

Tabitha licked her lips, vagina moist and tense from just looking at him.

She more than liked. She loved, and if she had to sit idly by and watch this man take off and put on another outfit without showing her new true sensual colors, she'd scream. "I like."

He glanced at himself in the mirror again, smoothing down the tie. "I have to tell you, I didn't think this green and purple would work, especially the pants, but now that I see it on me, I kind of dig it."

"You dig it, Moon Beam?" She smiled, thought her earlier image of him at Woodstock hadn't been too far off the mark.

"Yeah. I dig it." He came closer, leaned down and before she could react, chastely pecked her on the nose.

Tabitha sputtered, stood and pushed him back towards the fitting room. "You're wasting time, and you've got several more outfits to try on."

He caught her wrist and pulled her into the room with him, laughing as she fell against his chest and he pulled the curtain closed behind them. "I'd rather try on you."

"This is totally inappropriate, Eric."

"Who says?"

"I d—"

He bent his head and captured her mouth with his.

Tabitha tilted her head, let him explore every warm moist crevice, his tongue brushing hers as she buried her hands in his hair, reveling in the silken texture and pulling him closer.

His hands glided over her body, from the back of her short flouncy skirt, to the front of her silk blouse in one fell swoop, heating up her skin through her clothes.

Tabitha pulled away, breathless, one hand firmly planted in the center of his chest. "We can't do this. Not here."

His blue eyes glinted as he leered. "Not here implies somewhere else. Have some place in mind? Preferably close. My loft is free." He wiggled his eyebrows Groucho Marx style, dimples in full effect.

"That wasn't what I meant and you know it."

"What did you mean?"

"I mean, we can't do this. *At all.*"

"Sure we can. All you have to do is let it happen." He closed the space between them, reached for her, cupping a breast.

She gasped, not realizing he'd undone the top several buttons of her blouse and unlatched her bra until she glanced down and saw his hand against her naked copper tone flesh. "You're fast," she blurted.

"You have no idea." He pressed her against the wall, lightly pinching and rolling an already hardened nipple between his thumb and forefinger.

Tabitha moaned and Eric covered her mouth in a scorching kiss that sent her stomach spiraling in a pool of molten liquid draining straight out of her vagina.

"Is everything all right in there, sir?"

Eric dragged his mouth away from hers long enough to say, "Everything's fine!" He stared down at her, licking his lips like a hungry predator. "More than fine," he murmured, making slow sensual circles with a forefinger around her right nipple.

Tabitha moved away and slapped at his hand. "You're absolutely incorrigible."

"Guilty as charged."

She stopped herself from smiling. She didn't want to encourage him, not that he needed much encouragement to be the total scoundrel that he was.

God, when he looked at her like that—indigo eyes smoky and heavy-lidded, plainly proclaiming exactly what he wanted to do to her—Tabitha wanted to give in, give him anything he wanted, do anything to please him.

She had to get away from him before she fell any deeper under his spell.

Tabitha moved to the opposite side of the cramped room—not nearly far enough—warily watching him, didn't realize she was panting until she saw her breasts heaving from the corner of her eyes. She reached up to latch her bra and button her blouse with shaky hands under Eric's glittering watchful gaze, couldn't drag her eyes away from his. "You messed up my clothes."

"I was actually trying to get them off."

"You don't stop, and you'll mess up those clothes." She pointed her chin at his outfit.

"If I'm going to buy them anyway, will it make a difference?"

"Yes, it will. They'll know what we were doing in here."

He took a couple of steps towards her and before she knew it, he had her pinned against the wall again. "They already do," Eric whispered.

"Eric…" Her next words died on a groan as he lifted her skirt and palmed her sex.

He caressed her through the crotch of her pantyhose for several long torturous moments before he slid his hands up to the waistband and pulled down her panties and hose in one rough swift motion.

"Eric, please do—"

He got to his knees, buried his head beneath her skirt and in an instant, Tabitha felt his mouth on her.

Unconsciously, she gyrated her hips, grinding her pelvis against his mouth, felt him open and explore her with his fingers before his tongue penetrated her.

Tabitha gasped and would have tipped over had he not held her steady, gripping and spreading her ass cheeks as he pushed his tongue into her pussy as deep as it would go, burrowing and circling like some piece of earth moving equipment—how freaking appropriate!

She felt his fingers again, thumb and forefinger rhythmically stimulating her clit, zinging hot flashes of sensation straight to kitty town.

God…she was…going to…explode!

Tabitha bit her bottom lip hard to keep from crying out, tasted blood in her mouth as an orgasm crashed down on her sudden as an epileptic seizure. She stiffened, then convulsed as Eric got to his feet and held her close.

She lay her head against his chest—just resting, just catching her breath, she told herself—listened to his speeding heartbeat echoing the pattern of hers, slowly opened her eyes and stepped out of his arms to see him smiling down at her.

"C'mere, I'll kiss the hurt and make it better," he said and leaned close, smelling of her juices, tasting of her essence, caressing her lips with his, sliding his tongue into her mouth.

She let him kiss her, kissed him back for several mindless seconds before she got the strength to pull away and ask, "Why did you do that?"

"Kiss you?"

"No. You know what."

"Didn't you want me to?"

"No…no I didn't."

He stared at her, and she could see the unspoken accusation in his eyes, could hear it in her own mind.

Liar, liar, pants on fire. You wanted it so badly you were close to begging for it.

Eric palmed her cheek with one hand as he leaned in for another kiss, this one a light brush of his lips against hers, but no less potent or intimate than his last one. "Yes, you did."

"Arrogant bastard!" Tabitha jerked down her skirt, pulled up her panties and hose, and smoothed her clothes back into as much a semblance of order as she could before stomping out of the dressing room.

"Is everything all right, ma'am?" one of *Mikail's* salesmen asked, brows raised when he paused in front of her as she took a seat outside the fitting room.

She'd just insulted a man who'd gone down on her and given her an earth shattering orgasm—one like she'd never experienced before—and stalked out on him for no other reason than to *show him*. What she should have done was gotten down on her knees to thank him for showing *her* the incredible lightness of coming.

No, everything is not all right. "Everything's fine."

* * * *

"I don't understand why you're so angry with me. I was just being honest."

"Your version of honest leaves a lot to be desired."

"Version? There's only one version and that's the one that tells me you want the same thing I do."

"Will you just get off of it already!"

"I could, if I was on it."

Tabitha cursed and folded her arms across her breasts as she sat in the passenger seat of his Jeep, staring straight ahead. "Would you mind driving me home? Otherwise, I can call a cab."

He glanced at her, arched a brow. "I was going to offer, but I figured you didn't want to be anywhere near me for as long as it took me to get you home."

"Park Slope isn't that far from here," Tabitha said, and when he didn't respond, she turned to him and huffed. "If it's too far for you, I can call a cab, like I said."

"Calm down will you. I'll drive you." Eric put his key in the ignition and started the Jeep.

Tabitha sat beside him seething and determined to enjoy the ride in silence and gather her strength for the tussling match that would surely come once they arrived at her brownstone.

Christ, she wanted to strangle the man!

No one else in all her twenty-eight years had managed to arouse her dander more strongly than Eric did. Not her mother during one of her really bad binges, not her friends who fixed her up on blind dates against her wishes, and not Evelyn for introducing her to her brother in the first place.

She closed her eyes as if to escape the powerful emotions Eric inspired, and only succeeded in replaying her climax in the fitting room over again and again—his mouth on her, her pussy open and weeping beneath his indecent assault on her senses.

Tabitha shivered beside him, clutching her arms firmer, as if she could ward off her desire, as if she could stop her nipples from painfully tightening against her blouse.

He turned to her. "Are you cold? I could put on the heater."

She was cold and hot, and no heater or air conditioner could help her when the source of her mood swings and temperature changes was sitting right beside her weaving in and out of Monday evening traffic with the skill of an Indy 500 driver. "I'm fine."

Tabitha felt his eyes on her though he was wise enough not to comment on her lie.

She wasn't fine, and didn't think she'd ever be fine again if this man stayed in her life for longer than it took her to help him purchase a new fall and winter wardrobe.

God, what would happen if he wanted to continue employing her services for spring and summer? Could she really turn down his business? Sure, she wasn't hurting for clients, but any business needed satisfied customers, repeat business, and word of mouth to grow and thrive. And Eric was a legitimate client, when he wasn't acting in totally and sexually illicit ways. He could bring in new clients with a referral, he could keep her busy for years with his own wardrobe if his book did as well as she thought it would and his tour was as successful.

That was it!

He would be going on a book signing tour soon. He wouldn't be around to harass her and proposition her at every turn. He'd be too busy trying to please and ingratiate himself with the fickle book-buying public. He wouldn't have time to think about getting into her panties, wouldn't have time to think about sex.

Yeah, and if she believed that, there was a bridge in Brooklyn she should look into purchasing.

His writing hadn't suffered much since they'd met if the two articles she'd peeked in his glove compartment in a rare moment of nosiness were any indication. Which only told her that there was no correlation between his productivity or lack thereof, and his libido. When he was writing he wanted sex, and when he wasn't writing he wanted sex. He just plain wanted sex.

"I want *you*," Eric said, made Tabitha sit up straight in her seat and turn to gawk at him. "It's not just sex, Tabitha. I just wanted you to know that."

"How did you know what I was thinking?" she demanded.

"It's not hard to guess after what happened between us. I'm thinking about it too. Thinking about what I could have done differently, thinking about what would have made you more comfortable, feel more pleasure, come harder…"

Tabitha put up a hand in a stop sign. "Please, you don't have to elaborate."

"But I think I do. I think you think that this is just about me getting into your panties, wham-bam-thank-ma'am and nothing else."

"Isn't it?"

"No, of course not."

"So what, after you get some we're going to be this perfect inseparable couple? Is that what you're saying?" *Please don't profess your undying love and make me hate you for lying, Eric. I couldn't take that. Just be honest like you've been being. Tell me it's just sex. Tell me you want me to tie you down and eat you up and I'll believe it. Just don't tell me you care.*

Eric shook his head, hands tight on the steering wheel as he made a right turn to exit the thruway and enter onto the road leading to the residential tree-lined streets of her neighborhood. "Nothing in life is perfect. I'd be a fool to predict a perfect future for either of us. And in case you're not keeping count, I'm the only one in your scenario who *hasn't* gotten some."

Tabitha covered her mouth and coughed as she felt herself blush. He would have to remind her of that, wouldn't he?

"All I'm saying is for you to relax and—"

"Let it happen. Yeah, I got your hippie philosophy back in the fitting room. Unfortunately, I'm not in the habit of just *letting* things happen. I like a plan, a strategy, I like to know where and how I'm going."

"You want to steer your emotions with a road map?"

"There's nothing wrong with using some sort of diagram. I'd rather follow a guide than just blindly run willy-nilly into a situation without a thought to the repercussions."

"Want to know what I think?"

"I'm sure you're going to tell me regardless."

He smirked, pulled over to the curb beneath the shelter of a low-hanging tree a couple of blocks from her brownstone and turned off the ignition as he turned in his seat to face her full. "I think you just don't like giving up control. You want to put everything in a convenient category, put neat little labels on things. Your life, your job, your relationship with me."

"There *is* no relationship."

"My point exactly. There is. You just want to label it something other than what it is about, business between client and personal shopper, when you know damn well it's more than that, something you can't categorize, something you can't control." He shook his head, gritting his teeth as he firmly cupped her face between his hands. "A client wouldn't kiss you like this." He stroked the seam of her lips until she parted them, thrust his tongue into her mouth, drawing her closer, deepening the kiss as her heart pounded in her ears until she thought she'd go deaf.

Tabitha pulled away to stare at him. "That's where you're wrong, Eric. I can control this." She opened her door and put one foot on the sidewalk. "I can get out of this car and walk away from you just as nice as you please."

Eric got out of the Jeep on his side and ran around the back to catch up with her as she stalked up the block. He caught her arm and stopped her in her tracks. "Can you walk away from me that easily?"

"I can, yes."

He shook his head, laughing as he stared at her. "Just to prove a point? That you're a control freak who doesn't want to let nature take its course?"

"You're not ingratiating yourself with me right now."

"I'm not trying to, and you wouldn't respect me if I did."

"How do you know what I respect and don't respect?"

"I know you, Tabitha."

She glared at him, knees weakening at the dark gleam in his eyes, pussy clenching with lust. God, she wanted him. She wanted him to take her. Take her fast and hard, but knew that she'd fight him every step of the way, and only serve to prove his point, damn it.

You're a control freak.

"Let go of me." She tried to jerk her arm free, but he held fast, backed her against a nearby oak, dragged her hands up and over her head and held them there. "What do you think you're doing?" She felt her body trembling harder than her voice when she spoke, hot with desire and need, inflamed from his body heat.

He bent slightly at the knees, thrust a leg between her thighs, rubbed his knee against her center, slow firm circuits that made her wet just thinking of the way his big body blocked her, imprisoned her. This was so much more dangerous than the fitting room; they were out in the open.

She shivered at the thought, wondered if he'd really take her here, against a tree. Anticipation and fear warred as she closed her eyes against the smoldering look in his eyes.

He leaned close to an ear, lazily drew his tongue around the shell. "Say you want me, Tabitha. Say it just once, and get it out of the way."

"Let me go."

"You'll feel so much better if you say it." He pressed his knee against her sex more firmly, found her clit, the pressure he exerted and his deep persuasive tone doing strange things to her insides, liquefying them, making her want to melt against him.

"This can't happen."

"Ever?"

"Never."

He kissed her roughly, claiming her mouth, staking his title, branding her with his taste and spirit. "Never's a long time. Sure you want to wait?"

"I have to."

He looked at her, released her wrists, knee still pressed against her and making that sexy circular motion that had her panties wet and her clit engorged and pulsing.

Tabitha lowered her arms to her sides, but made no move to leave, just stared back at him as he replaced his knee with a hand, sweeping his fingers up her sensitized slit before sliding a hand into her panties to cup her.

She groaned as he pushed his finger into her like he'd done in his bedroom only they weren't in his bedroom and he didn't seem to have a qualm about it. Only stared at her as he drove his finger deeper and wiggled it around until he brushed her G-spot.

She writhed against him, whimpering low in her throat as he sped his thrusts, adding his thumb to the mix, deliberately flicking her clit in concert with his lunges until she arched her body into his, head thrown back against the tree, and violently came in his hand.

God, Oh, God, she'd just come against a tree outside, not two blocks away from her house!

Tabitha buried her flushed face against his chest, felt his hands soft and gentle in her hair as he murmured, "It's okay, baby, it's okay." before he slid a finger under her chin to lift her face.

She met his eyes expecting to find I-told-you-so smugness that would have sent her right over the edge, but instead found him looking at her with this confused expression on his face, as if she had just rocked his world, and not the other way around.

"C'mon." He grabbed her hand, led her away from the tree. "I'll take you home."

Chapter 9

EJ finished the final edits on *Reaching Out* a couple of weeks later and Fed Ex-ed them over to his editor at Renegade Publishing, before going about the business of finishing a short story and an article that he'd been in the middle of when he'd received the galleys.

He wouldn't think about Tabitha, wouldn't remember how sweet and tangy she'd tasted, wouldn't recall how tight she'd been when he'd slid his fingers inside her and she'd clamped her muscles around them as if her life depended on him pleasing her. He wouldn't wonder how snug she would feel around his cock when he thrust into her.

Damn it, he had to get over the woman! At least for now, until he could figure out a way to get into her company again without her flinching away from him like a nervous deer at a watering whole when she knows a predator is in the vicinity.

He had plans—and oh, wouldn't Ms. Lyons be so happy and proud of him to hear that. He knew what he wanted and was ready to go after it. He had patience, and was willing to wait her out for as long as it took, and knowing that maddening woman, it could take a while to make her see things his way and come around.

He'd been trying for the last couple of weeks to hook up with her, appealing to her sense of fun and adventure inviting her to the annual Halloween Parade in the Village; appealing to her obvious competitive nature inviting her out to a friendly game of racquetball. Just plain appealing to her sense of romance and inviting her out to a quiet dinner for two. She'd soundly rejected each and every overture he'd made so far, claiming business and a full schedule.

The one time he had seen her since their first shopping trip hadn't been worth mentioning, Tabitha stopping by a few days ago to drop off several bags of pre-approved fall and winter purchases she'd made. Black pleated chinos, several polo shirts in varying colors, cotton twill plaid shirts in black watch, red, her favorite gray, holly green, and check in cobalt and plum. For outerwear, she'd bought him a tan chamois suede jacket, and a long navy wool overcoat. And finally for footgear, she'd purchased a pair of Apache slip-on mocs; tan, insulated, calf-high, waterproof steel-toed boots, and ankle-high dark-brown leather harness boots.

No matter what he said or did, she wouldn't pause for niceties. No coffee or tea or soda, definitely no alcohol, and no nice-weather-we're-having conversation. Just came in, showed him what she'd bought, she even waited in the foyer while he tried everything on to make sure it fit of course everything fit perfectly, and came back out into the living room to model for her.

Just pretty damn unsociable. Just pretty damn Tabitha Lyons...or pretty damn afraid of him.

EJ grinned when he remembered her stopping not four feet inside his foyer with the packages, handing them over to him and not making any attempt to come further into his loft no matter how much goading or cajoling he did.

He had to give her credit for her bravery and determination. He knew that coming over to his place and seeing him in person had been the last thing on her wish list, but rather than fob off her duty on an underling or delivery company, she'd braved it and come over herself. Because that's the kind of person Tabitha was. If she said she was going to do something, she'd do it, no shirking or dereliction in her.

It was these very facets of her personality that made him admire her so much. Sure, he loved the package they came in, but physical attraction was just the beginning. He just couldn't get Tabitha to believe it.

Shit, he wished he knew what was going on in that woman's head!

For a brief second when she'd come over, he thought she'd been tempted to accept his offer of coffee, had noticed her curiosity—about what he'd do, how far he'd go—had seen that she'd been on the verge of accepting, but she'd fought off her natural inquisitiveness, her resolve to keep them on strictly business terms beating out her desire.

EJ stopped what he was doing, glanced at the monitor and reread the last couple of paragraphs he had written. Not too bad. He was surprised since he was so preoccupied with his plans for Tabitha, but then he'd always been able to find comfort and escape in his writing. Writing had always been his refuge, what he'd turned to time and again in the past.

In times of crisis, in times of celebration, he'd had his writing. When he had been lost, writing had helped him find himself. When he had been ill or in pain, writing had soothed him. When he had been down, writing had picked him up.

Just about the only thing his writing hadn't been able to do was help him save Sinclair, which was so ironic since it had been writing and art that had initially brought them together in the first place in second grade.

EJ had started out admiring her work in art class. The finger painting she'd been creating was so intricate and colorful that it gave him the feeling, even as a seven-year-old, that he was in the presence of greatness.

He remembered she'd glared at him, mumbling about his rudeness in standing over her shoulder while she worked, and why wasn't he at his own desk doing his own work.

"I finished it," EJ'd said as he held up his painting for her approval.

Sinclair glanced at it, just barely putting up her nose. "It's okay, I guess. What's it supposed to be?"

EJ shrugged. "The teacher said paint what you feel, so I did."

"You must feel goofy." Sinclair put the back of a hand— the only part of her hands not paint-smeared—against her mouth and giggled.

EJ wasn't one to be easily insulted and laughed with her, wanting to believe that she wasn't laughing at him.

His strategy worked.

Sinclair wiped a hand on her smock and stuck it out. "I'm Sinclair Donatelli."

"EJ Vega." He put his hand in hers and shook, hoping he seemed as adult to her as she seemed to him with the formality.

"EJ? What does that stand for?"

EJ shuffled his feet, averting his gaze. He'd never liked his name, didn't think it was anywhere near as cool as his older brother's name, Nick.

"Tell me. I won't laugh."

He glanced at her gap-toothed grin and returned it. "Eric James."

"Cool. I like it."

"You do?"

"Yeah. It's a cool name and cool initials. What do I call you?"

He told her to call him EJ, that everyone did, and from that point on, they were fast friends.

When EJ wrote his first adventure romance, it was Sinclair who'd done the illustrations.

Mr. Donatelli, Sinclair's father helped them mass-produce the finished product—a fifty-page work with half-pictures and half-story—made a hundred copies and bound them for sale.

Serious about her art and businesslike to the end, Sinclair set the price at a marketable buck a book—splitting the profits with EJ when *Lie Tei and Ming Toi*, an anime illustrated novelette, sold out the first day they offered it to their third-grade classmates. From there on, a lasting partnership was born.

From second grade to the end of junior high EJ and Sinclair were constant companions, so much so that everyone from EJ's parents to Sinclair's assumed that they were boyfriend and girlfriend, but the pair didn't become romantically involved until much later in their relationship. Ironically it was when they both entered separate high schools, each finally giving into the logic that they had been made for each other.

Where Sinclair was a somber, moody loner, EJ was an easy-going optimistic people person. Their personalities and ideals complemented each other in every way, and they constantly played off of each other's strengths and weaknesses.

EJ was just about the only one in the world who could pull Sinclair out of one of her blue funks and Sinclair was just about the only one in the world who could put him in one.

To everyone else, Sinclair was weird. She had even been tested for autism as a child and she'd confided that to EJ when they were ten, but to EJ Sinclair was just Sinclair, extremely talented, a little eccentric, and as deep as her heart was big.

So when Sinclair fell in with the post-punk, Goth crowd at her school—getting piercings in places that EJ wouldn't have imagined getting pierced, wearing the black make-up and clothes, EJ hadn't thought too much of it. He'd just attributed this new manifestation of his friend as Sinclair being Sinclair—adventurous, rebellious and ever changing.

Until he read one of her poems for her twelfth-grade creative writing class.

Sinclair's writing, more than her art, had always been full of dark imagery, as if she had to balance out one with the other, but there was something intrinsically bothersome about this poem that struck an unconscious cord in EJ.

Still, back then low- and no-tolerance policies had not existed. School shootings and today's level of student-on-student, student-on-teacher violence was unheard of when he and Sinclair had been in high school, so going to one of her teachers, or even the school principal, had not been a consideration. Not thinking the sentiments in her poem more serious than he could handle anyway, EJ confronted his girlfriend himself and asked her what the poem meant.

"It means what it means."

He should have known better than to let the subject go with just Sinclair's blunt response, had instinctively recognized something amiss in the text, especially the allusions to suicide and ambiguous sexual orientation, but he had no choice when she had gone into one of her moods directly after answering him, stomping off to her next class and not calling or speaking to him for a week after.

He never brought the poem, or its meaning, up again, and to this day regretted his laxity.

He should have seen the signs of her depression, her uncertainty; he shouldn't have accepted that last poem at face value, as "Sinclair just being Sinclair."

Damn, what he wouldn't do to have that last day back, to be able to know what she had planned and be at her house before she could go through with taking all those pills and slitting her wrists, even in death, his friend had been thorough.

EJ couldn't even take comfort in the fact that her own parents and few, closest friends hadn't had any more of an inkling than him. *He* should have known because he'd loved her.

But evidently, that had not been enough—not his love for her, or her love for him—to keep Sinclair going.

EJ didn't know why he now equated Sinclair's personality with Tabitha's. He just knew that instead of one face to haunt him when he laid down his head at night, he had two for entirely different reasons: Sinclair's death mask when he'd found her in the bathtub at her house and Tabitha's look of rapture when he'd made her come in his hand.

He squirmed in his chair now with unquenched hunger. Damn.

He didn't think he had wanted a female who didn't want him since sixth grade when he'd asked Carolyn Walker, an older woman at fourteen, to be his Valentine and she'd laughed at him before flatly turning him down.

Hmm. Scratch that. *Claimed* to not want him. Because EJ knew damn well Tabitha wanted him as much as he wanted her. He just had to make her admit it—to him would be good, but more to herself—before they could get over this intimacy hump to consummate what he knew was between them.

The phone rang and EJ jerked his head in its direction before rolling his chair to the end table by his easy chair to answer it. He knew it wasn't Tabitha Lyons, but something made him hope that his previous persistence had paid off, and perhaps she had gotten over her fear.

He didn't even glance at the caller ID. He wanted to be surprised, then berated himself when he picked up the receiver and heard who it was.

"Hey EJ."

"Hey Jade."

"I haven't heard from you in a while."

"Been busy." He didn't feel like confiding any more than that, and hated himself for his reticence. He'd never been at a loss for conversation with Jade. They had so much in common, a shared past in advertising. They could go on for an hour just talking about the job and all the characters they came across doing it. Relating a good pitch-meeting alone was enough to put each of them in stitches for a half-an-hour.

"So, uh, how's the book coming along?"

"It's coming."

"Finished those edits?"

"Sent 'em off to the editor today."

"That's, ah, good to hear."

"Jade, why'd you call?"

"If this is a bad time, EJ, just say so."

He'd hurt her, could hear the injury in her voice and immediately regretted being so blunt, although he'd never been one to hold his tongue, especially with Jade who'd never had a problem with his frankness. Jade had always given as good as she'd gotten, had never let a sullen mood or acerbic tongue get the best of her—not in business, or her personal life. She was a woman of his heart, her attitude about life so in synch with his own.

EJ sighed and closed his eyes, contrition pushing his tongue to make amends.

He shouldn't let a deprived appetite get the best of him. He never had. Then he'd never been deprived or frustrated where his appetite was concerned, at least not for very long.

Angela would say it was about time he'd met his match.

"It's a bad time, but not for the reasons you're thinking." Why was he rationalizing to her? They weren't married. He owed her no explanations about how he spent his free time but none of those justifications kept him from clarifying further. "I'm working, and just having a hard time getting the words down the way I want them."

"Maybe you're trying too hard, baby."

"Maybe."

"You probably just need someone to come over and give you a nice massage, work all that mean and nasty tension and writer's block right out of your body."

"Probably." Shit, he had no shame! At least his cock didn't, and that particular part of his anatomy was now standing at attention, tenting the front of his sweatpants in anticipation and clearly expressing its excitement at the possibility of sinking into an eager wet pussy.

EJ cupped himself, unconsciously massaging the most tension-filled part of his body as if trying to strangle the little sucker into submission and forgetfulness.

Then again, why should he deny himself? He had no one to answer to. Especially not Tabitha Lyons, who didn't want to give him the time of day, much less ease his tension, and could have cared less whether he was suffering or not...and he was suffering. Oh, hell was he, hadn't known just how much until he'd heard Jade's voice on the phone. Making everything right, soothing his wounded ego, offering the ultimate balm.

Jade was here, or she soon would be in a matter of minutes he was sure, just waiting for the green light from him.

Why shouldn't he give it to her?

"Where are you?" he blurted out.

"The question is, where and when do you want me?"

"The answer is here and now."

"Ooh, I love a man who knows his own mind."

EJ wasn't sure about knowing his own mind. Tabitha Lyons had him questioning every bold desire he'd harbored in the last two weeks. But he knew his cock and a multi-week dry spell was not only unprecedented—it was also totally unacceptable to the little guy, becoming more and more unacceptable to him. Time to show his friend he hadn't totally forgotten about his needs.

He signed off with Jade, rolled back to his computer about to shut it down and prepare for Jade's arrival when the phone rang again.

His heart started pounding right away, as if sensing Tabitha's nearness, which was ridiculous, since he didn't have any sort of bond with the woman, hadn't had a chance to forge one the way he would have liked.

He rolled over and picked up the receiver, disappointed when he heard Jodie Klein's voice on the phone, but immediately trying to cover his yearning with a bright and easy tone to match his publicist's.

She was calling with good news, had managed to set up several interviews with several major glossy magazines and *The New York Times*.

"How'd you swing that one?"

"I've got connections and I'm not afraid to use them."

EJ chuckled, liking her fearlessness and spunk, and tried not to let them remind him of the one person he was trying to forget.

"I'll call you once I have more interviews set up. I'm working on some contacts for the first leg of your tour on the West Coast."

"I'm looking forward to hearing from you then." EJ signed off again, staring at the phone and willing it to ring.

He'd never had a problem manifesting his destiny or exploiting a connection before, at least not one that existed.

But how could he connect with someone who was totally disconnected, someone who didn't *want* to *be* connected?

Chapter 10

Tabitha closed her eyes and rubbed her temples in a circular motion, trying to block out the memory of his deep smooth voice, and those big dimples. The memory of his mouth when he'd gone down on her...twice.

She shivered and opened her eyes to see Cynthia standing in her doorway, shaking her head as if disappointed with a star pupil who just refused to get it.

"When are you going to give in and g..."

"Let's not go there, shall we."

"I was just going to say when are you going to give in and go out on a date with him."

"Oh," Tabitha muttered, and glanced at her monitor. Not much there of urgency except a few questions her webmistress had forwarded from the website, surfers interested in the mechanics of her business in general and *Lyons' Style, Inc.* in particular. But the computer was as good a place as any in which to escape the prying curiosity of her capable assistant.

Cynthia crossed the threshold and took a seat in the chair opposite Tabitha's desk. She reached across to hand Tabitha several messages. "They're all from him. The last few are all the way from California."

"God, the man's a glutton for punishment," Tabitha bit out as she took them, chest filling with some unnamable emotion that he'd bothered to call her long distance. Then she popped her own bubble, rationalizing that he'd probably used some expense account and wasn't making any big sacrifice to call little old her. Except the sacrifice of his time and what was that meager investment if he finally got what he was after in the long run, namely her?

She'd managed to avoid him well enough for the couple of weeks leading up to his departure, except for that one unavoidable visit to drop off some clothes.

Tabitha had been so proud of her judgment in staying in the foyer, patiently waiting for him to try on each and every outfit. She hadn't sat down in the living room, had refused his attempts at making her feel comfortable and at home, refused to fall into anything that would make her visit look like anything besides business.

He'd tried on his outfits, modeled for her, and then after giving her thumb's up, Tabitha had beat a hasty retreat from his loft, hormones none the worse for wear thanks to her good sense and distance, though her libido had screamed at her for leaving so soon.

"Or maybe he just believes in the credo if at first you don't succeed," Cynthia said now.

"Well, he's barking up the wrong tree here."

"Is he?"

Tabitha glared at her, but didn't otherwise respond.

"I think he's nice."

"You don't even know him."

"And that's the point. Neither do you."

"Maybe I don't want to know him."

"Why not?"

Such a simple question, yet the answer to it was more than difficult for Tabitha to get a handle on, if not next to impossible.

How did he confuse her, let her count the ways?

Cynthia reached across the table at Tabitha's silence and grasped a hand. "What could it hurt? I know for a fact you're not seeing anyone, so it's not like your dance card is full."

"Did it ever occur to you that I like it that way?"

"Coward."

She said it in a teasing tone, a playful grin on her face, but it sliced just as deep as if she'd been dead serious when she said it.

It wasn't anything Tabitha hadn't called herself in the last few days—which was probably why Cynthia's gibe hit so close to home. If she'd had a good comeback, she certainly would have used it just to get the woman off her back and out of her office, but she had nothing except a feeble, "I'd rather not discuss this. Please go back to your desk and get to work."

Something in her tone and look must have tipped off Cynthia that Tabitha wasn't in the mood for a debate about the merits of her love life, or lack thereof, because her assistant quietly rose from her seat and headed for the door.

Cynthia paused at the threshold for as long as it took her to say, "I'll be at my desk if you need me." before she left and silently closed the door behind her.

Tabitha appreciated the woman's concern, but the lack of respect for her privacy was exactly why she didn't like being friends with the people with whom she worked. Exactly why she liked to keep the lines of formality in tact, because once they came down, people felt they had the right to go just a little further each and every interaction, and before one knew it, one's assistant was telling her how to lead her life and whom she should let in it, and calling her names, however jokingly.

Fine, she was a confirmed coward and control freak, and she was damn proud of both!

What was wrong with setting boundaries, exerting a little self-control rather than acting like a…a wanton harlot?

Tabitha swallowed hard, her mother's face instantly hovering before her vision—a bleary-eyed, belligerent drunk saddled with a daughter she'd never wanted, and who couldn't hold onto a man if her life depended on it.

It hadn't been her mom's fault, she told herself. The woman had been sick. Tabitha knew that now, intellectually recognized the symptoms then of what was today commonly known as bipolar affective disorder. It didn't help her feel any better about her childhood, about being abandoned at the Port Authority bus station by her mother not long after her dad had left.

God, she was hopeless! She'd thought she'd gotten over the desertion, but evidently it didn't take much to bring it all back: the helplessness, the fear, the loneliness and sense of failure pervasive to her soul even as an eight-year-old with not much control over her circumstances.

Despite knowing about her mom's illness, Tabitha couldn't get over the idea that had the woman exercised just a little more morals, been a little stronger…what? She might never have been born, is what.

How many times in her teens had she wished for exactly this? How many times had she let the kids in her neighborhood make her feel totally worthless because her mother was a substance abuser and a "kook"? How many times had she felt like less than nothing because her clothes came from the Salvation Army and Goodwill when all her classmates wore, if not the best gear, then gear that had been bought specifically for them first, and not castoffs from so many strangers? How many times had she had to listen to her dad's lame excuses about her mother's prolonged and sudden absences, holding her tongue when she knew the unfortunate truth? How many times had she had to fight for her mother's honor, even when her mother could have given a flying kitty about what people thought of her?

If there was one thing that she had admired about her mother it was her ability to block out what people thought of her, her carefree and eccentric ways. Of course, Denise could probably attribute most of that carefree attitude to her illness, but if Tabitha could have had just one-tenth of that ability, that one symptom of her mother's malady, she thought she might have been a much happier kid growing up.

But it just wasn't in her not to care. She cared about everything and everyone too damn much, though she knew she gave off the air that she didn't.

Case and point, Eric probably thought she hated his guts for seducing her their last time together when what she actually felt was…hell, she still wasn't sure exactly what she felt about that evening.

She knew for sure that she'd never felt more free and alive than the way he'd made her feel in that fitting room and against that tree, and Christ, it must have been something for her to be thinking about it weeks later!

She needed to get a life is what she needed, rather than moping around about something she couldn't have, some*one* she had thrown away simply because she was worried about what someone other than herself would think if she had accepted Eric's offering.

"You can run from me, Tabby, but you can't run from yourself," he'd said before bending his head to plant a kiss on her lips and turning to leave.

Tabitha stood at the top of her front stairs, hands balled into fists at her sides, wanting to punch him as she called, "Hey, Vega!"

He paused on the bottom step, holding onto the newel as he turned and grinned up at her.

"Don't call me Tabby."

"Why did I know you were going to say that?"

"You don't know me as well as you think you do."

"I know you, Tabitha."

He'd sounded so sure of himself, so sure of her, that he almost had her believing him, believing that he knew her better than she knew herself.

Well, damn it, he didn't know her! He knew a facsimile of what she presented to the world, and as far as Tabitha was concerned, that was all he'd ever know. All he deserved to know. All anyone deserved to know.

Tabitha slid her mouse across the pad aimlessly, staring at her computer monitor and not seeing the words on the screen, seeing only his face.

Sure, she'd succeeded in staying away from him physically, but what good did that do her when everywhere she turned the image of him haunted her, reminding her of how much she'd enjoyed his touches; reminding her of how badly her body had betrayed her?

She stared at the screen, determined to respond to at least a few pieces of e-mail before she left the office for another shopping trip for the unforgettable and seductive Eric. She already had several outfits mentally picked out, could just see him in them, and hated herself for looking forward to watching him model for her again.

Someone knocked on her door and Tabitha popped up her head as Cynthia cracked the door and peeked in. She had a chagrined look on her face that immediately put Tabitha on guard. What had that man done now, three thousand miles away, no less? "What is it, Cynthia?"

Her assistant shrugged and opened the door further to show the bouquet of red roses in a vase she had behind her back. "These came for you, so I signed for them." She walked the vase over and set it on Tabitha's desk. "They're from—"

"Yeah, I kinda figured they were."

Cynthia at least had the decency to cover her mouth with a palm as she chuckled. "He is persistent," she murmured.

"As acid reflux, and just as enjoyable."

Cynthia just smiled, her look doubtful as Tabitha leaned across the desk to sniff the roses and glance at the message on the card: *I saw these and they reminded me of you... velvety and thorny.*

Oh, he was good, a charmer until the very end.

"You're going to keep them, aren't you?"

"I see no reason to waste perfectly beautiful flowers."

"You want me to send him an official thank you note?"

"Etiquette would have us do no less."

Cynthia looked at her hopefully. "Any special message you want me to add?"

Like he'd get it? He hadn't so far, so why bother? Tabitha grinned as she tapped the card against her bottom lip. "Just a simple thank you for the flowers will do." Let him figure out the rest. That his romantic ploys were not going to work, that he and she were client and personal shopper, nothing more, and would never be anything more.

She glanced up when Cynthia hadn't left, arched a brow. "Anything else?"

"Uh, no, I guess not."

"Thanks, Cyn." She watched her assistant leave and closed the door before finally throwing herself into her work on the screen, suddenly feeling energized and rejuvenated.

* * * *

Tabitha had had a more productive day than the start of it would have ever predicted, shopping for the infamous Eric and two of her other clients.

She had to admit, she had more fun shopping for Eric though, probably because the end result would be to see him in the clothes and be at the receiving end of his appreciation and excited reactions.

Most of her other clients were well established and staid in their tastes. They knew exactly what they wanted and what they wanted it for. Tabitha's main job with them was essentially to do time-consuming legwork.

With Eric she was working with a blank slate, had the freedom to stretch her creative muscles, using her unique gift and "eye" for the art of dressing well to pick out what she knew would look good on him. She got to do what she had originally gotten into the business for—work with a client to define and refine his or her image.

Before Eric, she hated to admit it, her job had become routine, something she did to pay the bills, something she did because she'd been doing it so long. Shopping for Eric though, made her see things in a new light, everything fresh and fun, daring and dangerous…like the man.

God she hated him! And she wanted him so bad it hurt to think about him.

Arriving home, Tabitha retrieved her mail out of the lobby mailbox and headed up the stairs, antennae going up when she caught sight of a vaguely familiar surname in the return address area of something looking suspiciously like an invitation.

If this was another one of his tricks…Tabitha put a fingernail under the flap and slit the envelope open. She'd been right. It was an invitation from

Angela Calminetti to a surprise birthday party, and the guest of honor was, guess who? None other than Eric. Shit.

She couldn't not go. That would be rude. Knowing Angela from just their one meeting at the sidewalk café with Evelyn, his oldest sister wouldn't take no for an answer, business relationship or not.

Okay, he was a client. She had to go if only to be courteous and follow protocol, and that's what she would do. Be polite, cool and businesslike. Nothing more. Problem solved.

Tabitha guessed she couldn't really fault Eric for this latest event. It was a surprise party, something he was unaware of.

But she was sure he would not fail to take advantage of it to its fullest extent once he saw her at his loft among the other revelers.

Come to think of it, how were they going to swing giving him a surprise party at his own house without Eric knowing anything about it?

Tabitha wondered about it for a hot second before she shook her head with all the scenarios and possibilities. She finally came to the conclusion that Angela had everything under control; she seemed like the organized type to run a tight ship. She just knew *she* didn't want to be in the woman's shoes trying to surprise someone as sharp and slick as Eric.

Tabitha sighed now as she put her key in the lock, simultaneously dreading and anticipating the coming party though it was weeks away, already wondering what would be the perfect gift. Something not too intimate, but something unique, and that he probably wouldn't buy for himself. Could be clothes because he definitely didn't shop for those for himself, and she had such fun when she did it.

At least she had time to mentally prepare herself for the attack her emotions were sure to undergo surrounded by the Vega clan and seeing Eric in so personal an environment. A few weeks of time and habitual solitude enjoying a romance or two on cable with Vogue, munching popcorn, pigging out on Haagen Dazs and…

Tabitha froze when someone rose up from the shadows behind her as she slid her key out of the lock. She pivoted quickly, one hand grabbing her chest the other pointing her keys outward like a weapon before she recognized the tall, brown-skinned figure coming towards her.

"Hey Tabby-Cat."

"Damn it, Frankie! You scared the hell out of me." She punched her foster brother on the shoulder as he came closer and grabbed her in a bear hug.

"It's been a while," he said as he released her.

"Through no fault of mine."

"Are you going to invite me in?"

"Just like a man. Come and go as you please and just expect everything to be the same upon your return no matter how long you stay away."

"I love you too."

Tabitha glared at him, but couldn't hold it for too long when he smiled at her with those enviable pearly whites.

She reached up to ruffle his big curly Afro. "Either braid it or get dreads."

"You don't like my retro hair?"

"I like it fine. Just don't be surprised when you wake up in the morning and find most of it next to you on the pillow."

His eyebrows popped up, and he looked uncertain of Tabitha and his ability to charm for the first time since he arrived.

She burst out laughing at his shocked expression, turned to open her door.

When he didn't follow her in, she turned around with a devilish grin. "Change your mind about dropping by?"

"You don't scare me."

It seemed to be going around, the rumor that her bark was worse than her bite. Time to teach the men in her life a few lessons about her canines.

Chapter 11

New York Times Bestseller.

It was an achievement he'd dreamed about, distantly, but not an achievement he thought he'd reach until perhaps his third or fourth book. Not on his first. Not with the book of his heart.

But there it was in black and white. Number three on the list and quickly climbing, according to Jodie.

He vaguely remembered her mentioning he had entered the list in the number twenty slot, but hadn't been paying that much attention, being so on the go these last few weeks. Now he couldn't not pay attention.

"EJ, are you still there?"

Distantly he heard Jodie mention other newspapers and bestseller lists— *Publisher's Weekly, USA Today,* Independent Bestseller List, Amazon.com…

"I'm still here."

"Are you looking at the other papers I told you about?"

EJ flipped through the papers she'd indicated, saw *Reaching Out* listed in various positions at or near the top ten on the *Los Angeles Times* and *The San Francisco Chronicle* bestseller list.

"East and West Coast baby. You're in there!"

The book signings, and especially the round of radio and TV interviews that Jodie had set up, had no doubt been more successful than he could have predicted in getting his name and his title out there. Fourteen cities in fourteen days, chain stores and cozy independents throughout the west and southwest, and he still had seven more cities to hit in the south, a week to go before he headed home for Thanksgiving.

"I couldn't have gotten all this exposure without you, Jodie."

"Oh, please. *I* couldn't have exposed you without something to work with. Remember, I read your book. So it wasn't a hard sell."

Her sentiments seemed to sum up the general consensus. Everyone, including his and Sinclair's family, had loved the book. The reviews so far were all positive, most glowing, lauding his "unique voice" and the innovative fiction/non-fiction hybrid framework of the book.

He should have been more than ecstatic.

"Sinclair would be proud," Jodie said as if reading his mind, her voice low and solemn, a big change from her normally bubbly and bright tone.

Her words jolted him until he remembered his dedication in the front of the book and the acknowledgement in the back. Seems people really did read and pay attention to all that official and personal stuff authors wrote in their books in addition to the story.

Not a signing went by when at least one person didn't come up to him and express his or her sincere gratitude for how he'd handled a somber subject in such an optimistic, even humorous and realistic light.

Today Leslie Rubin, a Ph.D., member of American Association of Suicidology, and contact person for the Survivors of Suicide support group in Colorado had come up to him and asked if he'd present at her group's annual fundraising dinner.

As Tabitha had predicted, he'd received numerous invites like this— engagements to speak at writers' conferences, conventions, workshops, suicide prevention functions.

The latter touched him the deepest, had him wanting to ring Tabitha to tell her that her calculations had been on point. He felt as if she, more than anyone else he knew, would understand the significance.

He had, in fact, almost called her before he'd gotten Jodie's call, but chickened out at the last minute, and resolved to call her this evening after his signing at BookPeople, a locally owned, fiercely independent book seller.

He'd actually signed at the location the day before but decided to squeeze in another day when he'd been unable to accommodate all the customers who'd wanted a signed book, and the owner, who promoted local and new authors alike, had asked him to return.

EJ loved the cozy atmosphere of the store, a three-story, white brick place with long, ceiling-high windows on each floor overlooking the corner of Sixth Street and Lamar Boulevard in Austin Texas. Inside customers could find titles from obscure new age books to the latest *New York Times* bestsellers.

Readers seemed to get pleasantly lost in the labyrinth of shelves, and more often then not were drawn to all manner of the comfy and creative seating from wingback to barber's chair, needless incentive for true book lovers to stay awhile and get their fill. The place was his kind of homey, catered to customers and encouraged browsing.

Which reminded him. "Jodie, did you send that woman over to me today? She said she was a member of AAS?"

"Dr. Rubin. Uh, shouldn't I have?"

"I was just curious as to why you didn't set up an appointment with her like you did with all the other requestors?" He felt her shrug between his question and the long pause that preceded her answer, tempted to slide his shields down even more than they were already before he decided against it.

"I just thought you needed to meet and speak to that one face-to-face, let her tell you her story for herself. She sounded so sincere and eloquent."

She had been both, so much so that EJ had agreed to speak at her function without considering any of his other appointments. Luckily, it didn't conflict with any other engagements that Jodie had set up for him. It just fell pretty damn close to Thanksgiving and would have him flying out of town right after the holiday weekend. Not that he wouldn't have been on the go again to pick up with his book signing tour anyway. He couldn't have said no, especially when he knew, and Leslie had reiterated, the importance of reaching out, "No pun intended, Mr. Vega" to the masses during this high-risk time of year.

"So, did I do okay?"

"You did more than okay. I'm speaking on November 30th. I'll send you all the information as soon as Leslie sends me the brochure."

"Gee, that's cutting it close with all the other engagements you have coming around that time. You'll barely have time to spend with your family for Thanksgiving before you're off and running again."

"I'll be okay."

"You'd better be and take care of yourself, now. You're my favorite client."

EJ smiled, took the next words out of Jodie's mouth and said, "I'm you're only client."

She laughed. "I'm going to let you go now to bask in the glory of your feat."

EJ chuckled, signed off and as soon as he hung up from Jodie, the calls started to come in fast and furious.

First his agent Sal called to congratulate him, then his editor, John Chandler, who'd actually called him twice before and left messages, but EJ just hadn't had a chance to call him back before Jodie's call.

Chandler shared in EJ's pleasure, as excited as Jodie and Sal had been before him, then quickly got to the heart of his call: how the work-in-progress was coming along.

EJ wished he had better news to share, but considering his schedule, he was lucky he'd gotten as many chapters done as he had.

He was more than halfway through his current, had an outline for his third and had been jotting down notes for an idea for his fourth. He gave his editor all this promising news before he signed off with Chandler telling him to keep up the good work and doing whatever he was doing on his tour to keep *Reaching Out* at the top.

"I'll see you when you're back in town. Maybe by then you'll have more of that work-in-progress finished?"

As soon as he hung up with his editor the calls from his family started to trickle in, first from Emilia shouting out on a rare break from her job at Macy's. She only had a minute, but wanted to get in her congrats and say how proud she was. Next Nick called to congratulate his "baby brother," and tell him no way was he getting back any of his suits no matter how much he begged. Donna called a few minutes after EJ got off with Nick, then Evelyn and his parents soon after that, all congratulating him and saying how proud of him they were.

Finally, Angela phoned, as if she'd gauged her call for maximum effect, free to talk to EJ as long as she could without too much threat of being interrupted by any other family members.

EJ tried to cut her short after general how-do-you-do's, congratulations, and right before she would have gotten into his non-existent relationship with Tabitha. Except Angela brought him up short before he could disconnect when she said, "You know Jade's no good for you, EJ."

"Oh, hell, Angie. Will you quit showing off!"

"How else am I supposed to let you know I know about your little dish on the side? You won't introduce her to the family. I'm sure there's a reason for it."

"There is. I don't want the family in my business."

"Think about what I've said."

"I always do." EJ glanced at his watch. "Angie, I really have to get out of here. I've got to be at the bookstore—"

"Okay, okay, get going. I'll talk to you when you're back in town."

"All right. Bye!" He had all these people who were going to talk to him when he "got back in town" and not one of them was the person he really wanted to speak to.

* * * *

EJ made it to BookPeople at six p.m. and without a minute to spare, customers queuing up at the registers with his book in hand before he'd even arrived.

He got right to work, greeting people, signing inside covers as instructed, chatting with customers and giving out advice to a handful of fledgling writers.

At seven he broke for delicious homemade Texas fare, the store owners graciously providing dinner, before he circulated through the store and socialized with the customers, but especially the staff, whose recommendation cards sprouted irrepressibly on every shelf, exhibiting the employees' knowledge of genre, and fanaticism for their favorites.

By eight-thirty, the lines had started to dwindle and so had the supply of *Reaching Out* on the shelves.

EJ spent the last few minutes before his departure at nine signing the three copies that had been left on the shelf, and promising that he'd visit again when his next book came out if not sooner for another signing with *Reaching Out*.

He drove back to the hotel in record time, hopped in the shower then into a pair of boxers and comfortable jeans before settling down beside the phone to make his call.

Now that he was this close to speaking to her, he was nervous. He didn't know what it was, but he got a kick out of Tabitha trying to keep herself in line around him while she tried to put him in his place. He liked experiencing her in action.

He dialed the number. It didn't register that it was an hour later east coast time than the eleven o'clock he noticed on the hotel's bedside clock until Tabitha had picked up the line, only thankful that he wasn't in California or she really might have given him an earful.

As it stood, she sounded kind of peppy when she answered. Cautious but peppy.

"You're sounding wide awake at the witching hour," he observed.

"I should have known it was you. No one else would have the nerve to call me at this ungodly hour."

Ungodly? He stayed up until the sun rose when he was on a roll with his writing. Which, he guessed was why he couldn't hang with Ms. Lyons at seven a.m.

Rather than address her gibe he asked her a question of his own. "What are you doing up? You strike me as an early-to-bed, early-to-rise kind of gal."

"I splurge every once in a while."

"Really? What are you splurging on?"

"Right now I'm watching a movie."

He pictured her in red flannel pjs, matching furry bunny slippers with her feet up on a glass coffee table in front of her, breaking all the rules and balancing a big bowl of hot buttered popcorn in her lap.

EJ immediately got hard at the image. "What are you wearing?" he blurted, his curiosity about how close he'd come to the real deal overriding his fear that she'd back off and hang up at what she saw as sex talk.

The question didn't seem to put her any more on guard than usual, as Tabitha said, "I'm in my pjs and fluffy bedroom slippers."

EJ groaned, unzipped his jeans, slid a hand in and cupped himself. The little sucker had grown to painful proportions in the last minute.

Tabitha had probably thought her description would turn him off, had no idea her confirmation of his guess turned him on more, that he thought she'd be sexy in a buttoned-to-the-chin, floor-length granny gown, face slathered in cold cream and hair in rollers.

"So, to what do I owe the honor, Eric?"

"I wanted to speak to you."

"Eric—"

"I know what you're going to say. This isn't a good idea."

"It isn't."

"Tabitha, I wanted to hear your voice."

"Eric…"

He pushed past the chastisement he heard in her voice, needed to get this out in the open. "…and I wanted to thank you for making me get those suits, for talking me into dressing for success again," he said.

"No biggy."

"I've been invited to several speaking engagements where they'll come in right handy."

"I hear a definite southwestern twang in your voice. Where are you? I couldn't tell where you were from the area code that came up."

And she'd answered the phone anyway? Had she been expecting him, or someone else?

"I'm in Texas."

"Bush country, huh?"

Well damn, she'd snarled it as if she were a staunch Democrat, or maybe a Liberal. Which surprised him since he'd have figured her for a stone cold Conservative.

Sure, he'd voted for the guy, but he wasn't even going to go there and get into it with Ms. Lyons now, if ever. He had enough trouble trying to ingratiate himself and get into her heart...and her panties—hell, he had to be honest with himself on that last if nothing else—without adding a no-win political debate to the mix. "Yep, Bush country," he finally answered.

"How they treating you, Yankee?"

"Fine and dandy, and they loved the purple and green outfit."

"You wore it?"

"Damn right I did."

She chuckled, but stopped suddenly. "I read your book," she muttered, as if getting something unpleasant off her chest.

"And?"

"I told you you'd get asked to speak at important functions."

EJ grinned. The woman always had to have the last word. "Did you *like* it?"

"I loved it."

Damn, he hadn't thought she had it in her.

She'd spoken with no hesitation and such certainty that EJ thought it seemed as if she'd just been waiting for him to ask her the right question.

"You know I've gotten all these calls today from my family earlier to congratulate me on making all these bestseller lists, and none of them meant as much to me as hearing you say you loved my book."

"Oh, please," she sputtered. "I saw all those lists and reviews, by the way. Congrats."

"The dog accepts your bone," EJ quipped then asked, "Why didn't you call me?"

"I was making a desperate effort not to."

"Why?"

"Christ, you're like a five-year-old with that question!"

EJ laughed and she surprisingly joined him. "I missed you," he murmured.

"Will you stop! We haven't known each other long enough or well enough for you to miss me when I'm not around."

"The hell we haven't. Besides, in our case it's quality and not quantity."

"Okay, you've got me with that one."

Wow, he was batting a thousand tonight. Should he take his chances and swing for the fences? Before he changed his mind, he asked, "So, what were you watching? And have I totally ruined your movie night?"

"*You've Got Mail.* It's the DVD and I have it on pause."

"Ah, so either you're a Meg Ryan and Tom Hanks fan, or just a plain old romance fan."

"Meg Ryan and romance fan. Tom I can take or leave."

"Whoda thunk it?"

"Don't be such a smart ass." She chuckled.

"I can't help it."

"So, uh…how's the tour going? I'm assuming it's a success."

"It's going pretty well. It'd be better if you were here."

"And what purpose would I serve being there?"

"You could be my own personal cheering section."

"As if your head isn't big enough already," she deadpanned.

Christ, if she only knew!

EJ squirmed on the bed, turning from his side onto his back and to stare at the ceiling, picturing her face there instead of the sterile institutional shade of off-white.

"So, what are you doing up besides harassing me? I would have thought all that touring would have caught up with you by now."

"No, not yet. I'm usually more amped towards the end of the day than the beginning."

"Most vampires are."

"I vant to suck your blood," EJ intoned in his cheesiest Dracula accent, but it didn't stop Tabitha from giggling.

"Nut."

Shit, she didn't know how much he wanted to bust one right now, so bad he could taste it. To Tabitha he said, "Please don't use that word right now."

"Okay, how about lech?" She laughed.

EJ grinned, unconsciously stroking his shaft as he imagined peeling those pjs right off of Ms. Lyons where she sat. "I wish I was there right now watching *You've Got Mail* with you."

"Get out of here! You like chick flicks?"

"You'd be surprised. I'm a romantic deep down."

"Way deep down, I'll bet."

"Of course, my favorite movies are action, horror and sci-fi, not necessarily in that order."

"I can forego my chick flicks for *Aliens* any day."

"God, you too?"

"Of course, I do love Michael Biehn."

"You would."

"You have a problem with Mr. Biehn?"

"None," he muttered. "Only I'm cuter than him."

"Yes, you are."

"You mean that?" he blurted.

"You know you're gorgeous."

"It always helps to hear it." He took a deep breath before speaking again, didn't want to scare off the deer taking a sip at the drinking hole. "And by the way, you're gorgeous too. More than gorgeous."

"Thanks."

"I'd love to see exactly *how* gorgeous."

"I know you would."

Shit, they were treading toward dangerous ground and he had to play this very carefully, didn't want to hear the abrupt evil drone of a dial tone in his ear at some imagined insult.

Emboldened, EJ stepped out onto the ledge. "Arrogant, aren't we?"

"No more than you," Tabitha bantered. "And how would you achieve seeing how gorgeous I am?"

He liked that she always got back to the point, almost as much of a master at segueing as he was, liked that she sounded playful and ready for anything.

Maybe she was.

"Well, you make it difficult to say the least."

"I know, but you have your imagination."

"I do," EJ murmured, licking his lips before diving in. "Are you still wearing your pjs?"

"What else would I be doing with them, Eric?"

"You could take off your top for me." He held his breath, waiting as he heard noise on the other end, as if she were shifting her position on a leather sofa.

"I've unbuttoned it...all the way."

Damn, he couldn't believe he was doing this. He couldn't believe she was letting him.

In all his sexually active days, and there had been many, he had yet to have phone sex...phone sex with a beautiful woman that he knew personally, one he had intimately touched, smelled and tasted.

EJ closed his eyes, envisioned her smooth copper skin peeking at him from beneath the flannel material of her pjs, glimmering beneath the glare from the television screen. He could almost feel the flex of her trim abdomen, the slightly rounded curve of her belly against his pelvis as he imagined plunging into her. "What are you doing now?" he murmured.

"I'm waiting for you to take off your shirt."

"I don't have one on."

"Oh, you called me halfway prepared, huh?" She laughed, her voice low and throaty. "What *are* you wearing, Eric?"

He swallowed hard, mouth suddenly dry at her sultry tone. "Jeans."

"No shoes?"

"No, I'm barefoot."

"That's good. Because I like men in jeans and their bare feet."

Had he just heard her right? Did Ms. Tabitha have a foot fetish? "What about you? Did you take off those big fluffy slippers?"

"They're off."

"Have you taken off your top yet?"

"I'm waiting for you to touch me, Eric."

He shifted on the bed, trying to find a comfortable position as he completely freed his penis from his jeans and boxers, firmly massaging it from base to tip. "I want you to touch yourself, Tabitha."

"Is that what you're doing?"

"God yes."

"Good. I want you to pretend that I'm kneeling at your feet, that my mouth and hands are on you and I'm sucking your cock and fondling your balls."

EJ groaned deep in his throat, almost dropped the receiver to the floor before quickly catching it in mid-air by the cord, and cradling it between his left ear and shoulder again.

"Are you still there?"

"I'm here," he rasped.

"Good, because I'm touching myself and I'm thinking of you."

He listened to her breathless voice, the thought that she might be on the other end stimulating herself when he wanted to drove him closer to the edge. He bit his bottom lip and closed his eyes as he stroked his dick harder, faster, felt the pressure building at the base of his spine. "You are such a bitch, Tabitha."

"I know, but you love that about me, don't you?"

"Yes, damn it."

"I know you do, baby."

She paused for an interminable several seconds while he filled in the gaps, pictured her licking her luscious full lips and touching those proud mahogany nipples he remembered so well from their encounter in the fitting room. Her breasts had been so round and full, high and perky. Inviting. "Are you wet, Tabby?"

"Very. I'm dripping."

"Shit!" He gasped as the pressure heated and twisted in his balls right before it came to a head, and exploded out of his penis in a spurt of semen that seemed to keep coming and coming so strong and hard until he thought he'd discharged a life's span supply.

He lay on his back for several endless seconds, panting and trembling on the mattress, perspiration slowly drying on his torso in the coolness of the hotel room's air conditioning.

"Eric!" Tabitha shouted. "Eric, are you still there?"

EJ cleared his throat, opened his eyes and searched for the receiver, found it on the carpeted floor at his feet, scooped it up and put it back to his ear. "I'm still here."

"Did you come?"

"You know I did, you little witch."

She giggled, sounding simultaneously girlish and foxy, making him want to throw her down on her sofa and thrust into her so hard she'd know what the real thing felt like instead of playing these cat and mouse games long distance.

Hell, he had just had an explosive orgasm, and he was angry with the woman who'd been at its core for no other reason than he couldn't get his hands on her right then.

"Don't feel bad. I did, too."

"Did you?"

"And I thought of you the entire time. Thought of your big hands on my body, your long fingers inside me…"

If she didn't stop he'd be hard all over again, and he didn't think he had the energy to go another round with her, not on the phone anyway. In person was another story.

He wanted her live and in the flesh, and he'd show her what sensuality and multiple orgasms were all about, none of this 1-900-Sex-Talk shit.

"So, ah…" He cleared his throat again. "I guess you're going to get back to your movie now?"

"I'm not sure it'll measure up now. Tom *certainly* doesn't do it for me like you do."

"Watch *Aliens* then, and think of me in Michael Biehn's part."

"I'm already pulling out my DVD."

Chapter 12

God, she hadn't just *done* that! She couldn't have just had phone sex with the man!

Tabitha got up from the couch and ran to the bathroom to wash up and change into another pair of panties and a long T-shirt.

She hadn't been lying when she'd told Eric she was dripping. Her panties were soaked when she took them off and put them in the hamper.

She came back to the living room and stood in the center of the floor looking at the popcorn littering the polished parquet. Somewhere along the line she'd kicked the bowl off her coffee table and this was the result.

She vaguely remembered her feet flailing out in front of her when she'd hit her G-spot with a finger, imagining Eric's naked body glistening with perspiration beneath her, between her thighs as she straddled and rode him hard.

God, she was lucky she hadn't knocked over the entire table or broken anything, like the glass or some bones.

Tabitha smiled as she retrieved her mini-vac from the kitchen and tidied up the floor, had to admit that having phone sex with Eric had been worth the mess, and so much more stimulating than watching a romantic movie with Vogue, her cat.

Vogue screeched and dashed from behind the gray leather sofa and into Tabitha's bedroom when her mistress bumped the back leg of the sofa with the hand-held vacuum. "Sorry girl, but it's the truth," Tabitha said as if the cat had been insulted by her previous thoughts.

She finished cleaning as best she could, sleepy and tired but paradoxically invigorated at one in the morning on a weeknight.

She always came away from her encounters with Eric feeling like this—refreshed and happy, more alive and free than she'd ever been in her life, buoyant and hopeful like a child.

It worried her a little that this might be the false high, short-lived and precarious, that came before the fall into a dark and oblivious abyss. It worried her that she might be like her mother, that her current freedom and energy came at the price of her sanity, that what she'd just done with Eric had only been a small preview of what it would feel like to really let go. Just a small preview of something totally sinful and painfully unattainable.

Tabitha collapsed into a corner of the sofa, head in her hands as she wondered what she'd do when confronted with him in the flesh, how she'd react to him.

How could she face him?

Ha, that was easy. The same way she'd faced him after he'd put his face in her pussy and eaten his fill in a semi-public fitting room, or the same way she'd faced him after he'd made her come against a tree like a savage.

She'd survived each of those with minimal damage; she'd survive this.

Someone knocked on the door and Tabitha jerked her face out of her hands, heart pounding, still pumped with adrenaline after that little episode on the phone.

She went to answer the insistent pounding, quickly checking her face in the gilt-edged mirror in the foyer before she unlocked and opened the door.

"You didn't even look through peephole, did you?"

"Who else would be knocking on my door at one in the morning?"

Frankie stepped into the house and locked the door behind himself. "That's beside the point. You should be more careful."

"I'll remember that the next time I'm faced with one of your frequent and sudden absences." Tabitha flounced back to the sofa, dropped down into her favorite corner and scooped the remote up from the arm.

Vogue switched back into the living room to welcome Frankie home, rubbing her fluffy ecru coat against his denim-covered calves, walking back and forth between his legs as if she were completing an obstacle course.

Frankie picked her up by the scruff of her neck and cradled her purring form against his muscular chest, ensconced himself in the corner opposite Tabitha, stroking the little furball in his arms as he stared at his sister.

"What?"

"I worry about you, you know."

"You have a strange way of showing it." Why was she acting like this? She liked her freedom and solitude. Liked not having to pick up after a grown man who could give Oscar Madison a run for his money. Liked knowing where all her stuff was, being able to put her hands on things when and where she wanted and needed them, rather than having to search high and low for stuff after hurricane Frankie had gone through her house—showering, dressing, undressing, cooking—leaving general chaos in his wake.

"You were the one who thought we were better off parted."

"Oh, please don't throw ancient history at me in your defense. Especially when you wanted out as much as I did."

"No, I didn't," he murmured, eyes downcast.

Tabitha frowned. This was news to her.

"I just agreed with you because I knew you were right. I wasn't good enough for you. Not as a boyfriend anyway. There's a difference between agreeing with you to keep the peace, or fighting for something I wanted and possibly ruining a great friendship."

"I never said you weren't good enough for me."

"No, you didn't. But you didn't have to. I knew."

"Frankie—"

"It's no secret, Tabitha. You were going places. I knew that from the fist time I met you, knew that you were going to be someone, do things. I would have only held you back."

"Stop talking about yourself like a—"

"Loser?"

"If you're one then I'm one, too."

Frankie smiled, got up from the sofa and put Vogue back on the floor to loud feline objections. He bent over Tabitha and kissed her on the forehead before he headed for her spotless, stainless steel kitchen.

She crossed her fingers and said a prayer that he didn't start pillaging her fridge in search of something to ease the onset of another munchies attack.

He came back with a chilled beer in one hand and a coaster in the other.

Tabitha's eyebrows shot up in shock. Wow, you could teach an old sibling new tricks!

"Did you want one?"

She gave him a you-know-better stare, and watched as he chuckled and lifted the bottle of Corona to his lips to take a hearty gulp.

The only reason there were any beers in the fridge in the first place was because he was here and she was trying to be the accommodating "older" sister, a joke since she only had him in age by a few months.

Frankie finished half the bottle in one swallow, put it on the coaster and turned to Tabitha. "You're not going to turn into your mother if you have one drink, you know."

"Thanks for the tip, Freud, but I'd rather not."

He smiled. "Think you're going to lose all self-control?"

Tabitha rolled her eyes, got up and went to the kitchen to pour a glass of orange juice then returned to her seat in the living room.

Frankie was still in the opposite corner, staring at her. "What have you been up to while I was out?"

"Why do you ask?" She sipped her juice, casually put her glass down on the coaster.

Frankie shrugged, didn't take his eyes off of her. "You've got a lot of color in your face, and I'm wondering what put it there."

"I'm sure I wouldn't know."

"Hmmm."

"What's hmmm?"

Frankie grinned. "You're not still on the nun kick are you?"

"What?" Tabitha blurted. "What gives you the idea I'm on some nun kick?" *And if you knew what I was doing before you got here, you'd get that idea right out of your head.*

"You were practically living like one the last time I visited."

"Before the other day, how long ago was that?"

"My point exactly."

"Just because I'm not on the hard rocking, club trip like *some* people I know, doesn't make me a nun."

"I'd hate to think living in that Catholic orphanage all those years rubbed off on you."

"Oh, you!" Tabitha pulled the throw pillow from behind her and threw it at his head.

Frankie easily grabbed it from the air, chuckling as he cradled it against his middle. "I just want to make sure you've gotten over what happened with that guy. What was his name?" He snapped his fingers several times as he looked at her.

"Michael," Tabitha mumbled.

"Yeah, him."

"There was nothing to get over."

He arched a brow and Tabitha fidgeted under his piercing dark-brown gaze.

"You don't know the whole story."

"I know enough. You were both consenting adults and went into it with your eyes open."

"One of us did."

"He knew the rules of the game as well as you did. He played and he lost."

"But that's just it. He didn't know the rules. I barely did."

"No one told him to fall in love with you."

He made her out to seem like some *femme fatale*, when in truth she had been just as in the dark and desperate for someone to love as Michael. She'd just been a little better at hiding her need from one of the first guys in her life since Frankie who'd shown a sincere interest in her as a person, one of the first guys she sincerely liked. The biggest drawback next to Michael being her co-worker, an insurmountable one for Tabitha, was that he didn't do anything for her in the bedroom department, too staid and controlled, generating no heat. He reminded her of herself. Tabitha had gone into their encounter with the idea of a one-night-stand in the back of her mind. Her in the driver seat, her controlling the outcome—beginning, middle, and end, but she'd realized too late she wasn't cut out for the cold, love-'em-and-leave-'em life, didn't want to have control over someone else's emotional stability—his sense of self, sexual identity and prowess—didn't want that responsibility.

"He put his hand in the fire and he got burned. You can't spend the rest of your life regretting how it ended, believing you hurt him beyond repair. He'll live. Life goes on."

"And if you spout another cliché, I'm going to punch you."

He laughed, pulled her close and gave her a chaste peck on the lips. "I'm speaking from experience. Why should he have the luxury of all your sweet tea and sympathy? He's treading on my ground."

She couldn't say anything to dispute him because he was using the same justifications she'd used to dump Michael.

Frankie got up abruptly, and headed for the bathroom. "I'm going to catch a shower and hit the sack," he said over a shoulder.

She guessed that was her cue to hit the sack herself.

* * * *

"C'mon big guy. Up and at 'em."

Frankie burrowed further under the comforter as Tabitha circled the convertible, putting in her earrings and wondering if having a "real" sib was anything like this.

She went over to the sofa again, leaned over Frankie's head, cupped her hands in front of her mouth and yelled. "Up, up, up!"

"Aw c'mon, Tabby-Cat. Why you gotta be so mean?"

"No one told you to stay up till dawn playing video games."

"Ten more minutes." He turned his back on her, covering his head with the comforter as if for good measure.

"Yeah, I've heard that song before." Tabitha pulled off the comforter, thanking God he'd had the consideration to wear something to bed. She couldn't count the times he'd stayed over before and she'd discovered during one of her wake-up calls that he was in his birthday suit under the covers. "C'mon, get up. I don't care if you pack bags at the corner supermarket. You're getting out of here."

"I was. I mean I am." Frankie sat up and threw his long legs over the side of the sofa bed, big bare feet slamming onto her cold hardwood floors with such force she thought she was in the middle of a small-scale earthquake.

Vogue came out of her favorite hiding spot behind the sofa to rub against Frankie's ankles and purr.

Frankie obliged the little beast when she fell over onto her side and showed her stomach for him to rub.

"Have you no shame, Vogue?" Tabitha chuckled as she went back into her bedroom to get her trench coat and bag before returning to the living room to find Frankie had put up the bed, thrown on some jeans and was running a hand over his Afro as he sat in a corner of the sofa.

"Checking to see if it's all still there?"

He grinned up at her. "What's for breakfast?"

Tabitha froze in her tracks, trench coat half-on and half-off as she slammed a fist on a hip, arched a brow, and slipped into ghetto mode, something she did easily when Franklin Greer was around. "I know you're not expecting *me* to fix your big rusty ass some breakfast." Maybe having a sibling was something like this—if said sibling was a charming underachiever who looked like Lenny Kravitz on a good day.

Tabitha shook her head as she took a seat beside him on the sofa, already castigating herself for what she was about to do. She knew she'd regret it later but he was the only family she had. She wouldn't turn her back on him, couldn't. He'd saved her life more than once when she'd been in the system, the only positive remnant from her days in government custody, and she owed him.

She dug into her bag for her billfold, pulled out a twenty and handed it to him.

Frankie leaned in to give her a big kiss on the cheek and a hug. "I'll give it right back to you, sis, I promise. We've got a gig in the Village tonight."

"Sure." She'd heard that song before, too.

"Seriously. You'll see."

"Just get your ass in gear so I can leave for work."

Frankie bounced from the bed, gave her another peck on the cheek. "I'll be ready in ten minutes," he said as he headed for the bathroom.

"They're going to put that on your tombstone." Tabitha laughed.

God he was a pain, but exponentially ingratiating and she loved him more than anyone else in the world.

Frankie had been her first lover, for a little while there, her ideal man. Outspoken, protective and not afraid to stand up to the powers that be when they stepped on the little guy which invariably turned out to be her and their fellow foster system refugees.

When Tabitha had become an emancipated minor at seventeen and left the foster home where both she and Frankie had spent the last year-and-a-half, Frankie left with her. He'd had no choice after beating to a pulp their foster father when he'd come home to find the man high as a rocket and tussling with a terrified and half-clothed Tabitha.

She closed her eyes now remembering her rage and powerlessness, how close she'd come to losing her virginity to some crack and pot-smoking malingerer.

Instead she'd lost it to Frankie when they'd moved in together—her Black knight with shining pearly-whites. They'd made a go of it for a time before Tabitha realized that they were too different for the long haul and wanted very different things. Tabitha wanted to be a mover and a shaker, at least in her little part of the world at what she did best, helping people look good.

Frankie wanted to be a rock musician, and reminded her too much of what her biological father must have been like—what her mother had fallen for—for Tabitha to see anything else.

She loved him but couldn't be with him. They parted ways, so amicably in fact that every once in a while he popped up on her doorstep to let her know what it felt like to be responsible for someone else besides herself while reminding her of her past and that she wasn't totally alone in the world…and of course, to borrow a few dollars "until he got on his feet."

"Ready."

Tabitha blinked and stared at him from her place at the door.

When he said ten minutes, he really did mean ten minutes, she thought, glad that there were still some people in the world who meant what they said and said what they meant.

"Okay, let's go."

* * * *

Tabitha arrived at the office at eight-forty to find Cynthia already at her desk fielding calls and looking bright and peppy as ever. Like she'd gotten some. Ah, the perks of regular, new-marriage sex. She wondered vaguely if her look resembled Cynthia's, especially after last night, wondered how often she'd sported the new-man-in-my-life glow since she'd known Eric.

"Hey, you're looking chipper this morning," Cynthia said, proffering several messages as she answered Tabitha's first silent question.

"Is that another way of saying I don't usually?"

Cynthia shook her head, chuckled. "You always look fine. You just have a little extra something going on this morning, a little oomph."

"Oomph?"

Cynthia shrugged as the phone rang on her desk.

Tabitha headed toward her office and called over her shoulder before she closed the door, "I'll get that." She threw her trench coat towards the oak coat rack behind her door, and practically ran to answer the phone, breathless when she sat down behind her desk and said hello.

"Hello, Tabitha. This is Angela Calminetti, Evelyn and EJ's sister."

"Oh…hello, Angela."

"Were you expecting someone else?"

"Uh, no. Not really," she lied, knowing damn well she'd been hoping it was Eric.

"Oh, because you sounded a little disappointed."

"No, not at all." Tabitha arched a brow, wondered what prompted this call.

"I hope you don't mind, but I asked Evelyn to give me your number. I have a big favor I need to ask of you."

"A favor?" Her other brow joined its twin in her hairline.

"I know we barely know each other, but I think I can trust you to do this."

Barely wasn't quite the way Tabitha would put it, at least not on Angela's part.

She'd met the woman exactly once, and had come away from the encounter feeling as if her very soul had been frisked and mugged. The woman seemed to know her better than she knew herself, finishing her sentences for her, seeming to pull her thoughts and emotions from thin air to put them into words.

Tabitha vaguely wondered if she had this effect on everyone. "What is it you need?"

"I'm assuming you received my invitation in the mail?"

"Yes, I did."

"Well, we're hitting a little snag on how to get EJ out of his house for a little while. I mean Evelyn and I have keys to the loft in case of emergencies…"

"I was wondering how you were going to throw a surprise party in his apartment without his knowing."

Angela giggled and her warm girlish tone put Tabitha more on guard than relaxed her. "Yes, well getting in is one problem we've solved, but getting him out is one we haven't."

"The snag you mentioned," Tabitha prompted.

"You see, if any one of us, his sibs or his parents, try to get and keep him out for most of the day, he'll automatically suspect something. Besides which, when he's writing, which he's doing most of time, he tends to ignore our calls unless we 911 him, and we don't want to resort to such a measure for this."

"Of course not, but Eric and I aren't—"

"That close?"

There she was again, finishing her sentences. "Not really. I mean we're cordial and he's a client, but we really don't have the sort of bond that would

warrant us spending all day together, other than in a business capacity. I'm
sure he'll suspect something's up if I try to keep him away from his apartment
as well as if any of his siblings tried."

Angela's prolonged silence seemed to say she knew Tabitha was blowing
smoke up her ass and that she had already made up her mind she wasn't going
to take no for an answer.

"We both know that's not true," Angela said. "You know you're more than
capable of keeping my baby brother occupied. All you have to do is say the
word and he'll come running."

The simultaneous images that Angela's words evoked—of a helpless baby
and a loyal puppy— didn't quite agree with Tabitha's vivid images of the tall,
arrogant and sexy Eric.

Besides, what would they have done about this quandary had Tabitha not
been in the picture? They would have had to find some other way. The woman
couldn't have been counting all along on Eric and Tabitha being a couple,
could she?

Had Evelyn said something to her about that day she'd visited her
brother's apartment and found Tabitha there in the bedroom? True it had been
business, but with the Vega clan who all seemed to have some sort of sixth
sense about each other and the people in their lives, who knew what Evelyn
had sensed, or told her sister?

"Will you do it? The entire Vega clan will be in debt to you."

Oh, the woman was a master manipulator whether purposely or not,
instinctively knew all the right buttons to push. "I don't know," Tabitha
hedged, hated to be a pushover for anyone, friend or foe.

"We really need your help on this, Tabitha."

A mass request, not just from Angela but her entire family. All ganging up
on Tabitha in the interest of one of its members.

Tabitha wished she had someone as loyal and determined in her corner.

"I'll do it."

Chapter 13

EJ's plane touched down at JFK Airport a little after seven p.m., two days before Thanksgiving, the dark night sky twinkling with hundreds of stars that he never could have seen even on a clear day in the city, too many tall buildings blocking the view.

Out West, he'd had a different problem adjusting to all the smog and congestion, while in the Southwest the wide-open plains seemed to go on forever, uninterrupted by civilization. He'd enjoyed himself, worked himself to the bone every step of the way, but now he was home, and in the city where Tabitha lived and breathed.

EJ smiled, shouldered the satchel holding his laptop, practically skipping to the luggage carousel to retrieve his other bag, as eager as a puppy when its master arrives home after a long day away. Tabitha might as well have been waiting for him at the terminal for all his anticipation, and even though she wasn't he knew he'd see her soon, whether she knew it or not.

There was no way he would let too much time go by without touching base with her. He had to keep the little momentum he had with her going, make his presence known before she tried to forget what they'd shared.

He knew the woman's MO, how discombobulated and embarrassed she must have been when she'd hung up, probably a little in denial of what she'd done.

He wasn't going to be the dirty little secret she kept hidden in the closet with all her other little sex toys.

EJ frowned as he retrieved his Jeep from the airport parking lot, the image of his Tabby with a battery-operated latex penis between her thighs was inconceivable but vivid enough to harden his cock and simultaneously make him jealous.

If any penis was going to be between her legs, it was going to be his, and no other, not even one with a battery. Especially not one with a battery.

He was tempted to stop off at her house straight from the airport but didn't want to seem too eager or easy.

Instead, he drove home, arriving in a little under a half-an-hour, most of the traffic on the Grand Central Parkway going in the opposite direction of him, so he'd almost had the road all to himself.

EJ hit his loft running rather than exhausted and jet-lagged, quickly unpacking, showering, throwing on some jeans and a turtleneck, and getting comfortable as he booted up his computer and checked his phone messages.

Nothing he wasn't expecting—messages from his mother and Angela to see if he'd arrived home okay. Messages from Jodie about several more interviews she'd set up and a couple of appearances, readings to do in addition to his New York signings. A message from Jade.

The last glared at him more accusatorily than their final unconsummated time together.

Jade had not been happy leaving his apartment unfulfilled and he hadn't been happy trying to fake the funk and pretend that he wanted her when all he could think about was one pixie-faced, chestnut-haired woman who had his brains scrambled and his cock in a perennial exclusive state of readiness.

Jade had noticed this very state and wondered aloud why he didn't want to perform when it was clear to see he wanted her.

Not clear. Nothing about his life had been clear or simple since he'd met Tabitha.

But Jade had not been able to let it go, and even asked him if he'd already run out of the condoms she'd brought, not understanding that preparedness was the least of his issues with her.

There *had* been times when he'd come up short—with Jade, with other women—where he'd had to decline sex because he never had sex without a condom, never. It was why Jade had gotten into the habit of bringing over a supply of her own because she didn't like his coming up short with her.

EJ automatically dialed his mother.

He couldn't deal with Jade right now, didn't know when he'd be able to deal with her, if she even wanted to speak to him.

His mother got on the line now sounding breathless and rushed, worrying him for the split second it took her to say hello and him to ask how she was.

She'd been working out, she told him, and EJ laughed thinking of his almost seventy-year-old mother pumping iron, then asked about his father.

Mom had been worried about Dad the last time EJ had spoken to her, said the man had been working extra hard remodeling and getting the house in shape for the holidays. She wanted him to take it easy. She was ecstatic with the changes he'd made so far—finally turning Angela and Donna's old bedroom into Mom's computer room. Mom was an Internet junkie and loved to chat in over sixty chat rooms, which made him smile. They were turning Nick and EJ's old bedroom into an exercise room. He'd made Evelyn and Emilia's old bedroom into Mom's sewing room a few years ago.

"I swear, he doesn't act like a retired man half the time, EJ, and I keep telling him to get help or hire someone, but he won't listen."

"You know how Dad is. He likes to keep busy, and doesn't think anyone else can do the job as good as he can."

"He's usually right, but he's also seventy, not a spring chicken anymore."

"At least he's home."

"You're right, I shouldn't complain. It's just that I worry about him. You know he doesn't eat as healthy as he should, and he doesn't get as much exercise as I'd like."

"Don't Mom. Dad's a healthy active dude. He's going to be kicking for a long time."

His mother giggled at his description, and EJ's heart turned over at the reality that they'd been married almost fifty years, and couldn't have been closer.

They'd had their rough times raising six kids with Dad putting in eighty and ninety hour weeks—first in construction then building a successful landscaping business—and Mom a public school teacher who'd had to squeeze in enough time between parent/teacher nights at school to see to her own kids' needs with Little League, Boy Scouts, and ballet lessons.

They hadn't suffered from empty nest syndrome in a long time, too busy enjoying their twilight years. These days they spent their free time doting on Angela's youngest two girls and Emilia's boy and happily sending them back to their respective parents when a visit or baby-sitting gig was over.

"What's Dad up to now?" EJ asked.

"Oh, you know your pop. He's in the garage, restoring a car."

EJ smiled, remembered many a day as a child watching his dad work on someone's old Chevy in the family garage, remembered many a day as a teen helping him. He could see the pleasure on his father's face when he fiddled under a hood, rebuilt an engine or painted and buffed an old roadster to its former luster and glory.

Mom offered to call him to the phone, but EJ told her not to bother him, reassured his mother that she shouldn't worry about the old man, and told her he'd be seeing them in a couple of days for Thanksgiving before he signed off.

He dialed Angela immediately after, thanking his patron saint that he got her answering machine. He left a quick message, ready to escape to his computer and pick up where he'd left off with his laptop on the plane.

The phone rang as he typed Chapter Twenty on the keyboard and he ignored it until Angela's voice came over the airwaves after three rings.

"I know you're there, coward. Pick up."

Oh, those were fighting words. Never let it be said he let a puny woman push him around! Chuckling, he answered the phone.

"So, you made it back to the city in one piece."

"Got in a little while ago, and I was about to throw myself into some work," he said hoping she'd get the message, but he forgot to whom he was talking.

"So, how are things?"

"Angie, I just told you I'm trying to work."

"Work you can do any time. How often do you get to talk to your big sister?"

Lately, too often. To his sister he said, "Angie, I just got off the phone from Mom and I'd really like to try and get some work in."

"All work and no play, EJ."

He sneezed and heard Angela gasp on the other end of the phone.

"See that. You're running yourself ragged, probably coming down with something."

"One sneeze, and I have the bubonic plague?"

"Hey, we both know who you're talking to. You rarely get sick. Both of us do."

That was true enough. He often wondered if his and Angela's unusual good health was an offshoot of their gifts. "There's a first time for everything."

"That's why you should start taking better care of yourself. You're not getting any younger you know."

"Didn't I say I just got off the phone with my mother?"

Angela grumbled, "Oh, all right. I'll leave you in peace."

"You will?" he blurted out.

"For now. Just one more thing though—"

"Yes, I'll think about what you've said, old wise maharani."

Angela chuckled before saying good-bye and hanging up.

EJ immediately got back on his computer, but as soon as he was in front of the monitor he realized he just didn't have it. The magic he'd experienced with his laptop on the plane hadn't translated to the computer in his house. He got up, forked a hand through his hair to nape as he paced.

Shit, he'd had such grand plans, too, intended to spend at least several hours getting his foot in the door with Tabitha, then the rest of his time productively buried in his work-in-progress before the madness of Thanksgiving at his parents' house and going back on tour took over.

He knew what the problem was. He had unfinished business to attend. Business that had been started in Texas.

He thought about calling her first, but as tempting as the memory of their last talk made that, he knew she might try to brush him off, and he didn't want to give her that opportunity.

His best option was to go over there and corner the contrary woman on her own turf.

EJ grinned at the idea of seeing her in the voluptuous flesh, heart palpitating at the memory of that little chat they'd had on the phone. He hadn't actually come down from that rush of adrenaline and testosterone since he'd hung up with her a few nights ago, doubted that he ever would, looking forward to what they could do to top it.

EJ grabbed his keys from the pegboard at the front door, threw on his black leather jacket and headed out the door while he still had the balls to do this.

* * * *

On the brief drive over to Tabitha's place EJ managed to rein in his feelings and get them into perspective. Or more accurately, put a muzzle on his friend, and get his hard-on under control. He didn't want to go to her with a boner, let her know exactly how much she turned him on, how much of a hold she had over him. Like she didn't know either already.

He took the outside stairs two at a time, found her bell, rang it, and seconds later heard the sexy lilt of her voice over the intercom, the familiar tone exciting his friend all over again.

"Who is it?"

"It's me, Tabitha. Let me up."

"Who is me?"

"Don't play games. At least not until I get upstairs."

The buzzer instantly sounded, as he knew it would, sure she wouldn't want to discuss their business, even in a limited capacity, on the street.

EJ chuckled as he entered the downstairs lobby and headed upstairs.

Tabitha was waiting for him, leaning against the doorjamb, arms folded across her lush breasts as he cleared the landing and made his way to her apartment.

"You're looking good," he said.

"Thanks."

He grinned at her coolness, unruffled since he'd expected it.

She put a palm against his chest as he motioned to pass her and get into her apartment. "I didn't invite you in."

"Taking that vampire accusation a little too serious are we?"

She stared up at him, limpid whiskey colored eyes quickly weaving their spell as she dropped her hand and stepped aside.

EJ stopped just inside her hall, waited for her to close the door and precede him inside.

"You want something to drink?" She asked over a shoulder as she made a left into an immaculate stainless steel kitchen.

"Beer if you have it." Hell, he'd took a chance, not thinking that she would after the face she'd made when he'd offered her one at his house.

EJ made his way into the living room, not surprised by the sleek cool appearance of the furnishings, grinned when he saw the glass coffee and end tables beside the gray leather sofa.

He drifted further into the apartment, saw the plant stands, one catty corner to an overflowing teak bookshelf and another adjacent to the teak entertainment center. All the plants were perfectly aligned on their perches, queued up in size place, and with military precision. Their leaves were rich and green, obviously well tended and adding an air of warmth and humanity to their otherwise sterile environment.

Then he saw them, and couldn't help smiling, the elephant collection in the polished teak curio cabinet against the wall leading down the hall to her bedroom.

EJ went closer to admire the types and sizes, everything from a large gray porcelain elephant that took up the entire top shelf, to the smallest crystal ones proliferating on the bottom shelf. In between and crowding the remaining six shelves were gold elephants, silver elephants, brass elephants, glass elephants, ceramic elephants, even carved wooden elephants.

Had he known she had such a fetish, he would have showered her with elephants a long time ago, instead of wasting his money on roses.

EJ stood from his crouch and laughed when he spotted the signed collector's copy of Dr. Seuss' *Horton Hears a Who* standing open at the top of the shelf.

"What's so funny?"

He turned to see her with a Corona in one hand and a coaster in the other.

She handed him each then folded her arms across her breasts and stared at him like a school teacher who'd just caught one of her students scribbling obscenities on a bathroom wall.

"I was just admiring your collection."

"More like mocking it."

"No." He shook his head. "I dig it. I think it's cool."

She looked at him doubtfully, unfolded her arms and indicated the sofa. "Have a seat?"

He tipped his beer at her and took a seat in one corner while she took a seat in the opposite corner. "You were expecting me."

"Why do you say that?"

"I didn't figure you for a beer drinker."

"I'm not."

He waited for her to elaborate or confirm, but she wouldn't say anything else, so he let it go at that, decided he wanted to know more about this elephant craze of hers. "So, what's with the cabinet?"

"I would have thought it was fairly obvious."

"That you've got a thing for pachyderms? I got that. Just not why."

She shrugged. "Who says there's a deeper meaning than the fact that I just like them?"

"I know you, Tabitha."

"I wish you'd stop saying that."

"Just calling 'em as I see 'em, and I know you don't do anything without a reason behind it." He peered at her waiting for that peek for which he was so hungry, a tiny peek, given up willingly, without his trying to probe her, into the workings of her mind.

She must have stared back at him for a good two minutes—damn the woman was stubborn—before she finally broke down and threw up her hands.

"Fine, fine! If you must know, I don't just like elephants I admire what they symbolize."

He arched a brow. "And that would be?" He wanted to hear her say it, not assume that he had an idea, which he did, and not assume that he'd read Hemingway's *Hills Like White Elephants*, and loved because it was so dependent on dialogue.

Tabitha sighed as if he was wearing her down, and EJ smiled as she glowered at him.

"In most cultures elephants are symbols of strength, wisdom, patience, fidelity…there's just a whole laundry list of attributes that I refuse to go into right now, all right?"

"All right." He chuckled, moving closer. "Besides, we both know I didn't come over here to discuss your elephant fetish."

She glared, holding his look for as long as she could before she lurched to her feet and paced the floor in front of the sofa. She finally stopped in front of him, pointing an accusing finger. "I hope you're not expecting anything from me because of what happened the other night. If so, you're going to be sorely disappointed."

"Will I?" he murmured, stood and took two steps towards her.

"Stop it right there." She took two steps back.

He smiled at her, could almost imagine her wielding a crucifix to keep him at bay if she'd had one on hand.

"I think you have the wrong idea about me," Tabitha said.

EJ shook his head. "No. I've got the right idea. You're just sorry I know your secret."

"What secret?"

"That you're not just a control freak." He took another step towards her, circling until he had her in front of the sofa where he wanted her. Then he advanced until she tumbled backward on the cushions.

EJ instantly covered her body with his, catching her wrists above her head with his hands and holding her just so, letting his body adjust to her curves, sinking into the softness of her, immersing himself in her vanilla musk scent as she arched against him.

She calmly looked up at him while he slowly caressed one bare thigh and calf.

"I like the shorts," he murmured.

"I didn't wear them for you."

"Didn't you?"

"I like my comfort when I'm home relaxing."

"I'm glad they're comfortable, but they're still sexy." He lowered his head and nuzzled her neck, inhaling deeply, couldn't get enough of her creamy aroma, couldn't get enough of her trembling beneath him, her whiskey hued eyes darkening with lust. "Just like this muscle shirt. I was already hard listening to your voice downstairs, but I nearly came when I saw your bare athletic arms peeking out of the sleeves and these full breasts pushing against the white material, and this…" He curved his free hand around her slim waist. "Do you know what a smooth exposed belly does to me?" He caressed her navel with his thumb as if to emphasize his question.

"No, tell me."

"It makes me hot." He stroked her throat with his tongue, took one of her hands and guided it down until she cupped the hard bulge in his jeans. "I want you, Tabitha."

"I can see that."

He chuckled, sliding his hands beneath her to grip the delicious round ass that had been haunting his dreams since Texas and pressed her closer to his erection, simultaneously rubbing himself against her pussy. "Say you want me, too."

She groaned as he nibbled her left ear. "You know I do."

He almost gaped, shocked she'd finally admitted it. Not that he didn't already know. He could smell her desire, feel the moist heat leaking through her panties to the crotch of her jean shorts, couldn't wait to put his fingers inside her, couldn't wait to taste her.

EJ was so busy fantasizing about all the different ways he wanted to take her, enter her, worship her gorgeous body, he didn't hear the door unlock.

By the time he realized someone had entered the house this tall Black guy with a high bushy Afro was already standing over him and Tabitha on the sofa.

EJ leaped off of her and got to his feet.

"Don't stop on my account."

"Who the hell are you?"

"I could ask you the same question."

EJ grimaced as the dude swaggered into the kitchen as if he owned the joint, his blood beginning to cook in his veins.

"Eric…"

He turned on her as she coolly smoothed back her long hair as if waking from a nap and her placidity angered him as much as the big dude in the kitchen.

Tabitha stood up beside him as the stranger came out of the kitchen with a beer, and saluted EJ with it.

"Frankie this is Eric Vega. Eric this is Franklin Greer…"

Frankie proffered a hand, and just as EJ shook it Tabitha finished the introductions.

"My brother."

"Your brother?"

"Yeah, her brother. You got a problem with that, homeboy?"

EJ jerked his hand out of Frankie's grasp and turned to Tabitha. "If you don't want to tell me who he is—"

"I just did."

"Okay. Fine."

"You don't believe me?"

"Should I?" EJ arched a brow at her incredulous tone, angry that she wouldn't just fess up and be honest about who was her "friend."

He had plenty of friends of the opposite sex, and Tabitha was entitled to exercise that same option. They weren't exclusive, nowhere close. Cool. He could deal with that. He just didn't want to be slapped in the face with the evidence of her *Thoroughly Modern Millie* ideals, and he definitely didn't have to like how close she and "Frankie" obviously were.

The guy had a key! And he didn't look like any brother of Tabitha's. Not because he didn't look *like* her. He just didn't feel like a brother. He felt like a lover, or at least an ex-lover… living under her roof!

EJ turned to stare at the guy, felt the emotions right on the surface, the possessiveness, the desire and love, and suddenly turned on his heels to stalk towards the front door.

Tabitha followed him. "You're leaving?"

He pivoted, and when she would have collided with his chest EJ caught her by the shoulders and held her at arm's length. "It's obvious that I'm a third wheel here."

"Don't be ridiculous."

He glared at her for a long moment, arms itching to pull her close, ready to scan the truth, or at least the full story, out of her, but he had his pride, damn it. And evidently, she had her reasons for not wanting to level with him.

"Eric…"

He swooped down without another thought, took her mouth with his, biting and sucking her lower lip for a long glorious moment before sliding his tongue deep into her mouth and mating with hers. He came up for air seconds later to stare at her. "When you're ready to come clean about this, give me a call."

"Come clean?" She gaped.

EJ opened the door, stepped into the hall, and closed it behind him without another word.

* * * *

"You could have just told him the truth."

"So could you."

"Hey, that's not *my* job." Frankie took the seat recently vacated by Eric, sipped his beer.

"He should have taken my word at face value."

"Why? You don't take anyone's word at face value."

"Whose side are you on anyway?"

Frankie threw his hands in the air as if in surrender. "I ain't got no nickel in this dime. I'm just an innocent bystander."

"Ain't nothing innocent about you."

He chuckled. "I stopped Tabby-Cat from getting her swerve on," he teased.

"That's not funny." None of this situation was a bit funny.

The man had had the nerve to leave in a self-righteous huff. Like she had done something wrong or offended him in some way. He was the one in the wrong, and she would not apologize. Especially when *he* had popped up on her unannounced in those black jeans and that black turtleneck and black leather jacket, looking like a sexy sinful cat burglar, and sending her hormones into irreversible overdrive with his barely contained heat.

"What are you thinking?"

"Nothing you need to know."

"You really should have just told him."

"It wasn't something he needed to know." At least not yet. Maybe never.

"He'll come back you know."

"Since when are you such an expert on human relations?"

"I'm not an expert. I just know what I saw, and the look in his eyes when he left said he's going to come back, at least as soon as he realizes he fucked up."

"I'm glad you realize that he's the one who…fucked up and not me."

"Oh, I didn't say that. You both kind of fucked up if you ask me."

"Thanks a lot."

"Happy to help. Oh, and speaking of…" Frankie dug into a jeans pocket, extracted five crisp twenties and pushed them into Tabitha's hand. "Not that it comes even close to paying you back for all you've done for me. Or for me interrupting your groove session."

Tabitha laughed. "Are you sure?" She knew he'd be coming back for some, if not all of it.

He always did but who knew, maybe the tides were finally starting to turn.

"It's about time I started pulling my weight around here, at least for the time I'm staying." He gave her a quick kiss on the cheek, got up and headed down the hall to the bathroom, leaving Tabitha sitting in the living room with her head spinning.

God, there must have been a full moon out tonight. First Eric stopping over out of the blue, randy and ready and turning her inside out with his hot hands and his even hotter mouth, and now this. War and Armageddon were surely on the horizon.

Chapter 14

Jade knew EJ was home. She had spoken to Jodie and knew he had gotten back into town.

So why wasn't he returning her calls?

Even if he was writing, he eventually found a free moment to return her calls once he came up for air and realized that there was a big wide world of sex rushing by without him.

Jade didn't pretend he abstained when he wasn't with her. She knew how he was, knew she wasn't the only one EJ was seeing and that he would not do without for long, even though she knew that he could. Evidence of the latter plainly apparent the last time she'd come over and he hadn't wanted to do anything.

What was the point of her coming over? Sure she liked spending time with him, liked playing Scrabble and watching sports on TV with him., but half the fun of their relationship was the unpredictable excitement of their sex life. Without that, what was there to keep him close to her when he could get sex from another sexy stand-by if he wanted?

Someone like Ms. Uptight Personal Shopper.

Jade ground her teeth as she fine-tuned and finalized the concept for one of her latest campaigns. She'd soon be swinging the layout over to her art director to start on mock-ups.

Thanksgiving Eve and she was stuck in this place knocking herself out to ensure the agency met its deadline for a big retail account and that she kept her job for another day.

Jade flashed to her first campaign when she'd handled the advertising for her best friend's lemonade stand back when they were both seven and Jade had—bullhorn and hand-printed flyers in hand—announced the stand's grand opening.

She'd gotten the bug and been hooked ever since, hadn't yet regretted a moment in the business, loved working in an arena where her gifts for persuasion were rewarded and respected.

Lately, though, she wondered if perhaps EJ had had the right idea when he'd gotten out.

He certainly seemed happy enough these days, on the road pushing his bestseller and pushing up on Ms. Tabitha Lyons when he wasn't on the road she was sure.

She didn't know what little Ms. Uptight had that she or any of EJ's other past women didn't, didn't know what made her special enough for EJ to rebuff *her* advances, except perhaps her resemblance to Sinclair in that dark, tragic, naive damsel in distress sort of way.

Hell, it had been so obvious he had been thinking about another woman the last time Jade had been with him, and the only reason Jade knew the woman in question had been Ms. Lyons was her memory of the way EJ had acted when Jade had come onto him after his precious personal shopper had left.

She'd never seen him so absorbed with one woman, unless it was her, and the thought that she no longer held that place of distinction and honor in his life pissed her off almost as much as not getting off when an available and willing cock was in the vicinity.

"Hey Jade, I'm going out to get a quick bite. You want something?"

She glanced up to see one of the agency's programmers, Jeff Dudikoff, a bright young thing who'd just joined the company eight weeks ago and during one of the busiest seasons of any large ad agency right before the holidays.

Jade was surprised he seemed so amiable and upbeat this late in the day.

Her delay in getting the layout to her art director would surely put a crimp in any holiday plans Jeff had since his schedule was directly affected by the speed of work coming from his superiors, one of which was her.

She pulled a twenty out of her purse and handed it to Jeff when he crossed the floor to her desk. "Whatever you're getting."

"You're taking a risk."

She glanced up and noted a stud in his left nostril and left eyebrow, the several rings and studs lining each of his ears, the long sandy-blond hair, the shaggy-like whiskers, and the black polish on his fingernails.

He was a typical creative, an essential cog and the lifeblood of any ad agency, but so low on the totem pole and kept far away from the clients that it almost didn't matter how he looked or dressed as long as he could bear the heavy workload of generating completed products.

Jade noticed his grin and dark-blue eyes, that he had the most entrancing dimples she'd seen this side of EJ Vega.

He was kind of young at twenty-three, and normally blondes didn't do anything for her, but he was alluring enough to make her pussy tighten inside the crotch of her dress-down black pinstripe slacks wondering how he'd be in bed. Just to take the edge off of EJ's latest rebuffs.

At least until her next campaign. Because the competition wouldn't nearly be over until she got Ms. Uptight Personal Shopper out of the way and claimed EJ as her own once again.

* * * *

EJ sat in the family room with his brother, Angela's husband Federico, their three sons, and EJ's own dad watching a college football game on TV.

Dinner and seconds was a near-distant memory, everyone happily full and indulging in calorie-burning endeavors, like EJ's Mom who'd gone out for a walk with two of his sisters, while the rest of the women cleaned the kitchen—or lounging like satiated conquering Vikings enjoying the spoils of their latest raid.

EJ had spent the beginning of the day before dinner recounting tales of his life on the road, trying to convince his nieces and nephews that no, he didn't know Stephen King or John Grisham, while appeasing their curiosity of what it was like to be a "big time author."

Angie's son Vincent especially had been interested in his bestselling status, was trying to sell his parents on sending him to art school and using his uncle as an example that great success could be achieved in the creative arts.

EJ sheepishly tried to keep the peace between the boy and his parents, convincing him to at least study for a more stable career as a backup in case the art thing didn't work out.

Angie flopped down on their Mom's country floral sofa in the family room now and ruffled EJ's hair as their dad, brother and her sons stretched and went in search of more snacks during the commercial break.

"Thanks for what you did earlier with Vince."

He chuckled. "What kind of responsible self-respecting uncle would I be if I didn't try to steer him down the straight and narrow?"

"He really does look up to you."

"I look up to his mother." EJ leaned in and gave her a peck on the cheek.

"So, how are things going with Tabitha?"

"Wow, you let dinner and two football games go by before you dug in with that one."

"You are such a wise-ass." She playfully punched his ribs. "Well?"

"Who says anything's going with Tabitha, Ms. Matchmaker?"

"What have you done?"

Damn, there was just no hiding anything from the woman, and EJ doubted that he'd be able to hide anything from her even if she wasn't gifted. Angela was too intuitive, and too damn nosy to let anything like a busted relationship that she'd initiated get by her.

"I haven't done anything." At least that's what he'd managed to convince himself of during the last twenty-four hours. What else could he do? He had to stand by his decision, didn't he? Except when he thought of her—the bewildered look on her face, her surprise when he'd walked out—he wondered if walking out had been the right thing to do at all.

"Don't lie to me, EJ. I know you've done something to ruin it."

"What makes you think it's me and not her?" He crossed his arms over his chest in a childishly stubborn and defensive gesture that usually made Angela more tenacious and determined to get to the truth than not.

"Don't be such a spoiled brat. Own up to a mistake if you've made one."

Did she have to know him so well?

Angela laughed at the disgruntled expression on his face as their brother Nick came back into the room bearing three bottles of Heineken.

He took a seat beside Angela sandwiching her between himself and EJ. He handed two beers to her and Angela passed the extra one to EJ.

"Thanks bro," Angela and EJ chorused.

"She trying to fix you up with another of Freddie's friends?"

"For your information, I've already fixed him up with his soul mate."

"Do I hear wedding bells in the distance?" Nick cupped a hand around an ear and laughed before tipping his bottle to his lips and taking a long swallow.

"Not if he doesn't take what's wrong and make it right."

"Oh, shit, guru-sis is at it again." Nick shook his head. "I'm glad it's you she's after this time and not me, bro."

"I'm not after anyone. I just want to see my little brothers and sisters happy." Angela reached out to ruffle each of their fluffy dark heads, stood and glanced at EJ. "Remember what I said. Make things right." Then she left the family room.

"What the hell is Obi Won going on about this time?"

EJ shrugged, morosely sipped his beer before putting his bottle on the mahogany coffee table in front of the sofa.

Once again, his sister had struck the heart of the matter, and left him feeling as if he were a rebellious teenager who refused to do his chores or homework, except his refusal to apologize to Tabitha wasn't as simple or easy, especially when his mind was clouded with suspicion.

Before Tabitha, he hadn't realized he had a jealous bone in his body, and if that guy hadn't walked in the other night and interrupted them, he might never have realized it, happily going about his business thinking he was invincible and too easygoing to care.

Frankie's arrival changed all that.

He didn't think there was anything other than sisterly love between them on Tabitha's part. EJ had felt no passion in her for the guy, seen no overt signs of a sexual relationship and refused to believe that Tabitha would lead himself on with her words and her body the way she'd been, if she were serious about, or living with someone else. Call him a male chauvinist but he didn't imagine the woman promiscuous enough to do that, too chaste and principled to juggle more than one guy.

But the simple truth was his judgment was clouded with desire. As much as he tried and wanted to read her, EJ knew next to nothing about Tabitha Lyons except that he wanted to get inside her so badly he hadn't been able to function right the last couple of days thinking about it, and as far as Frankie was concerned, the only thing he knew for sure about him was that the man was in love with Tabitha; he'd recognized this as soon as he'd shaken Frankie's hand. This alone had him doubting any familial relationship and doubting Tabitha's words.

But who was he to doubt anyone, or begrudge Frankie his feelings when he was only in lust with Tabitha himself and promising nothing more than enjoyable and passionate several rolls in the sack that might or might not lead to anything more than he and Tabitha being friends?

More like enemies if Tabitha had anything to say about it because despite her big bad bold act, he knew she was too uptight not to take serious anything that happened between them, too passionate not to want all or nothing. Once she opened up and gave her trust, there would be no turning back for Ms. Lyons.

EJ had already made a commitment to open her up for him, to him, right from the beginning, and had no intentions on turning back either. Hell, he knew *she* wouldn't apologize, and when he got right down to it, he needed to swallow his hot-headed Italian pride, go over there, do a rendition of *American Idol's* Ruben Studdard's *Sorry For 2004* as many times as it would take her to forgive him.

Damn. She'd rub his face in it but good, if she didn't outright slam the *door* in it. *If* she opened it for him at all. He had to make it worth her while. Something extravagant, a grand gesture to show her his sincerity and EJ knew just the ticket.

"Damn, Angie got to you with all that guru talk, huh?" Nick asked now. "I can see that far-away, she-is-mighty-and-wise-and-I-am-but-an-ignorant-peon look in your eyes."

"Yeah, she got to me," EJ said and he wasn't thinking about Angie.

* * * *

Thanksgiving was days over and Tabitha arrived back at work bright and early Monday morning, put in a full day's work, another holiday come and gone with no romantic prospects.

Frankie had spent the holiday with her, she knew to keep her company more than out of any obligation to recognize traditional bonds. Almost as soon as he'd finished her modest holiday fixings, he'd been off and running to catch up with his rock group buddies, ostensibly to practice for a gig, and didn't return until well after midnight to raid her refrigerator for meager leftovers. He'd settled for a roast chicken sandwich and a hot chocolate with marshmallows that he consumed in front of the TV watching *Aliens* and reminiscing with Tabitha until bedtime.

Eric hadn't called all day Thanksgiving or the several days that had followed; she hadn't expected him to, and she certainly wasn't calling him.

She'd done nothing wrong, nothing to warrant his ire except tell him the truth and if he couldn't handle that, that was his problem.

Granted, she hadn't told him everything, but then who said he deserved to know? That he could handle her history when she barely could herself? Their relationship hadn't yet reached that level, and Tabitha wasn't sure yet whether she wanted to grant Eric the privilege and go there.

She still couldn't believe he'd walked out on her without a backwards glance and leaving in his wake what had been, for all intents and purposes, a warning: *When you're ready to come clean about this, give me a call.* As if she were keeping some grand detrimental secret from him. As if he were her freaking conscience!

It would be a cold day in hell before she dialed his number for anything other than to arrange an appointment to drop off new purchases. Even then she might resort to a delivery service, worth the extra expense to not have to see his smug, presumptuous face again.

Damn him!

Her buzzer sounded and Tabitha paused from cleaning the kitchen island to stare at it.

Against her better judgment, especially since he'd used it and interrupted her and Eric's getting their groove on, she'd given Frankie a key soon after his latest arrival. She was almost certain it wasn't him ringing the bell unless he'd lost it already, and she wouldn't put something irresponsible like this by him which was why she'd had the lock changed since his previous visit.

She stalked to the intercom fuming over all manners of imagined transgressions before she heard *his* voice and a sudden calm-before-the-storm enwrapped her. "What do you want?"

"Tabitha, let me up before I start ringing every buzzer down here."

"Don't threaten me, you pompous ass!" When she pressed the "Listen" button on the panel, she wasn't surprised to hear him laughing.

Damn it she wanted to slap him...and then ride all the frustration and lust right out of her body as she straddled him, his hard cock deep inside her.

She stood tapping her foot, arms folded across her breasts, waited several seconds, calling his bluff before she remembered who she was dealing with and buzzed him up.

This time he was in blue jeans and a navy turtleneck beneath a tan suede jacket and Tabitha's vaginal muscles spasmed at his brutal sex appeal as she held open her door and tried to harden her heart against the welcomed sight of him.

He had his hands behind his back, and a dimple-showcasing grin on his face that liquefied the tendons and muscles in her knees so much, she had to hold onto the doorjamb and concentrate not to founder.

"Flowers aren't even going to come close, Eric."

"I know. That's why I bought you this." He brought his hands from behind his back with a flourish and Tabitha couldn't stop a grin from spreading across her face.

He held a big fluffy, stuffed pink elephant up in front of his face, wiggling it back and forth before moving it to the side to peek at her. "For your collection."

"Come in, you pig." She stepped aside and let him in, surprised when he stopped just inside the door, turned to her and handed over the elephant.

"I only have a minute."

So many questions sprouted in her throat at that—*why haven't you called me, and where have you been all this time*—a couple of which never made it to her lips.

Tabitha settled for silence, just stared at him, waiting for an explanation, refusing to say anything first and let him off the hook.

"I just wanted to apologize for the other night. I shouldn't have jumped to conclusions."

"He's my foster brother," she blurted, wanted to slap a hand over her mouth, instead gritted her teeth and took a deep breath as Eric grinned at her.

"He's in love with you, you know."

"I know."

"And you still let him stay here?"

She shrugged. "I don't have control over his feelings. I only have control over mine, and they tell me that he's a good and decent person I want in my life for as long as he wants and needs to be in mine." She thought that should have been enough of an explanation, but should have known better where the male ego was concerned.

"How long has he been living with you?"

"Off and on? Years."

Eric grimaced and Tabitha grinned before she burst out laughing.

"Eric, he's family. He comes by every once in a blue moon when he's in town and needs a hand or a place to crash. I give them to him. End of story."

He stared at her and Tabitha could see the questions multiplying exponentially behind his eyes by the power of how many seconds he let tick by before he finally said, "Okay."

She had to fight not to sigh with relief in front of him, settled for hooking her free arm through his, trying to lead him further into the apartment.

"I wish I could stay, but I'm on my way to the airport."

Tabitha arched a brow, said nothing.

"I dropped by to see if you wanted to join me."

"To watch planes take off and land?"

"No, silly." He opened his jacket and slid a plane ticket out of his inside pocket. "I'm inviting you to come with me to Colorado."

"Colder than New York this time of year isn't it? I'd rather a trip to the Bahamas."

"I'm serious, Tabitha. I'm presenting at a Survivors of Suicide annual dinner and I'd like you to come."

Trying to hold in her excitement she said, "As much as I'd like to see you in action, it's kind of short notice."

"I know, and I'm sorry about that, but that's why I bought you an open round-trip ticket. My plane leaves in a couple of hours, but you don't have to leave now. You can meet me out there, if you decide to go." He took a folded brochure out of his pocket and handed it to her with the plane ticket. "This is the hotel where I'll be staying and the location of the dinner."

Tabitha took the brochure, staring at it for a long time, tamping down her natural instincts that had her wanting to leap into his arms and go with him as is, right now.

"I'd really like you to come, but if you can't make it, I'll understand."

She peered up into his eyes and knew right away that he was shoveling a load of bull. He was playing it cool, this close to acting the caveman, clubbing her over the head, throwing her over his shoulder and dragging her to the airport. She could see it in his intense gaze, the hungry demanding way his indigo eyes raked over her, just short of a physical yank.

It took everything in her not to tremble and succumb to the force of that gaze, to just play it cool like him and say, "I'll think about it."

Chapter 15

Fifteen minutes before show time and EJ was nervous as hell pacing the plush-carpeted corridor outside the Millennium Harvest House banquet room waiting to go on.

Tabitha hadn't shown up at the airport as he'd hoped even after leaving her at her doorstep with a deep soul-searing kiss that left her breathless, and his own head spinning as he descended the stairs to his Jeep, and she hadn't shown up at the hotel earlier today.

He should have just given up the idea a long time ago of seeing her at all, especially after that apathetic, "I'll think about it."

Either she'd been playing it cool, trying to make him squirm after his cold shoulder and the way he'd behaved the other night, or she really had no intentions of showing up.

He wasn't angry with her, just angry with himself for thinking that there was enough between them for her to want to travel all the way to Colorado on a moment's notice to support him the way she supported her foster brother. EJ shook his head trying to deny the specter of jealousy that still clung to him after Tabitha's explanations.

"So this is where you are! I've been looking all over for you." Dr. Leslie Rubin swept across the floor clad in an elegant, lace-trimmed navy dress with pearl buttons down the front and matching pumps. Her outfit agreed with the hall's décor—the crystal chandeliers and plush Persian carpeting of the lobby and fine linen table clothes, and fancy silverware and China of the banquet room inside.

She was slim and attractive in a Lindsay Wagner, Lifetime-Movie-heroine, widowed-mother-of-two-in-suburbia kind of way, the enthusiasm she had for her cause contagious.

EJ smiled as she approached, thought how much her maternal and assertive manner reminded him of Angela, sure that these characteristics served her well in her counseling position at the Platte Valley Crisis Center here in Colorado.

"Just getting some air and stretching my muscles before I go on," EJ said.

"We have a packed house waiting for you."

"I'm looking forward to presenting."

She put a friendly arm around his shoulder and squeezed. "Well, I'd better get back. I have another introduction to make before you go on." She gave him an encouraging smile before turning to leave.

EJ continued his pacing, paused and glanced at the large color placard outside the ballroom announcing the evening's program: *Sudden Loss and Traumatic Grief: Survivors' and Professionals' Perspectives.*

He had near-top billing on the card along with several esteemed doctors and specialists in the field of suicide and suicide prevention, and wondered whether his ranking came from his status as a bestselling author or as a survivor.

Either way it didn't matter, because Tabitha hadn't come and there was no one else with whom he wanted to share this grand moment, no one else whom would understand what this meant to him.

The lobby door opened several yards behind him, letting in the cold air from outside and EJ turned, heart dropping when he saw an older couple enter with overcoats draped over their arms as they made their way by him toward the banquet room. They nodded greetings. He nodded back and glanced at his watch, saw he had less than five minutes before he would be introduced.

Damn, he'd better head in. He didn't want to cut it too close.

He glanced at the door behind him one last time then turned, opened the large heavy mahogany door in front of him and headed into the banquet room to loud applause.

Dr. Rubin had already introduced him and EJ made his way to the podium, weaving in and out of the tables crowding the banquet room floor with eagerness and ease, his speech rehearsed so many times he could do it in his sleep. The theme so close to his heart he could extract and deliver its meaning with the comfort of someone who'd eaten, dreamed and lived it.

EJ reached the podium, briefly hugged Dr. Rubin before she left him to his own devices.

He shuffled his index cards a couple of times before taking a sip of the iced water Dr. Rubin had provided, then glanced out at the sea of tables, hoping one more time to see a familiar face, *her* face. That was when the door in the back opened and she stepped through.

He followed her all the way from the door to a table towards the rear of the hall, and there might as well have been a spotlight on her his eyes were so attuned to her every movement.

She glanced up at him, demurely smiled and gave him a thumb's up.

EJ grinned and went on autopilot.

He began by reading a passage from *Reaching Out*, one of the more poignant excerpts, one he knew hadn't failed to bring tears to his and Sinclair's parents' eyes.

The banquet room was pin-drop silent as he finished, and when he glanced out at the tables this time, he saw tears on many of the audience members' rapt faces.

He closed the book then started his presentation in earnest, finishing up twenty minutes later to deafening applause that he barely heard as he left the podium and made his way through the throng of well-wishers and congratulatory backslaps and handshakes.

Dr. Rubin stopped him as he neared the rear of the hall and Tabitha, shameless tears glinting on her face and arms outstretched. "Oh, my goodness, you were as good as I thought you'd be, better than great!"

EJ smiled, accepted her hug and returned it with equal warmth. Coming from a survivor of suicide, her praise meant more to him than appearing on a ticket with so many distinguished and accredited experts; meant as much to him as Tabitha's presence.

He watched her from the corner of an eye as he spoke with Dr. Rubin— hanging back in the shadows, one hand grasping the strap of her shoulder bag, the other clutching the handle of a piece of wheeled luggage—and he couldn't wait to get to her.

"I know it's quite a ways off, but I hope you'll think about presenting at our dinner next year?" Dr. Rubin asked.

"Just send me the information when you're ready and I promise I'll be there."

She hugged him again. "Thank you so much for coming, Mr. Vega."

"Thank you for having me."

Tabitha stepped forward as Dr. Rubin left, paused a foot in front of him. "You wore my favorite suit."

"I knew you'd come."

"I know you did." She nodded, tears welling.

"Hey, what's wrong?" He stepped close, wrapped her in his arms, glad for the excuse to touch her, her soft curves fitting next to his hard body as if they had been made for him.

"Like you don't know." Tabitha grinned.

"Honestly, I don't."

"I'm just…a little overwhelmed. I had no idea," she admitted.

EJ frowned. "No idea what?"

"That you were such a gifted speaker."

"Oh, so I was good then?"

"You know you were, smart-ass." She pulled away a little, playfully punched his ribs.

"Let's get out of here," he said, steeling himself for her rejection as he took her by a hand and led her towards the coat check, surprised when she willingly followed.

Outside, however, she paused at the curb, pulling on his hand.

He should have known her acquiescence had come too easily.

"Don't you have to say your good-byes and rub elbows and all that?"

"I've fulfilled my obligation for the night." He tightened his grip, headed for the garage where his rental was parked.

Neither of them spoke during the entire one-block walk, didn't say anything as EJ turned in his ticket, the attendant brought him his car, Tabitha put her luggage in the back seat, then got in up front beside EJ as he got in the driver's seat.

EJ had gotten several blocks away from the garage before Tabitha said, "I took a cab here straight from the airport."

"Oh, yeah?"

She nodded. "I didn't book a hotel room."

He briefly glanced at her. "No?"

"Nope." She shrugged. "Technically, I'm homeless and don't have a place to stay."

He smiled. "You've got a place to stay with me."

"I was hoping you'd say that."

She didn't say anything else until they got into his suite at the Marriott fifteen minutes later, and then it wasn't anything EJ wanted to hear.

"Can we just have something to eat and then hit the sack? I'm still kind of jet lagged."

EJ raised his eyebrows. "Jet lagged?"

"Yes, you know. The condition that occurs when you travel through several time zones."

Shit, she made it sound like she'd *time* traveled to another *universe* instead of taken a plane to another state. "I know what it is," he grumbled.

"I was counting on your understanding since you've been hopping from state to state for the last several weeks yourself and know how taxing it can be."

He nodded. "Yeah."

"I'm glad you understand, baby." She hugged him around the middle and laid her head on his chest long enough for his cock to twitch in recognition and her subtle vanilla scent to waft up to his nostrils. "I'm going to go take a shower while you order room service." She released him, lifted her bag onto the luggage rack, unpacked and just generally went about making herself comfortable in his Western style room.

EJ stood at the entertainment center/bureau frowning, fists on his hips as he watched her, his erection straining the zipper of his pants and threatening to burst through any minute.

Tabitha turned from hanging a dress in the closet, caught him looking at her and arched a brow. "What's the matter?"

He sighed. "Anything special you want to eat?"

"I'll leave that up to you, but something meaty and filling. I'm starving."

"Meaty and filling coming right up," he mumbled as he passed her to get to the phone atop the bedside table.

No way in hell was that king size bed going to be big enough for the both of them!

* * * *

The sun was barely up when Tabitha woke the next morning, body clock still two hours ahead operating on Eastern Standard Time.

She reached up to turn on the nightstand lamp, glanced over at Eric sleeping beside her, and didn't expect him to stir anytime soon.

She remembered turning over in her sleep and briefly waking during the night at one point around three a.m. to see him sitting up wide awake in the straight-back chair by the suite's work desk watching the news on television.

Tabitha leaned up on an elbow, resting her chin in her palm to get a better look at him. He looked exhausted and scrumptious with his black hair tousled around his head and she smiled at the idea that he had tried to stay up all night to stay away from her.

She hadn't lied when she'd told him she wanted to hit the sack early, nonetheless, she'd shamelessly teased him, insisting that the bed was more than big enough to accommodate the both of them when he'd refused to come to bed, mumbling something about sleeping on the suite's sofa.

He must have had second thoughts during the wee hours about being cramped, and finally swallowed his pride to slide in beside her.

Tabitha pulled back the comforter and sheet to check and see if he still had on his clothes. She wouldn't have put it by him to have gotten in bed with his suit on, armor to protect him against the big bad Tabitha-tease.

Nope, he'd taken off his clothes, clad in a pair of boxers and nothing else.

Yumm-y.

He had nice legs just like she'd thought—long, lean, well-delineated with muscles—and she couldn't wait to feel them flexing beneath her as she straddled him.

She hungrily dragged her eyes from his feet to his torso, taking in every detail of his athletic form in between.

She liked the way the boxers hugged his thighs and cupped his cock, as if gift-wrapping his package to offer as a present...to her.

Tabitha couldn't go another second without touching him.

She reached out her left hand, vaginal muscles contracting in anticipation, nipples pebbling and pushing against the soft cotton of her big T-shirt as she gently circled one of his flat nipples with a fingernail and stroked his bronze torso from muscled chest to hard, ridged abdomen. She paused for only a second at the light happy-trail of hair arrowing down from his navel to disappear beneath his underwear.

Tabitha slid her forefinger into his waistband, running it from one hip to the other before she dipped her whole hand in and gently grasped his firm shaft.

He did have a nice package, his size-twelve shoes and the bulge outlined by his trousers not lying. Oh, God yes, she could work with this!

Already he was hard and getting harder, penis warm and beginning to pulse in her hand.

She felt him shift and stiffen before she glanced at his face and met his wide-awake, clear-eyed blue gaze.

"I would ask what you're doing, but at this point, I don't care."

"I'm doing exactly what you want me to do," she whispered.

"I'm not dreaming, am I? Because if I am, don't wake me up."

"You're not dreaming, and you're not getting off the hook that easily." She flung back the covers, rose up on her knees and climbed on top of him.

He instantly put his hands on her hips and she let them stay there until she peeled off her T-shirt and tossed it aside.

Eric's eyes widened at the sight of her naked breasts dangling over him and that's when Tabitha decided to get tough, caught him by the wrists, and took his hands off her waist.

She slid his arms up over his head, held them there for a long moment, breasts tantalizing his mouth. "Hands to yourself."

"You can't expect me to—"

"I can and I do." She released his hands and sat astride him.

He peered up at her, wary and silent before he reached up with his right hand to gently pinch her right nipple.

She gasped, clenched her thighs around his lean hips and caught his wrist once more. "If you're not going to behave yourself, I'm going to have to take steps to ensure that you do." With this she hopped off of him, left the bed and sauntered over to the bureau across the room. She extracted two of his ties from the top drawer, smiling as she brandished them and returned to the four-poster bed.

He glanced up at her from his back, a cocky grin on his face, dimples in full force. "And what do you have in mind for those?"

"You know exactly what I have in mind, and if you're not a good boy, I'll have to retrieve two more to take care of your legs."

"I knew you had other reasons for me buying all those ties than to dress up my shirts."

"You're the one who gave me the idea."

He frowned until she reminded him of what he had said in her office. "I didn't put any ideas in your head that weren't already there."

"True enough." She leaned over him, looped one end of one tie around his left wrist, then leaned over him to loop and secure the other end to the post behind his head. "I'm curious, did you specifically order a room that had a canopy and four-poster bed?"

"I told you. I knew you were coming." He stared at her as she repeated the motions she'd just performed with his left wrist on his right. "I actually had something else in mind when I mentioned things to do with a tie that don't involve slacks and a jacket."

"I know you did."

He looked at her, suddenly turning serious. "Shit, Tabitha," he growled, trying the stability of his bonds before stopping in frustration. "You wouldn't ask me to do this if you knew how much I want to touch you, hold you."

"I'm not *asking* you to do anything, Eric." Tabitha draped her body over his, luxuriated in the feel of his hard chest against her breasts, the light sprinkling of soft hair tickling her nipples as she pressed against him. She closed her eyes and inhaled remnants of the cologne he'd put on yesterday, sandalwood and lustful male infiltrating her senses.

She sat up to stare down at him, licking her lips as she remembered how powerful and forceful he'd sounded at that podium last night, how elegant and sexy he'd looked in her favorite charcoal suit, vest and black T-shirt beneath.

God, it had taken every ounce of self-control in her not to fling herself across the lectern, a willing sacrifice to his erudition and raw charisma.

But she didn't have to use any restraint now, except what she used on him. She could do what she wanted with him, to him and she knew he'd love it.

Tabitha closed her eyes and groaned, felt him shudder beneath her and peered down at him, resting her palms on his chest as she shifted her pussy against his hard cock.

"Shit, you're killing me, woman!"

"Not yet."

He gritted his teeth and hissed as Tabitha slid down his body, grasping the waistband of his boxers in both hands and slowly pulling them off.

He lifted his butt and legs to help her completely divest him, and his penis jutted toward the ceiling, long, thick and fully erect.

Tabitha stared at him, every gorgeous hard inch, and licked her lips again.

He scowled. "What are you thinking?"

"Of how I'm going to do to you what I said over the phone."

"Tabi—"

She bent her head and crushed her lips against his, nibbling his full bottom lip for a long moment before thrusting her tongue into his mouth to tangle with his.

He writhed beneath her, straining against his ties.

She slid a hand down to his cock, gently fondled his balls, testing their weight, liking their naked springiness.

Tabitha swallowed his groans, dragged her mouth away from his, primed and ready to hunt up other pleasures to occupy her lips. She moved her head down to his groin, peeked up at him through her lashes as he panted beneath her.

She dipped her head to tease the tip of his cock, stuck her tongue in the slit and lapped the pre-come liquid that had collected there before closing her mouth over the head of his penis and suckling.

He pitched his hips towards her. "Oh, God, please…"

She gripped his firm ass, pulling him close, holding him still as she took him deep into her mouth, using her tongue to tickle the underside of his penis before sliding back up to taunt the head, circling her tongue around it several times.

"Tabitha, untie me. Please."

She had to admit he sounded cool when in fact she knew he was about to lose it, his legs trembling beneath her as he tried to hold back his climax.

She smiled around his cock, glanced up at his face, saw the desperate silent plea in his eyes right before she deep-throated him.

God he was huge! She was barely able to reach the base without gagging. She closed her eyes, concentrated on relaxing her throat muscles to accept him, then licked the base of his penis as she freed a hand from his ass to gently grasp his scrotum and stroke the soft flesh.

She felt him holding himself still through sheer force of will, his struggles as heady and hypnotic as his masculine scent, simultaneously lulling her into comfort-mode and exciting her.

She didn't know how long she stayed down on him, holding him deep and pulling hard on his shaft as if an extra thick milk shake were at the other end, but she soon felt him throbbing in her mouth, ready to burst.

"Tabitha…God…I'm going to come!"

She wanted him to, pussy soaking her thong just thinking about his fluid filling her mouth; chest expanding at the thought of her innate feminine power that had rendered him helpless, his complete surrender imminent.

She watched him strain against his body's needs and his bonds, face drenched in perspiration as he squeezed his eyes tight, clenched his teeth and worked his jaw muscles.

She stroked his balls more insistently, soliciting his release and with a low and urgent moan he finally let go, extending his legs, thigh muscles contracting around her as he gushed into her mouth.

He tasted salty and rich like the meatball and spaghetti dinner they'd had last night, but far more appetizing and wholesome.

Tabitha slowly dragged her mouth off of him, swallowing down every drop of his essence as she slid up his body to lie beside him.

"God." He gasped.

She giggled. "No, just me."

He turned to her, eyes radiant as if lit from a fire within, raking over her with hungry heat. "Can you untie me now?"

"What's your rush?"

"Tabitha."

She glanced up from idly stroking his chest, fingers frozen mid-caress, recognized the command in his voice. "What are you going to do when I untie you?"

"What do you think?"

Tabitha gulped, nervous yet too famished not to obey. She got up on her knees and reached over to the left post to untie that wrist, then did the same with the right.

She sat back on her heels, watched as he smoothed each wrist in turn, reinitiating the circulation, noticed the half-moons embedded in the palms of his hands where he'd clenched his fists, suddenly concerned. "Did I hurt you?"

"Nothing I can't handle."

"You're okay though?"

"More than okay." He looked at her one long moment before he caught her around the waist and flipped her onto her back. "My turn."

* * * *

"I'm not going to use these…" EJ gestured to the ties then flung them aside. "Because I've got a slight advantage over you."

"More than slight," she squeaked, warily watching him.

"And you like it that way, don't you, Tabitha?"

She nodded, surprised him—always surprising him—yelped when he reached down with one hand and ripped the thong from her waist. "Hey!"

"Hey, indeed." He bent and angled his head, lightly biting her left earlobe as he reached down and thrust one finger into her wet heat.

"Mmm," she groaned, twisting beneath him, arching her body towards his as he held both her wrists above her head in one hand and worked her into a fever with the other. "Please, Eric…I want you…inside…I want you inside me."

"Do you?"

She nodded again, nibbled her bottom lip, and his cock jumped in response, fresh memories washing over him as he watched her sinking her teeth into that swollen flesh above while he delved in her swollen flesh below.

"I'm going to make you come, Tabitha. Hard, and when you're done, I'm going to make you come again."

"Oh…Oh, sheesh."

He smiled, her body tight and pulled up like a bow, reaching, seeking as he released her wrists to strum her flesh like a violin, stroking her side from breast to knee cap.

"Please, Eric."

"You didn't listen to me when I begged."

"You vindictive bastard!"

He chuckled. "I never said I wasn't." He liked sparring with her, always had, loved her spirit, her strength and passion. And he intended to turn each of them on her as he turned her inside out with need.

EJ scrutinized her body from head to toe as if he were a surgeon deciding where first to cut with his scalpel.

He paused to focus on her copper skin, the rosy glow enticing, making his mouth water. "You blush pretty."

"I'm not blushing."

"You're burnished gold like a new penny. You're beautiful." He wiggled his middle finger inside her as if to accentuate his point, caressing the surrounding nerve endings inside before sliding in another finger and watching her eyes drift closed.

She panted, caught his wrist, holding his hand in place, trying to drive his fingers deeper as she pumped against them.

She was almost there, right at the edge, he could feel it—from the frantic movements of her hips, the hot moistness of her skin, her internal shudders riding up his arm—the idea of holding back and denying her, thus denying himself, exquisite torture.

"Uh-uh. Not so fast." He slid out his fingers and Tabitha whimpered then punched him in the shoulder. "That's not nice," he murmured.

"Neither are you."

He smiled before swooping down to claim her mouth again, tongue stroking the seam until she parted her lips for him and he plunged in his tongue to explore her mouth as if he'd never tasted her before. Each time he touched her fresh and new. Each time he kissed her a dizzying and different experience from the last.

"Eric..."

"I said I'd make you come baby, and that's what I intend to do." He reached past her, opened the nightstand drawer and retrieved a condom without looking.

She greedily stared as he opened the foil pack with his teeth and fingers before expertly rolling it over his penis.

"Yes, good, let's do this!" She settled her hands on his waist, caressing each hipbone with her thumbs in a conciliatory urgent manner that made him suppress a grin.

As she'd done to him earlier, he took her hands from his waist. "Good things come to those who wait, Tabby-Cat."

She bared her teeth, hissed at him and he glimpsed a hint of her namesakes in that instant that made his heart thunder with the idea of taking this fierce and fiery woman; flutter with the idea that this woman had taken and now owned him.

He settled himself over her body, cupped a perky bountiful breast in one hand, finally able to enjoy the full magnitude of her bosoms at his leisure. He bent his head to lave each hard nipple until they shone liked washed black cherries in the dim light of the room.

Tabitha squirmed beneath him, raked her fingers through his hair, fisted the long soft locks near the base of his skull and held him close, pushing her pelvis up against his rock-hard penis, and he groaned in painful ecstasy at the brief contact.

EJ wasn't going to be able to hold out much longer.

He slowly made his way down her body, leaving a moist hot trail of kisses and love-bites from her breasts to her stomach until he finally paused at the apex of her thighs where the musky-sweet scent of her desire wafted up to him in warm engulfing waves.

She grasped his hair and pushed her hips at him, and he met her thrust with an obliging flick of his tongue, hungrily licking her cleft. She released a primal noise that goaded him to dive in, tongue pushing by damp curls until Tabitha was mindlessly swinging her head back and forth on the pillow and begging him to take her.

He stroked her clit, slowly building a rhythm before he drove his middle finger into her pussy and her muscles clamped down and sucked him in.

"Oh, God, Eric, I want you. I want *you* inside me!"

He timed it to the minute, pulling out his finger, rising and carefully positioning himself between her thighs, penis hovering over her opening for one endless moment as he stared down at her and willed her to look up at him before he slowly slid into her.

"Oh…Oh, yes…"

"You are so fucking tight!" And hot and wet and she felt so good, just as he'd known she would, just as he'd fantasized. He thought he'd come from the rush of finally being inside her.

He paused half-way in, rotated his hips, then thrust deep, felt her canal stretching to accommodate his width and length, heard her sigh as he slid home inside her.

EJ did something then he'd never done with another woman, not even in the throes of his deepest passion: he slipped into Tabitha's mind as he slid into her body. The bond, the transition so natural he didn't even have to try hard, the effect of his entry echoing back to him with the force of a tsunami, making him feel what she felt.

He undulated his hips as if to test his theory, pulled out until just the tip of his penis brushed her vulva, torturing her with several quick shallow thrusts before he drove back in full, and ground his pelvis against her.

It happened again. He felt his own taunting, felt his own entry as if *she* had slid into *him*. He gasped, wrapped his arms around her and pulled her close, eyes shut tight, chest full as he tried to hold onto the feeling, hold onto her, the opportunity to get into her head, her heart, ephemeral and quickly slipping away.

Her shields were down, she was totally open and vulnerable to him and he might have had time to regret his invasion if Tabitha didn't stiffen in his arms at that very moment, her sudden orgasm crashing down and knocking the wind out of them both. She cried out, milking him, every drop as EJ released a hoarse grunt and stopped short of collapsing on top of her.

He rolled to his side next to her, panting as he reached out a hand and twined his fingers through her chestnut hair, the scent of strawberry shampoo from last night's shower still fragrant and fresh on the strands.

She turned her head towards him and he touched his forehead to hers as he lifted a lock of her hair to his nose and took a deep breath.

"That was nice," she murmured, stroking his chest.

"Nice? You are the mistress of understatement." He peered at her, and she was no longer reachable, her mind closed tight.

Damn, for an instant, just an instant, he'd had her. Not her thoughts, but her feelings. And she had been so in synch with him, and he in synch with her, that he knew it had been more than "nice" for her because it had been way more than nice for him.

"Maybe." She averted her eyes.

"Maybe," he whispered.

Chapter 16

He'd done something to her.

Tabitha didn't know what it had been, didn't know how he'd done it, but as soon as he'd entered her, when they'd made love, something besides the physical had happened, something on another plane, shifted and changed.

She hated thinking in terms of clichés, but she couldn't think of any other way to put what had happened between them, except eerie.

She was different, wouldn't be the same again, and didn't think she wanted to go back if it meant being without the intense feelings he evoked, if it meant doing without his wild and crazy sensuality or his warm and easy smile.

Sheesh, this scared her, scared the holy crap out of her. He scared her, and she hated feeling this way, tentative about a possibly life-changing moment, maudlin and wimpy and *open*. These sorts of emotions could only lead to disaster, always did.

She wasn't like this! She faced challenges and changes head-on, had been doing it ever since she'd been a little girl and left in the state's care. She'd had no choice, had no one to take the blows for her, or help her deal with changes, no one who *cared*.

"May I join you?" Eric pulled back the shower curtain, stepped into the modern spacious tub with her, and closed the curtain behind him before she could answer.

She glanced down his body, licked her lips and immediately got wet when she saw that he was fully erect, surprised that they were both turned on so soon after their last round just twenty minutes ago. "Obviously, that was a rhetorical question," she drawled.

"Obviously." He grinned.

"Did you order breakfast?"

"I love a woman with a one-track mind." He bent his head to kiss her right shoulder, caressing her arms from shoulders to fingertips before he twined his fingers with hers.

"I'm a woman with a hungry belly."

"And I'm a man with a hot and hard cock. What are we going to do about that?"

"Breakfast?"

"I don't think that's going to solve the problem."

She punched him in the gut. "Who's going to let room service in when they come up?"

"I will. This isn't going to take very long..." He bowed his head to lick her throat, pressing her against the slippery tile wall away from the hot spray of the shower.

"This is dangerous."

"I've got this." He held up a condom with a flourish, grinning widely.

"You know that's not what I mean," she said, her tone solemn. "We could slip and bust open our heads and hotel security will find our bodies days later horribly bloated and swollen after we've stunk the place up and the neighbors have complained."

"God you're morbid." He grimaced. "But don't think that's going to scare me off."

She looked at him, still worried and he picked up on her anxiety right away.

"Don't tell me you've never done it in a shower before."

She blushed, her coloring and silence telling him all he needed to know.

He leered and slid his free hand down to her slit, slowly pushed in a finger. "I'll walk you through it," he whispered.

Walk wasn't exactly the appropriate word, more like carry her through it, after he instantly sheathed his penis, reached down and behind her to lift her by the bottom and up into his arms.

Tabitha instinctively wrapped her legs around his waist, held on tight.

He pinched her round cheeks. "Mmm, nice cushion," he said, maneuvered her against his body until her vagina rested against the tip of his cock, slowly lowered her onto him as he thrust and completely buried himself in her hot moist depths.

She sighed when his penis filled her, clutched her pussy muscles around him and entwined her arms around his neck as she nuzzled his throat, nipping and sucking the skin there until he trembled.

Her nipples painfully pebbled and she took the edge off rubbing back and forth against his chest, squirming in his arms as he drove in and out of her with increasing force and speed until the friction became unbearable and she had no choice but to climax.

She fastened her legs around him, shuddering, vagina throbbing as his muscles flexed around her when he pressed her against his chest.

Tabitha came back to herself a moment later, raising her head to see his grin.

"Was that nice?"

She lazily moistened her lips with the tip of her tongue, nodded as her eyes drifted shut again, muscles spent with satisfaction. "Better than nice."

"Yes!" He pumped a fist. "Progress, that's what I like." He kissed her full on the lips, sweeping his tongue into her mouth, briefly sucking hers before someone knocked on the suite door outside. He pulled away to smile at her. "Do I have perfect timing or what?"

He put her back on her feet and she had to grab hold of the towel rack to keep from falling as she watched him get out of the shower and wrap a big fluffy white towel around his trim hips.

He glanced back at her and winked. "Be right back, sweetie."

He was gone in a flash, leaving her nerves jumbled and her mind more confused than before he'd come in.

Sheesh, the man was like a tornado sweeping through an area, leveling her defenses, leaving nothing but havoc in his wake.

But, oh, how glorious the havoc! And he knew it, flirting and wielding that deadly charm like a rapier against a beaten opponent only to turn and walk away as if he hadn't just committed symbolic murder.

How many other women had he called "sweetie" or "baby" in the past? How many women, besides Ms. Secret, did he still exercise his silver tongue on?

Tabitha had no illusions that she was the only one, or that she would be the last.

She shook her head suddenly, didn't want to think like that, didn't want to believe that she wasn't as special to him as he was to her.

God what had she gotten into when she'd hopped on that plane and come out here?

* * * *

When Tabitha came out of the shower minutes later, clad in a hotel robe and towel drying her hair, it was to the sounds of a Steely Dan song blasting over the radio.

She stepped out of the bathroom and into the suite to find Eric dancing around in his shorts, singing slightly off-key, and playing air drum and guitar between carrying the breakfast tray over to the room's table by the window.

The view of the Flatirons beyond of which she had heard so much on her flight over—stuck with a chatty elderly world traveler who just "loved the purple mountain's majesty of Colorado," —just barely rivaled that of Eric's tight wiggling derriere in his shorts.

"What is going on, Tom Cruise?"

"Tom Cruise can't touch this." He sang *Peg* along with Steely, pulled her in his arms and swept her across the floor, suggestively rubbing his lower body against her as he held her close, making her giggle. "You know, I used to fantasize about being a rock star."

"Really?" She tried to keep the chill out of her voice, but failed. Or so she thought.

Eric didn't seem to notice her sudden distance, expounding on his teenage dreams of having "hot sexy babes" throwing their panties at him on stage and slipping him their phone numbers backstage for a quick romp in a hotel room on the road.

God, was she doomed to attract irresponsible oversexed would-be Mick Jagger and Lenny Kravitz clones, reminded of her anonymous delinquent father for the rest of her days?

Eric hugged her close then held her arm's length, didn't notice her silence as he waggled his brows and asked, "Want to be my groupie?"

"Sheesh, is that all you men think about!" She pulled out of his grasp, drifted over to the window, back turned to him as she folded her arms tight across her chest.

"Why so serious? I was *joking*, Tabitha. You know, ha-ha funny joke?"

"It's not funny to me," she muttered.

He shut off the music and she felt him come up behind her, hands hesitantly hovering over her shoulders before he lowered them and she allowed him to turn her around to face him.

"What's wrong?"

"Nothing."

"Whatever it is, don't keep it bottled up. Let it out. We'll both feel better if you do."

"No, *we* won't, and I'd rather not talk about it."

"Christ, woman, what is it with you? One minute we're happily dancing around the room—"

"You were the only one who was happily anything."

"Liar," He glared at her, finished as if she hadn't spoken. "And the next minute, you're in a…a funk. What gives?"

"I told you, I'd rather not talk about it."

He stared at her long and hard, looked two seconds from putting her over a knee and spanking the answers he wanted out of her; or performing some other form of coercion that she didn't even want to consider from the glint in his indigo eyes.

Tabitha frowned, started as something brushed against her mind. It was the strangest sensation, intrusive yet eerily comforting, like fingers massaging her gray matter.

She stared at him as if for answers, confirmation, but he shrugged and quickly turned from her to go to the table, uncovering trays and bowls and sitting down before he glanced up at her and arched a brow.

"You said you were hungry, so I ordered a little bit of everything."

"Thanks." She joined him at the table, impressed by the colorful array and amount of food. Belgium waffles with strawberries and whipped cream, fluffy buttermilk pancakes, cold cereal, breakfast sausages, bacon, sweet ham, scrambled eggs, Western omelets, fresh fruit, melon, orange juice, milk, tea and coffee. "Is there anything left in the kitchen?"

He chuckled, rubbing his hands together. "I don't know about you, but I might be able to eat this entire spread all by myself."

"Do you mind, uh…" She averted her eyes, after all they'd done with each other couldn't believe she was acting shy around him, but she only thought to bring it up more out of self-preservation than any attempt at modesty and etiquette. "We're sitting down at the table to eat."

And I'd rather not distract my stomach from what it wants with what my lips would like to go down on. "Could you put on some clothes? At least a pair of jeans?"

He didn't seem offended, in fact looked downright pleased as punch when he stood, swaggered to the bureau across the room and slid into some well-worn blue Levi's before he sat back down across from her and smiled. "Better?"

"A little."

"It's going to have to do. I like my comfort just like you do."

Did he have to remind her about that night? Despite finally having had him inside her, she still hadn't gotten over that night of frustrated lust.

"Any thoughts about how you want to spend our free day here?"

Besides screwing each other's brains out in this hotel room? "There's the Pearl Street Mall, the Flatirons, inline skating…"

"What'd you do? Research before you came?"

"I like to be prepared." She shrugged, wanting to get out and see the sights, needing to get out of this hotel room with diversions and other people between him and her. Her sanity and emotional well being were at stake.

"Okay. After breakfast we'll get dressed and see what's doing."

* * * *

EJ had almost blown it back at the hotel, had pushed her too hard.

He knew she suspected something, if not exactly what he was doing, then that something wasn't quite right about their connection.

He didn't expect her to figure it out. Most people never did, too in denial and afraid of the bizarre to admit its existence, much less admit that someone could get inside their minds, and know their most secret thoughts.

He just wished. He hadn't come close, only scratching the surface of what was inside Tabitha, only brushing what made her tick. Why it was so important for him to know her so intimately when he'd never bothered to waste the energy or his gifts on any other woman with whom he'd been, was beyond him. If he got through sex shields up, emotionally in tact and protected against the nagging, what-are-you-thinking, this-is-the-beginning-of-a-beautiful-long-range-relationship, I-think-I-love-you harangues, he was usually more than a happy camper.

Being with Tabitha was different. *She* was different, gave off this distant, I-don't-really-care-about-you-except-for-the-sex vibe that made him hard just thinking about taking her. In this sense she was like Jade, but with a soft and innocent core beyond her hard edges.

He *wanted* to know about Tabitha, wanted to tell her things about himself that he'd never told anyone before.

He wanted exclusivity.

His cock twitched at the implied threat to his footloose and fancy-free independence. His heart twitched with something entirely different: capitulation. Damn!

"How are we doing over here? Bored yet?" She sneaked up behind him, sliding her arms through his to wrap around his waist.

He turned to her and returned her hug. "Me? I never get bored."

"This place makes it hard for anyone to get bored."

"Anyone who loves shopping."

"And I do!"

No kidding, he thought, smiling at her wide-eyed, childlike excitement.

He wondered how she could seem so stimulated by the idea of running around purchasing things when she did it for a living. Talk about loving your job. Or maybe it was one of those woman things, something in the X-chromosome.

She'd been on a high, flitting from store to store like a butterfly from flower to flower, browsing here, picking up a couple of items there, as if she'd never been let out off a leash.

The climate was unseasonably warm, perfect shopping and strolling weather and Tabitha had taken full advantage, must have dragged him to no less than ten different stores since they'd hit Pearl Street, and it was yet early afternoon, plenty of time left to hit more stores.

He'd actually seen one thing in a jewelry store window earlier in the day that had caught his eye and had sneaked off to purchase it on a whim before Tabitha had noticed his absence, back at her side in time fore her not to have missed him.

He couldn't wait to see her face when she opened it on Christmas.

Shit! He was actually planning ahead, planning his schedule around being with someone during a traditional holiday, doing traditional things like exchanging gifts on Christmas Eve.

He never did that, the last time he'd brought a girl home to meet his family when…God, the last time had been with Sinclair. He hadn't let another girl or woman get close enough to him since Sinclair to warrant the sort of honor meeting the parents represented.

"You haven't bought anything, have you?" She pouted, eyes glancing over his person in a gentle caress that he felt all the way to his scalp.

"How can I? You bought everything." He pointedly glanced at the two big colorful shopping bags—various boutiques, arts and crafts, and antique store names scrolled across their sides—at her feet.

"You exaggerate." She playfully punched his shoulder.

"Have you considered how you're going to get all that stuff on the plane? I only noticed that one small piece of luggage."

"I'll manage."

He arched a brow, knew what she was up to. "Don't think you're going to cram anything into *my* bags."

"You don't want my undies rubbing against your undies, spoiled-sport?" She stroked his chest and EJ's cock stirred, pressing against his fly.

"You are such an evil woman."

She giggled then pointed out Urban Outfitters' window. "Ooh, look! What's going on out there?" She grabbed her bags in one hand and his hand in the other and dragged him outside onto the pedestrian walkway where a crowd was gathering around three street performers captivating the crowds with their antics several yards away from the store.

Rather than Bongo the Balloon Man making animal creations out of a colorful supply of balloons, or the limber contortionist folding his body into a tiny box, Tabitha gravitated towards the nondescript older guy who had the biggest crowd around him.

They squeezed among the throngs, Tabitha standing on her tiptoes, peeking over shoulders and around heads and tempting EJ to put her on his shoulders so she could get a better look she seemed so young and eager.

"What's his shtick?" EJ asked.

"He's the Zip Code Man," a man next to them said and a woman next to him added, "Just give him your zip code and he'll guess your hometown."

"No way!"

"Yes, way. Go challenge him."

"Let's try it, Eric." Tabitha grabbed his arm and pulled him through the crowd until they were in the center, face to face with the Zip Code Man.

EJ glanced down at the price list on the small placard at the man's feet. Nominal, especially if he did what he said he could do.

He dug into his jeans pocket, pulled out a dollar and handed it to him. "10116."

"Thought you could trick me, huh? That's a P.O. Box zip, in Manhattan, by the way."

EJ's eyes widened. "Get out of here!"

"Care to try again?"

"Ooh, me, me!" Tabitha jumped up and down and raised her hand, and EJ handed the man another dollar.

Tabitha gave her zip code and the man paused, put a finger to his temple, closed his eyes like Johnny Carson's Amazing Karnack character, and finally said, "You're both from New York, but you, little lady are from the Park Slope Area in Brooklyn."

Tabitha gaped. "Get out!"

"I'll give you yours for free." The Zip Code Man turned to EJ.

"Okay." EJ gave him his residential zip code this time and again the man put his hand to his temple, closed his eyes and said, "You're from that infamous bohemian haunt, the Village."

This was creepy, and EJ was beginning to wonder what was the man's game, whether or not he was gifted like him and Angela, or just a well-traveled individual.

He could usually sense another like himself, surprised he didn't pick up anything from Mr. Zip Code Man when he gently reached out to probe him.

The guy just stared at him, smiled widely before bowing to his adoring fans, the crowd loudly applauding and whistling.

EJ proffered a hand, and firmly shook the man's hand, laughing. "You put on a good show, Zip Code Man."

He pulled EJ close, and murmured in his ear, "She's going to love your gift."

EJ pulled back, shaken, grabbed Tabitha's hand and made his way back through the crowds to stand beyond it on the walkway.

"What's the matter, Eric? What did he say to you?"

"Nothing." That had never happened to him before. He tried to tell himself there was some trick to the guy's insight. He and Tabitha were, after all, at a shopping mall where most of the people were either browsing or purchasing something for themselves or someone else. No stretch for him to guess that EJ might have purchased some item for a lady. Nothing to it.

"Eric?" Tabitha put a hand on his arm. "Are you okay?"

He glanced at her, tongue stuck to the roof of his mouth with a confession he'd had no idea he needed to admit until this moment, but he couldn't do it. He couldn't tell her about his ability.

God help him, he didn't know if he ever would.

Chapter 17

Their idyll was almost over and Tabitha didn't know whether to welcome or grieve its upcoming demise, didn't know where they were supposed to go from here.

She'd come to Colorado on a whim, so unlike her, not knowing what to expect and was leaving with more than she'd bargained for, so much more and less than she'd ever thought.

That's what life with Eric would be like, never knowing whether you were coming or going, never knowing whether he wanted and needed you the way you wanted and needed him because Eric, if nothing else, was a player. He knew how to talk a good game, she'd seen him in action more than once—with her, with Jade, with his sister, with Cynthia, and she could only imagine how many others—charming the panties off sundry females before the ladies in question even knew their undies were missing.

He slid in and out of character with the ease of a chameleon, at will—the charming client, the dutiful brother, the passionate and teasing lover, the accomplished and poignant speaker—until Tabitha wondered exactly who he was deep down for real.

She'd gotten a glimpse of another side yesterday, one totally unexpected and not exactly appreciated, at the mall when that Zip Code Man had whispered in his ear.

Whatever the man had said had badly disturbed Eric, something that he refused to talk about now almost an entire day later.

She'd tried to get him to open up, knew as she did that she was probably driving him further away coming off as the nagging prying girlfriend instead of a concerned friend and lover. A sure fire way to push away any guy, but she couldn't help trying to reach him.

He'd looked so out of sorts at the mall, and after when they'd eaten at a nearby sidewalk café—serious, quiet and ill-at-ease, totally un-Eric-like.

At one point, Tabitha had found herself carrying the entire conversation, what there was of it, watching Eric pick at the food on his plate, and after seeing him demolish that Hungry Man-style breakfast the other morning, watching him idly pick at anything edible without any intentions of eating it was reason for concern.

"You about packed?"

Tabitha turned from zipping her bag, stood straight to watch him come into the room from the bathroom. He was clad in a blue-to-match-his-eyes button-down shirt opened at the neck and tucked into a pair of blue jeans. She wanted to throw him down and eat him up right where he stood but restrained herself, just smiled and said, "All packed." She glanced at the bedside clock and added, "With plenty of time to spare, too."

"I knew I could count on you to get us up an hour before our wake-up call," he drawled.

"I never did trust those things."

He chuckled, sauntered over to her at the luggage rack and draped his arms over her shoulders before leaning in to kiss her lips. "I'm glad you came."

"So am I."

"It doesn't have to end here you know."

She swallowed, forcing herself not to speak, didn't want to hope. She hadn't thought he'd want to translate their little trip into anything long-range, mentally preparing herself for the big don't-call-me-I'll-call-you kiss-off once they reached New York, and here he was bringing up the future, because she sure as hell wouldn't have, not to save her and his life would she have said a word.

When she was silent for so long he asked, "So what do you think, Tabitha?"

"About what you said?"

"Yes."

She shrugged. "I guess it's something to think about."

He grimaced and she wanted to take back her cool tone, swallow at least a portion of her stubborn pride and tell him that she wanted to make a go of whatever this was between them.

She just stared back at him, watched his wounded eyes slowly darken with anger.

"Yeah, I guess it is," he muttered

God, tell him. Tell him you're sorry, you idiot! Don't let it end on this note, don't let him think you don't care…

"I'm going to get the rest of the bag—"

She put her hand on his arm to stop him and he froze to look down at her. "We've got some time."

He pointedly glanced at the clock with her. "Ten o'clock. Sure you want to push it?"

"We can do plenty in an hour."

He shrugged as if to say her offer in no way excused her insult, but she saw the steadily growing bulge behind the fly of his jeans and it told another story.

"C'mon." She slid her hand down to catch his hand, motioned towards the bed with a nod of her head. "Let's live a little dangerously."

"You know it's not just about sex, don't you?"

"What's not just about sex?"

"You and me," he stated. "That's not all I want from you."

"I don't know what more I can give you," she whispered, averting her eyes.

He ground his teeth as if he were dealing with an especially dense student. "Sex is not the answer to everything you know."

"I never said that it was."

"But you act like it."

"You, who's been trying to get into my panties from the moment I met you, have the nerve to lecture me?"

"I never misled you about what I want."

"No, you didn't, and now that I've come around to seeing things your way and given it to you, you're changing your tune."

He caught her around the shoulders, pulled her close and ground his mouth against hers in a rough kiss meant to show her he'd reached the end of his rope with explaining to her, meant to put her in her place and show her what she had driven him to.

She pushed her tongue out to meet his, slid her hand down to the crotch of his jeans and squeezed his balls none-too-gently.

He jerked back, cursed under his breath, scooped her up in his arms and carried her to the bed, unceremoniously dumped her in the middle of it.

She watched him warily, breathing hard as she backed away until her head bumped against the headboard behind her.

Eric put one knee on the bed, then the other, stalking her. He whipped out his hands to grab her ankles, pulled her back to him across the bed until her legs were dangling over the edge of the mattress.

"Eric don't—" She whimpered as he flipped her skirt up then gripped the waistband of her hose and thong before pulling both down her legs in one swift easy motion, leaving them bunched at her ankles, effectively imprisoning her legs and exposing her to him.

"You wanted a quickie?" He straddled her, towering above her on his knees as he unbuckled his belt, then unbuttoned and unzipped his jeans, watching her watch him.

"I never said—"

He leaned down and buried her mouth beneath his, searing her lips with brutal intent, thrusting his tongue and rolling it around in her mouth as if demanding she come out and play.

Tabitha's head spun at the ferocity of his raid, stomach rising and dipping with unquenched desire and liquid heat when he put a knee between her thighs and pushed her legs apart as far as they would go with her clothes fettering her ankles.

She squirmed beneath him, stared up into his eyes like a supplicant desperate for a handout and hated herself because she wanted him enough to sacrifice her conceit for his heated sexual attentions.

He knelt astride her again as if uncertain what he wanted to do to her first, but soon made up his mind when he drove a finger deep into her moist heat. "You're wet."

She bit her bottom lip, refused to say a word, just wanted him to do this and get it over with, off his chest and make her come like they both wanted.

That's all she wanted, she told herself.

Eric slid off the bed and got to his knees between her legs, the submissive posture—a ruse that didn't fool Tabitha one bit. He grabbed her thighs and pulled her further down the mattress until her legs draped over his shoulders and his lips were right where she needed them to be.

He closed his mouth over her, going to work on her clit, deliberate and determined as a dog sniffing out a buried bone, sucking and nibbling the swollen kernel of flesh until she cried out. Then he transitioned, seamlessly gliding his tongue from her clit to her slit, shoving deeply into her as he stroked her cleft and fingered her pussy in concert with his intimate kiss.

Before long she was arching off the bed, writhing beneath his sensual ministrations, grasping his hair tight and digging her stockinged heels into his back as she came and her juices flowed, copious and earthy, into his mouth.

He lifted his face from her pussy, took a deep breath and glanced up at her with an imperious and vain gleam in his eyes, as if to say his work here was done. Silently, he lifted her legs from his shoulders and got up to go to the bathroom.

Tabitha lay sprawled, spent and ashamed. Though he'd just gotten *her* off, she felt as if he had taken advantage of her, used her for *his* pleasure—because anyone who put that much effort into something must get *some* enjoyment out of it—proving that he could make her come at will.

She closed her eyes and listened to water running in the bathroom sink, seconds later heard him come out of the bathroom and opened her eyes as he sat on the bed beside her.

"Are you all right?" he asked.

"Shouldn't I be?"

He didn't answer, simply leaned back on his right elbow and gently cleaned her up with the warm soapy cloth in his left hand.

She glanced down at his zippered fly, saw that he still had a raging hard-on, then moved her eyes back to his face.

He didn't speak and she didn't either. If he wasn't going to address it, then she certainly wouldn't. Let him be Mr. Big-Tough-I-Don't-Need-You-To-Get-Me-Off Man. See if she cared!

But she couldn't stop herself from touching him, stroking his hard length through the rough denim as she stared at him.

He finally caught her wrist and held her hand in place, bent his head to kiss her, his lips and tongue now gentle and apologetic as he explored her mouth with slow deep relish.

She curved her fingers around him and he pressed closer to her hand, then jerked up his head and lurched to his feet.

"We'd better get going."

* * * *

EJ was an idiot and had punished no one except himself.

Damn, when he thought about her face, how she'd looked after he'd gone down on her, not like a woman fulfilled, a woman who had been tenderly taken care of, but one who had been mauled and violated to make a point.

He glanced at her now as she stood beside him in line to hand in their boarding passes.

She looked like a little girl, a refugee from parochial school in her white silk blouse, short blue pleated skirt and blue penny loafers. She was as dressed down as he had ever seen her since they'd met except when they had been out shopping yesterday and she had worn jeans, cross-trainers and a sweatshirt with Fashion Institute of Technology emblazoned across the front beneath a short black leather jacket.

He wanted to hold her, feel her slim compact form against him, sink into her generous soft curves again and again. More than that, he wanted to know her. Sadly, it appeared from the way she acted and the things she said that she didn't want anything to do with him that didn't involve getting her groove on.

In his heart he knew that was a lie, a façade like her perfect clothes and workaholic persona.

She was hiding God-knew what and it hurt him to know she couldn't trust him enough to tell him what was really on her mind; hurt him to know she wouldn't.

"Thank you, Mr. Vega, enjoy your flight with us." The attendant stamped, separated and handed back his pass, her smile just a little brighter than that which she had bestowed on most of the other passengers, brushing EJ's fingers as he retrieved his pass. "I loved your book, by the way."

He grinned. "Thanks so much. That's always good to hear."

EJ stepped to the side and waited for her to process Tabitha, noticed her smile disappeared, the sunny warm attitude she'd lavished on him non-existent, her tone cool when she addressed Tabitha.

"Thank you, ma'am."

Tabitha took her pass, smiled and said, "Thank you so much, I will."

The attendant frowned. "Will what?"

"Enjoy my flight with you."

EJ chuckled as she preceded him down the accordion corridor to their flight, past the gauntlet of airport security, attendants and other assorted airport employees until they finally made it onto the plane and to their seats.

Tabitha was silent as he stowed their carry-on bags into the overhead. Nor did she say a word as they sat down, put on their seatbelts or prepared for take-off.

Damn, he guessed that meant he was going to have to break the ice.

Normally it wouldn't have been a problem for him, but when the ice was in fact a gigantic berg to rival the one that had taken out the Titanic, slow consideration had to be given as to how to make his approach.

Tabitha finally let him off the hook when she turned on him, arms folded across her chest and spat, "Did you have to flirt so obviously with that attendant?"

"Flirt? All I did was thank her."

"I saw the way you were smiling at her."

"She smiled at me first."

"And treated me like chopped liver."

"How is that my fault?"

"Why there you are, little missy!"

Tabitha and EJ both froze and glanced to their left where a small elderly white-haired woman was grinning at them.

"Oh, hello, Miss Stanford. Funny meeting you here."

"Did you enjoy your stay?"

Tabitha cut her eyes back at EJ before turning back to Miss Stanford to answer. "For the most part."

"Oh, don't you let a little tiff with your boyfriend cloud your memories of the city now."

"He's not my boyfriend."

EJ wrapped an arm around Tabitha's shoulder and leaned close, peeking over her shoulder to smile at Miss Stanford. "She's just kidding."

"I thought so. You look like such a cute couple."

"Especially one of us. I think she is the most adorable thing." He gave Tabitha a squeeze and gasped when she elbowed him in the gut right before he reached across the aisle to shake Miss Stanford's small wrinkled hand. "EJ Vega."

"I know, the author." She held up his book and wiggled it back and forth. "I was at your presentation the other evening and rushed right out to get a copy. Finished it last night."

"Is it signed?"

"Why no."

EJ took an ever-present pen from his inside jacket pocket and reached for the book. He felt heat on the side of his face as Tabitha glared at him, but ignored it. "What would you like me to say?"

"To Edna, Loved your grand city as much as you loved my book."

EJ wrote out her message verbatim, then signed his name and handed it back to her.

"Oh, thank you so much. You don't know what a treat this is." Edna clutched the book to her chest, then took a deep breath and looked at him. "Well, I'll leave you two to your discussion now. Be good to each other."

"We will." He noticed the tick in Tabitha's jaw right before she turned on him again.

She muttered just loud enough for EJ to hear, "She leaves us to our discussion, but when I was by myself, she wouldn't leave me alone for one minute!"

"You probably looked like you needed someone to talk to."

She huffed, turned the back of her head to him, glanced at Edna Stanford and smiled before staring at the seat in front of her.

"Are you going to be like this for the entire flight?"

"Yep, the entire flight."

EJ smiled, wanted to tell her she was being childish, or even worse, a bitch, but knew better than to stick his hand any further into the lion's cage than it was already.

He sat back in his seat and glanced out the window to his right as the pilot's voice came over the loud speaker and the flight attendants did their spiel about safety and procedures to follow in the event of a rough, crash or water landing.

EJ had loved exploring the city with Tabitha, had loved this trip despite its relative brevity, and most of his pleasure came from the woman sitting beside him. Even if she was acting like an incredibly irritated lion with a thorn in its paw right now.

He smiled, eyes drifting shut as he tuned into her breathing, tentatively reached out and brushed against her mind. Prickly and cold, like her. He concentrated on smoothing and warming the rough boundaries, imagined a soft giving surface, something like a sponge, then pushed further until...EJ gasped in shock when he realized he was in!

She's a little girl, about seven or eight and pouring a fifth of Absolute Vodka down the kitchen sink, nervously stealing periodic glances over a skinny shoulder. In seconds it becomes apparent why she is nervous and speed is of the essence when a woman marches onto the scene and roughly jerks her free arm.

Tabitha drops the bottle and it crashes to the floor in a pungent puddle.

"What do you think you're doing, you little bitch? Do you know what this stuff costs?"

She whips out her hand and slaps Tabitha hard across the face.

Tabitha gapes and puts a hand to her quickly reddening cheek but does not cry, just stares up at her mother, unrepentant and fearless.

Flash to another scene, *she is about the same age, surrounded by crowds coming and going with head-spinning speed, and she is alone and waiting. She paces, stopping periodically to glance at passing female faces in the manner of a lost child looking for her mother.*

Soon a policeman approaches and asks her if she knows where her mommy is and Tabitha is forced to admit that she doesn't. She explains her mother left her alone while she went to purchase bus tickets, but her mommy's been gone a very long time now and Tabitha doesn't know what's keeping her.

As more time passes and her mother doesn't show up, it becomes apparent to the officer that her mother is not coming back. The policeman takes Tabitha away in a squad car to a precinct where she will wait the rest of the afternoon and evening away before arrangements are finally made for Tabitha's placement in a Catholic orphanage.

Flash to next scene, years later. *Tabitha is a teenager, the beautiful woman that she will finally become evident in the glowing copper tone of her complexion, the high proud angle of her cheeks and the defiant tilt of her full lips.*

But her long-entrenched bravado is soon put to the ultimate test when she is assaulted by a man who has forgotten his purpose under the influence, forgotten that he is in the business to protect and nurture and not abuse and take advantage of the weak and young in his care.

EJ moaned and shifted in his sleep, but couldn't yet pull away, other images flying at him, other images that wouldn't let go.

This time it is not of Tabitha but of *a woman, features cloaked in haze, unrecognizable, yet he feels a connection, a pull of familiarity right before the car she is riding in hits a retaining wall and she is flung forward against her seatbelt.*

"No!" EJ came awake with a start, confused and queasy, mind half in, half out of Tabitha's world, the images of Frankie storming into the room and pulling the man off of her and of the bloodied woman in the mangled car blending until they are one.

Shame instantly suffused him at the way he'd treated her back at the hotel. He hadn't raped her or forced her, but he'd come pretty damn close, rough and mean just to prove a point.

"Eric?" Tabitha shook his shoulder and he turned to see her almond shaped whiskey colored eyes turned on him in concern. "Are you okay?"

He focused on her face, barely nodded as nausea bubbled and he tried to re-engage his shields, block out all the fear and suffering, protect his sanity.

Since they'd made love it had become easier and easier to get into her mind and harder to protect himself, as if that first act of consummation had opened up the floodgates.

Be careful what you wish for...

God, he had wanted this, *asked* for it, and now that he had gotten it he couldn't deal...So much pain, so much chaos and misery, inconceivable to him that she was able to stay sane and function without crumbling beneath the weight of it all.

"Eric?" This time she cupped his chin, stared at him. "Are you sure you're okay?"

"I must have drifted off," he muttered.

"And had a nightmare." She frowned as she handed him a cup with ice and soda.

EJ gulped it down. He hadn't realized his mouth was so dry until this moment, the cool liquid immediately soothing his parched throat.

"I'm okay," he lied, the movie in his mind only now winding down, images still lingering, evocative and fresh.

The woman was going to die and it frightened him that he knew this with such certainty.

Telepathy he'd tolerated and accepted in one form or another since he was old enough to reason, so commonplace to him now that he took the resultant cacophony of strange voices and thoughts in stride, but he'd never experienced visions before, clairvoyance something new and alarmingly different.

Something that Tabitha had raised.

Chapter 18

Tabitha warily stared at him all the way from the plane to baggage claim, watched him closely until they made it out to his Jeep at airport parking.

She looked but she didn't speak, didn't know what to say, where to begin to address what had happened on the plane, still dealing with what had happened the day before with the Zip Code Man. Minor as was the incident, it bothered her because it had bothered him.

The silence in the Jeep was heavy enough to feel until it was like another living breathing presence in the vehicle with them stealing the air.

Tabitha felt like she was riding with a total stranger, as if she were a hitchhiker Eric had picked up on the side of the road. Which was so ironic since she thought she knew more about him, what made him tick, than she knew about her blood kin, yet he was stranger, more distant now than when they'd first met.

How they were going to part once they arrived in the city was anyone's guess, and Tabitha still didn't know how to approach his proposal.

It doesn't have to end...

She wanted to believe this was still true, that he still felt the way he had when he'd said it, that he still cared. That she hadn't totally alienated him.

Fifteen minutes into the drive Eric finally broke the silence.

"We're going to my house."

It wasn't a question, and every natural instinct in her wanted to argue with his high-handed tone, his presumptuous manner, but deep down she knew that there was nowhere else she wanted to be than at his house, with him, the only place she wanted to be right now.

She felt him glancing at her from the corner of an eye as if waiting for her reaction, and didn't know how she was going to respond herself until she said, "Okay." She almost choked on the timidity she heard in her voice but finally gave in to her desires rather than allowing her stubborn will any credibility.

She settled back into her seat and glanced out at the road ahead, other cars surrounding them and rushing by on either side in the dark, street- and traffic-lit night, and wanted to stop time, stop traffic, felt like her life was rushing by with their time together.

Tabitha drifted back to that scene on the plane and stopped herself from shivering.

She'd fallen asleep, too, almost as soon as Eric had, eerily connected to him in that moment, connected in a way that defied explanation.

She'd never felt so close to another human being than right then and when they'd made love, had always wanted to know what having a deep attachment to someone was like.

Even with Frankie, whom she loved dearly, she found her relationship wanting with him dropping out of her life more frequently than in. There was no opportunity to build meaningful ties beyond what they'd forged as teens.

She had no "real" brothers or sisters, no cousins or friends in whom to confide, had never felt the deficiency so desperately until now.

Tabitha cut her eyes at Eric, studying his profile as her heart lurched in her chest. He did things to her that no other man had ever done, even watching him drive—his powerful hands on the steering wheel, every small motion exuding silent confidence—turned her on, made her feel safe.

That's something else she'd never really felt with anyone before: safe.

God! Could trusting him be on the horizon?

Tabitha almost laughed at the absurdity, then noticed the figure waiting outside Eric's building and knew why trust was a long way off and security a memory.

Ms. Secret.

* * * *

EJ tensed as soon as he saw Jade, felt Tabitha tense beside him and stole a quick peek at her from the corner of an eye.

She sat ramrod straight in her seat, gaze aimed directly ahead, at Jade on the sidewalk.

He wanted to reach out and hold her, comfort her for all the injuries and injustices she'd suffered as a child—for what he suspected was about to go down—but how could he do that without revealing what he knew? Without revealing *how* he knew?

"Can't keep her waiting forever now, can we?" Tabitha whispered.

He started when he heard the challenge in her voice, just then realizing how long he had been parked at the sidewalk thinking.

Damn, there was no way this was going to be a good situation!

This was the first time these women would be seeing each other since he and Tabitha had consummated their relationship. She was no longer just his personal shopper he was trying to bone, and with whom he was flirting. She was so much more.

EJ unlatched his seatbelt, squeezed Tabitha's closest thigh and bent his head to say, "Stay here." He should have known better.

"The hell I will."

"Tabi—"

She undid her own seatbelt and got out of the Jeep before he could stop her, waited for him on the sidewalk.

"Hello Tabitha. Funny meeting you here."

"Not so funny."

"Jade, what are you doing here?" EJ asked as he joined them on the sidewalk, positioning himself in front of Tabitha, halfway between the women for good measure.

"I thought I'd drop by and surprise you, help you celebrate your best-selling status," she held up an expensive bottle of champagne, "but it seems someone beat me to the punch."

EJ felt the scathing look she raked over Tabitha as if Jade had sliced through *him*, and he could only imagine the damage her look did to Tabitha, though he knew she'd never show it.

"So you've resorted to slumming, EJ?"

"Slumming! I'll show you slumming."

EJ moved solidly between them now, blocking Jade from Tabitha's view as he confronted Jade. "I don't know what your game is," he lied. He knew exactly what her game was. She was trying to make Tabitha jealous, and that was not a game he wanted to play. "You shouldn't have come here, Jade."

"That's not what you said the last time we saw each other. In fact, you were rather happy to see me, especially when you were sliding your dick into me."

EJ caught her by her free arm. "What the hell is the matter with you, anyway? You know nothing happened between us the last time we saw each other, and what's more, you don't have any papers on me."

"Does she?" Jade jerked her chin in Tabitha's direction.

"I'll show you what I have on him."

EJ turned just in time to plant a palm in Tabitha's chest, tried to be as gentle as possible as he stopped her from charging ahead.

"Why are you protecting her?" Tabitha demanded.

"I'm not protecting her. I'm protecting you. You don't want to do this."

"I can handle myself."

"I don't doubt it, but why should you have to?"

"That's a good question, and we wouldn't be standing here trying to answer it if you'd been straight with her and me."

"I've never been anything but straight with you."

"Oh, really?"

"Let her go, EJ. Let's see what the little uptight personal shopper can do with this."

He glanced over a shoulder to see Jade poking herself in the chest as if she were a prizefighter or wrestler goading an opponent in the ring. God, he'd never seen her like this, shocked by her belligerence. The woman was always so cool and calculating.

Had he ever really known her at all? And who knew if her current show of bravado wasn't a form of calculation and control, a show put on just for Tabitha's benefit? There was no precedent for her behavior, he had nothing in their past together against which to judge her, and this was the danger of not being able to read people, especially women where he was already at a disadvantage. He never knew where they were coming from, or where they would be coming from in any given situation.

EJ turned back to Tabitha, saw her seething. The situation with her wasn't much better.

"I'll show her what I can do, Eric. Just let me go."

He caught Tabitha by an arm and walked her to the curb several feet away.

She jerked her arm out of his grasp, but didn't try to go back to Jade. "What are you trying to do? Get rid of me? Why aren't you getting rid of her?"

"He knows when to take out the trash."

"I'll show you trash!"

EJ pulled Tabitha against his chest and held her struggling form there until she calmed down. He pulled away to stare at her. "I'm not getting rid of you,

Tabitha. I just want you to go home so that I can handle this alone like I should have a long time ago."

"Go home?"

"Because *I'm* not going anywhere. This is a free country, and *you* don't own the street."

EJ turned and glared at Jade before he turned back to Tabitha. "I'll call you a cab." He told her as he pulled out his cell.

"Don't do me any favors."

"Please let me put you in a cab and I'll call you as soon as I straighten this out."

"I'd like to see how you're going to 'straighten this out.'"

"Tabitha—"

"All right. Fine. I'll go!"

EJ didn't know whether he should be relieved or not at her capitulation. The dark unforgiving look in her whiskey colored eyes told him he shouldn't be.

He speed-dialed a cab company, gave the dispatcher his and Tabitha's addresses before putting away his cell and draping an arm around Tabitha's shoulder. He walked her several more paces away from Jade, leaned his head close and kissed her cheek. "This isn't what it looks like, I promise you."

"I've heard that before."

"Not from me." EJ gritted his teeth, caught her face between his palms and forced her to look at him. If Jade and Tabitha didn't get the message from his actions, then he didn't know what else he could do to convince either woman of his feelings. "Tabitha, I will take care of this and call you. You hear me?"

"I hear you."

He didn't think that she did, didn't think she was interested in hearing anything from him, and really couldn't blame her.

Damn, this had turned into a worst case scenario in the span of minutes. The only blessing was that the women hadn't come to blows, and that was only because of his intervention. Who knew what would have happened had he not blocked Tabitha and held her back?

EJ shook his head, tamping down a smile at the image of his lioness in action. He didn't want to give her the idea that he found any of this funny, but the sight of her rushing at Jade like some avenging dark warrior filled his chest with a sense of protection and possession.

The cab pulled up to the curb in front of them several minutes later and EJ took Tabitha by a hand, led her to the back door and opened it. He squeezed her hand before leaning in to give her a lingering kiss on the mouth. "Remember what I said, Tabitha."

"I'll remember everything."

He put her into the back seat, gave the cabdriver her address again and handed him two twenties before hitting the top of the cab to send it on its way.

Then he whirled on Jade.

* * * *

Tabitha unlocked her door, and stormed into the apartment.

Frankie sat up straight on the sofa, eyes wide at the sight of her. "What in the hell happened to you?"

"Nothing." She took off her coat and flung it on the coat tree and stalked towards her bedroom.

Frankie leaped off the sofa to intercept her, caught her by an arm. "So, what happened on your trip? Did you hook up with him or not?"

"Yeah, I hooked up with him."

"And?"

"And nothing."

"If he hurt you…"

Tabitha glanced at him for the first time since she entered the apartment, tried not to grin at his violent glare as much as she wanted someone to go punch out Eric's lights, knew it would solve nothing. It especially wouldn't make her feel better, not really.

"He didn't hurt me, Frankie. I did this all to myself." It was true. He hadn't done anything. The hurt and breach of faith were all in her head, just didn't make her ache any less.

She pulled her arm out of his, continued to her bedroom and closed the door just as Vogue slid in.

"I'll give you five minutes to calm down, then I'm coming in and we're going to talk."

Tabitha smiled at the implied threat, then slid off her loafers and picked up Vogue as she headed to her queen size bed. She flopped back on the mattress, cradling the silky cat against her chest until she began to squirm and complain before Tabitha put her back on the floor. "Ingrate." She giggled, picked up her pink elephant instead and squeezed it to her chest. It was either squeeze it or rip off its head and scatter its stuffing around the room, but why take out on a defenseless stuffed animal what she wanted to do to one Eric Vega and Jade Aliberti?

Tabitha had given the elephant a name as soon as she'd gotten it: Erica, and the stuffed animal had already found a place in her heart, and a place of honor at her bedpost. She hugged Erica now as if for strength.

What were they doing now, she wondered, Ms. Secret and Eric?

Was he comforting her in Tabitha's absence, assuring Ms. Secret that there was nothing between him and Tabitha the way he'd assured Tabitha that there was nothing between him and Ms. Secret? Was Eric even now painting Tabitha as the bad guy in this scenario, the Big Bad Other Woman with whom he had made a mistake? Were Eric and Jade more serious than Tabitha had thought? More serious than Eric thought? Why else would the woman react the way she had outside his apartment, unless Eric had been leading her on in some way? The way he was leading on Tabitha?

She'd known going in that this would hurt—opening up and letting someone in always did—just didn't know how much, or that the pain would kick in so soon.

They'd barely consummated their relationship, and already she was feeling the familiar pangs of abandonment and loss, rejection and betrayal, the idea of them together, of that tall Amazon model touching Eric, or Eric wooing and whispering terms of endearments in her ear, almost more than Tabitha could bear. She buried her face in Erica's soft pink fur, closed her eyes and took a shaky breath. She would not cry. She would not. There was no need. Nothing had happened yet, and there was plenty of time for falling apart once she knew for sure what was going on, once she knew that he had actually broken what little trust she'd relinquished.

It wasn't like they were in love or had any great emotional investment with each other at stake, after all. Was it?

Frankie knocked on the door. "Tabby-Cat, open up."

Tabitha got up, not sure whether or not he'd break down the door, and not in the mood to test him or be tested.

The tears welled as soon as she saw his open brown face, as if his appearance and implied support were emotional triggers, the key to her tear ducts.

He took her in his arms and pulled her close as the tears fell freely, her chest emptying as the sobs escaped her throat in big hiccupping gasps. She hadn't cried since she was a teen, and certainly not in front of anyone. Not anyone except Frankie after he'd rescued her.

She'd never even cried in front of her mother all those years and hurts ago. No matter how many slaps and slights the woman had delivered, Tabitha had refused to show any emotion, any weakness, in front of the woman.

Even the nuns at the orphanage had had a hell of a time getting a rise out of her, and God knew they had tried. Tabitha often wondered if they'd sometimes found excuses to strike her extra hard, extra whacks, just to see if she would break down.

"It's going to be all right, Tabby-Cat. Whatever he did to hurt you, we're going to fix this and make it right."

She didn't know why she'd ever doubted the deepness of their relationship, their bond. Separations or not, dropping out of her life or not, he was here now, holding her, comforting her.

He was the only family she had. The only family she needed.

Chapter 19

EJ sat at his computer and played all the mind and time wasting games he could in two hours. Solitaire, Minesweep, Pinball before he switched to surfing the Net, ostensibly to research, but really wound up extending his time-wasting tactics. He popped in and out of game sites, and idly chatted on several listserves to which he belonged, anything to stay away from his work-in-progress. Anything to avoid the fact that he just didn't have it this morning.

He didn't want to admit how much that confrontation with Jade had shaken him, had shown him a side of her he'd never wanted to see, a side he'd wrought with his cavalier style.

How could he have been so blind?

He'd hurt not only Tabitha, but Jade with his no strings, you-go-your-way-and-I'll-go-mine philosophy, had had no idea of the depth of feelings she harbored for him, no idea of how long she'd felt the way she did for him.

EJ had tried to comfort himself in the knowledge that Jade was a sharp grown woman who knew the deal, that no one had forced her to do anything, but when he got right down to it, he knew that he had manipulated her as surely as she had tried to manipulate him last night, had strung her along for his own benefit—or more accurately for the benefit of his little friend. He'd accepted the physical pleasure she provided without thought that she'd wanted anything more in return for her favors than the luxury of an orgasm.

Had he made the same mistake with Tabitha?

Her reactions in the hotel room told him he might have, that she mistook his desires as just those of a physical nature. She'd accused him of coming onto her from the very beginning, and he had been, had never tried to get to know her, taking the easy way out and using his gifts to discover her past, rather than asking her about herself and exercising the patience and understanding it would have taken him to wait out her answers once she decided to open up.

Now he was afraid to ask her anything for fear of what she'd tell him, afraid that she'd expand on the horrible experiences he'd yet only glimpsed of her childhood.

Were her parents alive? Where was her biological father that he hadn't seen him in any of his visions? Only a strange man who'd tried to take away her innocence and a woman who was going to die a hideous death in a car crash.

EJ got up and paced the room several times, forked a hand through his hair as he glared at the computer monitor as if it was at fault for what had happened last night, for his inability to get any work done this morning. He really had to get out of the habit of blaming other things, other people for what was essentially his own fault.

EJ walked over to an end table, scooped up the cordless receiver and speed-dialed Tabitha's office. As expected, he got the nice assistant, Cynthia Lawrence, an attractive young newlywed whom, he knew, had a crush on him—so turned on the charm. He'd sensed a supporter in his past conversations with her, knew that if he had any chance in the world with Tabitha, at least in his dealings with her at work, he had to charm and get through her gatekeeper.

"I'm sorry, EJ, but she's not taking any calls."

He'd told her to call him EJ on their first meeting, and so far she was the only person in Tabitha's office who did. "I understand you have a job to do Cynthia, but you tell her I'm not hanging up until she picks up the phone. Will you give her that message?"

"I certainly will."

He waited a few minutes, didn't believe that Tabitha would actually make Cynthia hang up on a client, even if it was him, couldn't believe her anger had reached that degree of rudeness.

After he'd waited a good fifteen minutes—and he'd looked at his watch several times to confirm the length of his wait, shaking his head, she finally got on the line.

"What do you want, Eric?"

"I said I'd call you."

"I never said I'd speak to you when you did."

"Are you going to give me a chance to explain?"

"It took you all night to 'straighten things out'?"

EJ didn't want to discuss or remember last night. As far as he was concerned it was past history, and so was Jade, at least in her capacity as his lover. As a friend, he was sure he could only tolerate her sparingly, if she was still willing to be in his life on these terms at all, and with the way he'd left things with her last night, he wasn't sure she was willing. "Tabitha, all we did was talk and no it didn't take all night." He reached out, curious if their connection had evolved any further, whether the scope of his powers had grown. He'd received such intense images from her on the plane; he wouldn't have been surprised by anything he caught from her.

EJ hit a solid wall this time and couldn't break through.

"I don't have time for this, Eric. I'm at work."

"I'm going to be on the move a lot the next three weeks…"

"I know. On your book tour."

"But the signings are all going to be here in New York, so I won't be too far away from you at any given time."

"That's nice."

"Tabitha, I want to see you."

"I don't think that would be a good idea."

"For Christ's sake, haven't we gotten past all this?"

There was a long pause on the other end as he listened to her light breathing, tried again to touch her but couldn't.

Damn, this was frustrating!

"I thought we had, before last night."

"I can't talk to you over the phone like this. I need to see you."

"I have to go."

"Tabitha, don't hang up!"

But she did and left EJ talking to dead air.

He clutched the receiver in his fist so hard his hand turned tallow white.

Okay, he'd have to play hardball and go uptown to see her and say his piece. Make her listen to what he had to say. He was relatively certain she wouldn't make a scene and throw him out—not at her place of business—if he just showed up. Sure it was a dirty trick, but he had to use whatever advantage he had at his disposal with that woman.

* * * *

Cynthia stood at the door, arms folded across her chest, shaking her head as Tabitha hung up the receiver.

"I wish you'd tell me what happened in Colorado."

"It didn't happen in Colorado."

"Where did *it* happen, and *what* happened to make you scorn him this time?"

Tabitha wanted to tell the girl it wasn't any of her business, but didn't feel like alienating another person right now, didn't have the energy for the backlash.

She performed enough self-castigation and dished out more punishment on herself than anyone else could have. She didn't need incriminations from outside sources.

"Tabitha, he's such a nice guy. I don't see why you two can't make peace."

"Just because he's nice doesn't mean he's right for me."

"What makes him wrong?"

Jade Aliberti for one. To Cynthia she said, "He's too polygamous for my tastes, okay."

Cynthia frowned, disbelief plainly written across her face and Tabitha couldn't understand why.

The man was a player, it was plain for anyone to see. Unless he had charmed Cynthia so thoroughly in his brief visit and several phone conversations that she couldn't see beyond those gorgeous dimples to his true nature.

"Cynthia, I don't really have time to discuss this right now. So if you don't mind, I'd rather just drop it."

"Okay, if that's what you want."

"That's what I want."

Cynthia stood up straight from the jamb, gave Tabitha one last look before turning to go.

Tabitha knew she hadn't heard the last from her assistant on the subject.

Maybe she'd have to adopt a tough, do-not-mention-Eric-Vega-in-my-presence rule. But then Cynthia never did mention him by name, just referred to him as "he" or "him," though Tabitha knew for a fact Cynthia addressed him as EJ when she thought Tabitha wasn't in earshot.

Tabitha smiled as she glanced at her monitor and dug into her e-mail.

In a half-an-hour, she responded to most of them, and set up several appointments on her calendar before Cynthia buzzed her.

Tabitha pressed the "Listen" button on her console. "Yes?"

"He's here."

Sheesh, like God, he didn't even need a name.

Tabitha sat with her finger poised over the "Talk" button, unsure what to do.

Running and hiding wasn't an option, and the bastard knew that. Knew her all too well as he'd been claiming from the beginning, knew that she wouldn't make a scene not where she daily conducted business.

She clenched her jaw as she pressed the "Talk" button. "Send him i—"

He appeared at her door before she finished, expectantly poised on the threshold. "I was hoping you'd see me."

He was dressed in another of her favorite outfits—mint green dress shirt, purple tie, and purple chinos—the ensemble he'd had on during that infamous fitting room incident, and Tabitha wondered if his choice were purposeful. After only a second she decided that it was, because as well as he knew her, she thought she knew him, and Eric didn't do anything without a motive.

Her body vibrated with nostalgia, her pussy clenching with remembered excitement as she glared at him. "Come in and close the door behind you."

He shivered dramatically as he did what he was told. "Ooh, orders. I like a woman who knows her mind."

"You won't be liking me so much in the next few minutes."

"Is that a promise?"

She just rolled her eyes at him, didn't move from behind her desk as he grinned and made his way across the room in a sexy rolling gait that instantly got her hot and wet.

She followed his progress all the way from the doorway to the seat in front of her desk and watched him sit down.

He got comfortable, adopting that familiar laid-back posture she knew so well, with one ankle crossed over the opposite knee as he stared at her.

Tabitha momentarily averted her eyes, glanced at his shoes, a pair of black, well-buffed Kenneth Cole's, and thought that she had created a fashion monster; he'd turned into a male her.

"This is dirty pool, Eric. Even for you."

"What's dirty?"

"You know exactly what I'm talking about. The clothes—"

"You like?" He raised his arms from the sides of the chair and smiled.

Tabitha had another flashback, this one of him spinning around in front of her, modeling. "You know damn well I like it. I helped you pick it out. Like I said, you're playing dirty. Dressing seductively, coming over to my job when you know I can't—"

"Yell at me?"

"Don't be so sure."

"You wouldn't speak to me over the phone. How else was I going to get you to listen to me? If Mohammed won't go to the mountain—"

"Please spare me."

"Tabitha, Jade and I were only friends. Friends who had sex."

At least he was speaking about her in the past tense. "She was your fuck-buddy then."

He arched a brow, seemed surprise that she either knew the term, or was capable of using the infamous F-word. "That's all there was between us," he affirmed.

"She seemed to be under a different impression."

"I know that, but I straightened that all out last night."

"Is that what you told her it was between me and you? Just sex?"

"No," He shook his head. "And you know it. I've told you more than once there's more between us than just sex."

"How do I know what you've told her? How do I know you're not stringing us both along?"

"Because I'm telling you I'm not."

Tabitha peered into those indigo eyes, saw her own reflection staring back at her from the heated blue depths and her stomach flipped over then spiraled down to her core, suffusing it with the warm fluid of her desire.

She wanted to believe him; the sincerity in his voice, in his eyes, the total lack of subterfuge in his posture, told her that she probably should. Unlike him, however, she wasn't a body language expert. She only had her gut and instincts to go by, and she knew that each was totally lacking from disuse.

Because rather than exercise her intuition and put herself through guessing a guy's intentions, whether he was being straight with her, Tabitha tried to avoid the entire mating dance altogether. Those times that she couldn't avoid it, the minute a guy got close enough to ask about her family, her life beyond work, she backed off, ended the dance, no second dates allowed.

She'd ticked off a lot of well-meaning matchmaking acquaintances this way, but it was so much safer to keep her distance rather than rely on her rusty people-reading skills and risk falling for some silver-tongued devil's line.

She'd been out of practice too long, Eric the first man with whom she'd gone so far, the first man she'd come close to trusting since…God, she couldn't think of anyone besides her father before he'd left her and her mother, and Frankie.

There'd been another guy back in college, a young maverick as hungry as her for success but much more willing to step on anyone to get where and what he wanted than was Tabitha.

Taylor had been her second after Frankie, insinuating himself into her life when she'd been twenty-one and nearing her final days of college.

Before she'd met him she'd been a single-minded and serious student with one goal on her mind after she got her degree: start her own business.

She'd been building her resume since she'd left high school, picking up odd jobs here and there, but the most important one as a mystery shopper evaluating customer service at sundry businesses like restaurants and retail stores before finally snagging her dream job at Macy's as a personal shopper.

Taylor had approached her during lunch one day, said he'd noticed and liked her style and fashion sense—what she now recognized as appealing to her vanity—and asked her to help him with his. He promised to pay her well for the privilege of her opinions.

Only it didn't quite work out the way he outlined it, and her opinions gradually turned into outright shopping trips that ate up time she could have put into her real jobs. Tabitha chalked it up as needed experience, something extra to add to her personal shopping background.

She worked hard helping Taylor define and refine his image, haunting boutiques for just the right jacket, hunting in thrift stores for just the right accessories to dress up a particular outfit already in his possession.

She held up her part of their bargain, but when it came time for payment, Taylor always had an excuse, wielding explanations and promises with that quick and skilled tongue as he seduced her with his wicked smile and body.

For the hours she spent in his arms, she forgot about business, forgot about her plans, his wild sensuality and relentless pursuit of pleasure nothing she'd ever experienced before, satisfying the secret needs of her body, while he filled up her head with requisite assurances of commitment and coupledom.

However, once Taylor got what he wanted from her, an impressive new wardrobe at the expense of her ingenuity and talent, he dumped her. He was essentially her first and most important lesson never to mix business with pleasure, never to trust anything that came out of a good-looking man's mouth.

Tabitha glanced at Eric now, wondered where all her wisdom and reason had gone when it came to him, wondered what made him important enough that after her experiences with Taylor and Michael she was willing to believe almost anything he said, willing to forgo her personal hard-won credo. Willing to jeopardize her stability and freedom.

He rose from his chair as if he knew all the doubts she entertained, as if he knew she was teetering on the edge of saying good-bye and going about her life without him.

"Tabitha, we need to talk." He planted his palms on her desk, leaned in and kissed her on the mouth, his lips firm and searching as he finessed open her mouth with his tongue, demanding and getting entry.

She returned the kiss, kicking herself the entire while her tongue dueled with his, before she pulled back, breathless, several seconds later. "You said we need to talk. That was suspiciously not talking."

He shrugged. "But it's so much more fun."

Tabitha folded her hands on her desk, tried to assume a cool professional mien, and knew she was miserably failing when Eric circled her desk and stood before her.

She turned to face him, eyes level with his zipper before she raised them to his face, at a total disadvantage, didn't like the hold he had over her and quickly stood. He still towered more than half-a-foot over her, but at least now she wasn't as tempted by that enormous hard bulge in his pants.

Time to turn the tables.

"You have a birthday coming up soon, don't you?"

He narrowed his eyes. "December 19th. Why do you ask?"

"No reason," she said, but knew exactly how she was going to get him out of his house for the day, and that she was going to enjoy every minute of it.

She had been thinking about it since Angela had called her, but the idea only came to fruition just now as she reached for his tie and worked on loosening the knot.

"No reason, huh?"

"Just thought we could do something special. Spend the day together. My treat." If Angela's theory was right, then he'd jump at the chance.

"What do you have in mind?"

"Not sure yet. But I'll think of something."

"So how do I prepare?"

"Just be ready for anything when you wake up in the morning."

"Sounds kinky."

"Hmm, it is." She finished unknotting his tie, slid it from the collar of his shirt. "Speaking of kinky…you did wear this on purpose, didn't you?"

He grinned. "I couldn't help myself."

"Neither can I." Tabitha circled around him until they had switched places, and pushed him down into her executive chair.

He glanced up at her from the seat, eyes blistering and curious.

Tabitha's stomach trembled with the knowledge of what she was about to do. "Since you enjoyed your bondage so much last time…"

"I never said that."

"Did you lock the door?"

He smiled, and nodded.

"I knew you would when you came in."

"So you know me now?"

"I'm beginning to." She circled behind him, slid her hands down his shoulders to his wrists as she pulled his arms behind his back. "Just like I know you like this." She looped the tie around his wrists several times, finally knotting it firmly.

It suddenly occurred to her that it took a man totally comfortable and secure in his masculinity to let her keep tying him up as she pleased.

The thought fired a bolt of hot lust straight to her vagina, sizzling the juices inside.

Eric looked at her as she came back to his front, a silent question on his lips as if he didn't dare verbalize his concerns.

He tried his wrists, raised his eyebrows when he realized he couldn't get loose, that Tabitha had tied him to the bar at the bottom of the seat. "You really get a kick out of this power game, don't you?" he drawled.

"You tell me. Do I?" She slid a hand in her panties, removed it to wave and wiggle her fingers beneath his nose.

Eric flared his nostrils and hissed, tried his bonds again and muttered, "God, Tabitha."

"You're the one who decided to drop by my office uninvited, and I think that calls for some form of punishment."

"What if I didn't lock the door?"

"You're bluffing, and even if you're not..." She moved closer to him, a leg on each side of the chair as she stood astride him. "I'm willing to take that chance." She realized she was ready and willing to take all sorts of chances when it came to Eric and this scared her.

"You might want to check my front pants pocket, just in case."

She reached in, knew what she would find and smiled when she came out holding a foil pack. "Boy Scout motto, huh?"

He chuckled as she reached for his fly and unzipped his pants. She slid her hand into the opening, freed him from his shorts and he turned serious as his cock sprang free, long, thick and hard as it stuck straight up towards the ceiling.

Tabitha grasped him tight with one hand, relished the velvet-covered steel inside her fingers, felt him pulsing in her grip as she opened the foil pack with her teeth and free hand.

She released him only long enough to slide on the condom, toed off her shoes, then pulled down and kicked away her hose and panties before she straddled him.

He licked his lips as Tabitha put her hands on his shoulders to get her balance, and she stared him in the eyes as she positioned her pussy over his penis. Slowly, she lowered her hips, impaling herself on his shaft as he thrust his hips and sheathed himself completely.

They groaned in unison, moving as one, languidly at first before Eric picked up speed beneath her, pumping his hips in earnest as the chair began to roll across the floor.

She leaned in and whispered against an ear, "Eric, hold it still or we'll tip over."

"Or roll out the door into the reception area."

She giggled, felt his strong thighs flex beneath her as his passion built to bothersome levels and he braced his feet against the wood floor.

Tabitha unmercifully pressed down, grinding against him, riding him as hard as she could without disturbing the chair, clenching her inner muscles around his erection and crushing her mouth against his right before he loudly moaned. She absorbed the sound into her mouth, swallowing down the luscious sensation of his release as he shuddered beneath her.

"Christ," he bit out, trying his wrists again as she leaned in to kiss him, paying special attention to his full lower lip, lightly sinking her teeth into the sweet flesh as her own orgasm slowly dwindled, tissues intermittently spasming and tightening around him.

Finally regaining some control, Tabitha sat up straight, opened her eyes and smiled down at him. "So, was it worth the trip?"

"You're always worth the trip, Tabby," he whispered. "Always."

Chapter 20

EJ woke up with a monster headache on his big day, couldn't remember the last time he'd had one like it. Probably sometime way back in college when he'd woken up with a screaming hangover the day after graduation.

What a treat that had been, one he'd taken special care never to repeat. Until now.

Happy Birthday to me!

He groaned as he flung off the comforter and swung his legs out of bed. Just that tiny bit of activity made his head spin and pound until he thought there was a little man inside banging on a drum. Man he felt like shit!

He contributed most of his indisposition to the non-stop book signings he'd done the last few weeks. No less than two stores a day when he wasn't working on his work-in-progress or performing a reading at a library, or doing a radio or magazine interview that Jodie had set up. He hadn't had a minute of free time, and now his body was paying for it.

EJ had a flash of one of his last conversations with Angela and her warning him to start taking better care of himself. She would certainly get a kick out of telling him *I told you so* if she could see him now.

He staggered to the bathroom and cut on the overhead light, momentarily blinded by the brightness as he glanced in the medicine cabinet mirror. Ugh, dark circles under his eyes, crust in the corners, hair standing on end. The mug could frighten the dead.

He opened the cabinet and searched for something, anything to take the edge off of the pain, found what seemed to be a full bottle of Excedrin and checked the expiration date. He couldn't remember the last time he'd had use for them but evidently it had been during the last two to three years since the expiration date was fast approaching in a couple of months.

EJ took out three, popped them into his mouth and washed them down with a gulp of cold water. For good measure, he splashed cold water on his face to wake himself up. Didn't do much good except wet his hair and chest.

He stepped out of his shorts, turned on the shower full force, waited for the water to get hot and jumped in, aimed the detachable shower head at his aching shoulders and back muscles for several minutes before he soaped up, rinsed off and got out.

She'd said be ready for anything when he woke up in the morning, and he was ready for absolutely nothing except going back to bed and sleeping another six or seven hours before he even attempted to write a word.

Maybe she'd come later in the day, not the morning like she'd threatened. Maybe…

The buzzer in the kitchen sounded and EJ groaned. Towel wrapped around and riding low on his hips, he stumbled to the kitchen to answer it then rushed to the bedroom to throw on some boxers and jeans.

He wouldn't let her see him at less than his best, wouldn't give her any excuse to call off their day together.

EJ made it to the living room just as she knocked on the front door. He double-checked the clock. Yep, seven-thirty.

What could she possibly have in mind for them to do so early in the morning?

He opened the door to her glowing smile and had to stop himself from groaning again.

She was clad in blue jeans, a sweatshirt, cross-trainers and carrying a sports bag in one hand and a racquet in the other.

No, no, no…

"I thought I'd take you up on your previous offer and we'd make a day of it."

Any other time he would have been ecstatic to see her, but he'd been planning to rest up so that he'd be in top form for a date with her in the evening, maybe dinner and a movie. But this… "I made that offer almost two months ago."

"It's not still open?"

How could he say no to her, to the prospect of seeing her all hot and sweaty on the court?

"Sure it's open. I just have to get dressed."

"Make sure to pack extra clothes. Something casual, not too dressy."

He glanced at her over a shoulder and paused. "You want something to eat or drink while you're waiting?"

"I already had breakfast."

Damn, he knew she was an early riser, but what time did she actually wake up in the mornings? "And you've probably had a morning run and everything, huh?"

"Not today. I'm saving my energy for you on the court." She emphasized this little bit of information by spinning her racket handle in the palm of her hand.

Oh, boy, was he in trouble.

* * * *

EJ had found a small burst of energy somewhere between leaving his loft with Tabitha and them walking over to the Health and Racquet Club in Chelsea. Enough energy not to keel over from headache and body aches.

Tabitha, of course, had a membership to the club, one of which she regularly made use. Everyone at the place knew her, and greeted her with warm smiles and sincere wishes for a good workout.

EJ seemed to have left his game in October when he'd originally invited her out to play.

He beat Tabitha handily enough their first match, breaking her serve several times and winning by a score of fifteen to ten.

Tabitha made the next two games a lot closer, finally breaking through and beating him in the third and fourth games with lighting footwork and a powerful vicious serve that could have put Andy Roddick to shame. The girl was definitely one of those people who took a little while warming up, got stronger with each match.

He couldn't help thinking that she was somehow getting back at him for that fiasco with Jade outside his building weeks ago, never really forgiving him. She was as competitive as he had thought she'd be, played like she was out to get someone, and EJ knew that someone was him.

In this, their fifth game and the tiebreaker, EJ had battled back from a fourteen to eight deficit to tie the game, determined not to let a girl beat him. Not even if the girl was the bodacious and hot Ms. Lyons bouncing back and forth on the balls of her feet several feet behind him and clad in a pair of stylish aqua biker shorts with blue racing stripes down the sides and a matching Lycra-spandex midriff top.

He glanced over a shoulder, thought maybe that wasn't such a good idea when he got a glimpse of her bare tanned belly. That cute little inny and her skin glistening with a light sheen of perspiration were almost his undoing. "Ready, Serena?"

"Yes, and I take that as an extreme compliment."

"I meant it as one. She's one of my favorite players."

"Stop stalling and serve the ball, Vega."

He chuckled, set himself and served what he thought was a winner until, from the corner an eye, he caught the ball flying back at him. He had a second to duck out of the way and make a diving stab at the ball as it smacked the wall low on his backhand side.

"My ball." Tabitha switched up to the short line, bouncing the ball several times as she grinned at EJ over a shoulder.

"You got it, baby. Just don't wear it out."

"I don't intend to."

Damn, but she looked fierce in that outfit and those sports goggles, like she was at work and prepared to do serious damage.

Tabitha smacked the ball off the wall with unbelievable force, the little black missile bouncing just good, an ace that even at his six-three, with a more than three foot reach, managed to bounce out of EJ's range.

"Point game, Eric."

"Don't start counting your money yet."

She grinned, bounced the ball several times, and wiggled her butt back and forth as if for good measure, then served.

The ball came directly at the center of his body and EJ froze like a woodland creature in the glare of headlights, reflexes slower than normal. He barely had enough time to sidestep Tabitha's bullet and throw his racket at it to no avail.

"And that is game."

He jogged up to where she was standing and swinging her racket by its string. He hugged her around the shoulder with one arm and kissed her cheek. "Great game, Tabby."

She playfully elbowed him in the ribs at the moniker. "It was if I say so myself."

"Don't get a big head. I want a rematch."

"Any time."

Yeah, he thought, just not any time too soon. He needed time to regroup from today, had never been so tired in his life, doing his best to fake it and show Tabitha that he was up for any challenge she had in mind for him.

"So, what's next on the agenda?"

"Back to my house where we'll spend the rest of the afternoon before dinner and...hmm, I don't know. What do you have in mind?"

Sleep, Tabitha. Just plain old sleep. "I'm up for whatever."

"Good. Just what I wanted to hear."

God, what had he gotten himself into?

* * * *

Tabitha knew he wasn't himself and almost felt bad beating up on him at racquetball when she knew he wasn't feeling up to par.

He refused to give in to whatever it was that had a hold of him, just like a stubborn man.

If her guess was right, he probably had the flu, at least the beginning stages, and was deep enough in denial to wave it off as a cold or the sniffles. Time would tell. By the end of the night, if not sooner, he would surely give in.

She watched him struggle out of his jacket, moving much slower than how a healthy in shape thirty-something would after a thorough workout. There was more going on than just muscles that had had a drubbing on the court.

"You okay?" She arched a brow as she walked by him on the way to her bedroom.

Eric sprawled on the sofa, sports bag at his feet and garment bag slung over her leather recliner adjacent. "I will be after I get my second wind."

"I'm going to shower and change. Care to join me?" She thought maybe that would get him up, but his reaction time was a lot slower than she expected.

Eric remained on the sofa, eyes closed. "Go ahead and get started. I'll catch up with you."

"Okay." She stared at him for a long time, heart squeezing in her chest at the memory of how she'd worked him out.

Sheesh, he could have just said no and called it a day. She would have understood, but no, he had to break the tie, couldn't let *her* beat him at his game, no way.

Serves him right.

Tabitha thought it but didn't really feel it as she left him on the sofa and headed for the bathroom.

Five minutes into her shower, he came into the bathroom, moving like an old man, but joining her in the bathtub nonetheless.

"Oh, the poor baby. You look beat. I have just the medicine for you."

"You do?"

Tabitha soaped up her sponge, turned him around and gently washed his back. She lost herself for several moments, reveling in the broad muscled expanse, enjoying the flex and tone of his tendons and tissues beneath bronze skin. God he was so beautiful, sometimes it frightened her to touch him, that when she did, he would disappear in a puff of smoke as if he never existed. Just a dream.

"Go dry off and get in bed. I've got a treat for you."

"I can't wait."

He actually got out as she instructed, and that's when she knew he wasn't well.

How were they going to work out this evening? Could she talk him out of going out when she knew all those people were going to be waiting at his loft later on, counting on her to bring the birthday boy home?

Tabitha got out of the shower a couple of minutes later, clad in a bathrobe and trailing hot steam into the bedroom as she opened the bathroom door and came out.

Eric was sprawled on the bed face up, still and breathing steady.

She tiptoed over to the bureau to put on a thong and a bra, hung her bathrobe over the back of the rocking chair across from her bed.

"You never told me you have a cat," he murmured.

"It never came up."

"What's her name?"

"Vogue, and how do you know she's a she?"

He shrugged. "She looks like a she. At least the brief glance I got of her when she sped under the bed a few seconds ago."

"She likes to hide." Tabitha dimmed the lights and lit the aromatherapy candles she had strategically placed throughout her bedroom. Vanilla and spice and everything nice. At least she hoped so for Eric. "Is she going to be a problem? Are you allergic?" That's all she needed, for him to have an allergy attack on top of how lousy he was already feeling.

"No allergies. I like cats. Though I'm more of a dog person."

"You would be."

He chuckled as she opened the top drawer of her nightstand and pulled out her bottle of Tantra sensuous massage oil. She'd gotten it as a gift, part of an entire beautifully wrapped basket of sensual products, from Cynthia a couple of years ago, and had never found a reason to use it before now. But now seemed like the perfect moment.

Tabitha climbed onto the bed and Eric barely stirred. "Ready, tiger?"

"Grrr...ready when you are."

She giggled, pulled off his towel and said, "Turn over, Vega." before she could get a really good glance at his semi-erection and become anymore turned on. She was supposed to be helping him relax, giving a soothing massage, not getting turned on.

He winced, but obligingly turned over, folding his arms beneath his head and resting a cheek on his wrists.

The backside view was as titillating as the front, so much so Tabitha just sat back on her heels and admired his tight round butt for several seconds before smacking him on that delicious part of his body.

"Bondage *and* spanking? I'm going to have to do something about you."

She climbed on top and straddled him, liked the feel of him beneath her, liked the feel of his shoulders beneath her fingers as she gently caressed him.

Tabitha poured a generous amount of oil into her palm and rubbed her hands together before working the oil into his shoulders and upper back.

Eric groaned as she worked, completely still under her ministrations, never once moving or making a pass at her, never coming close.

She silently moved down to his lower back, enjoyed her work, pressing her thumbs into his spine and moving them in a slow circular motion as he sighed beneath her.

"That feels so good."

"Does it? I was beginning to wonder if you'd fallen asleep on me."

"I would never."

She moved further down his body to his legs, giving each thigh and calf the same thorough attention that she had given his back, working the oil into his skin as the luscious aroma mixed with his piquant musk and wafted up, making her stomach spiral with lust.

Tabitha sat back on her heels again, and gently spanked his butt. "Over, Vega."

He turned over, eyes closed as she climbed back on top of him, felt his erection poking against the seam of her ass, thought at least that part seemed to be functioning to capacity.

She massaged his chest, rubbing the oil into his skin, circling his flat nipples with a fingernail before bending her head to kiss his chest.

Tabitha abandoned the oil, kissed her way down his front until she reached the promised land, licking him from his scrotum to the moist head of his hard shaft. She kissed him, stuck her tongue in his slit before taking him into her mouth.

He moaned, bending his knees beneath her and burying his hands in her hair.

She tickled the underside of his penis as she slid her mouth down to the base then back up before slowly drawing him into her mouth again. She pulled for several lingering moments, forceful and adding her teeth before she came back up to tease his head, then swallowed him whole again, suckling until she felt him throbbing in her mouth.

He didn't warn her this time—probably too tired to care, too weak to stop—her only signal that he was about to come the tension she felt in his thighs, and the fierce grip he had on her hair as he pressed her closer to his groin and writhed beneath her.

Tabitha sat up and licked her lips as he trembled, still coming down from his climax.

He reached for her and she laid across him, resting her head against his chest and listening to the lulling sound of his strong heartbeat against her ear.

"Let's catch a few hours sleep before this evening?" he whispered.

She swallowed, feeling protective and tender. "Anything you want. It's your day."

Chapter 21

EJ woke several hours later, confused and achy as he turned to find himself alone in bed.

Tabitha came into the room just then, putting in her earrings and clad in a simple short-sleeved black dress, Lycra cotton material clinging in all the right places, and displaying her rich curves to their best advantage.

Sick or not, he appreciated her beauty and wanted to do right by her tonight, enjoy the evening she had planned for him. So far he was enjoying his birthday much more than he had thought possible when he woke up this morning, and despite still feeling like shit. He cleared his throat and immediately felt the swelling and soreness. Damn, this was not getting any better.

"Welcome back to the world of the living, sleepy head."

"How long did I sleep?"

"A few hours. I was beginning to wonder if you'd ever wake up this century."

EJ rubbed his eyes and sat up, realized he was naked beneath the comforter as it fell beyond his waist. He glanced at Tabitha's bedside clock then out the window.

"It looks later than it is."

It looked like what it was, six o'clock and he'd slept the day away. "So, what's on the agenda? Tennis under the lights? A little one on one basketball in the school yard?"

Tabitha giggled as she came over and sat beside him on the bed. She palmed a lightly whiskered cheek. "Just dinner at a restaurant of your choosing and a movie if you want. No working except a little mastication and getting from one location to the other."

"Sounds like a plan." EJ rooted around in the sheets for his shorts, found and put them on before he got out of bed.

His garment bag was already in the room draped across the back of Tabitha's rocking chair. When he reached out to retrieve the bag, fingers brushing the chair's varnished wooden back, a vision burst before his eyes with startling clarity.

Tabitha sitting in the chair, cradling and nursing a baby against her breasts.

EJ jerked away his hand and stumbled back a couple of steps.

"Eric, what's the matter?"

"Uh, I got a shock. You know, the carpet, friction…"

She came over to him, smiling as she slid her arms around his waist. "I know it's so hard to keep all that electricity all bottled up."

He grinned as he returned her hug.

If he told her what he'd seen, she'd never believe him. How could he get it out there in a way that wouldn't freak her out?

"Have you ever thought about having kids?" he blurted.

Tabitha froze in his arms, gawked up at him. "Sheesh, where did that just come from?"

EJ shrugged, trying to play off his question as if its answer wasn't all that important to him. Obviously, just throwing it out there hadn't been the best idea, but now that it was out there… "Just something I've been thinking about."

"There's usually a few steps that come before a baby."

"Yeah, I know." He waggled his eyebrows. "Hot unbridled sex without protection."

She playfully punched his shoulder, easily moved out of his arms. "That's not what I meant and you know it."

"I know," he said, suddenly serious as he pulled her back in his arms. "And in case you're wondering, I'm clean."

"So am I." She nodded. "I got tested two years ago, and I haven't been with anyone since."

His heart expanded in his chest at that little tidbit. He'd known it had been a while for her, just not how long.

"But that doesn't exactly address unplanned pregnancy and I'm not on the pill."

"Would that be so bad? Having a baby?"

She shrugged, moved out of his arms again and crossed her arms over her breasts as she turned her back to him.

EJ went to her, put his hands on her shoulders and pulled her back against his chest. "I know a lot of women might be scared away from having as many kids as my mother did."

She chuckled and turned around to face him. "Yeah, six is a bit much."

"But you would like to have a couple some day, right?"

"Someday, with the right person, at the right time."

Inwardly, he sighed, relieved she wasn't completely averse to the idea. "That I'm glad to hear."

He had deep feelings for this woman and didn't think he could further foster a relationship with her if she were against kids.

Deciding to push his luck, he said, "I'd want at least three, but we could compromise and have four, just to make things even."

"Two's an even number also."

"Hmm, guess it is."

"But we should talk about this at another time maybe. You, mister, need to get dressed so we can be on our way." She pulled out of his arms and left the room.

EJ quickly went into the bathroom, shaved, came back to the bedroom, unzipped his garment bag, removed and put on the black chinos and black turtleneck in short order.

Barefoot, he went into the living room where Tabitha was downing a glass of OJ.

She took her glass to the kitchen, came back and asked, "Any thought to where you'd like to go birthday boy?"

"Haven't thought about it."

"I hear Smith and Wollensky is a pretty nice spot. They're in Zagat's and the steaks are to die for. Ever been?"

"Uh, yeah. It's nice but not the most romantic spot in the world. More like a corporate, business lunch type place."

"Oh, I was kind of looking forward to sampling the food there, but it is your day."

"If you're interested in Zagat places but want a nice ambience..."

"I'm listening."

"The Shark Bar has great soul food, and good music. We could eat and dance off the calories." What was he saying? Dancing?

"Sounds like a plan to me."

* * * *

The man was full of surprises, but Tabitha guessed she shouldn't have been too surprised by his question. Not with all the assorted siblings and cousins and nieces and nephews he had. And after seeing the swarm of family pictures on his entertainment center, how could she not expect he'd want a couple of kids if not more?

"How do you like your food?" Eric asked.

"It's absolutely delicious! I'm glad you mentioned this place."

He smiled, reached for his glass of lemonade.

"I don't know why you didn't get a drink-drink. It's your day. You're supposed to be celebrating."

"Just being with you is celebration enough."

She glanced at his face, his peaked appearance plainly saying he wasn't well, but knew that he'd never admit it, determined to stick out the evening for as long as it lasted.

She'd seen him popping Tylenol from her medicine cabinet earlier, heart welling at the obvious pain he was trying to hide.

Tabitha thought of calling Angela and asking her to cancel the party. She just as quickly discounted the idea when she realized how late in the game it was to suggest such a thing. Not days before, but the day of. Eric would have to be dead for his family to abide a cancellation.

As she looked at him across the dimly lit table, she knew that he was probably feeling pretty damn close to death warmed over.

She'd gotten the flu exactly twice in her life and had been getting the shot religiously ever since, never wanted to feel so bad again.

She could ask Angela to reschedule. Nah, that was just as bad as canceling.

Tabitha glanced at her watch thought even now the Vega clan was probably gathering at Eric's loft waiting for her to bring him home.

Maybe she could suggest they wrap the festivities up early, she thought, inwardly laughing at ending something that hadn't even begun yet.

She could imagine trying to slow down and disperse the rowdy, close-knit group, knew that the Vegas probably partied hardy, in typical big-Italian-family fashion.

Tabitha and Eric quietly finished their meal—she the broiled salmon and he the southern fried chicken, both of them having collards, cornbread, potato salad and lemonade.

After the meal, Tabitha ordered the sweet potato pie with a dollop of whip cream on top for Eric and the chocolate mousse for herself. Of course once the desserts arrived they each sampled the other's dish as they had done with dinner.

"You're trying to make me fat," he said.

Tabitha smiled at the impossibility and said, "After our earlier workout don't you think we've earned it?"

"Thanks for reminding me."

She watched him try to cover a wince as he reached across the table to scoop up some of her chocolate mousse.

Tabitha checked her watch. They had a little time before they needed to be at Eric's, but she wanted to make sure. "I'll be right back. I'm just going to the Ladies."

Eric got up as she left the table, and she went to the Ladies' Room, stopped in the lounge to pull out her cell phone.

After three rings, no one picked up and Tabitha wondered if maybe anyone was at Eric's at all before she started to leave a message and Angela intercepted it to answer the phone.

The noise in the background was deafening, and she could only imagine the condition of Eric's loft.

"Hello Tabitha, how are you?"

"Sounds like you've got a full house over there."

"We do, and it's crazy, but we're getting everything all set up. We should be ready in another hour or so."

Another hour or so?

Her silence must have said it all, because Angela got back on the line and said, "I know it's a lot to ask of you, but do you think you could keep him out just a little longer than we planned. Until about nine-thirty instead of nine? Everyone and everything should definitely be here and in place by then."

"I'll, uh...I'll see what I can do."

"Thank you so much, Tabitha. You don't know how much I appreciate this."

"Sure."

210   Gracie C. McKeever

"How's everything going? Is he enjoying himself?"

She wanted to tell her that he was enjoying himself so much he was ready to collapse, but she didn't think that would go over so well with his overprotective older sister.

"He's having a nice time. We just finished dinner."

"Did he eat a lot?"

He hadn't, Tabitha realized, remembering how he'd picked at the chicken and collards, and just barely finished the potato salad. "He ate, but I'm sure he'll have plenty of room left over for whatever you guys are cooking up."

"I hope so, because there's plenty." Angela laughed. "How about you? How are you holding up?"

"Me?" God, she hadn't even considered how she was doing, surprised and touched that Angela had bothered to ask her. "I'm fine. Your brother is good company."

"He is that…"

Tabitha heard the "and" at the end of Angela's sentence, thought she could have filled in with a , "We always have a good time together" but didn't want to be too effusive or give Angela the wrong idea. Not that the woman didn't already have the wrong idea.

"Everything is all right between you two then?"

Tabitha frowned, wondered what stories Eric had been telling his sister.

Had he mentioned the Jade incident? Or maybe the Frankie incident?

She thought of asking Angela but in the end just said, "Everything's fine."

"Good, glad to hear it." Angela paused then said, "Well, I'd better get back to it. We're still putting up the decorations if you can believe that."

Tabitha laughed with Angela before signing off and hanging up.

She took a deep breath, left the lounge and headed back to their table and found Eric leaning on it with one elbow, chin in his palm as he watched some of the other patrons cutting the rug on the dance floor.

One of her favorite Sade songs was playing, and she decided she couldn't pass it up.

She approached the table from behind Eric and tapped his shoulder.

He glanced up with tired eyes that immediately brightened at the sight of her, and Tabitha's chest filled at the idea that she could do that to him, pep him up. That ability would definitely come in handy for the rest of the night.

"Care to dance, sir?"

"My pleasure." He stood up and proffered an arm.

Tabitha hooked an arm through his and they made their way out to the dance floor.

She put one arm around his waist and the other on his shoulder as he did the same with her, pulled her close as they slowly moved in synch to the beat of the music.

"If I haven't told you thank you for the day yet, thank you." He bent his head and tenderly kissed her on the forehead. "I had a great time."

"Even the racquetball?"

He laughed, and she could hear the mucus rattling in his chest. "Yeah, even the racquet ball. You looked as good in your shorts and top as you do in this dress." He lowered a hand to pinch her ass for emphasis and Tabitha slapped it.

"Behave yourself."

"But it's my birthday."

She giggled and rested her head on his chest as he held her tight against him and swept her across the floor.

Tabitha didn't think she could have enjoyed the day any more had it been her birthday, liked that he was so appreciative and had enjoyed his day, thought that the Vega clan appeared to be a very appreciative group overall.

The more she thought about his family all gathered at the loft waiting for them to arrive, the more nervous she got.

She hadn't considered before now just what the night entailed for her, hadn't considered what she'd be walking into, or how she'd act around Eric's family.

Would they like her? Would she like them? What would she do if they didn't approve of her? What would Eric do?

Tabitha already knew that Angela liked her, half-suspected that she and Evelyn were behind the scenes pushing Eric and her together, wouldn't put it by either sister to act as matchmakers.

She almost laughed at the idea that Eric needed anyone to find him a woman.

Sade's *Love Is Stronger Than Pride* segued into Billy Ocean's *Suddenly* and Tabitha quietly sang along with the opening bars as she pressed her hips forward and felt the growing bulge in his trousers.

Eric pulled back is head to glance at her and smiled. "You have a pretty voice."

"Don't sound so surprised."

"Not surprised. I just never had the pleasure."

"Wish I could say the same."

He laughed. "Are you referring to my *Peg* rendition?"

"All I can say is don't give up your day job."

"I already gave up a day job for creative pursuits. Once in a lifetime's enough."

She put her head back on his chest, felt his erection pressing against her belly, heard the sound of him inhaling the scent of her hair. She wasn't surprised when he leaned in to whisper in her ear, "Let's get out of here."

Poor thing. He was in for a surprise when they got home, and it wasn't her and him alone and in their birthday suits.

Chapter 22

EJ couldn't wait to get in bed and hold her close as he slept. Sex at this point wasn't even a consideration; he was too tired to entertain any form of it, and hoped Tabitha wasn't too disappointed especially after the way he'd rushed her out of the Shark Bar to get home.

He paused outside his loft door, bent his head to give her a lingering kiss on the lips. "I couldn't have asked for a better birthday than spending it with you."

"I had a good time, too."

"Will you stay with me tonight?"

"Um—"

"You can sleep in one of my T-shirts if you're worried. Or nothing at all." He leered, just couldn't help himself from teasing, even though he knew damn well he was in no condition to back up any proposition.

"That, uh, sounds like a plan."

He frowned. "Why are you so nervous?" He noticed she'd been jittery since they'd left the restaurant, wondered if it had anything to do with their earlier conversation about children, wondered whether she worried if he'd push the issue.

"I'm not nervous," she said

He peered at her an extra few seconds before turning to unlock his door. When he flung it open the lights inside came on in a blinding display and at least fifty people jumped up from behind furniture all screaming, "Surprise!" at the tops of their lungs.

"Oh, God." EJ covered his eyes with a hand and shook his head.

Tabitha came up behind him, slid an arm around his waist and whispered, "C'mon, birthday boy. Your guests are waiting."

"You were in on this." He stared at her, couldn't believe she'd managed to keep this from him all day, that he hadn't even thought to scan her and find out what she was thinking, what she had planned. He didn't know if that lapse was a good or bad thing, just that he felt comfortable enough with her to not worry about what she was thinking every second of the day.

Like a real, ungifted boyfriend.

"Oh, my goodness, and he's brought a girl," Emilia said as he and Tabitha entered the apartment holding onto each other.

"He hasn't brought a girl home to meet the family since—"

"Sinclair," Donna said, interrupting Evelyn.

A hush fell over the room and EJ quickly broke it when he muttered, "Technically, I haven't brought a girl home to meet the family now. I've brought a woman home to *my* house, you're all trespassing, and I should kick you out right now."

"Eric, be nice."

"Oh, that's so cute. She calls him Eric," Emilia said.

"And he *lets* her," Nick piped up.

"Oh, please, give it a rest and let's get on with my little surprise party," EJ quipped, trying to brush off his blushing, but liked that Tabitha was the only one who called him Eric. It gave their relationship a dimension of exclusivity he had never before considered.

He and Tabitha circulated the apartment together, EJ alternately trying to avoid kisses, accepting hugs and well-wishes, and introducing Tabitha to his family and friends.

He felt for the woman trying to remember so many names and faces—and he could see her actually trying, rather than just relaxing, having a good time and letting things happen—before they finally got to his parents.

"Hey, Mom." He leaned in to give her a hug and a light peck on the cheek, hoped he wasn't too contagious, because at this point he was sure he had the flu.

"Hey, bambino. Happy birthday." His mother squeezed him tight and returned his kiss, pulled back and eyed Tabitha with interest.

EJ's heart pounded as he wrapped an arm around her shoulder and pulled her close to his side as his father joined them. "Mom, Dad, this is Tabitha Lyons. Tabitha, these are my parents, Viviana and Joe Vega."

"Aren't you Evie's personal shopper?" Joe asked as he offered his hand and shook Tabitha's.

"Uh, yes I am, but now I'm Eric's, too."

"Oh, you're a little more than that." Viviana smiled. "I can tell by the way my boy looks at you that you're much more than that."

"Viv, don't stress the boy about his girlfriend. His brother and sisters are going to give him enough of that tonight."

"They certainly will." Viviana laughed, stepped to Tabitha, briefly hugged her before pulling back to say, "Welcome to the family, Tabitha."

"Enjoy yourself," Joe put in, slapping his son on the back and squeezing Tabitha's arm as he and Viviana left them to wander the living room.

"Cute couple," Tabitha said once they'd left.

"You think they're going to be saying that about us in a few years?"

"According to Miss Stanford, we already are a cute couple, remember?"

"Oh, yeah. I almost forgot." EJ put two fingers to a temple and massaged in a circular motion. "I am so out of it tonight," he admitted.

"I noticed, and you haven't even had anything to drink yet."

Before the words completely left Tabitha's mouth, Angela made her way over with two glasses of sparkling cider. "Don't be so rude, EJ. You haven't even begun to circulate." She handed one glass to him and one to Tabitha.

"I like what you've done with the place," EJ said and meant it.

The combination Christmas and birthday decorations and balloons alone must have taken an hour or more to put up. The spicy enticing aromas suffusing his apartment told him that his mother and sisters had knocked themselves out preparing the food.

"Thank you. I thought you'd appreciate it." Angela leaned in to give Tabitha a squeeze and kiss on the cheek. "Thanks so much for keeping him out. Your timing was perfect."

"Yeah, thanks for keeping me out, Tabby."

"Oh, don't get in a tiff with her. She was just doing what I asked her to."

"I'm not in a tiff. I'm just not going to make it much beyond an hour. I think I'm coming down with something." God, it killed him to admit that. Especially to Angela who would start hovering and fussing over him any minute.

With that thought his sister frowned and put a palm against his forehead. "You are feeling a little warm."

"Angie, I don't want to ruin everyone's good time, and I really don't want everyone to know," he muttered.

His sister turned to Tabitha, and both women shook their heads in unison and chorused, "Men."

"Look, I'll hang in as long as I can, but anything beyond midnight, and we're going to be pushing it."

"Well we'll just have to make sure we start wrapping it up around then."

"Promise?" he asked, hated sounding so pitiful, but whatever this was, it was really starting to come down on him.

Angie put an arm around his shoulder and squeezed. "You just do your part and smile when you open your gifts and blow out your candles, and call us even."

If his family, especially his sister, had gone through all this trouble for his thirty-fourth, what were they going to do next year?

* * * *

By eleven-thirty Eric had opened his presents to the expected oohs and aahs of his family and friends, and everyone had sang Happy Birthday to him before he blew out the candles and cut the first piece of cake

As promised Angela, with her take-no-prisoners efficiency and drill sergeant's bearing, got most of the Vega clan out of the loft and started the enormous task of cleaning.

The rest of Eric's sisters, Evelyn, Donna and Emilia, helped, washing pans, vacuuming, mopping and sweeping the loft into an acceptable state of cleanliness, while Eric went to bed and Tabitha endured the special brand of good-natured teasing and grilling that went with the territory of being Eric's "official" girlfriend.

"So, where did you two meet?" Emilia asked.

"Actually, Evelyn introduced us. She referred Eric to my personal shopping business."

"Aah."

"I'll bet Angela was in on that," Donna said.

"Why do you say that?" Evelyn arched a brow.

"I know how you two operate." Donna leaned close to Tabitha as she handed her one of the last pieces of Tupperware to dry. "You stay around us long enough, you'll learn that Angela is the family's official self-appointed Cupid."

"Really?" Tabitha didn't know what else to say to that, hoped the sisters didn't start revealing any deep dark secrets that Eric didn't want revealed or that she wasn't yet ready to hear. She was sure they were all quite capable of spilling any number of beans, especially the non-designated drivers who had downed generous amounts of alcohol throughout the night.

"And what does that make me then?" Evelyn asked.

"Her accomplice," Emilia said and she and Donna broke out into girlish giggles.

"All right, enough jabbering and more cleaning up so we can all hit the road and leave the two lovebirds alone," Angela said as she came into the kitchen and clapped her hands.

"All done," Donna said, handing Tabitha the last casserole pan.

Tabitha dried it and stacked it in one of the cabinets below the sink.

"How is EJ?" Emilia asked. "He looked a little run down towards the end of the party."

If she only knew, Tabitha thought. Her brother had been a trooper all day, run down long before the end of the party. "He hit the sack a little early."

"C'mon you guys. Carpool leaves in exactly five minutes," Angela said.

"We'd better go." Donna took off her apron and gave Tabitha a hug and a kiss. "Good to meet you, Tabitha. Hope to see you again real soon."

"Yeah, maybe you'll make it to our parents' anniversary party," Emilia put in as she gave Tabitha a hug, too.

"Maybe," Tabitha said.

"We'll meet you out at the van," Evelyn said to Angela. "Talk to you later, Tabitha."

Angela sighed once her three sisters left and turned to Tabitha. "Goddess, I thought they'd never leave."

Tabitha smiled, almost afraid of what was coming. "You threw a great party."

"You helped a great deal." Angela searched her face for a long moment, finally said, "I knew you were the one for him when I first met you."

"At the sidewalk café?"

Angela nodded.

"That had to be more than a year ago."

"Almost two."

And she'd sat on her knowledge that long before finally deciding to push her brother and Tabitha together? The woman had the patience of a saint.

"The time wasn't right," Angela said.

"I'm sorry?"

"Two years ago the time wasn't right for you two. You weren't ready for each other."

And we're ready for each other now?

Tabitha wondered, remembering all the little quarrels and confrontations that she and Eric had had since they'd met, remembering all the tender moments and torrid sex...

"Comes with the territory. Breaking up to make up. I like the make-up sex, too."

Tabitha felt herself blushing at Angela's conspiratorial tone. She was really going to have to start getting used to the woman's uncanny ability to so easily read her.

Angela smiled and caught Tabitha in a firm hug. "Take care of him. I'll call in periodically to see how he's doing."

Just like that she assumed that Tabitha was going to be here playing wet nurse.

Who was she kidding? She knew she would be here as well as Angela knew.

Tabitha walked Angela to the door, accepted another hug and kiss before seeing her out, finally locked the door and leaned back against it for a long moment before going to the bedroom to check on Eric.

She came up short on the threshold, just stood and watched him, heart melting at the sight that greeted her.

He was curled into a semi-fetal position, shoes off, clothes still on, and looking boyish and vulnerable with his hands folded as if in prayer and tucked beneath a cheek, his long curly lashes just brushing his high cheeks.

Tabitha's heart thudded so hard her entire body vibrated with the rhythm and an emotion she immediately recognized but feared putting a name to.

She loved him, plain and not so simple, and she had no idea what she was going to do about it except keep it to herself for now and hope that her knowledge didn't drastically affect the way she acted around him.

She wouldn't tell him, couldn't, not yet when she didn't know how to deal with it herself.

Tabitha took several steps across the floor until she reached the bed and noticed the bottle of Thera-flu on the nightstand and a handwritten note beneath it.

She picked up the note, and expectedly saw Angela's bold and precise penmanship.

Tabitha, I gave him a dose at eleven-thirty. He should need another at five-thirty. There's plenty of homemade chicken soup in the freezer with a cold compress and the thermometer is in the bathroom cabinet. Call me if there's anything I didn't think of. Talk to you soon, Love, A.

She smiled as she finished reading, folded the note and put it back under the bottle as she sat on the edge of the bed beside him. She reached out and smoothed a lock of hair from his face and just looked at him for a few minutes, still coming down off of a wonderful, hectic, happy, crazy and frightening day.

Eric tossed and frowned in his sleep, mumbling as he turned from his side onto his back.

Tabitha caught something about Sinclair and bent her head closer to hear.

"...why didn't you talk to me? Why didn't you let me help you?"

She wasn't exactly angry, refused to be jealous of a dead woman, after all, and it wasn't as if he had called Ms. Secret's name.

She knew from her read of *Reaching Out* and his presentation in Colorado who Sinclair was, and how important she had been to Eric before and after she had taken her own life. Obviously, the young woman had made an immeasurable impression on him that more than a decade later he'd dedicated his book to her and was talking to her in his sleep.

She hoped it was his sleep, and not that he was nearing a white light.

Stop being so melodramatic!

Just to be safe, Tabitha went to the kitchen to retrieve the compress and the bathroom to get the thermometer.

She went back to Eric and undressed him as quickly as she could. The chinos came off easily, but the turtleneck gave her a little problem.

He shivered as soon as he was down to his shorts and Tabitha covered him with the comforter, and turned up the thermostat a notch.

"Tabitha?" He looked directly at her, his eyes sharp and clear.

"Yep, it's me, and you officially have the flu, Mister."

"I know, and I'm probably contagious." He moaned, closed his eyes. "God, I hope I didn't give this to anyone."

"We're worrying about you right now."

"I know, but I really wouldn't wish this on my worst enemy."

"I know, you want to die right?"

"You mean I'm not there already?"

She chuckled, palmed a warm cheek.

He caught her wrist and stared up at her. "You shouldn't be here. I'm contagious," he repeated.

"Tell me about it. I've fallen ill with the Eric Vega bug a long time ago," she admitted, and stuck the thermometer under his tongue, then put the cold compress on his forehead.

Eric pulled the thermometer out of his mouth. "I'm serious. I don't want you to catch this." He coughed spasmodically, the mucus in his chest clearly audible now.

"I don't plan on catching your nasty germs," she teased. "I've had my flu shot."

"That doesn't make you indestructible."

"No, but it makes me less susceptible than some people I know." She cut her eyes at him. "You didn't get a shot, did you?"

"I never do, and with the shortage we had this year..." He shrugged. "I never caught it before, never had a problem."

"You've been lucky, but you've got it now, big time." She put the thermometer back in his mouth, got up and went to the kitchen to defrost some of the soup in the microwave.

When she was done, she measured a serving into a bowl, put the bowl on a tray, headed out of the kitchen and froze on the living room threshold when she saw Eric sitting at the computer with the thermometer still in his mouth.

Tabitha put the tray on the kitchen counter and marched to Eric at the computer. "*What* are you doing out of bed?"

He spoke around the thermometer and she caught something about getting chapters done. "Chapters smapters. Get back in bed." She bent and slid an arm around his waist to help him to his feet.

He got up willingly enough, but fussed as she led him to the bedroom. "But Tab—"

"But nothing!" She brandished her cell. "Do you want me to call your sister?" She didn't need to say which one, they both knew she meant Angela.

"No," he mumbled.

"I didn't think so." She walked him the rest of the way to his bed, helped him settle back under the covers. "Now stay put," she said before she retrieved the tray from the kitchen and made her way back.

She sat on the edge of the bed beside him, took the thermometer out of his mouth and read it with alarm. She remembered hearing that a child could sustain a higher temperature than an adult could and suffer less damage. Unless said child was an infant and had seizures? What was the standard here?

"What is it?"

"Uh, it's pretty high."

He frowned. "How high? Give me numbers."

"What are you? An accountant?" She quipped. "It's high enough for you to stay in bed and get some rest is how high."

"It's not a hundred-and-eleven is it?"

"What!" She peered at him, saw the dimples-showcasing grin through his peaked look and smiled back when she registered his joke. "No, Ralph Kramden, it's not a hundred-and-a-eleven. It's actually a-hundred-and-two. Satisfied?"

"Whoa, that's kind of high."

"I told you. Now will you stay put and get some rest?"

He nodded at the tray she'd placed atop the bedside table. "That for me?"

"It's not for me."

"You going to feed it to me?"

"No, smarty, you're going to feed yourself."

"What if I'm too weak? I am a sick man after all."

Tabitha smiled as he sat up in bed and she fluffed and propped up the stack of pillows behind his head. She picked up the tray and settled it over his lap before stuffing a napkin down the front of the T-shirt he had put on, and sticking the soupspoon in his right hand. "Now eat."

"Okay, Nurse Ratchet."

She chuckled and silently smoothed back that stubborn lock of hair as he ate.

He sipped down a few spoonfuls before he pushed the tray to the side and snuggled under the covers.

"You barely ate anything."

"I'm not really hungry. I'll try and eat some later." His eyes drifted shut. "I ache so bad."

"I know you do, baby." She forked a hand through his hair, preparing to dig in for a long night of nurturing and vigilance.

Chapter 23

EJ opened his eyes to see daylight outside and Tabitha sleeping in the recliner beside his bed with a blanket thrown over her lap.

Damn, how long had he slept this time?

He glanced at the bedside clock and winced. Nine-thirty? He'd slept what, ten hours? That wasn't too bad was it?

"Hey you." Tabitha stretched, flung the blanket off her lap, stood and draped it over the recliner back before coming to sit beside him on the bed. She reached out to feel his forehead. "I think your fever's broke."

Fever? Oh, God, had he been delirious? Spoken out of his head?

The last thing he remembered was sipping soup. Tabitha forcing some sweet and tangy medicine down his throat. Tabitha walking him to the bathroom. Tabitha forcing more soup down his throat. Tabitha forcing more medicine into him…the hours and doses vaguely blended into each other until the perennial image of Tabitha at his side with a spoon in her hand embedded itself on his consciousness, obliterating all other impressions.

EJ had a feeling he'd been asleep more than just overnight. "How long have I been asleep?" he blurted.

"Oh, not that long."

"I mean altogether."

"Hmm, about two days."

"Two days!"

"Off and on. You woke up for brief periods to take some medicine and have some soup and water. I didn't want you to get dehydrated or malnourished. Not that you took enough in as far as I'm concerned."

"You've been here the entire time?"

"Where else would I be?" She smoothed back a stubborn lock of his hair before sticking the thermometer under his tongue.

He pulled it out. "What about work?"

"What about work?"

"Your job, workaholic?"

"Oh, that. I'm self-employed like you. I can take time off at my discretion."

Self-employed. That's right. He'd been asleep on the job while she'd taken time off to take care of him.

What had he missed? "Did I get any calls?"

"Oh, plenty."

"Aw shi—"

"Not to worry. I took care of most of them."

"How?"

"I told your agent and your editor that you were down with the flu and you'd get back to them as soon as possible. The other calls I asked Jodie to handle."

"Jodie called?"

Tabitha nodded. "She was very understanding and concerned, but said to hurry up and get better, she's got some more appearances and interviews set up for you. You probably should give her a call when you can."

"I will."

"And of course Angela and your mother called. They'll want to hear from you soon."

"You've been a busy little beaver, huh?"

She shrugged. "We try."

He peered at her for a long moment, throat tight as he tried to form the right words. "Was I a good patient?"

She smiled, and he tensed, could only imagine what she would say.

"The best. You slept most of the time. Which is what you needed."

EJ flung off the comforter, sat up and raked a hand through his hair. He leaned in and kissed her on the forehead. "Thank you for taking care of me."

She blushed and he chuckled at the color that rushed to her face before he stood up on unsteady legs and aimed his body at the bathroom.

"Where are you off to?"

"I need a shower."

She just glared at him with a stern don't-overdo-it look on her face.

"I'm all better, thanks to you. Trust me," he assured her.

"Okay. I'm going to go tidy up a little. Make myself useful."

He smiled, and went into the bathroom. He didn't think she could have been anymore useful had she worked on his manuscript for him.

Damn, two days lost time.

He'd missed enough writing with traveling and promoting without having to deal with an illness knocking him down and out for the count for two days.

EJ tried not to stay away from his writing for more than a day. Even if he was blocked he forced himself to sit in front of his PC, free-write and let his imagination loose at least until a flower of genius popped up among a field of crap.

He quickly showered and shaved, threw on some shorts, sweatpants, a NYU T-shirt and followed his nose to the delicious aroma wafting from the kitchen.

"Had I known that I was involved with Florence Nightingale and Suzy Homemaker I would have gotten sick a long time ago just to partake in the fruit of your skills."

"Don't be a wise-ass or you won't get any of this delicious fare."

He stood leaning against the doorjamb, arms folded across his chest as he watched her flip, scramble and set breakfast on the table in a mouth-watering display of sausages, omelets and French toast and could tell everything *was* delicious.

"Well, don't just stand there. Come and eat."

"Yes, ma'am." EJ saluted, came to the table and sat opposite her. "Looks great."

"Wait until you taste it."

"Is that a warning or a seal of approval?"

She shrugged. "It's been a while since I cooked breakfast, but I guess it's like riding a bike. You never forget how."

"That's assuming you could cook in the first place, right?" He frowned as he sliced into a sausage link with his fork. "What do you eat for breakfast when you're at home?"

"Mostly oatmeal, or cold cereal."

"And you cooked just for me?"

"If you keep being a wisenheimer, I may be forced to replace that plate with a bowl of mush."

He laughed, poured syrup over his French toast, speared a corner and chewed with relish.

For the next several minutes he made short order of the two pieces of

French toast on his plate, the sausages and the two-eggs omelet and went back for seconds of French toast so that by the time he was through, he'd washed down a total of six with a large glass of OJ.

Tabitha was only halfway through her breakfast by the time EJ sat back, rubbing his belly. She stared at him and smiled. "Good to see your appetite's back."

"Everything was delicious!"

"Thanks. I'm glad you liked it."

He leaned forward, elbows on the table as he peered at her. "So, what are your plans for the rest of the day? You're not going to leave me and go to work are you?"

"I hadn't planned to but now since you're up…"

"Don't go." He caught her free hand resting on the table. "Spend the day with me."

"I've already spent the last couple of days with you around the clock."

"That doesn't exactly count. I was unconscious."

"And I had my way with you, too."

He raised his brows at the idea that she had taken advantage of him in his weakened state. Not that he minded, he'd just prefer remembering if it did happen. "Did you tie me up again?"

"I didn't need to. You were totally at my mercy."

He held her gaze, waited for her to crack first and was rewarded when she suddenly broke out into gales of laughter as she slid her hand out of his and covered her mouth.

"I had you going there, didn't I?"

"You always have me going, woman."

Her face turned suddenly serious as she said, "I do have to go soon. I haven't been back to my house in days, and Frankie's not the most reliable cat sitter. Last I heard Vogue was still alive and scratching but I don't want to push my luck."

He put his hands together as if in prayer and gave her his best Oliver Twist look "Please, one more day?"

She chuckled. "Okay, one more day."

"Good," he said then looked at her as a thought occurred to him. "So you wound up sleeping in my T-shirts after all?"

"They're comfortable but I will need to go home and change eventually."

"Hey, I've got an idea," he said, suddenly ecstatic at the thought of her spending the day with him. It had been too long, since Colorado that he'd enjoyed going to sleep and waking up next to her. "Why don't you read what I have of my manuscript while I work on finishing it?"

"Read your manuscript? Before it's done?"

She looked horrified and he rushed to relieve her. "I edit as I go so it shouldn't be too torturous on your literary sensibilities."

"I wasn't criticizing. I was…" She paused, took a deep breath as he waited. She finally stared at him, eyes searching and questioning. "Are you sure? I mean, it's your baby and I don't know if you should be trusting me with it just yet."

He laughed at her terminology, thought only a real creative person could understand the concept of producing something from nothing except a concept; understand how fragile was an artist's ego. "I can't think of anyone else I'd rather trust it to."

She hesitated still and he decided to tease her. "Unless you've already read it?"

Tabitha gawked as if caught in the act, fiercely blushed. "Okay, I admit I read some of your stuff in the glove compartment of your Jeep once."

"I know."

"But I haven't invaded your privacy since then."

Her choice of words struck a cord and he flinched as if she'd struck him.

"Are you still achy?" she asked, staring at him with an anxious expression.

"I'm fine. Just a few twinges here and there."

"So…" She stood up, clapped and rubbed her hands together. "Where's the masterpiece?"

He laughed, hungry for her approval and heart pounding with the idea of ultimate exposure as she followed him to the living room.

Sure, if he believed his own press and went by the best-selling lists and his bookstore appearances, millions of people had read and loved his book. Tabitha said she'd loved it herself. But reading an unedited work, a raw manuscript like she was about to do, was like being one of the first ones entrusted to care for a treasured newborn baby before it had a chance to be shaped and molded and even cut down by so many other hands.

EJ retrieved the printout from his workstation and handed it over to Tabitha who eagerly grabbed it from his hands.

"I feel like Miss Stanford. This is a real treat."

He laughed. "Remember, it's a rough draft."

She rolled her eyes, walked over to the sofa and curled up in a corner to read.

EJ stood and watched her dig in—the intent look on her face as she flipped pages, her grin and chuckle when she got to a humorous section—and smiled, as intent with her as she appeared to be with his book.

He lingered a moment more, admiring the soft glow of her skin beneath the halogen lamp adjacent the sofa and his heart stuttered then painfully sped when he realized an inescapable fact: he was in love with her.

Oh, damn.

* * * *

Tabitha knew from her other experiences with his writing that she loved his stuff. She loved his twisted sense of humor and his fast-paced narrative. She loved the way he started each chapter with a personal anecdote from his life. She loved the simple richness of his prose.

So when she flipped over the last page to discover she'd gone through two-hundred-and- fifty pages in a few hours, she was disappointed bordering on pissed.

Tabitha glanced up at Eric diligently typing at his PC, glared at the back of his head. "Where's the rest of it?"

He swiveled around in his seat to see her shaking the manuscript as if the missing pages would miraculously fall out of the stack. "You're finished already?"

"You know darn well I'm finished. Where's the rest?"

"Honestly, I didn't think you'd finish it that fast."

"Sure you didn't." Tabitha got up and marched over to his workstation, stared at the page number in the bottom left-hand corner of the monitor and gawked. "You're only up to two-hundred-and-eighty?"

"I did thirty pages!"

"And how many more do you have to go?"

"Estimating from my outline, about forty to fifty pages."

"Grrr."

He laughed. "What?"

"Do you realize you left me in the middle of a chapter?"

"I didn't know I had given you the beginning of Chapter Twenty-Three."

"I want the rest now."

"You want me to print up what I have?"

"Only if you've finished it...and you haven't." She pouted, suddenly brightened. "I could pull an Annie, hobble and chain you to your workstation until you finish."

Eric laughed at her allusion to Stephen King's *Misery*. "Every writer's worst nightmare."

She bent her head for a kiss, and he leaned up and angled his head to accept her lips. "Thanks for trusting me with your baby."

"So? How's it sound?"

"You know it's great. I don't even know why you're asking me."

"But I don't know. You're the first person to read it besides me."

"Your editor hasn't seen it yet?"

He shook his head, and she felt more privileged than when he'd first asked her to read it. "In that case, I should leave you to your work so your editor and I both can benefit from the fruits of your labor."

"Not so fast." He caught her by a wrist as she tried to leave and pulled her down onto his lap, put one arm behind her back, the other one around her middle and clasped his fingers to lock her close to him. "I'm due a break."

"Not when I'm waiting for those pages."

"You really are a slave driver." He bent his head to kiss her, smoothly slid his tongue into her mouth and drank long and slow from hers.

Tabitha felt his erection pressing against the seam of her butt, hard and insistent, liked his rebound time but vividly remembered his gaunt appearance over the last couple of days and pulled back.

"What's the matter?"

"I don't want to take advantage of your weakened state."

"Take all the advantage you want. I'm all better. Like I said, thanks to you." He bent his head for another kiss, but she pulled back.

"We don't want to move too fast."

"Speak for yourself." He moved in again but Tabitha pulled out of his grip to stand up and stare down at him.

She wanted nothing better than to spend the next couple of hours wrapped in his arms with him inside her hot and hard, and her wet and melting around him, but reality was beginning to sink in with the passing of the day and Eric's recovery.

The last couple of days had been pure heaven, not the nursing a sick man part, but the nursing a sick man with whom she was in love part. Spending so much time with him unaware had affected her on so many levels she couldn't even begin to name, given her a view of what it would mean to be with Eric at his best and worst. Doing what normal couples did. Nursing each other, feeding each other, teasing each other. In sickness and health. Through good times and bad. Till death do us part.

God, what was she thinking anyway? They weren't like that, nowhere near it.

Tabitha glanced at him across the room, still sitting in his swivel chair and staring at her.

She couldn't tell him. It was too soon. Too soon for her, too soon for him.

...You weren't ready for each other.

Tabitha couldn't help thinking that they still weren't. She knew she wasn't.

She turned suddenly and headed for the bedroom, not surprised when she heard Eric following behind her.

He stopped her at the threshold, catching her arm and turning her around to face him. "What happened back there?"

"Nothing. I just need to go, like I told you. I need to get home and change into my own clothes, sleep in my own bed, pick up some mail. You know, stuff."

"Stuff, huh?"

"Yeah, like my life."

He stepped back as if she'd slapped him and Tabitha immediately regretted snapping, at least for the few seconds it took her to realize that only her bitchiest act was going to get him up off her so she could get the fastest thing smoking out of there. She needed the distance to clear her head.

Tabitha realized she couldn't stay here another minute with him awake and staring at her with those all-seeing, all-knowing blue eyes and not spill her heart out to him...and that she could not do.

"You'll come back right?"

"Of course. I still have forty or fifty pages to read."

He grinned, but she could tell he was covering his disappointment.

And, Tabitha thought, if his disappointment was anywhere near as sharp and painful as her own, then he must be dying inside.

Chapter 24

EJ returned all his calls from the messages Tabitha had taken, scheduled some appearances and signings through Jodie for after the New Year, and took advantage of the next few days before Christmas working on his manuscript.

Rather than blocking him, Tabitha's sudden departure and absence inspired him, knowing that she had read more than half of it and was waiting for the rest with bated breath, incentive for him to finish the book.

That is, unless she was blowing smoke up his ass and just trying to get out of telling him how lousy she thought his stuff really was.

God, why did he let that woman get to him so easily? In every way, every day, she did something to either tick him off, or make him fall more in love with her, and she didn't even have to be in the vicinity to accomplish any of these feats. Because he lived on memories, images of his times with her so sharp and bright he ran on them for days and days after he saw her.

Good thing, too, since he hadn't seen hide or tail of her for the last three days and she hadn't bothered to call him, not even to ask him how he was.

Okay, so the phone worked both ways, but he had his pride, just like her, and he knew she was testing him, just like he knew he would break down and call her as soon as he finished this last chapter.

Driven, EJ dug in for the next hour and finished the last twenty pages.

The total page count had come out to three-hundred-and-fifty, fifty more pages than he had originally told Tabitha. Good thing she hadn't waited around for them because she might have chained him to the chair as she'd threatened.

Like that would have been torture?

EJ leaned back in his chair, palms against the back of his head, fingers interlocked, staring at the screen for a long while, reveling in the achievement of finishing another book.

He thought of calling his editor first, just to stall, but since he had beat his own personal deadline by a month and the publisher's deadline by two, he was in no great hurry to make that official contact.

Oh, hell, just call the girl and get it over with. You know you want to.

EJ saved his work to his C-drive, a disk and a CD before printing up the last hundred pages and closing the document.

He got up and paced several minutes before the Zip Code Man's words came back to him—*She's going to love your gift*—and pushed him over to the cordless on the end table. EJ speed-dialed her office number first, knew she'd be at work despite it being Christmas Eve.

"Lyons Style, Inc. Cynthia Lawrence speaking. How may I help you?"

"God, you're there, too?"

She laughed. "Hi EJ! I'm assuming you mean in addition to my boss?"

"Tell me you guys are at least leaving early."

"Actually you just caught me on my way out the door. Tabitha gave me the go-ahead to leave a little while ago, but I had some things to finish up."

"Don't keep that husband of yours waiting too long."

"I won't. Hold on a sec."

She put him on Hold and EJ's stomach churned with butterflies for the several seconds it took Tabitha to get on the line.

"Hi Eric. How's it going?"

"Fine. And what are you doing there?"

She chuckled. "It's only two-thirty and I'm leaving in a few."

He swallowed hard, couldn't believe she still made him nervous. "I finished the book," he blurted and wanted to rip out his tongue at the rough approach.

Smooth, real smooth, Vega.

But Tabitha's enthusiastic reaction made his awkwardness more than worthwhile.

"You did? When can I read it?"

"As soon as you come over?" He hoped she didn't hear the question mark at the end of that. Damn, he felt like he was asking Carolyn Walker to be his Valentine all over again.

"How about after I get off from work?"

"You're not just coming over for the book are you?"

"Of course not!"

"So you'll spend Christmas Eve with me?" He waited only a second before he decided she was about to say no and quickly added, "Unless you're spending it with someone else?"

"Don't fish. Who else would I spend it with except you?"

"Your brother maybe."

"He left for parts unknown. Found a note, my key and some money on the kitchen counter when I got home from your house the other day."

"And you're okay with that?"

"I told you, he does it all the time. It's how he operates. He'll be back. It may be weeks from now, months or a year."

"And when he does come back, he'll be welcome."

"Of course."

He knew he was going to have to learn to deal with this relationship of hers if he was going to be in her life. Knew he was going to have to get over his jealousy where Frankie was concerned. He also knew it wasn't going to be easy, and he for damn sure wasn't going to like it.

He would do it though, do what he had to to please Tabitha. Because he loved her. "So what time should I expect you?"

"Three, three-thirty?"

"Sounds good."

"Want me to bring anything?"

"Just yourself."

* * * *

Tabitha had been about to call him—seemed the longer they knew each other, the more in synch their brainwaves—when he'd called her.

Three days.

It had killed her to stay away from him so long with no contact at all, had killed her not to call him and hear that deep sinful voice.

As the week drew closer to Christmas the need to call him had intensified exponentially, pushing her hand towards the phone periodically throughout the days.

He was like an addiction she couldn't stay away from, her weakness, and Tabitha did not like addiction and weakness, especially in herself.

She remembered how in the beginning he'd said she wouldn't have respected him if he tried to ingratiate himself—as if he had to try—and he'd been right. That was one of the things she loved about him, that naked Sagittarian honesty, that take-charge and go for what you wanted attitude that he exuded in every thing he did.

It had certainly served him well in his career, his love life, knocking her off-guard and luring her in.

Tabitha made it to his building at three-fifteen, would have been earlier but had stopped off at the liquor store and the market on the way.

She had his gift, wrapped and tucked down in her bag, had had it made and been carrying it around with her for weeks knowing she planned to go over to his house and surprise him Christmas Eve.

She'd been on edge all day anticipating his reaction, feeding into her imagination with visions of an angry Eric, an argument between them and hot make-up sex.

He'd called, right when her own nerves had neared the breaking point and she'd been about to dial him.

Tabitha's heart pounded as she neared his loft, legs stiffly carrying her up the stairs after he instantly buzzed her in, her head telling her to turn around and run.

She spotted him as soon as she cleared the landing, standing at his door, leaning against the jamb, arms folded across his well-built chest, wearing a Santa hat, green Polo shirt tucked into a pair of blue Levi's and looking more sexy than any human being had a right to look.

"Merry Christmas little girl! What can Santa give you this Christmas?"

"The question is, what can this little girl give Santa." She grinned sensuously as he blushed, her heart tripping over itself anew.

As explicit and raw as he could sometimes be, from having sex in public to his raunchy sense of humor, she found his tender boyish vulnerability just as entrancing.

Tabitha held up the shopping bag holding a can of eggnog and a bottle of Cask and Crème Liqueur. "I didn't know how you were fixed for traditional fixings and didn't want to come empty-handed."

He wrapped his arms around her as she neared, kissed her slow and deep on the lips before pulling away to hold her at arm's length and stare at her. "There's nothing empty about you, Tabitha Lyons." He slid a hand down, twined his fingers through hers and drew her into the loft. He waved to his little Charlie Brown tree with a flourish. "Just waiting for decorating."

Oh, God, she couldn't speak and it felt like her chest was going to explode.

Tabitha pushed the grocery bag into his hands and rushed to the bathroom.

"'Was it something I said?"

She closed the door, squeezed her moist eyes tight, took several deep breaths and tried to get a hold of herself. Sheesh, she'd been on the verge of hyperventilating, crying in front of him for no good reason except an attack of mushiness!

Tabitha turned on the faucet, splashed cool water on her face, took several more deep breaths and prayed she didn't have a breakdown in front of him.

It's just a tree, she told herself. Just a tree.

Despite the fact that she'd never had one growing up, that her mother had never let her father get one because she didn't want to "buy into all that commercialism shit," this tree was no big deal. No big deal at all.

Yeah, right.

When she emerged from the bathroom a couple of minutes after going in, Eric was anxiously waiting at the door.

"You okay?"

She nodded, sure her eyes were red or that some other part of her body gave away her instability—he was a body language expert after all—but he didn't address her sudden disappearance and for that she was more than grateful.

"Thanks for the spirits and especially the eggnog. I forgot to get some."

"I could drink it all year round if they sold it and since I don't drink—"

"Don't tell me you're going to make me drink alone."

"I, uh…"

"C'mon, today's a celebration. You have to have at least one drink with me." He took her by a hand, led her out of the bedroom and into the living room. "So, have any experience decorating a tree?"

"A little," she lied, but figured with her eye for style and fashion she could wing it. "At least it's not a big one." It wasn't quite Charlie Brownish, just a shade shorter than she was.

"The big one is at my Mom and Dad's. I figure since we're going over there for Christmas, I wouldn't get a big one for just us."

"We are?"

"Are what?"

"Going to your parents' for Christmas."

"Hey, I'm sorry. I just assumed…" He paused, took both her hands in his and gave her a serious look. "Will you come with me to my parents' house for Christmas?"

"Uh, yeah sure."

"Please hold down your enthusiasm until tomorrow."

She laughed, heart pounding a mile a minute. She tried to talk herself down, convinced she could handle a major holiday with the Vegas. She'd made it through a surprise party after all. Christmas should be a piece of cake.

"Oh, and while we're at it, I might as well invite you to my parents' anniversary party."

Tabitha hedged. They were wading out of girlfriend waters and into something entirely deeper, more committed and permanent.

"C'mon, you might as well go for broke since you're coming Christmas."

"When is it?"

"New Year's Eve. We always have a little shindig for them with the immediate family, but this one's going to be a big one, their fiftieth."

"Wow."

"We can go over there, bring in the New Year, and still go out and party if you want."

Did he realize that going to his parents' for a fiftieth wedding anniversary was party enough, and more than she ever did on New Year's? More significant and real.

Against her better judgment she finally gave in and said, "Okay."

"Okay you'll come? Or okay, you want to party?"

"I want to come. I'm not much for partying though."

"We'll have to put a stop to that if you're going to hang around us."

"You and your big family." She smiled, realizing she still had on her coat when Eric put his hands on her shoulders and turned her around to remove it.

He took it over to the coat tree, hung it up and made his way back to her. "So, are you hungry? Or do you want to build up your appetite working on my pitiful tree?"

Tabitha walked over to the tree standing in a place of prominence behind his sofa, and circled it a few times. "It's not pitiful. It's got potential." She turned to him. "Where are the decorations?"

He pointed her to a stack of boxes several feet away, and for the next hour they dug in filling out the tree with gold and silver tinsel, colored lights and balls.

Eric handed Tabitha a light-up angel and she reverently placed it at the top of the tree, stepped back and waited as he cut off the living room lights and cut on the Christmas tree lights.

*I will not cry. I won't...*God, she'd had no idea she had such a squishy streak!

Tabitha started when Eric sidled behind her and slid an arm around her shoulders.

"Nice work," he murmured.

"I had help."

He turned her in his arms and kissed her, mouth tasting of the sweet and potent liqueur she'd brought, almost as intoxicating as his natural flavor and scent.

She groaned and opened to him completely, enfolded him in her arms, holding him close as she met his tongue with fervor and his erection insistently pressed against her belly.

"I want to hold your naked body in my arms so bad, Tabitha. You don't know how long I've wanted to feel you against me again." He backed her against the wall nearby, quickly going to work on her blouse's buttons.

When he talked like that he made her feel like the most desirable and secure woman in the world, though she knew the truth. That he couldn't love her near as much as she loved him, and that he wouldn't hang around for as long as it took him to realize he'd made a mistake in dumping the exciting and exotic Ms. Secret, for the boring and staid Tabitha Lyons.

Eric parted her blouse, exposing the top of a sexy lace teddy. He splayed a hand against her abdomen, reverently stroked the black and silver nylon spandex with a thumb, material blocking his way to her skin, pulled down one strap and cup with his other hand, revealed a naked breast and bent his head to greedily suckle.

She closed her eyes and arched against him as he completely removed her blouse, tossed it aside, jerked the teddy down to her waist, then unbuttoned and unzipped her trousers.

Tabitha frantically worked on the button and zipper of his jeans, reached into his fly once it was open, freed and grasped his hard shaft as if it were a life preserver.

"God, I can't wait to have you," he growled.

"You don't have to." She squeezed him for emphasis, caressed and teased the slit in his head and absorbed his groan as he leaned in to kiss her mouth again.

He stripped her of pants and teddy in short order, picked her up in his arms and balanced her on his thighs as Tabitha twined her legs around his waist and arms around his neck.

"Take me now, Eric. Right here!"

"I'm going to." He fiercely bit and sucked her neck as he poised her directly over his jutting cock, and Tabitha knew that she would have to wear a turtleneck or scarf for the next few days to cover the mark of ownership that would surely be cropping up on her throat.

She was so wet, he barely had to thrust before he was sliding through her sheath all the way to the hilt. He alternately rolled and pistoned his hips in silent desperation, lightly biting and licking her pebbled nipples as Tabitha met his plunges with her own strong thrusts.

A few minutes later, she came with a keening whimper, face pressed against his shoulder, teeth firmly sinking into the soft flesh where shoulder and neck met as he violently shuddered and climaxed an instant behind her.

She kept her head on his shoulder as he walked her to the bedroom, lay her on the bed, and proceeded to finger and lick her to multiple orgasms again and again for the next few hours.

* * * *

EJ absently caressed her breasts and belly, comfortable and barely wanting to get up for food as he lounged naked beside her.

"I guess we should get up to eat," she whispered, reading his mind. "If only to refuel for another go-round."

"I like your thinking, woman."

She giggled as he pressed his face against her stomach and blew a long and loud raspberry against her flesh. "Get up, silly."

"Before we eat, there's something we need to talk about."

"I know what you're going to say. We didn't use anything."

He arched a brow. "And you're all right with that?"

"It's done now."

"Coming from someone who likes to plan for everything, that's awfully nonchalant of you isn't it?"

"I guess it's the company I keep." She shrugged and when he just stared at her, she sighed and said, "Look Eric, whatever happens happens, and we'll deal with it then. Okay?"

"I guess it will have to be." He leaned in to kiss her lips, then pulled back and said, "I have something for you."

"I have something for you, too."

"Wow, we can do a real-life traditional exchange of gifts on Christmas Eve!"

She laughed and he realized how childish he must have sounded, then the seriousness, the implications of his words must have sunk in because her face almost instantly fell.

"You're not going to run off on me again, are you?"

"No, of course not. I just…I don't do traditional very well."

"Who doesn't do traditional?" he asked rather than saying what he really wanted to say.

He had so many questions to ask her, so many things he wanted to know about her childhood besides the flashes he'd gotten. How much worse could it have been? Had there been any bright spots?

He remembered that first time in her office when he'd teased her about selling cookies door-to-door, realized how far away from that reality her life had been.

I was entirely too busy with more important activities to indulge in that particular whimsy.

So much unsaid in that sentence, what had been left out so telling.

He wouldn't push, he told himself. Whatever he got from her from now own she would give of her own volition. It was beyond time that he more strictly abided his personal code. He'd abandoned it far too easily, for too long and Tabitha deserved better from him.

She deserved her privacy.

EJ reached into the bedside drawer and pulled out a gift-wrapped, long slim box, and proffered it.

She gaped at it for so long before she took it, her look tempted him to break the promise he'd just made himself, but he didn't need to scan her to know how afraid she was.

She glanced at him before she put out a shaky hand to take the box. "It's jewelry."

"Open it and see."

She ripped the paper so meticulously and slow he was ready to snatch the box out of her hands and open it himself.

Finally she revealed the burgundy velvet box, paused a long moment before she flipped it open and gasped at the sight of the jade elephant with ruby eyes suspended from an eighteen inch, twenty-four-karat gold, Italian link chain.

"Oh, it's so beautiful!" She carefully lifted the elephant from its velvet cushion, caressing the smooth jade and rubies with a thumb before turning her back to him. "Put it on for me."

EJ happily obliged, watched as the turned and showed off her new necklace.

The stones and chain looked flawless against her copper skin, the gold and rubies catching and gently glinting beneath the light of the room.

"Thank you so much. I love it!" She put her arms around his neck, hugged and kissed him long and hard before she pulled away to get up. "Now yours."

Tabitha retrieved her bag, pulled out a nine-by-twelve gift-wrapped box and EJ's heart fell at the notion that she had bought him a sweater or some other clothing before he realized Tabitha wouldn't do anything so uninspired.

He smiled as she handed him the box, didn't care what it was, her closeness, her reaction to his present, was gift enough.

EJ didn't waste time opening his gift, quickly ripped away the paper, and flipped open the box to see the silver and crystal plaque inside. His heart smiled at the engraving as he pulled the plaque out of the box: *Best Writer In The World Award, to Eric James Vega, for his unflinching attention to narrative excellence and entertaining creative prose, from your Biggest Fan.*

"You are crazy!" He laughed, pulled her against his chest with one arm and hugged her tight before releasing her to admire his plaque.

"I take it you like it?"

"I love it and I'm going to hang it right over my computer so I can see it whenever I'm stuck. It'll make me kick myself into gear and get unstuck."

"Speaking of, isn't there a little matter of me getting my greedy little hands on the rest of that manuscript?"

She could put her greedy little hands wherever she wanted but he guessed the manuscript and some food would have to do for now. "C'mon, let's go get you some sustenance."

Chapter 25

Tabitha spent more time during her half-day at work fingering her new jade elephant—nestled against her breastbone and that she never took off, and staring off into space contemplating her and Eric's Christmas Eve together than doing any work.

When he'd pulled out that box she'd been on the verge of running again, and had it been a little square box and he had gotten down on one knee, she probably would have.

This was serious, had been serious for a long time; the minute she'd hopped that plane and jetted to Colorado things between them had changed, had ceased to be light and airy, or teasing and joking.

Surprise parties, Christmas Eve as a couple and Christmas with the big and wild family meant serious in anyone's book, especially her raised by Mr. and Mrs. Dysfunctional, brought up in a broken home before she'd been abandoned to the system.

On top of all this, she knew that Eric had not treated another woman with the attention and trust that he'd so far shown her; knew that he had not exposed his family to any other women, not even the inimitable Ms. Secret. Her heart swelled with the knowledge but just as quickly beat with the distinctive rhythm of alarm and anxiety.

How was she supposed to measure up to his expectations? How could she continue to entertain a relationship with him, when she wasn't ready to tell him how she felt, or show him the same level of trust he showed her?

Tonight she would be bringing in the New Year with Eric and his family. That was momentous enough in itself, but the fact that they were going to be celebrating a union that had lasted half-a-century and survived six kids in this day and age, filled her with an equal level of dread and hope that exactly coincided with her ambivalent feelings for Eric.

She knew that she loved him, which was one of the only things that she was certain of, but was love enough?

There'd been a time as a child when love and stability were all Tabitha had craved and dreamed of, all she'd thought she'd needed to be happy and normal like all her classmates and neighbors. Now she knew that there was a lot more to happiness, and for her it began with loving herself enough to relinquish and entrust that love to someone else.

She wasn't sure yet whether she was ready to take that step in the relationship.

Cynthia knocked on the jamb and smiled when Tabitha looked up.

"I thought you left an hour ago," Tabitha said.

"I had some stuff to clear up."

"I think you've been hanging around me too long."

"It's only two and I've still got time to get home and pamper myself before my and Dillon's night on the town."

"Time Square?"

Cynthia nodded, smile widening. "Our first time and I can't wait."

"Better you than me."

"What about you? What's on the agenda for you and Mr. Vega?"

"You don't have to front, Cyn. I know you call him EJ and it's okay."

Cynthia sighed at being let off the hook, then brightened once again. "So, any plans?"

Tabitha shrugged, tried to play off how much the coming evening meant to her. "Just going over to his parents' house for an anniversary party, then ring in the New Year from there."

"Wow, the parents. Sounds serious."

The girl had no idea, and Tabitha wasn't going to tell her, scared enough as it was without Cynthia reminding her of what she had gotten herself into.

She tried to shrug it off by mentioning the surprise party and Christmas, didn't realize she was digging herself deeper in Cynthia's estimation until her assistant widened her eyes in awe.

"So, where's the ring?"

"We're not *that* serious."

"If you say so, but I've seen the way he looks at you, and it's serious."

Eric's mother had said something similar.

What way was he looking at her that Tabitha was missing? She swore all she saw was lust. Sure, there was some tenderness, some compassion but did he love her?

"So whose anniversary is it?"

"His parents'. Their fiftieth."

"Wow!" Cynthia suddenly got all dreamy eyed and sighed again. "I hope Dillon and I make it that far. Of course, we have to make it to one first, huh?"

"You will."

"I wish you were as certain about your relationship as you are about mine."

"I wish you would go home to that man of yours and start your celebrating." Tabitha got up from behind her desk, walked to the door and shooed Cynthia out. "Go on. Go home now."

Cynthia giggled, leaned in to give Tabitha a hug. Tabitha returned it.

"Have a good time," Cynthia said.

"You, too, and be safe."

As soon as she was alone Tabitha went back to her desk and shut down her computer. It wasn't like she had gotten that much work done today, but it was either come to work and play at being busy, or stay at home and drive herself crazy with thinking about tonight.

By now she would have cleaned the house to within an inch of its inanimate life had she stayed home, and probably still would with the time she had to kill between now and tonight when Eric was due to pick her up.

No use putting it off any longer, she had to go home sooner or later.

Tabitha retrieved her coat and bag, shut off the lights, locked up her office and left.

As soon as she made it home a little under an hour later, she dumped her bag in the corner by the coat tree, got out of her clothes, and checked her messages.

There was one from Frankie wishing her a belated Merry Christmas and a Happy New Year and saying he had found an apartment in Los Angeles, was adjusting to the wild and crazy Hollywood scene and doing well with his band. He left a number for her to reach him and said to give him a call sometime.

So he'd finally settled down and gotten his own apartment. Tabitha hoped this new stability lasted for a little while and wasn't just a fluke.

The other one was from Eric confirming that he was going to pick her up at nine.

There was a long pause between his message and sign off of "I um…I'll see you later." and Tabitha wondered what he'd been about to say.

She played the message several times just to give herself a little thrill listening to his rich baritone over and over again while she ran a hot bath with one of her favorite Body Shop oils. Once the bath was full, Tabitha abandoned her bathrobe, picked up a paperback from her bookshelf and settled into the tub with a drawn-out sigh, muscles singing with gratitude.

She tried to get into the book, a recent purchase of the fifth installment in a vampire romance series on which she was hopelessly hooked, but as soon as she finished the first page, she knew she wouldn't be able to get into it, not so soon after reading Eric's *Body Language*.

His voice haunted her, his twisted sense of humor contagious.

She mentally revisited certain passages, admired his view of human nature, especially his perceptiveness where women were concerned.

Where did he come up with his ideas? What made him such an expert on body language?

In his foreword he paradoxically claimed not be, stating outright "I'm no expert. You don't have to listen to me, but I'll tell you this, I know what I know. And after two decades of growing up in a house full of the female gender, I especially know about the body language of the fairer sex. Trust me."

She realized she did trust him, more than she trusted anyone else in her life, even Frankie. No, much more than she trusted Frankie. Frankie was her past, still her brother who she'd always love, whom she knew would never harm her, but Eric was her present and future. She trusted him with her safety and her life, was beginning to trust him with her soul.

Tabitha got out of the bath an hour later, wrinkled like a prune, refreshed and secure enough in her feelings for Eric to look forward to tonight with more hope than the dread she had felt earlier. She dried off, made herself something light to eat, settled in front of the television and watched just enough of some mindless, I-slept-with-my-husband's-brother-and-may-be-pregnant-with-his-baby themed talk show to start doubting her feelings all over again. Tabitha shut off the television, set her alarm clock for eight, and decided to take a nap.

As soon as the clock went off a couple of hours later, she jumped up, instantly awake, and started to get ready.

Since he'd liked the black dress she'd worn on his birthday so much, Tabitha decided to wear a similar one, but this dress was red and perfectly went with the necklace Eric had given her. She put on a pair of matching pumps to complete her outfit.

She carefully made up her face, only putting on a light touch of blusher and lipstick, then brushing and leaving her long hair down beyond her shoulders and framing her face in glistening waves.

She was ready by eight-forty-five and not yet concerned since she knew Eric didn't do early, though he'd gotten better about watching the clock since she'd known him.

By nine-fifteen with no sign of him, she did get concerned. By nine-thirty, she was annoyed. By nine-forty-five she called his loft, got no answer and left a curt message. Worried, she called his cell, was directed straight to voicemail, and left another message. By ten-thirty she was concerned, annoyed, angry, pissed, frightened, and had such a severe flashback to her mother abandoning her at Port Authority, no-one could have told her that she wasn't that unloved and unwanted eight-year-old girl again.

What was wrong with her that no one wanted to stick around? What was wrong that people kept walking out of her life right when she got used to having them around?

God, how could she let him make her feel this way? So helpless, vulnerable and like yesterday's trash?

By eleven, Tabitha left the house on her way to Eric's loft.

* * * *

At seven o'clock in the evening, EJ's world had turned upside down.

He, the rest of his siblings and his mother all lingered in the waiting room on the Coronary Care Unit of Long Island Medical Center hoping to hear good news about Dad.

EJ had been in the middle of putting the last touches to his outfit before going to pick up Tabitha when his mother had called him from the hospital to say that Dad had had a heart attack and she was at the emergency room with Angela and Evelyn.

EJ'd immediately stopped what he was doing, got all the pertinent information he needed and ran out to his Jeep to rush to the hospital.

He arrived an hour after Viviana's call, cell forgotten at home and without a way to call Tabitha to let her know what was going on until he hunted up a phone.

By the time he reached his mother and sisters in the emergency room however, all thoughts of calling Tabitha were replaced with thoughts of whether or not his father would survive the night after having—what the doctors had told Viviana looked like—a moderate heart attack.

Viviana, however, had her doubts, relaying to Angela and Evelyn their father's frightening chest pains, pallor and out of breath state when the ambulance had rushed him to the emergency room.

That had been hours ago and since EJ's arrival, Emilia, Donna and Nick had joined the family for a waiting room vigil. By ten-thirty, EJ remembered to borrow Nick's cell, was on his way outside to make his call to Tabitha when a doctor came out with news of how their father was doing. He paused to listen, promised he'd make his call as soon as he heard what he needed to from the doctor.

The diagnosis was better than the family had hoped, confirming that Joe had had a moderate heart attack, been stabilized and was resting comfortably.

The doctor told them what had probably caused the attack, what treatment he and his team were planning on utilizing to correct the problem, and what the family and Dad could expect in the next few days as he recovered and before he was sent home.

"He should be able to return to work or engage in strenuous activity in about four weeks or so."

EJ was so preoccupied with the doctor's youthful appearance he almost interrupted him a few times throughout his spiel to ask the man how old he was and where were his credentials. He wisely remained silent and absorbed the man and his team's prognosis with the rest of his family, comforted by the doctor's unflinching confidence, insight and tact.

After the doctor had outlined the steps that Joe would need to follow to take better care of himself and prevent another heart attack, the family was allowed to visit with Dad in stages. Two individuals at a time, until just Viviana sat with her husband for several minutes before coming back out to the waiting room with her children.

It took some doing, but Angela and her siblings convinced their mother that she needed to go home and get some rest so that she would be bright and strong tomorrow when she came back before Dad went in for his bypass.

Angela volunteered to take Viviana home, a no-brainer since she wouldn't have allowed anyone else to do so, and considered it the most logical course of action as she lived the closest and had easier access to her parents' house.

The rest of her siblings left for their homes under Momma Angela's orders, all promising to meet at the medical center tomorrow to await the outcome of their father's surgery.

Nick hung back for a minute while EJ finally made his call to Tabitha and got voicemail.

EJ frowned, barely felt his brother nudge him in the shoulder as he left a hasty message.

"She probably couldn't wait for you and went partying without you, bro."

"That's not funny, Nick." The last thing he needed on top of everything else that had gone on tonight was the idea of Tabitha dancing the New Year's Eve away in some other guy's arms.

She wouldn't, would she?

Nick plucked his cell out of EJ's hand and headed for his car. "Just call her again when you get home. Maybe she stepped out for a minute or is taking a hot bath to relax and get you standing her up off her mind."

"Thanks for your constant support."

"Don't mention it."

He had to take everything Mr. Play The Field Smart Aleck said with a grain of salt. It wasn't *his* woman not answering the phone after all. Nick did drive-bys, and didn't let women come to his apartment, always rendezvoused at his sexual target's house, didn't allow jealousy and possessiveness in his world.

How could a cool playboy like this sympathize with EJ's quandary?

By the time EJ made it back home it was already eleven-thirty, and he was still coming down off an unpleasant adrenaline rush that he had been on since his mother had called him earlier in the evening.

He didn't remember Tabitha until he was parking in front of his building and by then he was anxious to speak to her, and knew she'd be totally pissed when she heard from him.

EJ came up short at the entrance of his building when he saw who was standing there waiting for him.

"Hello EJ."

"This is a very unpleasant taste of déjà vu, Jade, and I'm not in the mood for drama now."

"No drama this time."

He noticed her shy stance, her uncertain tone as she approached holding a bouquet of flowers and a bottle of champagne.

"I acted like a total bitch the last time I was here and just wanted to come by and apologize, wish you and Tabitha a Happy New Year on the off-chance you were here." She peered at his Jeep then frowned at him. "Where is Tabitha?"

"She's not here right now. I'm on my way upstairs to call her." He must have looked more troubled than he sounded, more troubled than he wanted to come across, because Jade was immediately at his side, putting her free hand on his closest arm.

"Are you okay?"

"My father had a heart attack tonight," he blurted. One simple question, and his facade cracked, emotions on the verge of pouring out of him at Jade's concerned glance.

He'd been holding up his mother and sisters at the hospital most of the evening, calming them and assuring them in the absence of his father and older brother. All the while beyond assurance and peace himself thinking about the pillar of a man he knew as his father flat on his back and at death's door.

"EJ, I'm sorry. Is there anything I can do?"

At that moment she ceased to be his and Tabitha's nemesis, and became the woman he had gotten to know at Smith and Wollensky, the playful, teasing and sensuous woman with whom he had become friends before lovers.

"I'll be fine. I just need to settle in and grasp everything that's happened before I go back to the hospital tomorrow."

"Do you want me to keep you company until Tabitha gets here?"

He swallowed, unable to speak, focused more on keeping the tears from welling, silently nodded as Jade slid an arm around his waist and walked with him the rest of the way to his building.

"We'll go upstairs and you can tell me everything over a glass of hot tea."

He stared at her profile and she must have felt his look as she returned it and smiled.

EJ peered in her eyes and saw no malice or calculation, just sympathy and sincerity.

God, he wanted to believe that that's all there was, hoped that he wasn't misreading her again, too emotionally drained and weak to delve any deeper than the surface.

"Sure," he finally murmured, and let Jade lead the way up to his loft as if he was a lost little boy; at that moment, he felt like one.

EJ unlocked the door with his key, and once inside, Jade took over, ordering him to change into something comfortable while she made a pot of tea in the kitchen, at home in his house and giving orders as if she had been born to it.

Funny how, in all the years they had known each other, he had never seen this domestic, maternal side of Jade. He wasn't sure if he could get used to it, but welcomed the warmth of her company and concern for now.

By the time EJ emerged from the shower, washing off the antiseptic and medication-laden smell of the hospital from his skin, clad in a pair of well-worn jeans and a T-shirt, Jade had finished making the tea and was settled into a corner of his sofa sipping from a cup.

He felt underdressed in his own house, getting the full impact of the fancy evening wear Jade was wearing once she'd removed her overcoat and waved a hand at her outfit. "You were on your way to a New Year's Eve party or coming from one?"

"I was on my way to see you." She rose from the sofa and sauntered over to him as he stood on the threshold of the living room, paused for a moment to peer up at him before throwing her arms around him in a tight hug. "I'm really sorry to hear about your father, EJ," she whispered.

He returned her hug, pat her shoulders, already feeling better since arriving home and eager to be reunited with Tabitha and explain to her all that had happened to him tonight. He realized Jade would have to leave before any of that occurred and was prepared to eat major crow once he reached Tabitha. "I appreciate your being here for me, Jade." He caught her by the shoulders and pulled away slightly to look at her. "But I'm going to be all right now."

"I know you are, EJ, but I'd still like to keep you company for a little while longer, just to make sure."

"Jade…"

She stood on her tiptoes and reached for his lips with hers before he could stop her. Her mouth closed over his, tongue working past his lips in a sinuous passionate demand that EJ could not, in good conscience, obey.

Breathless, he pulled away and glared down at her. "This can't happen, Jade."

"Why? Because you're committed to Ms. Personal Shopper?"

"Her name is Tabitha."

"I know what her name is, and I know she could never love you the way I do. The way I've loved you ever since high school." She pulled him into her arms again, burying her face against his neck and inhaling deeply.

Since high school? EJ pulled away again to gawk at her. "What do you mean since high school?"

"Very well, if you must know…" She sighed before her face suddenly brightened with a smile. "I'll actually feel better once this is out in the open."

"What the hell are you talking about?" EJ had a bad feeling about this, didn't like the look on her face, or the signals he was picking up from her aura—stronger than usual, not the vague readings he usually received—as if she had finally let down her mental shields and opened up her inner self to him.

To what did he owe the occasion?

"You should know I've had my eyes on you for a long time, as far back as when you were with Sinclair."

"You…you knew Sinclair and me in high school?"

"I was acquainted with Sinclair. You, I only knew from afar."

He found the first hard to believe. Jade was not Sinclair's type of friend. Jade was the cheerleader, popular girl type that dated the captain of the football team. She was actually the type that Sinclair despised, the clique-y girl that looked down on every one else who wasn't like her.

Sinclair, as beautiful and intelligent as she had been, had been anything but popular except to him. She had gone out of her way not to be popular, like EJ's brother Nick, a rebel to the core.

All of a sudden snippets of that poem came back to him—*She's in your life now, like a pit you can't shake, jaws clamped down tight on your ankle, How to chew through the bone…*

When he had initially read those lines he had thought it was just typical teenage angst, typical dark, melodramatic Sinclair. Now he knew it was so much more; more sinister and ominous.

"It was you!" EJ stumbled away from Jade as she advanced with this cool, self-satisfied look on her face.

"Trust me, EJ. It was for the best for everyone involved."

"What the hell are you talking about?"

"She wasn't good enough for you, EJ, wasn't strong enough. She would have brought you down eventually. It was just a matter of time."

"Who are you to make decisions like that for me? For anyone?"

"I'm the woman who's in love with you." She approached, arms outstretched, and hugged him before he could stop her.

He stood numb and unmoving in her embrace, incredulous and in shock.

EJ caught her around the shoulders and held her away from him, saw the cold calculating look in her blue eyes, a look he'd only briefly glimpsed outside his loft when he and Tabitha had returned from Colorado, and he knew that Jade didn't know the meaning of love.

All this time he had been sleeping with the enemy and hadn't known it until now.

"You killed her," he blurted but Jade vehemently shook her head.

"I might have made some suggestions, given her some gentle prodding, but I didn't kill her. Your girlfriend did the final exit all on her own. At least she was inspired in the end."

"You bitch."

"I did it for you, EJ. I did it all for you."

"You crazy, manipulative…" He abruptly pulled her into his arms, closed his eyes and held her tight, crushing her in his arms, mindless hate and rage for her melding with his blind naïve love and memories of Sinclair until he didn't know whether to kick Jade out or squeeze the life out of her to exact revenge.

He didn't know who he was more disgusted with: Jade for urging Sinclair to her death or himself for letting his dick override his good sense; letting his ethics keep him from trying to probe Jade more extensively in the beginning.

Would it have made a difference had he tried? Would he have been able to penetrate her defenses or would it have been as impossible as reading Sinclair and Tabitha had been?

EJ slowly emerged from his emotional haze to feel her arms come around him, feel her pressing her body, grinding her hips against him, and shuddered in revulsion.

Abruptly, he pushed her away, grabbed her by an arm and dragged her unyielding form towards the door. "I want you out of here now, Jade. If you stay in my sight a minute longer, I can't be responsible for my actions."

"You're making a mistake."

"The only mistake I made was in letting you into my life without question. I'll regret that for the rest of my life, but that won't stop me from trying to rectify it now." He opened the door and pushed her out into the hallway. "Don't ever come near me or call me again."

"But EJ, I did it for you."

"You did it for yourself."

Jade flung herself in his arms and he instantly pushed her away right before she slapped him hard across the face.

And that's when EJ noticed Tabitha emerge from one of the nooks in the hallway and slowly make her way over.

Christ, how long had she been standing there? And what was going through that fertile brain of hers?

Chapter 26

Tabitha examined her feelings during the entire ride up to the Village, finally coming to the conclusion that she was numb rather than angry or disappointed. Of course, this changed as soon as she arrived, paying the cab driver before getting out to walk up to the building.

She glanced up at his window, saw the lights on and the silhouette of a man and woman in a passionate clinch behind the shades.

Bile quickly rose to her throat and she swallowed it down, almost choking on the bitterness and betrayal.

She waited a moment to see what they would do, rewarded with the man grabbing the woman's arm and dragging her off.

Probably to the nearest bedroom to finish what they started.

Tabitha gathered her strength and headed towards the front door.

Luckily, a couple of New Year's Eve revelers, party hats in place and blowing colorful tin horns, were on their way out of the building. Tabitha caught the door as they exited. The revelers wished her a Happy New Year and she automatically wished them the same, surprised that her brain and vocal cords were working.

She headed up the stairs with one thought on her mind: to catch them in the act and end things right here right now. A not-so-clean break that was way overdue, probably since they'd arrived back from Colorado.

This needed to be done, she told herself. She just hadn't wanted to admit it before now, hadn't wanted to admit that she had let her hormones make an important decision for her yet again, hadn't wanted to admit that she might be exactly like her mother.

Tabitha hit the landing just as a door opened, ran to hide behind a dark nook several feet away, and watched Eric drag Ms. Secret out into the hallway.

She closed her eyes, emotions threatening to choke her as she kept her silence.

Obviously, they were having some sort of lover's spat. Question was, over what?

Had Ms. Secret given him some her-or-me ultimatum? Did she want him to break it off and stop straddling the fence between the two of them and Eric refused? Did he want to have his Tabitha and eat his Ms. Secret, too?

"Don't ever come near me, or call me again."

"But EJ, I did it for you."

"You did it for yourself."

Tabitha had had enough, her legs moving her away from the wall and out into the open before she had a chance to think about what she was doing and that's when Ms. Secret flung herself into Eric's arms.

He instantly pushed her away and Ms. Secret slapped him hard across the face.

Eric glanced up then, eyes wide as he noticed Tabitha's approach.

"Tabitha, it's not what you think."

"Oh, I think it's exactly what she thinks."

"Jade, get out of my sight or I swear I'll call the police and slap a restraining order on you so fast—"

"Oh, don't put on a show for your girlfriend when you know what we were doing together before she got here."

Eric turned and frowned at Tabitha as if asking for assistance with the crazy woman before he turned back to glare at Ms. Secret and point her towards the stairs. "Get out," he growled.

"Fine." She pouted, turned to go, but paused in front of Tabitha for one more parting shot. "He's all yours, honey. Hope you like leftovers, because I warmed him up nice and good for you."

"Why you—"

Eric caught Tabitha around the waist and pulled her back and up into his arms, had her feet dangling several inches off the floor, forcing her to helplessly watch Ms. Secret flounce down the stairs in all her smug bitchy glory. "Let me go, Eric," she bit out.

"Are you going to listen to reason?"

"Let me go, damn it!"

He did and as soon as her feet hit the floor, she turned on him.

"You son-of-a-bitch!" She slapped him across the cheek in the same spot that Ms. Secret had just slapped him, almost winced at how much his face must hurt, only almost, because he couldn't have been hurting as much as she was hurting right now. Damn him!

"Tabitha—"

"I don't want to hear anything you have to say." She turned on her heels to leave but Eric caught and pulled her back into his arms again.

"Let go of me."

"Tabitha, please listen to me."

"I said it once, I'll say it again: you don't have anything to say that I want to hear."

"I told you it's not what you think."

"Why'd you send her away this time and not me?" she blurted, curiosity getting the best of her. "Got your fill of Ms. Secret and now you want to take a turn with Ms. Boring and Drab?"

"What are you talking about?"

"Never mind what I'm talking about. Just let go of me." She kicked out, struggling against him.

"Tabitha, stop it right now! Don't make it into something it wasn't." He turned her around, held her by the shoulders, at arm's length, just avoiding her knee as she raised it up towards his jewels with serious intent. "Will you look at me and listen for a minute!"

Something in Eric's voice made her stop and stare at him, and for the first time since she had arrived she noticed his appearance. He looked totally exhausted. Not exhausted from any physical or sexual exertion, not exhausted from any pleasurable activity at all. He looked emotionally depleted, eyes sunken in his face with dark circles beneath.

She recognized his expression, the same grief-stricken and haunted expression she used to see in the mirror after her father left, after her mother abandoned her, after the nuns told her that her mother was never coming back for her and that she shouldn't waste her time hoping.

Tabitha finally registered his loss, afraid to find out how serious and extensive but asked anyway, "What happened?"

"Before I tell you I want you to come here and listen to your messages."

"But I—"

"No, you come in right now." He dragged her into his loft and stalked her over to the cordless on the end table.

Reluctantly, she picked up the receiver and dialed her number, feeling like an inconsiderate jerk because she had a feeling what she was going to hear.

Tabitha listened to her outgoing message, entered her code after it had played, chest tightening when she heard his voice—low and with an unmistakable quality of sadness to it.

"...if you're there, pick up...Look, I don't know where you are, but give me a call when you get this. My father...he had a heart attack tonight and, um...Just give me a call, okay?"

She hung up the receiver, clinging to her dignity with everything in her, wanting to save face, unable to trust him, or her heart, completely. "This message came in forty-five minutes ago. When did it happen? Why didn't you call me then?"

"I forgot my cell when my mother called me and once I got to the hospital I just...I didn't remember to call you until after we knew my father was going to be okay and were all leaving the hospital and on our way home. I borrowed Nick's cell to call and leave my message." He finished with a shrug, arms raised from his body, palms up, his look so contrite and sheepish Tabitha wanted to forgive him on the spot, but she couldn't yet, couldn't go down without a fight.

"You didn't remember to call me but you remembered to call *her*?"

"I didn't call her. Jade was waiting outside when I got here."

Tabitha had a flash of that night they'd arrived back from Colorado to find Ms. Secret standing outside his building and her heart melted a notch.

"She stopped by to apologize for the way she acted the last time she was here."

She shot up her eyebrows, couldn't believe he had fixed his face to say that to her. "Don't tell me you believe her!"

"I did before she—"

"Give me one good reason why *I* should believe anything that woman says."

He caught her by the shoulders, stopped just short of shaking her. "I'm in love with you and she doesn't matter to me."

Okay, that was two and she had to stop herself from gaping, stop herself from unwisely blurting out her own feelings, silently looked at him for a long moment.

"Tabitha, nothing happened," he murmured. "And when I tell why, you'll know I'm telling the truth."

She stared at him as he closed his eyes and took a deep breath, heart hammering as she waited for him to gather himself.

Before he spilled his guts she had known only bits and pieces about Sinclair, all minute pieces she had learned from his book, but nothing substantial.

By the time he finished explaining what had happened between him and Jade, explained what he'd learned about Jade and Sinclair, Tabitha was near tears with Eric.

She hadn't known how appropriate her designation for Jade had been, how deep the woman's animosity and jealousy went for any woman who got near Eric.

"Do you believe her? That she didn't actually kill Sinclair?"

"I believe she hated Sinclair enough to want her dead. But I don't believe Jade raised a hand to do her in. I sincerely believe Sinclair did that all on her own."

"If pushing someone to suicide was a crime..."

"Then I'd have her arrested in heartbeat."

"But I guess since it's not..." Tabitha shrugged, uncomfortable with all she'd learned tonight and not knowing how to approach him, reluctant to touch him for fear that one or both of them would shatter beneath the emotional strain. "How's your father doing?" she finally asked.

"He was stable in the Coronary Care Unit before we all left. He's due for bypass surgery tomorrow."

"Oh, God, I don't know what to say, Eric." She'd had a lousy childhood, sure, but as lousy as it was, she had no experience with almost losing someone to illness. She didn't know what she was supposed to say or how she was supposed to act around him.

She could only imagine what he must be going through, remembered how it had felt when her father walked out on her and her mother.

"You don't have to say anything. Just your being here is enough."

She wished that were true, but she knew he needed much more than her presence, much more than assurances and platitudes. The man had just found out that the woman he'd been sleeping with off and on for years had been, in more than a roundabout way, responsible for Sinclair's death, on the same night that he'd found out that his father had had a heart attack. What could she say to ease the shock and pain of this news? Tabitha felt like anything she said at this point would be trivial and meaningless.

He held his arms out for her and Tabitha silently walked into them, burying her face against the soft cotton of his T-shirt for a long moment, relishing his sweet-spicy musk and hard muscles.

"You look nice tonight," he murmured. "I'm sorry I wasn't here to bring in the New Year with you."

She pulled away to glance up at him, wanted to tell him they'd have next year, plenty of next years, but her throat clenched with too many broken promises, too many disappointments to believe that, much more to tell him.

* * * *

EJ woke early, before the sun began to rise outside his window.

Tabitha was deeply asleep beside him.

He turned to stare at her for a long silent moment, the idea of waking her making his fingers itch until he realized how much he enjoyed watching her girlish features relaxed in slumber.

God she looked so soft and vulnerable! He loved her so much he didn't know what to do with himself, and now after last night his secret was out.

EJ got out of bed as quietly as he could, tried not to let the fact that she hadn't returned his I-love-you bother him. The notion that she didn't reciprocate his feelings a weight pressing on his chest, a lance piercing his heart with a pain he hadn't felt as sharply since Sinclair's death.

He swallowed hard as he cut on the light in the kitchen.

He'd make breakfast, get his mind off of the omission, think about how she'd looked when she'd opened his Christmas gift, think about how to make her look like that every day of her life with him.

However long that lasts.

He wanted it to be forever, as unrealistic as that duration appeared, especially with someone as wounded and unpredictable as was Tabitha Lyons.

EJ shut off his maudlin thoughts and went on autopilot as he got out the ingredients he'd need to make a filling and tasty breakfast.

An hour later Tabitha came into the kitchen clad in one of his university T-shirts, a blue NYU number that reached a couple of inches above her knees and gave him a delicious peek of copper, toned thighs.

The image of those thighs wrapped around his waist, imprisoning and squeezing him tight nearly knocked the breath out of him.

As it was, EJ had to close his eyes tight and take a deep breath as she padded across the floor on bare feet, leaned up on her toes to kiss a cheek.

"I know I've got a serious case of bed head, but it's not that bad, is it?"

He opened his eyes to leer at her. "You've never looked sexier. Or more edible."

She chuckled, gave him a lingering kiss on the lips and said, "Happy New Year."

"Happy New Year to you."

She stood on her tiptoes to peek over his shoulder and see what was cooking. "Ooh, pancakes. Much more edible than me."

"I don't know about that."

"I wonder if they're as good as my French toast."

"Do I hear a challenge? Because we could have a cook-off right here, oven mitts off."

"I like a man who takes his cooking so seriously." She glanced at the marble island where a stack of fluffy pancakes was in a serving platter next to a plate of bacon and sausages.

"You don't cook like this often, do you? Because if so, we're going to have to start working on lowering your cholesterol and fat intake and soon."

His heartstrings jerked at the allusion to them being together for any length of time. "You plan on being around long enough to see the results?" he asked. He couldn't help himself and almost regretted his words at the traumatized look on her face. Almost.

"I do."

He frowned, purposely dense, staring at her until she elaborated.

"I plan on being around to see the results. That is, if you want me to be."

EJ gritted his teeth, angry with her for dancing around the issue, angry with himself for letting her.

He needed to be a man, just lay his cards on the table like he had already laid his heart.

Tabitha almost instantly soothed his ego, calming his stormy thoughts when she sidled behind him, put her arms around his waist and leaned a cheek on his back a moment before he turned from the stove, holding the last pan of pancakes aloft. "I don't want anything to happen to you, Eric. I don't want you to—"

"Have a heart attack like my father?"

She nodded as she released him and stepped back.

EJ flipped the finished pancakes onto the batch on the island and turned to face her again. "I don't plan on it."

"I know you don't plan on it but things happen."

"I had a clean bill of health my last physical four months ago, and my cholesterol is a healthy one-sixty-five in case you're wondering."

"I should have known you'd know the numbers. I think you were an accountant in another life, Eric."

He chuckled and hugged her. "What about you?"

"A pretty healthy one-seventy-five."

"Hmm, we're going to have to work on lowering that a little, just to be safe."

She cut her eyes at the breakfast on the island. "Not with meals like this."

"I don't eat like this often, in answer to your earlier question."

"That's good to know."

They separated and silently took seats at the island adjacent each other.

"You're beginning to sound like my sister," he said.

"Angela?"

He nodded.

"She is rather protective of you."

"You can say the word. It's *over*protective, and yes she is."

Tabitha giggled as she helped herself to a few pancakes and a couple of bacon strips while EJ related how Angela and Evelyn had run out onto the field during one of his Pee Wee League games when the pitcher had clocked him in the head with a ball high and inside.

Tabitha doubled over hysterically laughing as he described how his father and other siblings had to run out onto the field and pull Angela and Evelyn away from the poor kid.

When she'd caught her breath she looked at him, face solemn. "Your family is so close."

"We are." He waited for her to fill in with something about hers, just any little tidbit to feed his curiosity and she surprised him when she said, "I guess you know I'm not. Close to my family that is."

"I guessed."

She was silent for along time, eyes averted before she looked at him again. "You might as well know my father—or the man I knew as my father—left home when I was about eight. My mother abandoned me in a bus station shortly thereafter."

He waited as long as he could for the rest, knew that there was more, but couldn't let on that he knew, and didn't want to discourage her from sharing the part of herself he'd been needing her to share. Finally he gave in and said, "You said the man you knew as your father. I'm guessing he wasn't really."

"My mother...God, I can't believe I'm telling you this. I've never told anyone..."

He caught a free hand and squeezed, urging her to go on as his heart squeezed in his chest, urging him to share more than the I-love-you he already had.

"My mother married my dad when she found out she was pregnant, pushed me off as his. My biological father was, or is, some rock musician she...screwed backstage after a concert, and the result was *moi*."

Oh, God, it was coming together. His comment about wanting to be a rock star, how she'd suddenly turned cool when he'd asked her to be his groupie. "You never knew him at all?" He had such a big immediate and extended family the idea that she didn't know half of her heritage, where she came from, was inconceivable to him.

She shook her head. "My mother was, uh...is, since I guess she hasn't been cured, a manic depressive, what we know as bipolar affective disorder."

"That must have been rough on you."

She shrugged. "It made for a pretty unpredictable and colorful childhood . At least when she was around and not on one of her many trips and sprees. She disappeared a lot when I was little. Before that final disappearance."

He wanted to tell her that he'd never leave her like that, that he'd never disappear but the words clogged in his throat.

"So, now you know."

Like these few facts made up her entire life story, but at least it was a start. He could work with it. They could work with it. "Now I know."

She searched his face as if for support or contempt and he wasn't sure which she thought she'd find, or which he transmitted, tried to make his expression as neutral as possible.

"Would you like to come with me to the hospital to visit my father? Unless you have other plans?" He automatically slid down his shields anticipating her response.

"Of course I'll come with you. What other plans would I have?"

He caught the unspoken *besides being with the man I love* and instantly, but far too late to matter, slid up his shields.

EJ swallowed hard at the idea of his treachery, having invaded her privacy yet again. but damn it had been worth it to know how she felt, that he wasn't drifting alone in a sea of emotions, that he wasn't alone in the world with his feelings. How was he ever going to tell her about himself now?

Chapter 27

Tabitha didn't know what to do with herself surrounded by so much warmth and concern and natural affection. She should have been used to it by now having spent so much time with Eric's family, but she didn't think she'd ever get used to Emilia's bright, ever-present smile, Donna's sarcastic wit, Angela's protectiveness for each and every one of her younger siblings, or her ability to read everyone's needs and thoughts in an instant, and Nick and Evelyn's outspoken opinions that made Eric's honesty pale in comparison.

Actually, the entire Vega clan suffered from the latter, along with a healthy dose of affection of which the family had been unconditionally showering her with different levels from hugs and kisses upon greetings and departures, to careless touches on the arm or back during idle chit-chat. She was so unused to the closeness, the touching she was starting to feel like she was a weirdo and an ingrate, but couldn't stop her claustrophobia around them.

Tabitha was currently on a break, down at the floor's vending machine getting a few cans of soda for the family and taking her time before returning.

She was ashamed of herself for her cowardice, but every time Angela or Viviana glanced at her they reminded her of Eric's declaration and all the things she could have said to him, but hadn't. Reminded her of all the things she could have with him if she were just honest and told him how she felt.

Tabitha made her way back to the waiting room where Eric and his mother and siblings had been gathered since ten this morning, almost four hours ago.

She handed Viviana, Donna and Angela the sodas that they'd requested and took the empty seat next to Eric.

He immediately put an arm around her, kissing her temple as he squeezed her arm, making her feel wanted and missed.

She realized that was a Vega trait, too. At least one they'd exhibited in abundance with her, making her feel welcomed whenever she arrived and that she'd be missed when she left.

"No news yet?" she asked for lack of anything else to say.

"Nah, not yet."

"We're going down for a smoke," Evelyn announced as she and Nick stood from their seats and headed for the elevators.

Tabitha followed them with her eyes, for once wished she had the vice if only to get her out of the room, afraid of having to be a solid column of strength if bad news came down from the doctor.

Sheesh, you're a pessimist!

She wasn't even prepared for good news, couldn't conceive of it, though she hoped and prayed with everyone else, for a positive outcome.

"Are you okay?" Eric asked.

"I should be asking you that." She glanced at him, twined her fingers through his, enjoying the warmth of his hand, the lifeblood pumping through his veins next to hers.

She had so much on the tip of her tongue, so much she wanted to say to him but old mistrust and fear kept her mute.

She used to think she was fearless, at least where making decisions in her life was concerned, but since she'd met Eric, especially since last night, she feared everything about their relationship, especially the feelings he evoked. She feared their unknown future together, and she feared a future alone and bereft of his easy humor and positive outlook. She feared his love and the burden it had placed on her the minute he'd said the magical three words. She feared the burden her own feelings placed on her, growing heavier and heavier by the day.

Why not relieve herself and tell him?

Because she knew in her heart that the repercussions of letting out all those emotions would be far more than detrimental to her well-being and the health of the relationship than keeping it to herself. Surely telling him would be so much easier than keeping everything in, restraining herself like she'd been doing since she was a little girl. Holding in her fear, her love, her trust because there was no one in her orbit that deserved them, much more who wanted them.

The doctor came into the waiting room then and everyone was instantly on his or her feet.

The scrubs-clad young man barely looked as old as her, but Tabitha was immediately comforted by the slight smile on his lips.

He made a beeline straight to Viviana, put a gentle hand on her shoulder and told her how her husband's surgery had gone. "He did very well, Mrs. Vega. We'll be bringing him from Recovery soon and you'll be able to visit with him for a little while but not too long. He needs to rest up and build his strength so that he can leave in a few days."

Viviana grabbed one of the man's hands with both of hers and vigorously shook it as she thanked him for his efforts and time.

Nick and Evelyn came back into the room as the doctor was leaving, joined their brother and sisters to gather around and hug their mother.

Tabitha stood just outside their circle, her heart in her throat and tears in her eyes, more thankful and relieved than she could ever remember being.

The circle broke and Eric automatically went to her, pulled her into his arms and kissed her on the lips. He pulled away after a moment to stare at her. "What are you doing over here?"

"Just thinking."

"Pretty hard from the looks of it." He frowned, pulled her close again. "He's going to be okay." He murmured it as if to reassure himself.

"How could he be anything but with all of us in his corner praying for him?"

"Were you?"

"Was I what?"

"Praying for him?"

"Of course I was! What, you think I'm a total heretic?"

He shrugged, didn't seem to get her little joke. "I didn't want to assume you were religious in any way. Everyone's not."

She wasn't really, didn't consider herself any particular denomination, but had a particular aversion to Catholicism in any form. "What about you?" she asked then wanted to bite out her tongue when she realized what she'd asked, except that Eric was totally unoffended by her question.

"Lapsed Catholic," he said sheepishly. "But every once in a while, like now, I remember my roots, and all the old prayers and habits come back."

"Your mother's pretty devout."

"You can tell, huh?" He smiled, glancing in Viviana's direction. "I can't knock it. It gets her through the rough times."

"Like today?"

"And others." He looked at her, indigo eyes deep and serious. "My mom was diagnosed with breast cancer several years ago," he whispered.

"Oh, no! Is she…?"

"She's been okay for a long time now, achieved remission six months after her initial diagnosis with no recurrence."

"I'm so glad." Tabitha sighed, looking over a shoulder at the picture of strength, good health and wisdom that was his mother.

"It was touch and go for a little while, but her faith and the doctors got her through."

"I'm sure having all you guys around helped, too." She smiled. "I know this must be extra hard for you. Your father being ill and all."

"He's pulled through the worst I think. We'll help him get through the rest."

She threw her arms around him then, held tight, trying to absorb all the love and positive energy he harbored for his family and that they harbored for him, but held onto her own love, keeping it to herself and close to her heart like a talisman against bad tidings.

She wondered if she had had more faith or prayed as a child, would her mom and Dad still be together and in her life.

* * * *

EJ didn't know to what he owed the closeness he and Tabitha had been experiencing the last couple of days. He was only thankful for her being next to him when he went to bed at night and woke up in the morning.

It frightened and excited him that he was so attached to her, used to her company, accepting it as his due.

He waited now as she unlocked her door, stepped in front of her to enter the apartment first, cutting on the lights and glancing around before he let her come in.

"You know you really don't have to do that."

"Habit. You know like sitting with my back to a wall in public, or only letting the woman walk on the inside, away from the curb and traffic."

"And they said chivalry is dead."

"Not with my mother alive and kicking. She'd kick my butt if I didn't hold the door or give up my seat for a woman."

Tabitha kissed him on a cheek. "Shame the chivalry doesn't translate in bed when you make me sleep on the monster side, near the door."

"Hey, I take the window!"

She chuckled as she removed his scarf, hat, coat, and hung them on the coat tree.

"Seems like one of us is still a little overdressed." He leaned in to kiss her throat, licking his way up to gently bite her chin as he removed her coat and threw it in the general direction of the coat tree.

Tabitha tossed her keys towards the peg board by the door and hurriedly got out of her clothes, standing naked before EJ in the living room as he hungrily licked his lips and stared at her like a piece of steak.

"Last one to the bedroom is a rotten egg!" Tabitha broke into a sprint and EJ followed, removing his clothes along the way until he was down to his shorts by the time he reached the bedroom.

Tabitha was lounging back against a pile of pillows, legs invitingly spread so he could see her juices glistening beneath the bright overhead lights of the room.

He wondered vaguely if she had stuck her finger in and spread her cream around to tease him when he came in.

EJ stood at the foot of the bed for an interminable moment admiring her body—the lush

curves and firm muscles, the rich chestnut waves flowing across the pillows and down over her shoulders, the red-painted toenails on her small dainty feet—and his already hardened cock twitched as if to remind him that he was fully loaded and ready for action.

He slid down and stepped out of his boxers before crawling across the bed until he'd reached his goal.

He planted a palm on each thigh, spread her wider, pushed his face between her legs and inhaled deeply.

She quivered beneath his touch and he splayed open her lips with his thumbs before sliding in his middle finger slow and deep.

Tabitha whimpered, closed her eyes, and arched toward his hand, writhing beneath him as she licked her lips. "Oh, God, Eric. I want you. I want to feel you inside me."

"You will. I just have to take care of something important first..." He paused to lick her, up, down and sideways before thrusting his tongue inside and teasing her clit with a thumb and in rhythm with his strokes.

"Eric..."

He popped up his head long enough to say, "You taste so good, I could stay down here all night. Forever."

"I have other plans for that tongue of yours." She ended her sentence on a gasp when EJ flicked her clitoris with his tongue before gently nibbling and suckling the hard kernel of flesh.

He slid up her body until he was balancing his weight on his palms, each planted on opposite sides of her face. "You deprive me of one of my favorite joys in life. What possible plans could you have for my tongue than what I was doing?"

She reached up and softly bit his full lower lip, sliding her tongue into his mouth and kissing him deeply as she moaned and raked her hands through his longish black hair. "Don't tease me, or you'll be sorry."

"Threats?" He smiled, but had already decided to put her and himself out of their misery.

He reached over to the bedside dresser where he'd left the box of condoms he'd brought and left the other day and Tabitha caught his wrist.

"I want to feel you."

EJ arched a brow, searching her soft features. He didn't know what she was up to, whether she wanted to start working on those two kids now to which they had once alluded, and didn't want to examine his feelings on the matter too closely or he'd chicken out. "Are you sure?" he asked.

She nodded, reaching down to caress his balls before gently squeezing them. "I've never been more sure."

He didn't know what held him together, what held him back at the drugging look in her whiskey eyes, just wanted her with such an intensity all thoughts of love, marriage and babies took a backseat to his desire.

EJ gripped her hips as he mounted her, thrusting hard and burying himself deep within her, rolling his hips with steady athletic precision, luring Tabitha into the dance until she was matching him thrust for thrust and pant for pant.

Within minutes, he felt the pressure irrevocably building in his scrotum, pistoning his hips, massaging his shaft against her canal until he couldn't hold himself off any longer. Still, he gave her a chance to change her mind, didn't know from where his restraint came. "Tabitha, are you sure? I'm going to come."

"Yes...yes! I want you to, Eric. I lo—I need you. Just hold me and come."

He burst at her words, at her almost-confession, spurting free in her channel as her inner muscles clenched around him and milked his cock for all it was worth.

Slick and sated, he shuddered in her arms as Tabitha trembled and clung to him with her arms and legs, squeezing him tight to her. "God, I never want to let you go!"

"You don't have to, Tabby." He peered at her and she averted her eyes and in that second he was on the verge of telling her. Telling her everything but the moment past as soon as she pierced him with her gaze, a sad smile on her lips.

He didn't know what was worse: that she didn't believe in him enough to tell him how she felt, or that he didn't believe in their relationship enough to be honest with her.

Either way, he needed to stop lying to Tabitha and soon.

Chapter 28

Tabitha woke up early the next morning pleasantly sore and invigorated.

She should have left well enough alone, but decided to tempt fate, couldn't resist waking him with a few light licks to his penis.

He was instantly awake and aroused, softness a distant memory.

"Isn't it me who's supposed to wake you up out of a sound sleep poking you in the butt in the middle of the night?"

"I figured I'd beat you to the punch. Don't like being poked in the butt in my sleep."

"Where do you like to be poked in your sleep?"

She grinned before she went down on him in earnest, fondling his balls and licking and sucking his hard shaft from head to base.

"God..." He clenched his teeth and caught her around the shoulders to lift her off of him.

"I wanted a little snack before I started breakfast and you ruined it."

"I'll give you a snack."

Her interrupted blowjob segued into tender mind-blowing lovemaking that left Tabitha near tears and the on the verge of breaking.

She still went off to work a couple of hours later without telling him how she felt.

She did, however, arrive a few of hours later than her normal time, determined to take it a little easy, especially after what had happened to Eric's father and how close she had come to losing Eric over a stupid misunderstanding.

Life was too short and she needed to start taking it easy and enjoy what she had with him for however long it lasted.

Cynthia arched a brow when she walked through the door.

"Sorry I didn't call."

"Hey, you're the boss. You can come in when you please."

"How was your New Year?"

"Great! We watched the ball drop, kissed each other and a bunch of strangers and got out of Dodge as fast as we could to have a nice bottle of champagne at home."

"I'm glad you enjoyed yourself and made it home okay." Tabitha passed the desk to go to her office before Cynthia came from behind her desk to stop her.

"Before you go in, you have a visitor."

It couldn't have been Eric since she'd just left him lounging under the comforter in her bed. He was the only person she could think of that Cynthia would leave alone in her office. "You let them in my office?"

"He says he's your father, Tabitha, and he has some bad news about your mother…"

Tabitha's emotions went on high alert, running the gamut from rage to confusion to happiness and back again.

She stalked toward her office and barged through the door trailing Cynthia's bewildered, "…but I thought your mother was dead."

Tabitha slammed the door and the man standing in the middle of her office started and slowly turned to her.

It was him, looking a little older and more dignified with gray at his temples and a little rounder in the middle than she remembered, but with the straight and erect posture that made him appear as trim and tall as he'd always seemed to her when she'd been a child.

He was the man she'd known as her father for eight years before he walked out. Not that she blamed him for that. If she could have left Denise she would have, too, but she hadn't had a choice, and *he'd* left her all alone, on her own to deal with the madwoman.

How dare he come to her office, she suddenly thought, and wondered what it was about the men in her life sneaking up and ambushing her at her place of business.

"Tabitha…" He started across the carpeted floor, arms outstretched and Tabitha put up a hand like a stop sign, glared at him.

"What are you doing here?"

"I have some bad news about your mother."

"So I heard." She peered at him, saw the tears behind his lightly tinted tortoiseshell-framed glasses, her stomach somersaulting. "What sort of bad news?"

"You mother...she's dead."

"No..." All these years she'd been alone, believing her mother and father alive out there somewhere, but just not wanting her, and here was solid evidence that she really was motherless. "You came here just to tell me that?"

"I didn't want to tell you something like this over the phone."

"Why tell me at all? Why track me down after all these years?"

He lowered his head, looking so abashed she almost felt sorry for him. "I thought you were dead until very recently."

"Why would you think that?"

"When your mother tracked me down in New Jersey, that's what she told me."

She'd tracked him down? In New Jersey? Is that where her mother had gone when she'd left Tabitha alone in that bus station? Running off to find her husband? "You've been together all this time?"

He nodded, his Adam's apple bobbing.

Twenty years! Living the married, childless life in New Jersey, building a life together without her and they didn't seem to miss her until now.

The thought numbed her, chilled her to every angry, violated bone in her body!

"How could you do that to me? You left me. You left me alone with her and then you accepted her back no questions asked."

"That's not exactly how it happened, Tabby—"

"Don't call me that! You don't have that right anymore."

He nodded as if agreeing. "I'm sorry. I couldn't stay any longer. It was tearing me apart to watch her slip further and further away, watching her destroy herself little by little every day."

"What about me?" God, she hated herself for asking, for sounding like a whiner. She didn't need him anymore, didn't want to need him.

But here he was standing in her office twenty years older and looking older than that, grief and probably guilt weighing down on him.

Something he'd said earlier suddenly dawned on her. "She told you I was dead?"

Edward nodded. "I took her word at face value, never thought to question her."

The implications, the irony almost made her laugh. All these years she'd been denying her mother's existence, killed her off in her heart and mind, and here the witch had done the same to Tabitha. "How did you find out I was still alive?"

"Your mother told me before she…before she died."

She watched the tears roll down his cheeks, and tried hard not to feel any sympathy for this man who hadn't been her father for more than two decades, longer than he had spent being a father to her. "So she came clean on her death bed, huh? How absolutely freaking melodramatic of her. How absolutely freaking like her!"

"Tabitha, I'd like you to come to the funeral."

"No freaking way. I wrote that woman out of my life a long time ago. I wrote *you* out of my life for that matter. You've *both* been dead to me for a long time."

"Tabby…" He tried to hug her but Tabitha stepped away.

"Don't." She couldn't let him in. He'd only hurt her again.

"You won't be able to live with yourself if you don't get this closure."

"Like you suddenly care about my mental well-being?"

"I know you may not believe it, but I do."

"You're right. I don't believe it." She pointed him to the door. "Please, just go."

"Tabi—"

"Go. Get out now!" The anger boiled over as she opened the door. Anger for being abandoned so many times in her life she could no longer keep count. Abandoned by the man who'd provided the seed to her mother to make her, although he at least had an excuse, since he probably hadn't known about her to begin with. Abandoned by the man her mother had married. Abandoned by her mother.

How much rejection was she supposed to take?

Edward drifted toward the door, his gait slow and lumbering, so unlike the sure and capable man she used to know as "Dad."

She couldn't let herself care a lick about what he used to be. What he used to be meant next to nothing to her. Just like *he* meant nothing to her.

Tabitha closed her door and sat down behind her desk. She waited a solid twenty minutes, just sitting in silence and doing nothing except staring into space, giving him plenty of time to get out and away from her and her office before she gathered her satchel and headed for the door.

"I'm going home for the day, Cynthia. If I get any calls, just call me on my cell."

"Oh, okay."

Tabitha didn't give the girl a chance to ask the obvious question before she stormed past Cynthia's desk and out the glass door.

* * * *

Showered and clad in jeans, EJ hadn't long gotten up when Tabitha's phone rang and Cynthia began leaving a message.

He intercepted the voicemail and picked up the phone when he heard his name. "Hi Cynthia. What's up?"

"Tabitha had a visitor here this morning, someone claiming to be her father, and he upset her pretty bad."

"Father?" He wondered which one. The step or the biological?

"Yes, they argued and then she kicked him out. That was about a half-an-hour ago. Tabitha left here a few minutes ago herself. I think maybe you should be on the lookout for her."

"Thanks for the head's up, Cynthia. I will." No sooner did he hang up, than someone knocked on the door.

EJ went to the door thinking maybe Tabitha had forgotten her keys in her rush to leave her office, but when he opened the door he was confronted with a middle aged man who looked about as upset as Cynthia had said Tabitha had been when she'd left.

"You must be Tabitha's father."

"She's told you about me?"

"She's mentioned you a time or two. I'm Eric Vega, her boyfriend." EJ proffered a hand.

"Edward Lyons."

As soon as Edward shook his hand, EJ had a flash of the woman in the car, the accident, crushed metal and spilled blood everywhere.

He staggered, grasping Edward's hand extra tight as he squeezed his eyes closed.

"Are you all right?"

He opened his eyes to stare at Edward, nodded. "I'm fine. I just need something cold to drink. Can I get you something?"

"Ice water would be fine."

"Coming up." EJ headed for the fridge, poured himself and Edward ice water and brought the two frosted glasses back to the living room.

He'd thought twice about getting a beer, but didn't want the old man to get the wrong impression about Tabitha's beau. He was already home in just jeans in the middle of the day during the week. Drinking before noon probably wouldn't go over too well, despite the fact that he thought he might need some alcohol to get through the next several minutes.

"Your name sounds familiar. You wouldn't happen to be related to the author EJ Vega, would you?"

EJ smiled, felt heat rushing to his face as he blushed. No matter how many times people recognized his name or complimented his work, he never tired of or got used to the acknowledgment. "Actually, I'm EJ Vega. It's Eric James."

"Ah, I thought you looked familiar. I recognize you from the picture on your book jacket."

"So you've read *Reaching Out?*"

"I…I was in the midst of reading it before my wife died. I haven't been able to pick it back up."

"Tabitha's mother?"

"Yes, she was in an automobile accident New Year's Eve and died of her injuries a couple of days later."

Damn, she'd had her accident the same day his father had had his heart attack. How ironic was that? And how ironic that Tabitha had only just begun to reveal her family ties to him only to discover the most important one severed by death.

No wonder the kid had walked out of her office upset. EJ was almost afraid of the condition she would be in when she got home. He realized he wouldn't have to wait long, however, when he heard her key in the door.

Dear Lord, he could just imagine the picture he and Edward made, sitting on the sofa, chatting nonchalantly when Tabitha opened the door.

She was much more calm than she'd been when Jade had met them out front of his loft after they'd gotten back from Colorado, seemingly slow to burn this time.

"God, I can't get away from him," she muttered as she slid her key out the lock and hung it on the pegboard. Louder, she asked, "What the hell is he doing here?"

Edward stood and turned to his daughter at the front door. "Tabitha—"

"When I asked you to leave, I didn't just mean my office. I meant my life."

"Maybe you should go Edward. I'll talk to her."

"So it's Edward?" Tabitha's eyebrows shot up. "My how friendly we've become with my boyfriend behind my back."

"Tabby—"

"I told you not to call me that!" She turned her anger from her father to EJ. "And don't think you *talking to me* is going to change my mind about this."

"I'd better go." Edward eased by Tabitha to the door, paused on the threshold and spoke to her back. "You should see her laid to rest, Tabitha."

She ground her teeth, jaws furiously working. "Yeah, yeah, so you said. For closure. How about you close this!" She turned to give him the finger and EJ came forward to wrap his arms around her before she went after the man.

"I love you, Tabby. I never stopped."

"I told you before, and I'll tell you again. Get out of my house and get out of my life."

"Tabitha…"

"Why is this so difficult for you? You've got practice, it should be easy."

EJ winced as the man finally stepped out into the hall and closed the door behind himself.

He caught her by the shoulders and turned her to face him.

"Don't say it. You think I was cruel."

"Among other things."

"Well pardon me for not having a big warm loving family like yours. Call me Miss Dysfunctional."

"Tabitha, stop it."

"I don't want to talk about this, Eric."

"You need to."

"I'm about tired of people telling me what I need to do!"

He slid his shields down, just a tad, and was immediately punished for his nosey invasion when a collage of painful images bombarded his senses, almost sending him to his knees. He slammed his shields shut again.

How did the woman live with all that agony buried inside her without succumbing?

"You not only need to…" He put his arms around her again, pulled her close and held tight. "You want to."

"He left me, Eric. He *left* me, left us, and then she tracked him down and the two of them went their merry little way as if I never existed!"

"He didn't know you were still alive."

"It doesn't matter. He'd already left me with the madwoman."

"You don't mean that, Tabby. You don't want to think ill of her like that."

"Why not? Because she's dead? It doesn't change what she did to me, what…what I went through when she left."

He felt the tears before he saw them flowing out of her eyes, felt the sobs wrack her slim body as he held her against him.

"She's dead, Eric. My Mom's dead."

"I know, baby, but it's going to be okay. You're going to go to that funeral and put this all to rest. Put her to rest."

"I'm afraid. I'm so afraid I'm going to wind up like her, be like her, be a…" She shook her head against him, the rest of her words muttered against his bare chest.

He didn't need to hear her, because he knew.

She didn't want to be a madwoman.

Chapter 29

Tabitha started the week off after the visit from her father going back and forth with Eric to the hospital before his father was finally released home after a week and with a clean bill of health.

Joe's doctors expected him to make a full recovery, predicting a lot of years left for him to spend with his family and friends as long as he followed medical advice which of course included eating right and exercising.

Eric's mom had started laying down the law in the hospital before her husband was even released, told him he was going to accompany her on her morning walks as soon as he got out of the hospital, stressed he needed more exercise than just what he got mowing the lawn and fiddling with the engines of his classic cars.

Tabitha loved hearing Eric's stories about his father's recovery and his mother's drill sergeant demeanor when it came to getting her husband back in shape. As much as she wanted to, however, she knew she couldn't continue to bury herself in his family triumphs forever, had to face her own family, or what there was left of it.

The day after Eric's father's release from the hospital was her mother's funeral and Tabitha woke up with butterflies in her stomach as if she weren't going to see her mother laid to rest, but instead going for a visit after so many motherless, empty years.

When would she stop looking for her mother's love and approval?

Eric was already up and half-dressed, clad in black slacks, shoes, a black shirt and a black silk tie. He seemed more eager to get this day over with than she did.

"Finally up?"

"I didn't sleep too well."

"I know. I felt you tossing and turning." He came to the bed, sat down beside her and grasped a hand. "It's going to be okay. I'm going to be with you every step of the way."

She squeezed his hand back. "I know." If it hadn't been for Eric's constant harangue over the last few days about family ties and obligation she wouldn't be going to the funeral at all, but he'd finally gotten through her defenses with the same thing her father had said: she needed closure, and she would regret it for the rest of her life if she didn't see her mother laid to rest.

Tabitha still doubted the wisdom of going, had no idea how she'd react to seeing her father, but Eric convinced her to try and forgive if not forget, to resolve her issues with her stepfather while she had the chance.

"You never know what's around the corner, Tabitha. Who knew my father would have a heart attack? I'm lucky he survived, that he recovered and I have more chances to show him how much I love him, how much he means to me. You've got that same chance with your father. Don't let it slip away..."

God, did the man have to be so wise and right about everything?

She should have been upset with Eric for running interference between her and her father but couldn't find it in her to be angry, especially after what had happened to his father. She knew Eric was feeling extra sensitive about father-child relationships and understood he wanted her to reconcile with her stepdad before it was too late.

She had loved him once when he was her whole world. Could she love him again when he hadn't been in her world for so long?

Eric leaned in to kiss her forehead now, and caressed her hair before standing and sauntering back to the mirror to finish knotting his tie.

Tabitha got out of bed, took a quick shower and put on her all-purpose black dress before she styled her long hair in an elegant and sedate chignon.

Eric came over to her, black suit jacket on as he cupped her face and kissed her on the mouth, sliding in his tongue for a lingering French kiss as if trying to transfer his strength to her.

"I'm okay, Eric." She finished putting in her diamond studs then made her way to the living room to retrieve their coats.

Eric drove them to Butler, New Jersey in a little under two hours, getting them to the church several minutes after the ceremony had already begun.

The church, though sizable, was packed with mourners.

Twenty years worth of friends and acquaintances. Twenty years worth of Fourths of July, Memorial Days, Thanksgivings, Christmases and New Year's Eves. Twenty years worth of birthdays. Twenty years worth of anniversaries.

They had built a life in New Jersey, carved out a nice little existence without her.

She swallowed the giant-sized lump in her throat, realized she was jealous that they had been able to be happy without her, or because they had left her.

Maybe it had taken her father leaving to make her mother come around, realize what she had lost, that she had had a good man who worshipped the ground upon which she walked, and she needed to straighten up and fly right to get him back and keep him.

From the information that Eric had insisted on feeding her from her stepdad over the last few days, despite how much she'd tried to block it out, her mother had been taking her medication regularly, had been clean and sober all the way up until the accident, and hadn't had any of her lapses or black-outs in more than nineteen years.

It was a drunk driver that had ended her life, Tabitha thought ironically. Her mother had never done anything small time, or easy. Why should she die that way?

What a way to start the New Year.

Tabitha sat in the back of the church with EJ and listened as the priest read a few choice sections from the bible, then called her father up to give the eulogy.

She felt the tears welling as soon as he reached the podium, but held them in.

I'm not going to cry. I'm not.

He hadn't seen her slip into the church at the last minute, and she was still hoping to escape his knowing she had come, until he glanced up from his notes and noticed her.

Once he tearfully mouthed "thank you" then spoke of her mother, and what a good and loving wife she'd been, a caring and generous neighbor, giving anecdotes to illustrate the pastoral life they'd led as man and wife in suburban New Jersey, the dam finally broke, tears flowing down Tabitha's face uncontrollably.

Eric put an arm around her shoulder and she leaned her head against his chest and let the tears flow, the realization that her mother was really gone finally hitting her.

The casket was closed at her father's request, everyone's point of reference a recent picture that had been blown up to ten-by-fifteen and sat on a brass stand adjacent the coffin behind the podium.

When the ceremony came to an end, rather than file past the coffin, the mourners filed past the photo.

Tabitha remained in her seat in the back with EJ until the church was empty and only then did she go up front and pause at the picture. She fingered the glossy covering as if she could feel her mother's spirit, touch her mother one last time. She closed her eyes and imagined her mother at the bus station, the last time she'd seen her alive. Her mom had been happy that day, extremely happy, one of her manic moods, her excitement rubbing off when she told Tabitha they were going on a trip.

Tabitha didn't remember now how long she'd waited, except that when she'd realized her mother had left her and wasn't coming back, she'd never dreamed her disappearance permanent. Her mother always came back, if it was days and weeks later, she always did.

But not that last time.

Eric grasped her arm. "Tabitha, your father's waiting outside. He wants us to ride in the limo with him to the gravesite."

She shook her head. "Tell him we'll follow the procession in your Jeep."

"Tab—"

"I can't be with him right now. Not yet."

Tabitha didn't know what he said to her father outside, but a minute later he was coming back alone to retrieve her and take her to his Jeep.

The gravesite was fifteen minutes away, and most of the mourners who'd attended the funeral were at the graveside ceremony.

Despite her father and EJ's persistence, Tabitha stood several yards away from the grave, couldn't take being too close to all the mourners who knew her mother, did not want that familial pressure or responsibility yet, maybe never; did not think she could deal with being the "daughter of the deceased."

After the ceremony, Tabitha lingered behind for several moments with Eric. She waited as her father shook hands with his and her mother's friends and well-wishers until the graveside was finally deserted except for her, her father and Eric.

Hesitantly, her father approached, paused in front of her and caught her by the shoulders.

Tabitha had thought she was all cried out before he touched her, before he stared at her with those contrite and grateful brown eyes shining with tears behind his glasses and the her own tears started to flow all over again.

He pulled her into his arms as if it was the most natural thing in the world for him to do and Tabitha went with him, letting him hug her close as her body wracked with sobs.

"Thank you for coming, baby."

She didn't know what to say—thanks for inviting me, didn't seem quite appropriate—so she remained silent.

"She would have been proud of the way you turned out."

Without any help from either of you. Would she ever get rid of this bitterness?

She pulled away to peer at him, said "I'm glad I came." and realized that she meant it.

"I am, too."

"Dad...I'll...I'll call you sometime."

He looked at her as if she had just made his millennium and the clog in her throat grew when he whispered, "I'd like that."

Eric bid her father farewell, caught her hand and led her back to his Jeep at the curb.

He twined his fingers with hers and gently squeezed until she looked up at him. "You did good, Tabby. I'm proud of you."

"That seems to be going around"

He chuckled as he helped her into the passenger seat and they began their journey back to the city.

* * * *

EJ had helped Tabitha lay her ghosts to rest, now he had ghosts of his own to lay to rest.

He wasn't too thrilled about it but knew it had to be done, because how could he expect her to be honest and open with him, trust him, when he wasn't being honest and open with her?

He didn't want to be in another relationship where there were secrets between him and the other party. He didn't want another Sinclair. He didn't want another Jade.

EJ unlocked the door and let Tabitha into her apartment, tossed the keys up on the pegboard by the door and hung up his overcoat.

Tabitha followed suit, hanging her coat beside his then kicking off her shoes and padding to the sofa in her stocking feet. She collapsed in a corner with a loud sigh. "I'm drained."

"I know. Me, too."

"It's been quite a week."

"But we made it through." He sat down beside her. "It was a nice ceremony."

"Nicer than I thought it would be. Although, I'm not really sure what I expected, but that's just like my mother. Full of surprises until the very end."

"Are you really going to stay in touch with your father now that you know where he is?"

Tabitha shrugged, and he realized it was too soon after the funeral for her to start dealing with family reunions.

One trauma at a time, Vega. You've got a trip to lay on her already without adding trying to repair a Grand Canyon deep, decades long, father and daughter rift.

She put out her arms and grinned. "Come here, you."

He moved closer, accepted her hug, felt her soft breasts pressing against his chest and got instantly, indecorously hard.

Not now, not now! "There's something I have to tell you." He pushed away from her and held her at arm's length.

"Wow, that sounds serious, and in case you haven't noticed, we've both had more than our share of that in the last several days."

"I know, and I wouldn't do this to you if I didn't think it was necessary."

"Eric, what is it?"

Rather than tell her, he reached out and scanned her.

It was difficult getting through. Even with all they'd shared, all they shared now, even with their bond, she still had her guard up, a natural wall she erected against the world. And unfortunately, the world included him.

EJ tried again.

"Eric, are you...did you just...?"

His moment of truth. She'd either believe him or she wouldn't. Hate him or not.

His stomach dipped at the latter, but he nudged her again, a gentle push against her barrier and this time Tabitha gaped and lurched to her feet, stumbling away from the sofa.

"You're wondering why you felt so connected to me all of a sudden. Why it feels like fingers are caressing your mind."

She gawked, said nothing, but he heard every thought now, loud and clear. Instead of closing herself off, she'd dropped her armor as if she wanted him to prove himself, as if she needed him, anyone, to see her, know her insides.

"I know you don't want to hear what I'm about to say, don't want to believe—"

"You read minds!"

"Not all the time. Just when I drop my shields. By necessity I keep them up ninety-five percent of the time. Either that or I'd go out of my mind with all the cacophony."

"What about the other five percent?"

"I, um…I scan thoughts. It's like a mind-touch I use to, um—"

"This is just plain ridiculous, and if I weren't so grief-stricken right now, I might be able to enjoy your twisted attempt at humor."

"It's gotten easier to scan you since we made love. You were a pretty tough nut to crack in the beginning though."

"And this description of your…your *talents* should endear me to you? Knowing that you've been tinkering inside my head?"

"Now you're wondering what kind of sick, Penn and Teller parlor tricks I'm pulling."

She took two steps forward. "Stop it. Just stop it now. You're talking crazy."

"I know I should have told you sooner. I—"

"Lied to me."

He saw her eyes change from disbelief to acceptance in the instant the accusation left her mouth and his heart dropped. "Not intentionally. My abilities just never came up. It's not exactly the sort of subject you can just bring up in idle conversation."

"You had your chances," she murmured.

"Tabitha—"

"At the hotel when we were all cozy. You wanted me to open up and give you the lowdown on *my* life, yet you weren't willing to do the same."

"It wasn't like that."

"You're not just a liar, didn't just deceive *me*. You're a fake."

"What?"

"You have, *had* me, the world, fooled thinking you're a body language expert when in fact you know what people are thinking, don't *need* to read any facial expressions or unspoken language. You can just go the easy route, fall back on your—"

"That's not how it is!" God, she knew how to hit him exactly where it hurt the most, attacking his ethics, his integrity, each of which he had forfeited to know a little more about her. And her allegations hurt him so much because he knew they were correct, every last one of them.

"I know exactly how it *is.*" She glared at him, hands clenched. "You're a cheat *and* a liar."

"Tabitha…" He paused, put his hands out palms up, flinched at the look on her face. He didn't need to read her mind to recognize the look of someone who'd been hurt and betrayed too many times in her past. Someone who found it hard to trust and had just had their reasons—not to trust anyone, not to open up—justified.

"Is Angela like you?" she blurted.

He'd wondered when she'd ask, helplessly nodded.

"God, how many more in your family?"

"Just us two that I know of."

"I'm sure if there were more you'd know about them." She sneered, moving beyond incredulity and disillusionment straight to anger, and he didn't blame her.

"You've done this to me before. You've scanned me, been in my mind."

EJ saw the realization dawning in her whiskey colored eyes, mind clicking a mile a minute, her words clearly an accusation.

He stood and went to her, surprised when she let him catch her by the shoulders, but then he saw her face, the expression of disgust, and sensed her going suddenly, totally cold inside. She'd re-engaged her shields—armor, walls, gates, barbed wire and electric fencing—all up and locking him out.

There was a sign on the outside of her gates he could clearly read, her last thought glaring like neon: *I trusted you.*

It didn't escape him that her meaning was in the past tense.

The thought suddenly occurred to him that Tabitha was gifted, too, just in a different way, able to block any efforts of reading her, able to stop in its path any telepathy aimed at her.

He wondered if she had any inkling, but knew better than to bring up any possibility of her own talents now. She'd probably think he was crazier than she already thought, might think he was projecting his "illness" onto her, calling her a madwoman by default.

No, telling her would definitely do more harm than good, especially if she thought he was trying to evade the subject.

"Get out."

Her words jolted him, at first he'd thought he was hearing her thoughts again.

EJ glanced at her, tried again for one desperate probe and she went ballistic, put her hands against his chest and pushed him towards the front door.

"Get out, get out! I want you out!"

"Tabitha, don't use this as an excuse to break us up."

"I don't need an excuse. *You* did this all on your own." She started pummeling his chest, crying and screaming at him and EJ didn't realize he'd back-stepped to the door under her attack until he felt the solid wood against his back.

Tabitha took a deep breath, closed her eyes for several long seconds then opened them to stare at him.

The look in her eyes chilled him.

He saw the raw open wound that was her past and realized that he had hurt her more by not coming clean sooner than any cheating or infidelity ever could.

There wasn't any hate or malice to her look. Those, he thought, he could have dealt with, but her look was one of someone betrayed—something he'd promised he'd never do to her—innocence not lost, but crushed.

"I never want to see you again, Eric."

He turned from her—*too easily, way to easily, fight for her, Vega, fight!*—swallowed hard as he opened the door and stepped into the outer hallway. He waited with his back turned to her, couldn't bear to see that look of betrayal on her face again, especially knowing he had put it there.

The door closed behind him with a quiet snick, but it might as well have been an emphatic bang.

He had lost her.

Chapter 30

I know you, Tabitha.

He'd said it so many times since meeting her that she had begun to believe it. Now she understood *why* he'd said it. He'd been reading her mind all along. She'd been operating with him at an utter disadvantage. It wasn't enough that he had the kind of raw sex appeal that turned heads, melted knees and sizzled brain cells. He had the ability to read minds!

How much of her past had he known before she'd told him? Had he been humoring her when he'd asked her about herself, all the while knowing who and what she was, intimate with all her weaknesses and strengths, laughing at her behind her back? Storing up details and information to use against her when he pleased?

Telepathy. Mind reading. The stuff of science fiction and Stephen King novels!

Tabitha still didn't quite believe it, almost wished he were crazy. That might have been easier to deal with than a boyfriend who could read minds. At least she'd had experience with the former, knew a little about the mentally ill, much more than she ever wanted to know actually.

Leave it to her to fall in love with…with someone so different, outside the realm of normal. Like her mother. The madwoman.

When he'd first told her about his ability, that was the first thought to cross her mind—even with the proof, the probe and scan he'd performed—that he was a madman.

God, how could he do this to her? How could he lie to her with a straight face, sleeping next to her all those weeks, seducing her—not only with his body and his words, but his mind—and still smile in her face as if he were the innocent little Boy Scout from his past? How could he do that to her?

We only hurt the ones we love, darlin'.

Her mother used to say it to her all the time when she'd disappointed her daughter yet again, going missing on important holidays, neglecting to come to a Parent-Teacher conference, neglecting to show up for a school performance in a play or a musical, knocking down her daughter's already miniscule self-esteem at every turn.

Nope, Denise hadn't coined the phrase, but she had definitely perfected it, put her own southern twang and good-natured twist to it.

Tabitha had thought she'd found Mr. Right in Eric, had thought he deserved all her trust and more. And for a moment there, he had deserved it, had earned her love and trust.

By lying to you.

She closed her eyes on the screen in front of her and swallowed hard.

She'd been operating on autopilot for the last two weeks, trying to act as if an Eric Vega didn't exist, and that was near impossible to do.

Everything she did, everywhere she turned were reminders of him.

Erica sitting at home near her headboard in all her innocent pinkness. The jade elephant she never took off, snuggled against her bosom like a promise. The scent of his aftershave lingering in the linens and air of her apartment, even after so many days had gone by.

She was beginning to think Eric had other abilities, like spell-casting, perhaps that he'd put a hex on her, something that caused her to think about him night and day, unable to forget him, unable to hate him.

Unable to forgive him.

Theirs had been a whirlwind romance, moving fast, catching her imagination and her heart from the first, culminating in no more than three months by Tabitha's estimation.

She thought she might have been in love with him from that first meeting, and the visit to his closet, that had sealed the deal. Sealed her fate.

Tabitha remembered all the times they'd spent together, the good and bad, the funny and sad, the silly and serious. He had been so sweet to her, so supportive and giving, even at the end right before he had told her about himself.

She kept coming back to that day, wondering what had driven him to fess up. He didn't have to, especially with the gifts that he possessed, could have realistically gone on hiding it from her for years.

But he hadn't, had volunteered information that he knew would be unfavorable in her eyes, indeed damaging to his credibility, when he hadn't had to. God knew it had to have been difficult for him to tell her—it had been difficult for her to listen and realize that he was telling her the truth, especially once faced with irrefutable facts of his treachery and power—yet he had told her.

Because he'd felt guilty? Or because his moral code wouldn't let him go on living a lie?

Should it matter why he had opened up to her? Shouldn't the fact that he finally had opened up be her only yardstick for whether or not she should forgive him, but much more, trust him again, trust him not to violate her?

She still loved him, knew that she'd never stop.

But was love enough?

Tabitha had been asking herself this question for the last two weeks, fending off Eric's relentless calls to her home and office, his barrage of flower deliveries to same, close to caving in so many times, but somehow she'd held onto her anger and dignity long enough not to dial his numbers, not giving in.

She had to decide whether she could live with a man knowing he had the ability to read her mind—whether he used it all the time or not—had to decide whether she was mentally and emotionally prepared to deal with the fact that he could know her thoughts any time he pleased.

Sheesh, Tabitha didn't know what angered her more. The idea that he could read her mind, or the idea that he had lied about it.

Cynthia knocked on the doorjamb and stood on the threshold of Tabitha's office until her boss glanced up to acknowledge her presence. "…and the New Year started so promisingly, too."

"Don't start."

"What start, I'm just making a comment."

"I know what you're trying to do, and it won't work. Not this time."

"Would it make a difference if I said he's called several times today?"

"No, it wouldn't, and what makes today any different than the last two weeks?"

Cynthia shrugged, lips trembling, actually seemed on the verge of tears.

"Cyn, what is it?"

"I just hate to see you guys break up for no good reason."

Not that Tabitha *could* tell the girl the reasons for the break-up—she imagined how well that would go over, just call the men in white coats now—but she just wouldn't, valued her privacy too much.

She realized that was another issue she'd only so far scratched the surface of. Not just the fact that Eric had lied but that, however good intentioned his motives had been, he'd violated her person, stepped over well-delineated boundaries before they'd even had a bond.

She stood and crossed the floor, opened the floodgates when she took the girl in her arms as Cynthia's slim body trembled with her sobbing and the tears fell.

Oh, goodness, she was taking this as hard as Tabitha. Probably had something to do with being a newlywed and still in a fresh, on-the-verge relationship herself. Maybe the girl felt threatened, thought bad relationships and break-ups might be rubbing off.

Tabitha pat and rubbed Cynthia's back, calming her down as best she could, considering she didn't have a whole heck of a lot of experience dealing with hysterical females, finally pulled away to peer at her assistant.

"Don't worry about us, Cyn. Okay? We'll work it out." She realized as she said it that she meant it, knew that she had to put an end to her own and Cynthia's pain as soon as possible.

It was past time.

* * * *

EJ had gone through the last two weeks like an automaton.

Book signings, interviews, library appearances—he'd said the right words, smiled in all the right places, put his John Hancock where asked and when asked—doing just enough to get by and function, nothing more.

Today he was at an independent bookstore in the Fordham Road section of the Bronx; he liked the small independents, the personal Mom and Pop touch that they provided. Nowadays he needed plenty of the personal touch just to remind him that he was a living breathing functioning human being who needed to feed his heart with as much human contact as possible just to validate his existence.

Damn, he could be melodramatic when he put his mind to it, but he had reason, though he wouldn't dare admit it out loud.

Angela had been bugging him for the last couple of weeks trying to pry from him any information about Tabitha that she could get. Problem was, he wasn't giving, and this ticked her off as much as the idea that he had done something to ruin the relationship.

EJ had finally had to tell her to lay off that his life was his own and whether Tabitha was in it or not was his concern and not his older sister's. That had put her in her place for about an hour before she called him back, contrite and apologetic, but still subtly asking what was going on with him and Tabitha.

Four days ago he'd finally told Angela what had happened, how he'd broken the news to Tabitha and that she hadn't taken it very well. Angela, surprisingly, didn't have any all-purpose, save-the-relationship advice to give him, just gently commiserated and tried to make him feel better with it's-for-the-best platitudes that made him feel anything but better.

For the best? Like hell it was.

If he were half the bold and bodacious bastard he'd been when he'd first met Tabitha, he would have marched right over to her apartment or job and made her listen to him, but no. He was trying to give her space to deal with the shock, space to come to terms with what he was and could do, trying to let her deal with her recent grief.

Bullshit!

Back when he'd first met her he hadn't had anything to lose. He hadn't had anything like his heart at stake, lying out in the open for the world to see and know that here was a man who'd been kicked in the ass by love. It was easy then to be a bold and bodacious bastard, not so easy now when the woman with whom he was in love had the very ability to crush him to dust with just a word or a look. Or no word and no look.

Could he really blame her for shunning him, for shutting him out of her life? Had he been in her place he might do the same thing, probably would, knowing what a high value he placed on honesty.

Hypocrite. Coward!

If the people on this line had had any sort of sympathy and pity for him, they'd quietly go away so that he could leave and suffer the rest of the afternoon in solitude.

EJ signed another book, handed it back to the customer with a mumbled thanks and took the next book.

After another hour, and another fifty signed books—suffering a severe case of writer's cramp since he'd been at signing this afternoon for the last two hours and the line was only now showing signs of letting up—a reader silently placed her book on the table, stepped back and waited.

He didn't look up right away, just glimpsed the high-heel pumps, fingernail polish, and long elegant copper tone fingers—his only hints that the customer was a woman.

EJ consciously tried to slow down his speeding heart, didn't want to get his hopes up. But he'd recognize her vanilla musk scent, that sedate coral polish anywhere.

Yeah, like they only sold one bottle to her. *Get a grip, Vega, get a grip!*

He cleared his throat, took a deep breath, but still didn't look up. "What would you like me to say?"

"To Tabitha: If you forgive me, I'll forgive you, and we can start this relationship thing all over again, Love, Eric James Vega."

"Hmm, that's interesting phrasing. Long-winded, too." It took everything in him to keep his cool and not jump up and down screaming Hallelujah because she was forgiving him.

"I thought it apropos."

He took another deep breath, began to write out the statement, and right when he got to his signature and would have put his *nom de plume*, she reached out her hand and caught his wrist.

"I want your full name, just as I dictated it. For positive identification purposes."

"Identification purposes?"

"So I'll know who to bring it back to if I'm not one hundred percent satisfied."

"What if I told you your satisfaction is guaranteed from here on out?"

"I'd say I need some proof of that fantastic claim."

He raised his eyes then, saw her beautiful hesitant smile, didn't know how he stayed in his seat as long as he did without jumping across the table to grab her in a Hollywood hug and kiss her senseless right on the floor of the bookstore.

"Hi," she murmured, and he wondered why she seemed apologetic when it had been him who'd almost ruined their relationship.

"Hey." EJ peeked around her to see only one other customer on the line behind her, a senior aged woman with an indulgent smile, clutching her book against her breasts like a precious treasure, patiently waiting for her turn.

Tabitha stepped aside as he glanced at his watch, realized that the official book signing had been over a half-an-hour ago, and he'd managed to handle everyone who'd bought a book and been on line.

The elderly woman stepped forward, grinning widely now as she handed EJ her book.

"How would you like me to sign this?"

"To Margaret: I'm on my way to propose to my girlfriend, thanks for being so patient and waiting while we worked it out, Eric James Vega."

He glanced at her and smiled, started to write and stopped when she cleared her throat.

"I'd like your full name also. Not just for identification purposes mind you. I just like the sounds of it. An honest and solid name."

"Why thank you, Margaret. My mom and Dad thought so, too, and I try to live up to it every day." He finished signing the book and Margaret took it with a wink at Tabitha.

"Does he, young lady?"

"Does he what?"

"Live up to his name?"

Tabitha peered at him, her look a combination of admiration, forgiveness, and lusty love, smiled and said simply, "I believe he does."

Margaret left them with her thanks and well wishes, and then the storeowner came to the table to shake EJ's hand and congratulate him for selling out stock.

"Thanks for hosting the event." He smiled, eyeing Tabitha behind the owner, anxious to get at her as soon as possible, too much time and space between them. Too much.

"We've got your book on order, so you're welcome back in for another signing whenever you're ready."

"I'll make sure and do that."

As soon as they were alone this time, EJ got up and came from behind the table to properly greet his future wife. He wrapped her in a warm and tight hug, welcoming her back into his life and elated that she had found him worthy.

Her lips were hot and hungry against his, tongue and teeth ravenous as she sucked and bit him into a total state of arousal.

"Let's get out of here. I need you." She caught him by a hand and led him out to his Jeep.

EJ didn't know how he was able to stay on the road with her sensual musk wafting out to him and her sexy thighs only inches away as she sat belted in the seat next to him, but he made it downtown to his house in record time and in one piece.

They ran up the stairs together, hand-in-hand, and EJ quickly opened the door, letting Tabitha into the loft behind him, and went to work on removing her clothes and his.

They left a trail of jeans, turtleneck, T-shirt, shorts, silk blouse, skirt, bra, and thong in their wake as they made it to his bedroom. In a tangle of arms and legs they collapsed onto the king size mattress, enmeshed in the sheets kissing and fondling each other into a heated haze.

"I love you, Eric. I'm sorry I never told you, sorry I never said—"

He put a finger to her lips, removed it only long enough to replace it with his mouth, hungrily attacking her full mouth with a ferocity he hadn't known himself capable.

When Eric pulled up for air after several seconds, Tabitha said, "I'm pregnant." at the same instant he said, "Marry me."

They stared at each other and burst out laughing, then suddenly turned serious.

"That's not the only reason you came back, is it?" EJ asked.

"No. I came back for you." She paused, stared at him as she caressed his smooth bare torso, paying particular attention to his nicely muscled pecs and flat nipples. "You didn't just ask me to marry you because I'm pregnant did you?"

"I'm old fashioned, but that's not why." He grinned and felt her tremble as he slid a finger into her moist heat, reacquainting himself with her very sensitive and responsive tissue. "I don't want to make a liar out of Margaret."

"Mustn't displease the fans."

"With that in mind…" EJ dove between her legs to explore his favorite cavern and relearn all the treasures he'd ever discovered between Tabitha Lyons' beautiful thighs.

Epilogue

Wantagh, Long Island—Twenty-One Months Later

Tabitha watched James Edward Vega toddle his way across the backyard's rich lawn, away from her and toward his grandfather Edward's outstretched arms.

At one he was an affectionate, but thoughtful and serious baby who preferred the one-on-one attention of his parents or another adult here and there, but once the group grew larger than three or four, he became antsy and searched the crowd for his parents or another familiar adult he could tolerate.

He tolerated few except his grandfather Edward and the Vega brood, accepted his father's big family about as well as Tabitha had when she'd first been exposed to them, which gave him a big head start since he'd begun his adjustment early, from birth.

Tabitha guessed it helped that he had the unflinching and daring blood of Eric's family running through his veins.

He yet preferred the quiet, creative and cerebral pursuits his grandfather Edward favored, the two spending hours together coloring in James' various coloring books, and working with Playdough and erector sets so much that Tabitha thought she might have a budding architect or artist on her hands.

Angela came over and plopped down in the lawn chair beside her. "Well, how's the little mother-to-be doing over here?"

"Shh! I haven't told Eric yet." Since she didn't get the usual morning sickness like so many women, and she already didn't drink or smoke, and followed a pretty good diet, there'd been no change in her habits to tip her husband off so he hadn't yet guessed.

"Whoops." Angela slapped a hand over her mouth. "I'm sorry. I get so excited over these things I just forget myself."

"I know. I do, too." Tabitha chuckled, rubbing her belly and glancing out over Joe and Viviana's large backyard where a raucous volleyball game was in full effect—Angela's and Emilia's kids and a few of their friends against the Vega siblings.

She watched Eric make a diving rescue of an attempted winner. Nick tipped and passed Eric's save to Emilia who spiked the ball right between her son Anthony and Angela's girl Danni.

Laments of "no fair" and "bruiser" rose up from the Calminetti/Gallo side.

"Mom!" ten-year-old Anthony whined.

"Hey, we're here to play, kid. You guys said no shorts, no prisoners. We're just playing by your rules. We're here to win!"

Tabitha laughed as she watched Emilia whoop and high-five her siblings.

She knew she was pretty competitive, but had nothing on Emilia, had gotten a glimpse of her sister's-in-law competitive spirit her first Fourth of July picnic at Joe and Viviana's when the gang had played softball. Emilia had slid home so hard she'd knocked the ball out of her then nine-year-old son's glove.

"She tries so hard to be a mother and a father to him," Angela murmured, and Tabitha had a feeling she knew what was coming.

Where was Angela's accomplice when Tabitha needed her? "She's done a good job with him," she said.

"Yes, but she can't teach him how to be a man."

Oh, oh.

Evelyn trotted over just then and grabbed a can of soda from one of the ice-filled coolers on the long picnic table behind Tabitha and Angela.

"Whew, I needed a break. Em is brutal even for me. Don't let one of us miss the ball.

She's all over us like...like EJ on Tabitha."

Tabitha felt blood rush to her face at the allusion to her and Eric's sexual antics. Admittedly, they didn't know how to keep their hands off of each other, even after almost two years of marriage. She hoped they remained at least as randy for the duration.

Evelyn and Angela laughed as Evelyn took a seat beside her sister on the foot of her lounge chair. "So, what's going on over here? Picking out baby names?"

Tabitha shot Angela a look. "Is there anyone you haven't told?"

Now Angela blushed, sheepishly smiled. "Evie's the only one."

"Okay." Sheesh, she'd tried so hard to keep this a secret until just the right moment, but with a sister-in-law who was telepathic it was hard to keep any secrets.

Eric had given her a few pointers, showed her how to fortify her already strong shields and engage them at will, but for some reason, Angela seemed more immune to her armor than Tabitha's own husband.

"I think Eve is nice," Evelyn said now.

"You would," Angela said.

"What would you call her? Because we all know it's a her." Evelyn smiled and patted Tabitha's stomach.

"Angie's a nice name, and in case it's a boy, Angel is even better."

"Of course." Evelyn rolled her eyes, and Tabitha chuckled at them.

Aunts. What was the kid going to do but accept their wild and crazy antics as they endlessly doted on her?

"Why don't we change the subject before Eric gets suspicious and comes over here,"

Tabitha muttered.

"Oh, right. Don't want to spill the beans," Evelyn said, peered at Angela. "So, who's your next project since you're on a roll, Ms. Cupid?"

Angela grinned. "I'm not sure yet, but I think Nick is a good candidate."

"You have someone in mind?"

Tabitha put her hands over her ears with the proper amount of histrionics and said, "This is info my virgin ears do not need to hear," but couldn't help listening anyway.

"No, but I'm keeping a lookout…"

Who would Angela use as an accessory when she was trying to hook up Evelyn, Tabitha wondered and glanced at Angela to see if she'd caught the thought.

Of course she had, was smiling like a cat left with a bowl of cream.

"Actually, there's a colleague of his who should be here shortly."

"You're not talking about Slany Breeze!"

Tabitha had heard about Ms. Breeze, and according to Nick during any of his numerous gripe sessions—and, of course, he was biased—Slany Breeze was a real man-eater who thought her shit smelled like lavender sachet.

"I most certainly am," Angela answered her sister.

"They'll kill each other."

"He'll be nice. Besides, I invited her over under the guise of a truce, initiated by her friendly rival, Nick."

"And she agreed to come?"

"It took some convincing, but I mentioned that Nick wanted to apologize for the hard time he'd been giving her on their last project together."

"And she didn't wonder why Nick didn't call himself?"

"I didn't call her. I sent her an e-mail from his address."

How she'd managed that, Tabitha did not want to know, only gaped as Angela turned her gaze toward the back porch where a statuesque, auburn-haired, green-eyed beauty had just arrived and was standing on the top step surveying the backyard as if it were her domain. Clad in green silk pants, matching tank top and red designer sandals, she did not look like she was ready to play anyone's volleyball or chow down on a mustard-slathered hot dog at a Labor-Day-picnic-slash-one-year-old's-birthday-party.

"The Fourth may be two months past, but when Nick sees Slany, he's going to blow up like a professional fireworks display," Evelyn observed.

"Why should my bro blow up, pray tell?" Eric had silently sidled over before his sisters or Tabitha realized. Just what she had been afraid of all along.

He grabbed a bottled water from the cooler, opened it and took a long gulp before splashing some on his face.

Angela winked and Tabitha quickly stood, hooked both her arms through one of Eric's and pulled him to the side, away from his sisters and the porch.

He smelled good, sweet-spicy musk of his aftershave blending with his perspiration to form a potent pheromonal aperitif that instantly put all her female hormones on high alert, as well as gave her another good reason to get close besides dragging him away from the action, but she didn't move near quick enough.

Eric glimpsed Slany on the back porch eyeing the action on the makeshift volleyball court and gaped. "Isn't that—?"

"How do you feel about Denise for a girl's name?"

"Huh?" Eric turned to her and gawked.

This wasn't really the way she wanted to share her news, but desperate times called for desperate measures and from the approving look on Angela's face, Tabitha guessed she'd made the right move.

She glanced over a shoulder to see Nick stalking towards the back porch and led Eric away as fast as she could.

"Denise is nice. Any particular reason?" He automatically reached for her stomach, rested his palm against it and smiled. "Are you sure?"

"Got the confirmation last week and was just waiting for the right time to tell you."

"And what makes now the right ti—?" Eric cut himself off as a loud shouting match broke out behind him and Tabitha, Nick and Slany's voices rising in anger.

Tabitha led Eric further away, shaking her head, didn't think another zip code would be far enough to get away from the heat and outrage of Angela's latest victims.

Poor Nick and Slany.

Tabitha had a feeling it was going to be a stormy courtship—if they didn't rip each other to shreds and dispense with courtship altogether.

"Nick's going to have to fight his own battles," Eric said before Tabitha could respond to his aborted question. He caught a hand and led her towards the front of the house, away from the line of fire. "Let's you and I discuss this name business in more detail, Mrs. Vega."

"Gladly, Mr. Vega."

He leaned in, cupping a full breast and hungrily kissing her on the lips as they entered the house and closed the door behind them.

BENEATH THE SURFACE
The Matchmaker, Book 1
THE END

www.GracieCMcKeever.com

SIREN AUTHORS: GROUP BLOG
Siren authors discuss their books, writing, and everything else
http://sirenauthors.blogspot.com

SIREN BOOKS: NEWSLETTER
Keep up with new releases and special events
http://groups.yahoo.com/group/SirenBooks/

Siren Publishing, Inc.
www.SirenPublishing.com

4124604

Made in the USA
Lexington, KY
23 December 2009